A Witch's Guide to Love and Poison

ALSO BY AAMNA QURESHI

Young Adult:
The Lady or the Lion
The Man or the Monster
When a Brown Girl Flees
My Big, Fat Desi Wedding

Adult:
If I Loved You Less
The Baby Dragon Cafe

AAMNA QURESHI

HODDER CHILDREN'S BOOKS

First published in Great Britain in 2025 by Hodder Children's Books

SRD

Text copyright © Aamna Qureshi, 2025
Illustrations copyright © Melissa Castrillón, 2025

All rights reserved.

No part of this publication may be reproduced, stored in
a retrieval system, or transmitted, in any form or by any means, without
the prior permission in writing of the publisher, nor be otherwise circulated
in any form of binding or cover other than that in which it is published
and without a similar condition including this condition being
imposed on the subsequent purchaser.

A CIP catalogue record for this book
is available from the British Library.

Hardback ISBN 978 1 444-97871 1
Paperback ISBN 978-1-444-98088-2

Printed and bound in India by Manipal Technologies Limited, Manipal

The paper and board used in this book are made
from wood from responsible sources.

MIX
Paper | Supporting
responsible forestry
FSC™ C104740

Hodder Children's Books
An imprint of
Hachette Children's Group
Part of Hodder & Stoughton
Carmelite House
50 Victoria Embankment
London EC4Y 0DZ

The authorised representative in the EEA is Hachette Ireland,
8 Castlecourt Centre, Dublin 15, D15 XTP3, Ireland
(email: info@hbgi.ie)
An Hachette UK Company

www.hachette.co.uk
www.hachettechildrens.co.uk

For Sara,
my sunshine

'*A Witch's Guide to Love and Poison* is an enchanting tale of magic and sisterhood. With a charming romance and whimsical forest backdrop, Aamna's writing sparkles on the page!'
Zulekhá Afzal, author of Dancers of the Dawn

'Brimful of whimsy and charm, *A Witch's Guide to Love and Poison* had me hooked until the very last page. I loved the dynamic between Bisma and Xander, and the sisterly relationships were delightful. Highly recommended!'
Heather Fawcett, Sunday Times bestselling author of the Emily Wilde series

'*A Witch's Guide to Love and Poison* is the perfect blend of cosiness, magical mystery and romance, with a grumpy sunshine romance you'll never forget'
Anam Iqbal, author of The Exes

1

It was Bisma's eighteenth birthday, which meant it was time for goodbye.

But there were hours until then; she would not think of it now. Instead, Bisma got up from her bed: a soft spread of leaves above a thick branch molded perfectly for her body.

She stood and stretched, looking around the room she occupied in her home, a massive treehouse in the center of the Enchanted Forest. The other girls weren't as comfortable with heights, but Bisma loved the feeling of being above the entire world, so her room was the very highest. It suited her just fine. With seven of them occupying the home (Baji Eva the eldest at twenty-one, and Deeba the youngest at two), Bisma relished the quiet up here.

Walking across the weathered wood floor, Bisma went to the center of her room, where the tree's massive trunk rooted all the rooms together. She stuck her head through the opening, down the stairs that twisted and turned around the trunk, connecting every portion of their home.

She heard her sisters rising, already bickering over morning chores. Baji's voice rang out clearest as she ordered them all about.

Baji was the title for the leader of their family; her actual name was Eva, but when she became the head, she was called Baji out of respect.

And now it was almost Bisma's turn to become Baji.

Pushing aside the twinge in her heart at the thought, Bisma stepped on to the staircase. Rather than going down to join the others, she went up, climbing onto the roof of her room, then up higher on to another thick branch well above the treehouse. She sat down, pulling her knees to her chest, and inhaled a deep breath of fresh, sweet air, savoring the taste of earth on her tongue.

The first time Bisma had gone into town, she'd eyed the neat homes in the village along the way: little cottages, one or two storey tall. *How boring*, she'd thought. *And stuck on the ground, too!* Her home was a plethora of connected rooms built on thick tree branches on the biggest tree in the Forest, and from up here, they had the very best view.

The sun warmed the sky with color, rising higher and higher, shimmering over the tops of the green trees, turning the leaves a fiery gold. From here, she could see the outline of the glistening Mirror Lake, its waters a perfect bright blue, as though it was a stroke of paint.

To the east, she saw the meandering shape of the Rushing River, the waves roaring white and gray as they dashed forward. Beyond that, she knew the Forest led straight to the Cliffs, which then cut off to the ocean. Birds flitted through the sky, their wings violet and red, chirping their morning songs.

Bisma had known the Enchanted Forest her entire life, but it seemed there was always more to see, more to explore. Her magical home, the very best place in all the world.

Turning her wrist, Bisma looked down at the mark on her skin, a simple black tree that branded her as an Unwanted Girl. This was what the villagers called her band of sisters, and they had long since adopted it themselves. An unwanted child, Bisma had been left on the outskirts of the Forest as a baby. She was lucky in that sense.

Some of her sisters had similar experiences, but others had come to the Forest willingly, having nowhere else to go. Not all who came were accepted by the Forest, and she had heard the stories of how frightened her sisters had been to plunge into the dark woods, not knowing if they would survive.

But those who were accepted were accepted wholeheartedly; strangers one day and sisters the next.

Bisma listened to the faint sound of her sisters down below. She could hear five-year-old Nori, up to her usual mischief, most probably bothering two-year-old Deeba. Twelve-year-old Azalea would be hiding away from her chores, while nine-year-old Mei would be assembling breakfast with fifteen-year-old Luna.

Inhaling another sweet breath of mossy air, Bisma enjoyed the view of her forest. She stood and walked along the branch, balancing perfectly along the curve until she reached the very end. Bisma did not bother to look down; she simply jumped.

Wind whipped across her body as she fell, and Bisma let out a shriek of delight, unable to help herself. Her stomach gave out as the ground hurtled up toward her, growing closer, closer—Until a branch reached out and caught her. Bisma laughed, hair falling over her cheeks.

'Thanks, Forrie,' she said, as the branch gently deposited her onto the floor of the Forest. The branch waved at her, then slithered back into place in the treehouse.

Bisma sighed, looking up at the house. She didn't want to go in just yet, or she would be stopped a hundred times with baby Deeba demanding cuddles and Luna wanting to once again ask if she thought the baker's son had told her to have a nice day in a general sort of way or if he'd meant that he specifically wanted *Luna* to have a nice day, a question Bisma had already answered about seventeen times.

But really, she wanted to avoid the cheerful birthday wishes—and the harsh reality that accompanied it. Just a little longer.

Turning her back to the treehouse, Bisma skipped along. Whistling with the birds chirping up above her, she passed the vegetable garden and the chicken coops as she made her way down to the well for a drink of cold water, then meandered down to the stream to wash.

Stripping off her clothes, Bisma bathed in the cool stream, as she had hundreds of times before. She washed her long hair with lavender soap, watching the dark brown waves grow straight and ink-black in the water. The familiar scent calmed her, and she sank deeper into the water.

When she was done, Bisma saw there was a fresh outfit laid out for her on a branch, along with a drying cloth. It was a new dress; she recognized Azalea's hand on it. While the twelve-year-old hated chores, she loved sewing and was always making new outfits for the sisters.

The Forest had brought the clothes out for her. 'Thank you, Forrie.'

The wind whistled in response as Bisma got dressed. The dress fell to mid-calf and fit like a glove. It had short cap sleeves and was in her favorite color: a deep emerald green with black embroidery on the body.

She pulled the strings on the corseted bodice and tied them into a little bow, then admired the mehndi on her hands. She had applied it two nights ago and it had finally fully darkened.

Bisma twirled, watching the fabric of her dress lift with the movement, then fall back down, as soft as a sigh. She walked over to a still pool of water to look at her reflection. The dress really did look beautiful.

Her dark hair was beginning to dry and curl. Bisma usually let her unruly hair flow freely or tidied it into a simple braid. At most, she would add a string of motia, the sweet jasmine scent staying with her the entire day. But today, she knew Mei would want to do something special. The nine-year-old was always insisting on doing her sisters' hair in complicated fashions they had no need for, and today Bisma would indulge her.

She made her way back to the treehouse, picking mint leaves on the way and chewing on them to freshen her breath. She passed by a burst of sweet rosemary and plucked some sprigs to press onto her wrists, inhaling the lovely scent.

As Bisma walked home, she ran her hand along the wildflowers—pink, purple, orange, yellow, and blue—touching her hand to the soft petals. Sunlight shone through the leaves from above, highlighting all the brilliant colors.

Every bit of the Forest was overgrown and alive, not like the neat squares of grass in the villagers' estates. She had been horrified the first time she saw the villagers of Old Town mercilessly cutting away at the earth's natural beauty.

Finally, Bisma made it home. She looked up at the treehouse, hearing the chaos from outside. She climbed up the winding stairs and entered the main area of their home, which was decorated with cushions in various colors, pitchers filled with flowers, hanging pots and pans, and shelves lined with mismatched teacups and plates.

'Morning!' Bisma said.

All the commotion inside the house stopped.

It was silent for a half a heartbeat, then they all exploded with noise. Six girls shrieked and cried out and tackled her with hugs. Bisma kissed each of her sisters.

'Happiest of birthdays, angel,' Baji said. She held Deeba in one arm, then came to hug Bisma with her other. Bisma hugged her close, and Deeba wrapped her little arms around their necks, squeezing both of them.

'Do you like the dress?' Azalea asked, brown eyes lit up with excitement.

'Let's play!' Nori cried. Her thin, wiry frame jumped up and down, upending her already messy hair.

'Finally, you're here,' Luna said, exhaling dramatically. 'I am *starving*.'

'Breakfast is ready!' Mei said, pointing to the picnic baskets. 'Just need to pack the tea and milk.' She went to the kitchen, where water was boiling on the stove.

'Tch, Mei, leave it,' Baji said. 'Azalea, go help her.'

Azalea rolled her eyes, tossing her brown hair aside. 'I made Bisma's dress! I think I've done enough.'

Baji gave her a stern look, but Azalea was hardly fazed. *Twelve-year-olds.*

'It's alright, Baji, I can do it,' Mei said. She was a thin girl with straight, jet-black hair that was cut short, skimming her chin. Since her hair was so silky, it was hard to do much with it, which was why she loved doing her sisters' hair.

'You've been cooking since the morning,' Bisma said, going over to help Mei. 'Besides, I need you to do my hair.'

'Hey, I helped with breakfast, too!' Luna complained. Bisma sat down on the wood floors so Mei could do her hair and Luna came and sat across from Bisma, dark brown eyes sparkling. She had a beauty mark next to her lip, and her hair was a deep honey color. 'Haru said not to overwork the batter when you make scones.'

Bisma bit back a laugh. Luna took every opportunity to bring up the baker's son, her latest crush. At fifteen, Luna had a new crush every few months.

'I helped Baji with the jam!' Nori said, bouncing over and dropping into Bisma's lap.

'Oof,' Bisma said, as Nori elbowed her in the gut. Bisma played with the five-year-old's hair, straightening the blonde curls into something resembling neatness.

None of the girls looked similar; they were all different. The closest in likeness were Bisma and Deeba, who both had deep brown skin, but Deeba was a shade darker, and her features were different to Bisma's. Nori had pale white skin, while Azalea had a tawny skin tone, and Mei's was more of a fawn. Luna had olive-colored skin, and Eva's was dark chestnut.

'She really did help with the jam,' Baji said, coming over with little Deeba, who waddled on her own feet.

'Remind me, who made Bisma's dress?' Azalea added pointedly, squeezing in beside Bisma to run a hand along the fabric of her outfit.

'Thank you,' Bisma said. 'It's perfect.'

Azalea beamed with self-satisfaction. The girls all sat together as Mei finished styling Bisma's hair. Afterwards, Bisma looked in the mirror, and she saw her own dark eyes fill with joy.

'It's beautiful, Mei,' Bisma said. 'Thank you.'

Small tendrils framed her face, but the rest of it was pulled back, and Mei had wrapped the braid with a few strings of motia, the little white flowers a stark and striking contrast against Bisma's dark hair. Coupled with the small gold baliyan Bisma always wore on her ears and the freshly dark mehndi on her hands, she looked fit to go to a ball.

'It really does look so pretty,' Azalea said. She batted her eyelashes at Mei. 'Do mine, too?'

'Can we *eat*?' Luna asked, clutching her stomach. 'Haru says the scones are always best when they're fresh.'

Azalea pretended to vomit, then muttered to herself, 'If I have to hear about the baker's son one more time, I swear . . .'

Baji and Bisma exchanged an amused glance.

'Yes, let's go eat,' Baji said. As their eldest sister and leader, hers was the final say.

They gathered up the picnic baskets and made their way down the treehouse, comforting chatter filling the air. Azalea was going on about how she desperately needed new fabric to make a blouse or she would just *die*; Luna was reciting a love poem she had recently read; Nori was hopping and twirling, as hyper as ever.

They walked through the Forest, and Baji pointed out different mushrooms and berries to Mei, who declared whether they were safe to eat or not—something they were all taught when they first entered the Forest. They stopped at a hill with a view of the Rushing River and sat in the shade of an elderberry tree on a picnic blanket that was the yellow of sweetcorn and sunflowers.

Then the girls eagerly set about unloading their breakfast: jars of glistening blueberry jam and orange marmalade, warm crumbly scones, savory egg and spinach pie, lots of toast and salted golden butter, bottles of cold milk and pots of strong black tea, and a vanilla cake with bright red strawberries and thick sugared cream.

'This is amazing,' Bisma said, heart swelling. She looked around at her sisters, feeling nostalgic for this moment already. After today, everything would change.

Her gaze snagged on Baji, whose eyes welled with tears.

Bisma opened her mouth to speak, but Baji gave her a bright

smile, blinking her tears away. As painful as this was for Bisma, she knew it was worse for Baji.

'Let's eat!' Baji declared. The girls did not need to be told twice.

They dug in, passing plates and cutlery and teacups and sugar, eating until their stomachs were full. Then they spent the day playing in the sun.

Around midday, they all gathered back onto the picnic blankets and huddled together to nap, cuddling close and warming one another with their bodies in the cool shade of the elderberry tree. Patches of sunlight shifted through the gaps of the leaves above them as they slept.

When they woke, they ate again, then raced to the Rushing River, splashing each other with cold water. They picked flowers and made bouquets; Bisma made each of her sisters gajre to adorn their wrists. They talked and bickered and teased and laughed.

It was a perfect day. Everyone was on their best behavior—even Azalea—and before Bisma knew it, the sun was setting, the sky shifting from bright cerulean blue to a dark purple.

The sight filled her with terror; she didn't want the day to end. Bisma wished she could reach out into the sky and hold the sun in place, just for a while longer. *Please, just a few hours more*, she implored, but even the magic of the Enchanted Forest could not stop time.

Goodbye was inevitable.

'It's time,' Baji said, her voice solemn and thick. They all grew silent. Quietly, they packed up their things and made their way back to the treehouse, walking slowly, prolonging the end.

They could only put it off for so long. Soon they were back at the treehouse.

It was time for goodbye.

'I'm going to miss you girls so much,' Baji said. No, not Baji anymore—just Eva. Now that Bisma was eighteen, it was time for *her* to become Baji.

'Deeba, give me a hug,' Eva said, crouching down. Deeba was too young to truly understand that this would be the last time she saw Eva. She waddled into Eva's open arms, hugging her; Eva held her close, kissing her cheek.

Then she stood, holding her arms out for Nori.

'You'll be back, right?' Nori asked, face scrunched with confusion. A streak of dirt marred one cheek; she rubbed at it, smearing it further.

'No, sweetheart, remember?' Eva said. Her eyes shone. 'I have to go now, but Bisma will take care of all of you. She'll be your new Baji, and she's going to be wonderful.'

Baji was the title of the head of their family. Like Bisma, on Eva's eighteenth birthday she had been bequeathed the title, and like Bisma, she had said goodbye to her own Baji, a girl named Silke that Bisma remembered well.

Silke would be twenty-three now, but Bisma had not seen her since she had left the Enchanted Forest.

'Come, give me a hug,' Eva said. She hugged Nori, then said goodbye to Mei, then Azalea, then Luna.

'I'll walk with you,' Bisma said. Eva nodded; she turned to the girls, as if to tell them to go up and get ready for bed, then stopped herself.

Eva looked at Bisma, who felt unsteady by the sudden responsibility.

'Girls, wash up and change for bed,' Bisma instructed them, her voice shaking. 'I'll be back. Luna, you're in charge until then.'

Luna nodded, putting an arm around Nori. Mei held one of

little Deeba's hands, while Azalea held her other. With one final smile, Eva blew them a kiss. She looked up at the treehouse—her home—then turned to go. Bisma walked alongside her.

The Forest was dark now, but they could move through the woods with their eyes closed. Moonlight shone down from above. The air was chilly. Bisma rubbed her arms. They walked in comfortable silence until they reached the edge of the Enchanted Forest.

It was time.

Bisma threw her arms around Eva, holding her tight.

'Don't go,' Bisma said, though she knew it was futile. She pulled away, clutching Eva's forearms. 'I'm not ready, Baji. Can't you stay just a little longer?'

'Not Baji anymore,' the older girl replied with a sad smile. 'Just Eva, remember? I'll have to get used to that again. Same as you'll have to get used to being called Baji.'

Bisma released a long breath, eyes filling with tears. It felt as though a piece of her heart was being carved out.

'The rules are the rules,' Eva whispered, her voice wavering. 'You know how the Forest is.'

The Enchanted Forest had a mind of its own. It welcomed girls who were unwanted or had nowhere else to go but with the strict stipulation that the eldest would become Baji on her eighteenth birthday and remain only until the next girl came of age.

In three years, when Luna was eighteen, Bisma would be leaving just as Eva was now. It felt like a cruel punishment, always having to say goodbye.

Things had always been like this, since the Enchanted Forest took in the first girl hundreds of years ago. The rules and traditions had passed down over and over. The girls did not quite understand *why* the Forest had its rules, just that it did, and they needed to obey them.

'Won't you write to us?' Bisma whispered. 'To me, at least? I won't tell, I promise.'

Eva sighed. 'I wish, but you know I can't. None of the elder bajis ever have, and besides, I don't think the Forest would allow my letters to reach you even if I did.'

'But why?' Bisma asked, angry. 'It isn't fair.'

'Darling, if you spend all the time I'm away wishing for me to come back, how will you ever adjust? How will any of the others?' Eva said. 'You need to trust and rely on yourself, so the girls can, too. The system is the way it is for a reason.'

Bisma didn't understand why it was like this, but she did not see the same frustration on Eva's face. Eva seemed to understand why it had to be this way; perhaps when Bisma was done with her tenure as Baji, she would understand, too. But for now she felt nothing but anxiety.

'Now I really must go. Look . . .' Eva said, drawing up her wrist. There was a black tree inked onto her skin; it was the mark of the Enchanted Forest. They all had them, but Eva's was fading fast, nearly gone.

'I'm afraid,' Bisma whispered. Raising five girls under the age of fifteen—caring for them, protecting them, nurturing them—was no easy feat.

'So was I,' Eva said. She squeezed Bisma's arm. 'But you'll figure it out, and you'll have the Forest to help you. I know you can do it.'

But Bisma wasn't as patient as Eva, nor as clever or kind. She loved her sisters, but love was not always enough.

'I have to go,' Eva said. The mark on her wrist was nearly gone now. Once it faded, she would not be allowed back into the Enchanted Forest. She would go and build her life somewhere else, somewhere new, just as the previous bajis had done before her.

Bisma had no idea where any of them were; once they left, they did not stay in the Old Town and they did not return.

'I hate this,' Bisma said, eyes welling with tears. 'I'm going to miss you.'

Eva cupped Bisma's face in her hands. 'We'll see each other again,' she said, her voice a promise.

Hope flared in Bisma's heart. 'Really? How?' Bisma asked quietly.

'I'm not sure,' Eva replied, nibbling on her lower lip. 'But it's what my baji told me.'

'Where will you go? How will I find you?' Bisma had a hundred questions, but Eva just smiled, leaning forward to kiss Bisma's forehead.

'Just trust me,' Eva said, and despite the fear unfurling in Bisma's chest, she did. She trusted Eva with her life. She pulled her older sister into one last hug.

'Be good,' Eva whispered. With that, she walked away into the thick fog and disappeared.

'But that's just it,' Bisma whispered to no one in particular. She stood alone in the quiet woods. 'I'm not good.'

2

*D*isaster did not strike until two weeks later.

The first week was spent in a mourning period; the treehouse was quieter than it had ever been, and a somber mood filled the air. It took the girls some time, too, to remember to call Bisma 'Baji'.

There were chores to be done and lessons to be learned, and Bisma was in charge of all of it. There was no one above her; the responsibility was hers and hers alone.

Slowly, Bisma began to understand why Eva had been sad but hopeful on her last day; why the Unwanted Girls had to leave the Enchanted Forest when the next girl came of age. It was so they could become something more than a caretaker, so that they could live lives of their own.

To be the Baji forever was untenable. As much as she loved

them, in a way, Eva must have been glad to move on to another adventure. To live a life that was entirely her own.

It was all-consuming, looking after five girls, but such was the role of the Baji. Bisma would do what she needed to do, just as she always had, just as Eva and the bajis before her.

Deeba needed constant attention, and the older girls took turns with her.

'Why does she always need a diaper change during MY shift?' Azalea asked. Wrinkling her nose, she held Deeba at arm's length. Deeba giggled.

'Give her here, I'll do it,' Mei offered, holding her hands out for Deeba. Though she was three years younger than Azalea, she was far more responsible. Azalea went to hand Deeba off, but Bisma gave her a stern look, making Azalea stop in her tracks.

'Azalea, it's your shift and so it's your responsibility. I didn't hear Luna complaining when Deeba threw up on her.'

'*I* did!' Azalea whined in outrage. 'Luna was being a big baby about it.'

Bisma narrowed her eyes. She tried to keep her voice level. 'Still, Luna took care of it. Just like you will.' Azalea rolled her eyes, muttering to herself. '*Without* attitude,' Bisma added.

Azalea scoffed loudly. 'Oh, so now I can't even have an attitude!'

'Keep complaining and you'll be cleaning the chicken coops tomorrow,' Bisma warned.

Azalea promptly shut her lips tight, but not before giving Bisma a long-suffering look.

Bisma's heart twinged; she hated to be the bad guy, but she would need to grow used to disciplining her sisters or the entire house would fall into disarray.

There were a million things to do and manage that she had not realized, and at the end of each day she felt she had missed something (or twelve things) and ruined even more. Then, the next day, it would start all over again.

The chickens and goats needed tending to, the house needed to be cleaned, there was food to be cooked, dishes to be washed, fruits and vegetables to be picked, clothes to be stitched, pottery to be made, lessons to be taught (not to mention manners and etiquette!), furniture to be mended, and the Forest knew what else!

Of course the work was divided among the six of them—well, five, since Deeba was a baby, and honestly, she was a task on her own to be taken care of—but to organize the tasks and divide them fairly was the Baji's job—*Bisma's* job.

She had never realized how much finesse it took to keep a household running smoothly! If even one day Bisma forgot to remind one of the girls of one of their tasks, it upended the careful balance of the *entire* day, giving them all headaches and terrible moods.

In a house full of girls, bad moods were to be avoided at all costs if they were to survive, otherwise their quaint, cozy little home would soon become a butcher house.

That day, Luna sat at a table in the main room, painting the dried pottery she'd made recently. The first floor of the treehouse consisted of the kitchen, their dining area, and the living room, and it was where they spent most of their time.

The rooms were stacked above, and because they were small, they each had their own rooms, except for Deeba; she rotated rooms, since a two-year-old couldn't be left alone for the entire night.

Sunlight streamed in through the open windows, carrying in a soft breeze and the scent of pine and blossoms. It was the beginning of autumn, but warmth still remained in the air when the sun was out.

As Luna painted, and Azalea watched Deeba, Bisma was tasked

with teaching five-year-old Nori how to read, and neither of them were enjoying it one bit. There was a school for the villagers' children in Old Town, but the Unwanted Girls were not welcome there, so they taught themselves.

'Sound it out,' Bisma begged, reaching out to tuck Nori's blonde hair behind her ear. 'Cat. Cuh-Cuh-Cuh—ah-ah-ah—tuh-tuh-tuh.'

'Uh, K? O? D?' Nori attempted, getting it wrong for the seventh time in the past three days.

Bisma released a long breath.

Mei was in the kitchen, baking a pie for dinner, and the smell of potatoes, cheese, and thyme was making Bisma wish she was enjoying a nice meal out in the sun rather than suffering through a spelling lesson.

'Cat,' Bisma said again, looking into Nori's blue eyes. Her hair was a mess; Mei had done it this morning but Nori had pulled it all out from the two intricate braids. 'Come on, cuh-cuh-cuh . . .'

'Baji, I'm hungry,' Nori whined, throwing her book to the side.

'Baji, I'm hungry, too,' Azalea whined, joining them in the main room with Deeba on her hip. She plopped onto the sofa, lifting her feet up and balancing Deeba on her knees, bouncing her up and down.

'Higher!' Deeba cried, the word lispy.

Bisma got up and went to the kitchen to find some snacks. She looked around at the hanging pots of fresh herbs and glass jars overflowing with flowers to the stacks of mismatched plates and delicately painted teacups. Finding some fruit, she sliced and prepared fuzzy pink apricots and smooth green pears, licking the juice from her fingers. She brought the fruit to the table, and they all gathered round.

'Hey, that's mine!' Luna cried, as Azalea swiped a pear slice from her hand and cackled.

Bisma gave her a stern look, and Azalea shut her mouth, though a smirk remained on her face.

'Baji, my shoes,' Mei said, coming over sadly with something in her hands.

Bisma set down her sliced apricot and held her hands open for the shoes, which she lifted to find that the fronts were broken through; Mei's feet were too big for them now and she would need a new pair.

And that meant Bisma would have to go into town. She hadn't been to town since Eva left. The realization startled her. The past two weeks had passed by in such a blur. It felt like only last night Eva had left them.

'I'll go to town and get you a new pair,' Bisma said, standing. She groaned as her back cracked; she felt she had aged two years in the past two weeks.

There was no time to worry about her decaying bones; she needed to check the coffers to see how much coin they had. While the Unwanted Girls were mostly self-sufficient, they did need money for things they could not easily make, like shoes, or fabric for new clothes, or pans for cooking.

Bisma sold her poisons, and the other girls kept productive with what they could: Azalea sometimes did stitching, Luna would read to a kind elderly woman in town, and Eva used to sell painted pottery.

'I can go!' Luna said, brown eyes lighting up like struck matches. She jumped up. 'I can stop by the bakery, too, and pick up some bread instead of baking a loaf.'

Bisma gave her a look, and Luna's cheeks reddened with a blush.

'Real subtle,' Azalea cackled.

They all knew why Luna was so enthusiastic to go to town, and to the bakery, no less.

'No, I'll go,' Bisma said. She needed a moment out, anyway. Besides, it was a good excuse to take her cart. Bisma was a skilled garden-witch and could grow a number of berries, leaves, and plants, and so she sold potions in town and earned a good bit of coin that way.

There weren't many witches in Old Town, which helped her business, for it meant the vegetation she grew was not so easily accessible, and the potions she brewed were unique. Magic itself was special to the people of Fairendelle, the kingdom in which they lived, but—luckily for Bisma—it was not so rare as to be feared. In her home, at least, it was a delightful and pleasing rarity; Bisma enjoyed how her sisters squealed in awe whenever she grew a plant from the dirt.

In fact, most magic was not extraordinary; it merely helped people in their trade. There were some witches who excelled at cooking (kitchen-witches); some who were masters of stories (quill-witches); others who were good with animals (shepherd-witches); and so forth.

In the villages of Fairendelle, none were so powerful that it made them significant, though in bigger cities, such as Whitebridge, there were some quite powerful and famous witches, and in Castletown—the crown city—the most powerful witches served the king on a special council.

In Old Town, however, Bisma and the few other witches were not given such respect.

Bisma was struck by the realization that she hadn't gardened since before Eva left. *Good grief.* She needed to get back to that. She didn't have any open orders—she'd delivered all the ones before her birthday—but she needed to go to town to receive more orders to then make more money. As Baji, it was her responsibility to provide for the girls.

Finishing off her apricot, Bisma stood and brushed a stray curl from her face. 'Alright, I'm going to town,' she declared, making sure each of the girls heard her. 'Luna, you can't come because you are in charge while I'm gone.'

'What!?' Azalea groaned, huffing out her full cheeks. 'Why is Luna *always* in charge?'

'Because I'm the oldest after Baji *and* the most mature,' Luna replied, lifting her chin. She twirled, her pink dress flaring out.

'And because we like Lulu better,' Nori said innocently. She exchanged a mischievous glance with Mei, who laughed. Even Bisma's lips quirked at that, while Azalea was not the least bit amused.

'Baji! They're disrespecting me!' Azalea said, turning to Bisma with her jaw dropped. Then a hard look entered her brown eyes. She turned back to the younger girls. 'In six years when *I'm* Baji, I'm going to remember this.'

The girls hardly cared. Luna snorted.

'Baji, I'm coming, too!' Nori asked, scampering away to grab her little boots. She pulled them on, her hair falling in front of her eyes.

'Those are on backwards, angel,' Bisma said, helping Nori put them on correctly.

The girls did not go to town often, for it was not safe. The Unwanted Girls were treated like second-class citizens, if that. Many villagers regarded them like feral animals and avoided them as though they carried the plague. And so the younger girls especially were not allowed to go without an older one.

After sliding on her black boots and tying the laces tight, Bisma grabbed her leather purse, preparing to go. There was a slight chill in the autumn breeze, so she slipped on a thick cardigan as well, made of the softest yarn. This was her town cardigan; it was crow black. While Bisma adored all the wonderful colors of the Forest, when she went to town, she always wore dark colors as a sort of armor, to encourage the villagers to stay away.

'Baji, I'm ready!' Nori said, already having made quick work of putting on a sweater that looked too big for her.

'Good job, sweet,' Bisma said, pushing back Nori's wild hair. They were all set to go. Leaving Deeba, Azalea walked them to the door of the treehouse, donning an innocent expression.

'When am I allowed to go to town alone?' Azalea asked, batting her eyelashes. 'I'm almost thirteen. I think Luna went alone when she was thirteen.'

'Nice try.' Bisma gave her an unamused look. 'You know you're not allowed to go alone until you're *fourteen*, and you are currently only one month past twelve.'

'That's basically thirteen, which is basically fourteen!' Azalea cried.

'Your math skills leave something to be desired,' Luna sang from the table, while Mei giggled.

'Luna,' Bisma said, fixing her with a stern glance. 'Behave. And take care of the others. We'll be back soon.'

With that, she ushered Nori toward the stairs. Nori jumped from the highest step, her squealing laughter filling the air. A branch reached out to catch her as she went hurtling toward the ground. Bisma met her at the bottom, then walked over to the garden to grab her cart.

When she didn't have orders to drop off, she went to town with her pushcart. She had ordinary potions, like peppermint tea for upset stomachs, or elderberry syrup for a cold, or lavender essence for an antiseptic, or dried white willow bark to chew on to relieve pain—but what she was really *known* for was her poisons.

There were sleeping drops—made of valerian, a pink flower

that Bisma used magic to grow for the wives who did not like their husband's advances in the night. (And if those husbands happened to pass in the night, well, that was none of Bisma's business.) Then there was itching powder made of nettle and sumac; a hogweed spray to cause potential blindness; monkshood to cause numbness; yew-berry jam to cause discreet death; and a variation of other such products that sold quite well to the women of the village.

Of course they had to be discreet. Bisma had been notorious as 'the Unwanted Witch' or 'garden-wench' ever since she was ten and made her first potion—or, well, *poison* might be more accurate.

There were few witches in their area, and even fewer skilled ones, but Bisma was a truly gifted witch, her talents further cultivated by the Forest. She had always been talented at gardening, able to grow things from the earth with magic, like ripe fruits out of season, or herbs for cooking, or pretty flowers for her sisters.

But she became truly infamous when she was ten. Aged seven, Luna had just arrived in the Enchanted Forest and become an Unwanted Girl, and Bisma was excited to have a new sister.

Except little Luna never spoke. Whenever anyone approached her, she flinched as if injured and hastily stepped away. She seemed to be afraid of her own shadow.

It took Luna months to open up, and that was when Bisma learned that Luna had been abused by her father until it had become so unbearable that she had run away to the Enchanted Forest, prepared to face death rather than live in her own home another moment.

When Bisma learned this, she had been angry—angrier than she'd ever been. And she would only grow angrier.

One day in town, a villager spat at Luna. 'Shame on you!' the old woman said. 'Running away, sullying your family name!'

Luna covered her mouth with both her hands to stop from crying out; her body shook with the force of repressed sobs.

'Don't you know why she ran away?!' ten-year-old Bisma cried, standing in front of Luna. 'Her father hurt her!'

But the villager did not care, nor did she listen. With a final disgusted glance, the old woman walked away.

Luna quietly cried. Bisma fumed.

Their baji whisked them away, scolding Bisma for lashing out. 'You could have been hurt,' Baji had said, her voice afraid.

But Bisma wasn't afraid; she was angry.

Another visit to town brought them face to face with Luna's father. He was a broad, short man with a mustache and dark eyes the same color as Luna's. Luna froze in front of him, her breath a gasp, but her father walked straight passed her like she wasn't even there.

'If he was kind to me,' Luna whispered to Bisma that night, as they lay together in Luna's bed, 'I would go home. So long as he didn't hurt me again, I would go home.'

'No, Luna, this is your home now,' Bisma said, hating to see Luna upset. She wanted to hold her sister, but Luna did not like to be touched.

A wretched feeling was growing and twisting like a vine within Bisma, sharp and prickly. No matter how she tossed and turned in bed, the feeling would not relent. Sleep refused to come. It was as if her insides were riddled with the sharpest thorns.

Unable to bear feeling so helpless, Bisma got up and went outside. She ran down the stairs, out into the dark forest, tears coursing down her cheeks. She felt like vomiting, and she ran to her garden to inhale the sharp scent of mint, but even that did not help.

The moon shone above her as she fell to her knees, crying out. Bisma sank her hands into the dirt and felt the Forest pulsing beneath her palms, magic calling out to her. This was more potent than anything she'd felt before; it felt like clutching a lightning bolt straight from the sky.

As Bisma cried, a plant grew from the earth. She had never seen it before, but she somehow knew exactly what it was and what it could do.

She stopped crying.

Wiping away her tears, she plucked the plant, then went up to her room, where she crushed the leaves into a paste.

Then she went to the kitchen and gathered cocoa butter, beeswax, and a little bit of coconut oil to mask the nasty smell. She had made hand cream before, but this was a special product, made for one person in particular.

The next time Bisma went to town with one of her older sisters, she snuck off. Disguising herself, she went to the local blacksmith, Luna's father. The last time she had seen him in town, she noticed how very insecure he was about his hands from the way he walked with them behind his back, as if hiding the soot-stained fingers, the blackened nails.

'This is a cream that can fix all marks!' Bisma said, pitching it to him. She brought up her flawless hands. 'See? I have used it myself for years. I will give you a good price.'

Luna's father seemed hesitant, so Bisma pressed into his insecurity. 'Use this and no one will be able to tell you are a blacksmith,' she said, giving him a small sample. 'Your hands will be as clean as the bookshop owner's.'

Luna's father spread the sample across his hand, smelling it. The cream melted into his skin; he seemed impressed by its magic and bought it, thanking her as he went.

Then Bisma waited. She did not tell her sisters, in case it did not work, but somehow she knew it would; it was only a matter of time.

The next time she came to town, a week later, she slipped away to the blacksmith's shop, taking Luna with her. They both saw that it was being taken over by another, while Luna's father wept.

His hands were covered with pus-filled blisters that they could see even from a distance.

Bisma could not help her wickedness; she smiled, and stepped forward so he could see.

'You!' he cried, looking at her, recognition flaring through his face, shoving his raw, bleeding hands in her face. 'What did you do?'

'I don't know what you mean,' she replied, lifting her chin. He shouted, reaching for her, but she was quick and moved away, twirling as she did, a delicious satisfaction coursing through her. The commotion caused people to come out into the square and watch.

Let them, she thought.

Luna's father turned to the villagers. 'The Unwanted Girl! She sold me a cream and this is the result!' He lifted his hands for all to see.

Horrified gasps spread through the crowd. The plant had done precisely what Bisma had wanted it to. While at first it would have softened his skin, urging him to use it more and more, eventually, it would have rotted his hands. She could only imagine the constant agony he was in, the blisters bursting every time he tried to touch something.

Luna stepped forward, slipping her hand into Bisma's, holding tight. It was the first time Luna had willingly touched anyone. Bisma squeezed back.

Luna's father looked to Luna, realization dawning on him. 'You did it on purpose,' he said, disturbed.

'Every time you reach for a cup of tea, or try to lift your tools, the pain will remind you of what you did. And you will suffer every single moment of every day until you are dead,' Bisma said, a wicked smile spreading across her face. The blacksmith looked as though he would be sick.

As they walked away, Luna let out a long breath. She leaned her head on Bisma's shoulder. Finally, the twisting vines inside Bisma eased.

After this incident, Bisma became quietly notorious. Everyone heard about what she had done and why, and villagers began reaching out to her for similar products—not quite as harsh, but of varying degrees.

Soon Bisma had a booming business on her hands.

She did not need to advertise her poisons; people did that for her. Wives and daughters told one another of Bisma's skills, keeping the matter discreet.

What was *not* kept discreet was the fact that Bisma was clearly bad news. Unwanted Witch. Garden-wench. An abomination. Vile, twisted, cruel. Rotten to her core.

Good, Bisma told herself. *Let them be afraid*. There needed to be someone to fear, and if it was her, then so be it.

Her reputation, however, did not come without its problems. The villagers hated her more for it; she was spat at, had garbage thrown at her back when it was turned. For months the grocer refused to sell to her specifically, but would sell to her sisters after they pleaded, though at an outrageous price.

Bisma felt no remorse. How could she? For Luna was no longer afraid.

Luna no longer worried that her father might find her and hurt her again. She stopped flinching when the other girls hugged her, and then at thirteen she had her first crush and went on for weeks and weeks about how the boy who picked apples had brushed hands with her when he handed her an apple in the orchard one day.

While Bisma's poisons—as well as the family she'd found in the Enchanted Forest—gave Luna that ease, it also meant that forevermore Bisma had to be on guard in town. Even more so as Baji now, when the Unwanted Girls were her responsibility.

As she passed through the village with Nori, Bisma's body tensed, alert. She looked down at Nori, who was bouncing.

'Behave,' she ordered, her voice stern. 'And hold onto the cart. Understood?'

'Okie-dokie!' Nori said, but she was already looking around, buzzing with excitement at the change of scenery.

They entered the town square, where Bisma did her business and everything they needed could be purchased. At the north end was the tavern, the Apothecary, the mayor's office, and the inn. The west end held shops for shoes and fabric, along with a seamstress's store; the south end was where the paint store and bookshop were, along with the potter's and the blacksmith's; and the eastern portion held the meat stores, the bakery, and the fruit and vegetable stands. The storefronts were all different colors, the names painted in different styles, though they were a bit old now, the paint chipped.

The town was overcrowded, as well. Whenever Bisma came, she was struck anew by just how many *people* there were. She was so used to her little family having free rein over the entire Forest, which of course they shared with the birds and animals and bees, but it was not nearly the same as dozens of people crammed into this one square, shopping and chatting and laughing. It was so *loud*.

As Bisma pushed her cart through the square, she felt uneasy. People nudged each other and pointed, staring at her and Nori. Bisma glared back at all of them.

In town, she always donned her most feral scowl, and her

withering glare, and the hard set of her jaw, like a rabid animal prepared to pounce at any moment.

'Don't smile,' Bisma ordered Nori, who was happily skipping.

The Unwanted Girls were disliked, and if they showed happiness, it only encouraged further bullying. The villagers were always keen to remind the girls to be miserable, so they put on the facade of unhappiness and the villagers stayed content, and more importantly stayed away.

As Bisma approached the shoe store, a woman grabbed her child and shoved her out of Bisma's sight, as though Bisma was an evil force that children needed to be protected from.

Despite herself, Bisma's heart twinged. They were strangers, but when they looked at her like she was evil, it only made her feel like an even worse person.

If she behaved like a monster and was treated like a monster, did that make her a monster?

It does not matter, she reminded herself. She did not need them. All Bisma could count on was the Unwanted Girls and the Enchanted Forest. They may be unwanted elsewhere, but they were wanted by each other.

It was better for the villagers to be afraid of her.

Then they would leave her alone.

3

After selling orders to her usual customers, then collecting new shoes for Mei, Bisma went to the bakery for those chocolate chip muffins the girls loved. At least Old Town wasn't filled with all bad characters. The baker and her family were kind, good people.

Bisma waved at the baker and her husband, then at their son behind the counter, who donned an apron.

'Hello!' Haru said. He was a sweet-faced boy of fifteen with silky black hair; it was easy to see why he was the object of Luna's daydreams.

He looked over Bisma's shoulder, as if searching for someone.

Bisma lifted Nori up so she could wave at Haru. 'I'm afraid she's my only companion today,' Bisma said, giving him a small smile. There was no one else in the bakery, so she did not have to worry about maintaining her surly attitude. 'Eight muffins and a loaf of bread, please.'

He gathered her order, and she paid.

'Please tell—' He broke off, looking away. His ears tinged pink. 'Tell your . . . sisters I send my regards.'

Bisma nodded, trying not to laugh at the poor boy. 'I will.'

She stashed the goods on her cart and left the bakery, Nori beside her. Once outside, Bisma's smile immediately faded. She glared at passersby, scanning the crowds before looking to Nori. 'Ready to go home?' she asked.

'Aw, Baji!' Nori pouted. 'A little longer!' She held onto the edge of Bisma's dress, pulling. 'Please, please, please!'

'Tch, Nori,' Bisma said, unable to say no.

She looked up and was promptly distracted by a familiar figure. As her heart rate spiked violently, and her glare hardened, Nori took the opportunity to skip back into the bakery to Haru. Though the figure was across the square, she would recognize that obnoxious face from any distance.

Xander Chapman.

He strode toward her, and even his walk was detestable, those ridiculous long legs clad in black trousers made of fine material and leather boots that were so clean, they shone. His strides were confident; he practically sauntered.

He wore a white blouse with billowing sleeves and a waistcoat that accented his slim waist and outrageously broad shoulders. The waistcoat was emerald green, the same shade as his eyes. The only thing worse than the waistcoat was his hair: silky locks that were the deep copper-brown of leaves in autumn and which added a good few inches to his already towering height.

More than a handful of village girls stared at him, pointing and giggling. Bisma's hands tightened around her cart as he approached.

She considered making a run for it, but knowing Xander, he would only chase after her.

Deplorable man.

'Well met, Bis,' he said, standing in front of her. He flashed her a brilliant smile, showcasing his perfect teeth and those deep dimples in his flawless cream-colored skin.

One of her eyes twitched. That was another thing. He sometimes called her by a nickname, as though they were intimate friends.

'Alexander.' She put as much disdain as she could into each syllable. She did not even know if Alexander was his full name, but it was the opposite of calling him a nickname. Not that he cared; his lips spread into another easy smile.

He was *always* smiling.

And why wouldn't he? What worry in the world did he have? He was rich, loved, respected, beautiful, and . . . good.

She hated him and his perfect life.

He had both his parents, and they were madly in love with another, and it was clear that their only child had been born of that love and was doted on as a result. He had spent most of his youth in Whitebridge receiving a private education and had returned to Old Town a few years ago, where he had easily slotted into his family's business, made friends with just about every local, and had girls falling at his feet wherever he went.

The very people who spat on Bisma as she walked past practically kissed the ground Xander walked on.

And like the spoiled, bored man that he was, he was constantly trying to entrap her.

Why else would he go out of his way to see her whenever she came to town? Xander had no reason to be interested in her in any genuine way. He had everything a guy could want—why would he ever want her, an Unwanted Girl, and the very worst one at that?

He looked at her with those glittering green eyes and charming smile, asking her questions in his posh velvet accent, only to seduce and humiliate her.

Bisma had heard the stories from her elder sisters when she was younger; how the boys of Old Town loved to place bets to see who might tame one of the Unwanted Girls, how they would pretend to be enamored by them only to drop them once their conquest was complete.

Bisma had seen first-hand how Eva had fallen in love with a villager who had only been playing with her. He broke her heart, and Eva cried for weeks.

Even then, Bisma had not heeded her older sisters' warnings, until at the age of sixteen, she grew feelings for a villager of her own and faced the very same fate.

She had sworn she would never fall for it again.

No matter how adamant Xander was with his ridiculous attentions, bringing her flowers or sweets or, worst of all, kind words and an even kinder gaze, she would not succumb to his nefarious plans.

Case in point: Xander pulled a flower from his breast pocket and held it out for her between long, slender fingers. She watched as the yellow petals morphed to dark emerald green to match the birthday dress she was wearing beneath her black sweater.

Xander was a garden-witch—just like her—but he was an obnoxious show-off, where Bisma was not.

He bent forward, and she inhaled the spicy sweet scent of cloves that always emanated from him. With a smile, he held the flower out for her. She plucked it from his hand and held it between her mehndi-covered fingers. His face grew pleased, dimples appearing in his cheeks.

Until rot spread through the flower, darkening the petals till they shriveled. Bisma dropped the flower and stomped on it, grinding it into the dirt for good measure.

Rather than be offended, his smile only deepened. *Stubborn ass!*

He placed a hand on his heart. 'You do know how to make a man feel special.'

'Man?' she asked, looking around. 'Where? I only see an overgrown boy.'

'I am a year older than you, you know,' he said in his know-it-all voice. 'And on that note, happy belated birthday. That was what the flower was for, by the way. Before you mercilessly killed it.'

She narrowed her eyes; he was thorough. How did he find out when her birthday was?

Then, as if realizing something, his smile faded. His expression grew somber. 'Oh, that means Eva must be gone. You must miss her.'

Even the people of Old Town knew about the Enchanted Forest and its rules. With his words, Bisma's heart felt as though it had been pierced with a dozen tiny thorns. Before she could stop herself, her eyes teared up. He was cruel, rubbing salt into her wound in such a manner, reminding her of her grief.

She had been sorry to have been away from town for so long, but now she felt she should have stayed away longer if only to avoid *him*.

'I haven't seen you in some time,' Xander said, changing the subject. His eyes sparkled. 'Old Man Hughes was asking for a potion for his stomach ache, said what you'd given him had helped, but not quite enough.'

She'd given him a simple potion that should have alleviated his pain, but the fact that it hadn't meant that this was no simple stomach bug; likely, the old man had an infection. She'd need to use the root of karu—a deep blue flower, spotted with green and white—to make a potion for him, something Xander easily could have done.

She arched her brow. 'Not clever enough to make it yourself?'

She wondered why he hadn't taken the chance to steal a customer from her while she had been away. These past few years, Bisma has had consistent and loyal customers, but it was nothing compared to Xander's family business. The Chapman Apothecary had been around since Old Town was founded over two hundred years ago; most of the villagers bought directly from the Apothecary, which was why most of Bisma's clientele were those looking for poisons, not potions.

Xander shrugged easily. 'Hughes is your customer.'

She frowned. His kindness was a trick, she was sure. The wind blew through his copper hair as she regarded him closely. He let her, not the least perturbed by her assessing gaze, whereas the other villagers avoided her glance the moment she set it upon any of them.

'You know,' he said, 'if you supplied your potions to the Apothecary, we could work together and you wouldn't have to worry about delayed shipments.'

There it is. It wasn't enough that he planned to seduce her, now he wished to control her business, as well?

'I would rather poison myself than work with you,' she said.

At that, he grew tense. He lowered his voice, stepping closer. Heat ran through her at his proximity. 'You really ought to stop with all this poison business,' he said sternly.

Indignation ran through her. 'Who are you to tell me to stop?'

'Why must you argue?' he asked, which was rich, since *he* was the one always arguing with *her*. 'It's just not . . . right,'

How condescending. Perfect Xander with his perfect life. What did he know?

'I don't care for what is right or wrong,' she lied.

'You should,' he said, eyebrows furrowing. He looked concerned.

'Last week a man was so ill he could not swallow anything but water and stale bread for five days. It was a peculiar case.'

Bisma was familiar with the case, of course, because she was the one who'd poisoned him.

The man in mention was a father of four and spent all his wife's hard-earned money on liquor. His wife had discreetly approached Bisma for a poison that would make liquor repellant to him, and the poison Bisma had concocted was meant to do just that. It wouldn't have killed him to survive on stale bread and water.

Of course she couldn't tell Xander that. Her clients trusted her to keep their secrets; their confidentiality was paramount. While Xander may have been able to tell that the drunk was poisoned, the man himself would not be able to. It was why many of her poisons were subtle, for the protection of those soliciting her business.

'I healed him,' Xander said. Irritation flared through her, and she glowered. Xander hardly noticed. 'You need to be careful,' he warned. 'I spotted your handiwork; others may as well.'

'You only noticed because you're a garden-witch, too,' she replied. 'You know your potions.'

'No,' he said, his voice softening. Something turned in his expression, the severity giving way to tenderness. 'I know you.'

A shiver ran down her spine. She felt hot and cold at once as she looked up into his eyes, noticing how large his pupils had become. His eyes were dark, the lids lowered as he gazed down at her.

The breath lodged in her throat as she scanned his face, her heart hammering loudly in her ears. Xander took a step closer, the warmth of his body infiltrating her space. He smelled like herbs and earth and rain, like sinking her hands deep into the dirt, magic sprouting plants in response.

Despite the warning bells ringing in her head, Bisma took a small step forward. He lifted an elegant hand as if to touch her face.

She jolted. *No!* she scolded herself.

She scowled, taking a big step back.

He looked startled and dropped his hand.

'Don't you have somewhere to be?' she asked, making her tone as nasty as possible. 'Fellow puppies to play with?'

'Yes, always.' He laughed. 'But none quite as pretty as you, darling Bisma.'

'I assure you my bite is as bad as my bark,' she threatened.

'Now that's something I'd be keen to experience,' he said, eyes flashing with heat.

Her pulse raced. She couldn't look at him; she was afraid she might do something asinine, like blush.

Instead, Bisma looked over his shoulder and saw that the mayor's office and inn front seemed to be busy with preparations.

Xander turned and followed her gaze. 'Ah, my Uncle Fred is coming to town for a few months,' he said. 'Perhaps you've heard of him? He's a brilliant architect. He has ideas to modernize Old Town.'

'What an oxymoron.'

Xander smiled. Irritation—with an undercurrent of hopeless despair—ran through her. No matter how rude she was to him—no matter how she tried to keep him away—he was always amiable and good-natured, a silly smile forever plastered on his face.

'Clever,' he replied. 'I am lucky we were never in class together or you'd have taken my spot as first student.'

While before she was merely vexed by him, now she was angry. He was *mocking* her.

Unwanted Girls were not allowed in the town's school, and rich boys like Xander went away to bigger cities for proper education at boarding schools.

'I am surprised to hear you were the first student,' she replied, this time finding no difficulty in making her voice scathing. 'But while your charms may have worked on your brainless teachers, they don't work on me.'

He looked wounded.

Another ploy! Well, she would not be swayed by the injured expression on his sweet face.

'I didn't mean—' he began.

'I know what you meant,' she snapped.

'Bisma—'

'It's Unwanted Girl to you,' she said. None of the other villagers cared to learn their names, and the only reason he did was to trap her. Every time he said her name in that deep voice of his, part of her tugged closer to him, ached for him to say it again.

To hear her name whispered by him, to taste it on his tongue.

A shiver ran through her.

The problem was Bisma knew how lovely the build-up of being ensnared was, the rush of being kissed, of being touched. It was so easy to remember the thrill of it and to forget the pain of the aftermath, the agony of heartbreak.

But she would not forget. She would *not* repeat the same mistakes.

'Good day,' she said, making to leave. She looked to the bakery to call Nori once more, only to realize Nori was no longer there.

Bisma swore under her breath.

Concern covered Xander's face. He stepped forward. 'What is it?' he asked, his voice tender.

'Nothing!' she cried. 'Leave me alone.'

She grabbed an itching power from her cart, flicked open the cap, and blew the powder into the air. Xander jumped back and she hurried back to the bakery to ask Haru.

At the bakery, Bisma heard Nori's laughter. Relief flowed through her for a second before her heart froze with dread. The laughter was not coming from in front of her but from behind.

From . . . *above?*

Bisma turned, gasping. Nori had climbed one of the trees in the square. She loved jumping off the tall trees of the Enchanted Forest and having a branch reach out to catch her.

Dread gripped her heart.

'Nori, no!' Bisma screamed, already running.

In horrifying slow motion, she watched as Nori grinned and jumped from her branch. From that height, the fall would kill her.

Bisma pushed her body, running as fast as she could. *Please*, her very being cried out. *Please let me reach her in time.*

She did not.

But Xander did.

He ran toward Nori at the same time she did, but he was closer, and as Nori's body came careening down to the unforgiving ground with alarming speed, he threw himself forward, catching her at the very last second.

Xander broke her fall with his body, holding onto her.

'Nori!' Bisma cried, running to reach them.

Though confused as to why the branch had not caught her as it did in the Enchanted Forest, Nori still laughed, amused. Stupid child!

Xander helped Nori to her feet, his copper hair a mess, his immaculate clothes streaked with dirt. With a pained groan, he stood, cracking his neck.

Bisma grabbed Nori from him, shaking her. 'Why did you do that?' she cried, hands digging into Nori's arms. Her heart was beating so hard she worried it might break through her ribs.

Seeing the worry in Bisma's expression, the amusement vanished from Nori's face. Her bottom lip trembled. Then she began to cry.

'Bis—' Xander began, face alarmed. She ignored him, focusing on her sister. Nori tried to prise herself free from Bisma's arms, but Bisma only held on tighter to the little girl.

'We are only safe in the Forest!' Bisma hissed, shaking Nori again. 'Do you understand?'

Nori replied by wailing, her face wet with tears. Villagers gathered round to watch, not even bothering to whisper as they made comments. Bisma did not care; she pressed into Nori's arms.

'Tell me you understand!' Bisma yelled.

'I-I do,' Nori cried. 'I do.'

Bisma released Nori, but the terror in her body did not release her. It was a physical thing, gripping her the way ice covered branches in winter.

If Xander hadn't caught her . . .

Bisma could picture the girl's broken body bloodying the earth below. The sight seared into her mind.

She was Nori's Baji; Nori was *her* responsibility.

'She didn't mean to,' Xander said, his voice soft. 'You need not be so harsh.'

Bisma whirled on him, face wild. Seeing her vicious expression, he pressed his mouth shut. He held his hands up, but the concern in his eyes made her want to claw at him.

His concern was aimed not only at Nori but her too.

She could not bear it a moment longer. Grabbing Nori, Bisma went back to her cart, then back to the Enchanted Forest.

It wasn't until they were home that she could properly breathe.

4

After the disaster with Nori, Bisma kept away from town for some time.

She sent Luna and Mei to drop off potions and poisons, and Azalea to pick up the things they needed. Nori went with Luna on one of the occasions; the little girl recovered quickly, even if Bisma had not.

The very same evening as the near catastrophe, Nori was back to laughing and playing with Deeba, the two-year-old shrieking with glee as Nori tickled her, while Bisma replayed the moment again and again in her mind: the startling speed with which Nori had hurtled toward the ground and the riotous pound of Bisma's heart as she had run toward her in vain.

She thought also of Xander, how he had saved Nori. The concern in his eyes. How he had run toward her without hesitation. *Why had he done so?*

Bisma did not tell anyone what happened. She would not worry her sisters, and other than them she had no one else to tell. She was their baji. They had faith in her. They believed she would protect them, take care of them.

Even if she was not worthy of such faith, she would not break it.

Bisma recalled how when she was younger, her bajis always seemed so sure, so calm. They were never frightened or worried, so now, even if Bisma was not as confident as her bajis had been, she would at least uphold the pretense.

She knew how much comfort it gave.

But as the days passed, Bisma still felt frayed. She felt heavy, burdened. Each night, the scene replayed in front of her, though this time with a horrific end: Nori falling from that perilous height and colliding with the unforgiving ground, her little body crumpling instantaneously into a gruesome breakage of bones and blood.

To distract herself, Bisma spent time out in her garden. The women of the village sometimes left her orders for poisons in the earth at the edge of the Enchanted Forest, which the Forest then delivered to her through various means: either through woodland creatures, which resulted in little teeth marks on the paper, or through the soil, which left the letters damp and streaked with dirt.

The letters were always deposited in her garden, waiting for her; the Forest was very helpful in that regard. She knew, also, that the Forest only sent her the letters it wished for her to receive, otherwise she would have an abundance of hatred to sort through daily.

While the feel of dirt beneath her nails and the smell of fresh plants did ease her worries, she felt terribly lonely, like vines were tightening around her, rooting her in place.

After a morning spent making poisons and an afternoon spent delivering them, she returned home, ready to lift her feet and rest. The girls were all doing their own thing: Deeba was napping, Nori was playing with the Forest trees, Azalea was working on embroidery, and Luna was reading poetry.

Mei was frying sesame dessert buns, the smell of the sweet dough filling the treehouse with a delectable scent. (Out of all of them, Mei exhibited signs of being a witch: her skills in the kitchen were impressive for anyone, let alone a nine-year-old.)

The evening gave them these quiet moments as they all recharged on their own before colliding back together at dinnertime. Bisma gave her sisters kisses and snagged a hot sesame bun before heading up the winding stairs to her room.

There, she took off her sweater and pulled her hair loose from its braid. Looking around, she rearranged some of the flowers in their vases, then refreshed the dried lavender hanging from the ceiling with new sprigs.

Suddenly, the room felt too small, too quiet. A strange suffocating feeling overcame her. Her throat tightened. It felt like there was something inside her that needed to get out, but she was too tired to go down to her garden and use her magic.

Without thinking too much about it, Bisma took out a piece of paper and quill and ink, then sat down on the floor, crossing her legs. She set the paper down and smoothed it across the wooden floors. Perhaps writing would help. Tapping the quill against her lips, she felt the worn feather end brush against her skin.

Then she stopped.

She had no one to write to. Bisma couldn't write to Eva or any of her other bajis.

Still, she felt like she needed to write, to somehow fill the echoing emptiness of her solitude with words, even if they were only her own. She was no quill-witch—a master of words—but even so, she put the quill to paper and wrote.

I don't know why I am writing this, or to whom, I just know that I am so lonely I don't know what to do with myself. I don't want to be alone with my thoughts. I am afraid, and perhaps if I write what I feel down onto paper, I can expunge these dreadful feelings from within me.

I wish Eva didn't have to leave. I know I am eighteen, that it is time for me to be Baji, but doesn't the Forest understand that I am not capable? How can it entrust these girls to me? I am ashamed of what happened. Nori might have been lost to all of us, only because of me.

What should I do? What can I do? My eyes well with tears as I write this. I know I have no choice but to carry on, and I will do my best, but what if my best is not good enough?

What a stupid question. I know my best is not good enough, for I am no good.

Setting her quill down, Bisma stared down at the paper. She did not want to read what she had written so she folded the paper in half, then into quarters, then into eighths, until it was a little crooked square.

Where to put it? She did not plan on sending it, for she had no one to send it to, and she did not want to leave it lying around in case one of her sisters got their hands on it. Bisma slipped the square into a gap in a vine around one of her windows.

Which begged the question: *why write at all?* Was it not futile, fruitless? What was the point?

But Bisma found the act cathartic, as if by writing the words down, some of the overwhelming emotion from within her had been removed. It felt . . . soothing.

Then she heard a howling gale from outside. Bisma furrowed her brows, alarmed. Such wind only came when the Forest was upset. She shot to her feet, about to investigate when she heard a cry from below.

'Baji! Come quick!' Luna screamed. 'It's Mei. She's been poisoned!'

5

Bisma rushed down to the main room, then dashed to the kitchen, where Mei was lying on the floor.

'What happened?' she cried, falling to her knees by Mei's side. Mei was unconscious, her silky black hair spread around her head like spilled ink.

The veins of her arms were an unnatural dark blue. Bisma had never seen anything like it before. The girls were right; it was a poisoning. It could not be anything else. Rage whipped through Bisma, fire-hot.

Mei's chest gently rose and fell; Bisma forced herself to focus. At the very least, Mei was breathing. The girls were all gathered around her: Luna's eyes were wide as she held sleeping baby Deeba; Azalea looked horrified, a hand covering her mouth; and Nori was pulling at Mei's hand with both of hers.

'Mei, wake up,' Nori said, her little voice worried.

Bisma felt the skin of Mei's arm, which was freezing cold. She ran a hand along Mei's dark veins, which were raised. She didn't understand the symptoms.

'Get blankets,' Bisma said. 'And a pillow for her head. Did she fall?'

It wasn't good that Mei was so cold.

Azalea ran to get blankets, while Luna said, 'I think so but I'm not sure, none of us actually saw. I heard a thud and when I turned around she was on the floor.'

'I asked her to bring me a snack,' Nori said, eyes welling with tears.

'Shh, it's okay,' Bisma said, putting her hands on Nori's shoulders. 'It isn't your fault, sweet.'

But whose fault was it?

Who would poison Mei, and how did they do it?

Bisma set those questions to one side; she had to focus.

'Get her up onto the sofa,' she ordered. 'And get her warm. I'll be back.'

Mind racing, Bisma ran down to her garden. Wind howled around her as she went directly to her cart. Bottles clinked together as she rummaged through potions, trying to find something, anything.

Finally, she found a generic cure-all that she sometimes sold with her poisons, especially to mothers with small children who were afraid of their children accidentally ingesting poison. The cure-all wasn't guaranteed to be an antidote, but it was better than nothing.

Grabbing the dark pink bottle, Bisma ran back up to the main room of the treehouse, then dashed to the kitchen. The cure-all was made of gullshamdani, a purple flower with hairy-toothed leaves; the root was dried then crushed, but to be effective it needed to be mixed with milk and sugar.

'Baji,' Nori called, her voice worried.

'Just a moment,' Bisma said, making the mixture, using her magic to stir it more quickly. 'Done.'

In three large steps she was back in the main room, where Luna had set Deeba down and was sitting beside Mei, holding her hand as it dangled off the sofa. Bisma went down on her knees beside her, lifting Mei's little head up, Mei's dark hair soft in Bisma's shaking hand.

'Azalea, Luna, help me hold her up,' Bisma said.

Azalea did as she was told, holding Mei up from the other side, while Luna held Mei's head from beside Bisma. With Bisma's free hand, she opened Mei's mouth and with the other, dribbled in some of the cure-all. Pink liquid wet Mei's lips, a drop falling down her chin and onto her dress.

'Tilt her head back a little,' Bisma ordered.

The girls did as they were told, and they watched with bated breath, waiting to see if Mei would swallow.

At last, Mei's throat moved.

'Sit her up,' Bisma said.

Azalea and Luna helped lift her up fully and Bisma sat on the sofa behind her, so Mei could lean against her. The weight of her sister felt both too heavy and too light. 'Nori, angel, can you rub Mei's feet please?'

Nori nodded. Reaching under the blanket, she rubbed Mei's feet as Bisma waited. 'Luna, Azalea, her hands,' Bisma said, and they began to rub her hands.

They all held their breath, watching.

Finally, Mei's veins lightened, the dark blue color leaving them almost entirely. Warmth returned to her fawn-toned skin. She coughed, then groaned.

'Mei, honey, it's Baji,' Bisma said, rubbing her arms. 'Can you open your eyes?'

Slowly, Mei blinked, then opened her eyes. Her dark eyes took in the sight of all her sisters; her face furrowed with confusion.

'What happened?' she asked, her voice hoarse.

The girls looked at each other, then to Bisma.

The problem was Bisma didn't know either. And she was *supposed* to know.

'You fell,' Bisma said, not wanting to worry Mei.

She controlled the narrative; if she panicked, then the other girls would, too. Bisma forced a smile as Mei looked back at her.

'Oh,' Mei said, trying to smile. 'How silly.'

'Yes,' Bisma said, forcing a smile on to her own face as well. 'Very silly.'

'It's so cold,' Mei said, snuggling close to Bisma, who wrapped her arms tight around the nine-year-old.

Her skin was still icy, though not as freezing as before. The cure-all may have worked for now, but it hadn't solved the root of the problem. Bisma could still see the remnants of the poison inside Mei; her veins still bulged slightly, and they were darker than they should have been.

'What—' Bisma began, but she stopped when Mei yawned.

'I'm so sleepy,' Mei said. She leaned heavily against Bisma.

'Let's get you to sleep, then,' Bisma said. She would have to ask her questions later to uncover what exactly had caused such a reaction, what Mei had eaten or touched.

'Come on,' Azalea said, helping lift Mei to her feet. As much as the dramatic twelve-year-old complained about chores, when it counted, she was there for her sisters. Bisma gave Azalea a grateful smile.

They guided Mei to her room, Luna trailing behind them with Nori and Deeba. Mei's room was neat and clean, her desk covered with herbs set out to dry. Above them hung ribbons in various shades, ribbons she used when doing up any of her sisters' hair.

Bisma helped Mei settle in her bed, then tucked her in with blankets.

'Do you need anything?' she asked, sitting beside her.

Mei languidly shook her head, eyes already drooping closed. A few moments later, Mei fell asleep, her breathing soft but steady.

The other girls still seemed worried, so Bisma gave them all a reassuring smile, pulling Nori close to her, stroking her blonde curls.

'Everything is alright,' Bisma said, forcing herself to sound bright as she led them out of Mei's room. 'Who's hungry? Let's get ready for dinner.'

'I'm starving,' Luna said, helping Bisma break the tension.

'Weren't you just reading poetry?' Azalea said, arching a brow.

Luna gave Azalea a confused look. 'What precisely is your point?'

'Aren't you always going on about how you could just *live* off books?'

Luna scoffed. 'I was being hyperbolic.'

'Riiight.'

Bisma laughed, and the other girls followed suit, giggling. The tension dissipated from the room as they busied themselves with setting the table. Azalea had been helping Mei with dinner tonight, and it was a dish of soft cheese drizzled with honey, a fresh loaf of bread, and a salad with dried cranberries, nuts, and sweet potatoes.

As they ate, Bisma's thoughts strayed to Mei, who thankfully slept peacefully. If she had been disturbed, or her condition grew worse, Bisma knew the Forest would alert her.

Bisma fought the urge to go down to her garden to start whipping something together. She knew that if she panicked, the girls would as well.

So Bisma ate her food and chatted with her sisters. After, she checked in on Mei, whose skin still had a bluish tint to it. Her condition had not grown worse, but it had not improved, either.

'Time for bed,' Bisma announced.

They all cleaned up and got ready for bed, and only after everyone was asleep did Bisma go down to the garden, lighting the hanging candles so that she might see in the dark.

She worked on a few different potions by candlelight, her mind running through possibilities. She grew a pashanbhed—the flowers pale pink with a deeper rose flush in the center—then crushed the rhizome; it was often used to cure internal infections. But what if it wasn't an infection, and instead was something she had ingested?

Karu was used for stomach aches, so if this poisoning had been caused by something Mei ate, the root of the blue-flowered plant could be used to cure her.

Or perhaps the right course of action was to use yellow cobra lily? The plant itself was poisonous, but it was also used to cure certain snake bites. Could it work if Mei had been bitten by something venomous?

Alone in her garden, panic flared through her. She was running blind; she didn't know what to do. She had a working knowledge of various plants and their uses, but she didn't have enough experience, exposure, or education to know which would be correct, which would be best. Her work with curing potions was low-level: basic medicinal herbs, like peppermint tea for upset stomachs, or elderberry syrup for a cold, things like that, things she could easily make and sell.

This was not her expertise, but she knew whose it was.

Bisma clenched her jaw. She would rather chew off her own hand than reach out to Xander, but maybe he didn't need to know. His family's apothecary would surely have cure-alls more effective than hers, as well as other ingredients she could mix to create a cure of her own.

She looked up at the moon; it was night. The Apothecary would be closed. She could sneak in and grab what she needed and he would be none the wiser. Yes, that would work.

She quickly checked on the girls. Their home was quiet (well, Nori was snoring) and everyone was fast asleep. Grabbing her sweater and pouch, she snuck out, making haste through the dense trees until she was out of the Enchanted Forest, heading for Old Town.

The autumn night had a bitter bite to it, wind scraping against her, but she hardly felt it. Her blood was running too hot with worry for Mei, as well as rage at the thought of someone trying to hurt one of her sisters.

When she arrived in town, everything was closed, doors shut and locked. The square was empty and silent, dark save for the few lamp posts that stayed lit through the night.

She walked over to the Apothecary—one of the largest buildings—and slipped behind the building to the back door. As she did, it began to rain. Under the gray clouds, she broke off a little branch, infusing it with her magic, willing it to become what she needed it to.

Her magic came easier to her in the Enchanted Forest—as easy as breathing, really—but outside the Forest, it required more of her energy. Even so, the branch gave way and morphed. She used it to pick the lock, which gave way quickly.

Bisma crept into the shop, which was filled with rows and rows of potions and powders and salves. The potions were housed in the typical Chapman Apothecary special glass, which was made especially for them and imported in from Castletown. It smelled strongly of various herbs, though the one that stuck out most to her was the sweet, spicy scent of cloves, so strong she could taste it. *Xander's scent.*

The thought sent a jolt down her spine. Shaking her head, she pulled a candle and match out of her purse and lit it, holding the light up as she made her way through the aisles, reading the different medicines.

There was an entire aisle dedicated to beauty products, which wasn't shocking to her in the slightest; no wonder Xander's cream-colored skin and copper hair were always immaculate. He probably tested all his mother's potions.

After a little while, she heard a noise, but assumed it was just the wind outside, picking up intensity as the rain fell harder. Bisma continued down the aisle, turning bottles to read their ingredients. Allspice for relieving aches, arugula for fertility, nutmeg for colds . . .

Finally, she found the section of cure-alls.

She set her candle down and grabbed a few different ones, sneaking them into her purse. She held one up, about to open the cap to take a sniff when someone grabbed her from behind.

A hand clamped over her mouth to keep her from screaming out while an arm wound tight around her waist. Her heart thumped wildly in her chest.

Bisma whirled around, and her assailant immediately dropped his hand from her mouth.

'Bisma?' Xander said, confused. His arm was still around her, his grip strong. He held her in a near embrace, and she could smell the rain and earth on his sweet skin. Standing this close, she had to tilt her head back to look up at him.

His copper hair was a mess, as though he'd just woken up, but his green eyes were vivid and alert. He was in his shirtsleeves, the blouse open at the neck to reveal the long line of his pale throat, which was wet with rain, glistening.

She could feel his pulse racing and felt her own quicken in response.

Foolish. 'Let go of me,' she snarled. She struck him with her elbow, and he stumbled back.

Once he'd caught his breath, he straightened up. 'What are you doing here?' he asked, brows furrowed. 'You're not a thief.'

He looked at her with confusion, and irritation flashed through her. If it was anyone else catching her trying to rob their family's business, they would have been livid. But not Xander. He only looked concerned, his emerald eyes warm.

'What are *you* doing here?' she countered, avoiding his gaze.

'Someone saw a light and came to inform me.' He furrowed his brows. 'Now answer the question, Bisma. What are you doing here?'

Hearing her name on his lips made her shiver and she forced herself to take another step back. 'Nothing,' she snapped, trying to brush past him. As she stepped away from him, he reached out and caught her wrist, pulling her back.

'What's wrong?' he asked, velvet voice low with worry. 'You can tell me.'

'*Nothing*,' she said. But her voice was lacking its usual bite.

He still held onto her, his slender fingers soft yet firm around her forearm. That was when he noticed the bottle in her hand.

'Something's wrong, what is it?' She did not reply, and he stepped closer, his tone gentle as though she was a wild animal that might scare easily. 'Bis, let me help.'

She would not be in his debt; she would not let him hold power over her—not any more than he already had, which was dangerous enough.

'Please,' she said, hating how her voice trembled. 'Just let me go.'

With a sigh, he stepped back.

Not looking at him, she ran.

She didn't stop running until she returned to the Enchanted Forest, until she returned home.

Mei was sound asleep in her bed, and Bisma set a pillow on the floor beside her, lying down. She reached up and took one of Mei's hands; it was still cold, but not colder than before. Bisma would try the Apothecary cure-all in the morning. Maybe rest would do Mei good.

She would be fine, Bisma reassured herself. *Perfectly fine.*

The next morning, mercifully, Mei's condition was the same. The girls were relieved to find their sister stable, even if her skin had an unnatural blue tint to it.

'Come, let's have a picnic in the main room,' Bisma suggested, helping Mei to the sofa there.

'I got the blanket!' Nori called, bringing over the yellow picnic blanket. Azalea helped her set it up, while Luna and Bisma retrieved the breakfast items from the kitchen.

They brought all the goods to the floor in front of Mei so they could eat breakfast together. Mei stayed bundled in blankets, holding Deeba in her lap as Deeba talked in broken sentences of gibberish.

After Mei had some breakfast, Bisma fed her the potion from the Apothecary and was relieved to see that throughout the day Mei's condition seemed to be getting better. By the afternoon, Mei had enough energy to get up on her own, and the blue tinge from her skin was almost entirely gone.

They were nearly in the clear. Soon, Bisma would investigate what had happened, but until then, she focused on the girls, on things going back to normal.

The tension of the night before left their home entirely. By evening, even Bisma was feeling relieved, the sight of Mei's darkened veins already morphing from reality to memory.

Outside, it began to drizzle, then pour, and they all gathered round the windows, looking out to watch the rain soak the earth, dribbling down the leaves of the trees.

They ate together at the table, a hot basil tomato soup with gooey grilled-cheese sandwiches, their fingers shining from the butter, and everything was alright.

Until it wasn't.

An hour after dinner, as they were all busy with their own things, Mei stood from the sofa and promptly collapsed. The blankets fell from her body, revealing dark blue veins across her arms and legs.

'Baji!' Nori shrieked.

'Mei!' Luna cried.

They all rushed to her side. Dread curdled through Bisma. She touched a hand to Mei's skin; it was freezing and tinged a deeper blue than last night.

The cure-all must have faded.

'I thought she was better!' Azalea cried, her voice accusatory as her brown eyes flicked to Bisma.

'What's happening?' Nori asked, petrified.

'Maybe try this?' Luna said, bringing the cure-all from the Apothecary forward from the kitchen. 'Baji?'

They all turned to Bisma.

Bisma opened her mouth to respond, but nothing came out. She didn't know what was happening, and anxiety iced through her. Her sight began swimming; she felt faint.

Bisma swayed, then jolted upright. She heard a sniffle and saw that Nori and Deeba had both noticed. They looked at her with concern, afraid. They were all so small.

What was she doing? Bisma couldn't let them see her unraveling. Her heart pounded against her chest, drawing pain with every beat.

'I need a moment,' she said, her voice high. Her gaze jumped to Luna, who looked frightened as well.

'Go,' Luna said. Bisma hesitated; she didn't want to leave them for even a second, but she needed to compose herself.

She felt a hand on her back; it was Azalea, pushing her. Without thinking further, Bisma ran up the stairs, going all the way up to her room.

Now that she was alone, the anxiety overcame her completely. Her vision blurred with tears as she gasped for breath, everything inside her tightening and twisting.

She was so scared. She missed her baji, all the bajis that had come before her. She didn't want this responsibility. How could she take care of the others? She hardly knew how to take care of herself!

What was she doing? What was she doing?

Her thoughts spiraled, and she felt like a fish caught in a net, pulled out of the water and flopping this way and that as it struggled to breathe.

Then she spotted something on her bed.

It was a neatly folded piece of paper. It had no seal but was covered with streaks of dirt, as if it had come from the earth. The Forest must have delivered it to her.

Curiosity needled through her anxiety, and she clung to it, hoping to clear her head. She walked to her bed and took hold of the letter, unfolding it.

She began to read.

I received your letter, which I was very surprised to be the recipient of. Please do not be alarmed by my response, for I feel you did not expect your letter to be received. I must confess I know who you are, though I will not divulge who I am, except to say that I am a long-time admirer and wish only to be your sincere friend. It seems you are in need of a friend, and, as it so happens, so am I.

I understand loneliness. Being surrounded by loved ones, yet still feeling completely and utterly alone.

Perhaps we can be lonely together.

As for what you should do . . . what else can you do but your best?

And if you feel your best is not good enough, then try again . . . and then try harder. That is all you can do.

What you must not do is give up. Or give in. Then you have truly lost, and you do not seem like a girl who likes to lose.

Hoping to be your friend.

Bisma exhaled deeply. The letter was short—it took only a minute to read—yet focusing on the words had helped her calm down. Her heart felt a little steadier.

She wondered who had written the letter. For a moment, she thought of Xander, but he would never waste his time writing her a letter. His aim was to play with her, while this letter was genuine. Kind.

Who was this mysterious writer? They had not even signed their name. The Forest must have delivered the letter she had written, but to whom?

It did not matter. She trusted the Forest, and for good reason. Reading this response had quelled the panic that had been rising in her like a tide, threatening to drown her.

Bisma wiped her cheeks, brushing away her tears. She took a deep breath, then exhaled. She listened to the sound of the rain falling outside, taking in the sweet scent of petrichor that was thick in the air.

She grabbed a cup and stuck it out of the open window until it filled, wetting her hand in the process. Bisma gulped down the cold rainwater. Finally, the noise in her brain calmed, and she could think.

She knew what she needed to do.

Pushing her hair back, Bisma went down the stairs. Her sisters turned to look at her when she entered. They were all huddled around Mei's body, clinging to one another: Luna, Azalea, Nori, and Deeba.

Bisma went and crouched down next to Nori.

'It's going to be alright,' she said, running a hand over her blonde hair. 'I promise.'

Nori released a breath, some of the tension leaving her. She nodded. 'OK, Baji,' Nori said quietly.

Bisma kissed her cheek, then stood, turning to Luna and Azalea.

'I'm taking Mei to town,' she declared. 'All of you go to sleep. Mei will be fine.'

'But—' Azalea began, gearing up to argue, like always.

'Trust me,' Bisma said, her voice surer and stronger than she felt. Even so, she felt better than she had before.

'We do,' Luna said, her hand on Azalea's arm, and Azalea nodded.

It gave her some strength to know that there was someone out there who knew her pain—someone who had read her words and taken the time to respond. She would do her best; it was all she could do.

'You heard Baji,' Luna said, nudging Azalea. 'Time for bed.'

Bisma gave Luna and Azalea a hug. The older girls held onto her tight, and Bisma heard Luna's breath catch.

'Everything's going to be fine,' Bisma repeated, squeezing their shoulders.

With that, she went down the steps and into the rain. 'Forrie,' she said. 'Bring Mei down.'

A branch curled up into the treehouse and a moment later brought Mei down. Bisma had her cart ready, emptied of its contents, and the branch gently laid Mei down on the cart. She was shivering.

'Luna!' Bisma called. 'Blankets!'

Luna and Azalea tossed blankets down from the treehouse. Bisma did her best to cover her sister, whose skin was now tinged purple, the veins bulging dark blue.

Bisma's stomach turned at the sight, but she pushed past it and instead pushed the cart forward to leave the Forest.

As she sped down the path to Old Town, the Enchanted Forest bent its branches so that leaves would provide cover from the rain. Even so, Bisma was soaked by the time they made it to the village outside town.

Heart beating painfully, she pushed her cart down to the most expensive street, the one with the biggest, most extravagant estates. She ran past the neat and tidy lawns, until she found the one she was looking for.

'Hold on, Mei,' she whispered, her voice cracking. 'Just a little longer, I promise.'

She stopped in front of the intricately designed door of a grand house and lifted her hand. Hoping he would answer, Bisma knocked hard with her knuckles, then stepped back, waiting.

She had nowhere else to go.

Rain poured down, soaking her further as she waited for the door to open. Bisma turned to look at Mei, who was whimpering lightly, the layers of blankets above her also growing heavy with water.

Bisma knocked again, hard enough to bruise her hand and rattle her bones.

'Please,' she whispered. Hot tears filled her eyes and fell down her cheeks, mixing with the cold rainwater. She wanted to fall to the ground and sob, to let the earth take her.

But then she remembered the letter: *What you must not do is give up, or give in.*

She would not give up. She would not give in.

She knocked again.

Finally, the door opened. Light flooded out into the darkness, blinding her for a moment as a silhouette approached her.

'Xander,' she choked out. 'I need your help.'

6

'Bisma!' Xander cried. His face flooded with emotion as he took in the sight of her: drenched in rain, eyes red-rimmed. Immediately, he stepped toward her, slack-jawed with concern. His gaze shifted to Mei on the cart, and he sucked in a breath. 'Come in.'

He reached to pull her inside, but she resisted. She didn't want to drip all over the immaculate floors of his polished home, nor did she wish to be inside his expensive cottage, which looked cozy and clean.

She loved her home in the Enchanted Forest, she did, but being here made it glaringly obvious that this—his decadent house, his perfect life—was never an option given to her.

'To the garden?' he asked, sensing her hesitation. His voice was soft but clear above the rainfall.

She nodded. Then, with a shuddering breath, she moved to push the cart with Mei, but his long fingers came over hers, taking the load from her hands. His hand was warm; she cherished it for the moment it was over hers.

Xander sped Mei to the garden, then into an adjoining greenhouse, and Bisma followed close behind, cold rain falling across both their skins.

When they entered the greenhouse, she was glad to be out of the rain. It was a beautiful building, the size of a small cottage, rainwater rushing down the glass panels.

The greenhouse was filled with tall plants, reaching up to the ceiling, as well as various hanging pots and even more pots covering every table surface. The greenhouse seemed to be for Xander's particular use; it had none of the clean organization of the Chapman Apothecary.

In a corner, she saw a rumpled bed, the blankets undone. Her cheeks heated; she looked away. Her gaze fell to Xander, who had cleared a table and was covering it with blankets. She went to help him, taking the opposite end of a blanket, then smoothing it down.

He smoothed it from the opposite end, until they both met in the middle, their hands brushing. A jolt went up her arm and she shivered.

Xander scooped Mei into his arms—oh, she was so small, being held so!—and set her down upon the blankets.

'Mei, it's okay,' Bisma said, reaching for her sister's hand.

Mei was trembling, her chin quivering as though she was in great pain.

'How long has she been like this?' Xander asked, wasting no time in beginning to examine Mei. He checked her eyes, her mouth, her pulse, searching and feeling for things beyond Bisma's understanding. Immediately, she could see how competent he was, how efficient. That soothed her worry a little.

Bisma explained the past day, how she had given Mei the cure-all from the Apothecary, which had seemed to work until it didn't.

'So that's what you were doing at the Apothecary,' Xander said, more to himself than her. He let out a frustrated sound before turning to look at Bisma over his shoulder. 'Bis, I wish you'd told me. I could have helped.'

'I had it under control!' Bisma snapped, then broke off because of course she hadn't; the proof lay before them both.

At least Xander had the good grace not to point it out.

'She was fine,' Bisma continued, sounding defeated. 'But now she's worse. It wasn't like this yesterday.'

'The cure-all would have provided temporary relief,' Xander explained. 'But the poison remained inside her, festering.'

He left Mei's side then, moving easily to one of the other tables. The sound of clinking bottles filled the air as he searched for something, then she heard his quick 'Aha!'

Xander returned with a small purple vial. She noticed it wasn't the special glass that the Chapman Apothecary used. This was ordinary glass from the local shop, and it held a thin liquid, clear like water but with a cloudiness to it. She recognized the smell of chamomile and something else, perhaps valerian root? But it held other notes she couldn't recognize or decipher; it was a high-level potion.

'What is—' she began, as Xander returned to Mei's side.

Xander released a breath, then turned to Bisma. His green eyes were bright, vivid.

'Everything's going to be alright,' he said, placing his large hands upon her shoulders. They were warm, and she was too in need of comfort to push him away. 'I promise.'

Xander turned back to Mei and gently lifted her head, emptying the liquid into her mouth.

'What are you doing?' Bisma cried, but it was too late. Her heart

A WITCH'S GUIDE TO LOVE AND POISON   63

jumped into her throat Mei's throat moved as she swallowed. A few moments later, the trembling in Mei's body ceased.

'It was just something to help her sleep,' Xander said. 'She's in pain.'

Bisma struck his back, and he turned to her, face alarmed. 'You don't do *anything* without telling me first!' she cried, her voice vicious.

He blinked. 'Alright,' he agreed. 'I won't.'

She knew she should be thankful—he was helping her, after all—but she couldn't help but claw at him.

'We need to get the poison out of her system,' he said.

Xander left Mei's side to rummage through various pots, searching for something; Bisma could see his mind was whirring through different combinations and ideas.

She felt utterly useless in comparison. Treatment was never something she'd ever dealt with; she didn't even know where to start. Instead, Bisma turned to Mei, taking her little hand in her own and giving it a squeeze. 'Everything is going to be alright,' she whispered. 'I promise.'

'I'll be right back!' Xander called.

Before she could reply, he vanished from the greenhouse, and a few minutes later he came back with a bucket of slimy black creatures. He set the bucket down, then pulled two out, holding them up for her to see. They wiggled in his hands.

'Leeches!' he said proudly, smiling at her in the most absurd manner.

She gave him a look that she hoped expressed just how deranged she thought he was.

'What on earth—' she began, then watched as he dropped them into a mortar. With one hand, he crushed them with a pestle, then with the other he picked and threw in a few drops of tea tree oil.

'This should bring the poison to the surface,' he said. 'Then we can get it out of her.'

'Can I help in any way?' she asked, coming to his side.

'Actually, yes,' he said. He handed her the pestle. 'Keep crushing, gently, to make it into as smooth a paste as possible.'

She nodded, doing as she was told, then watched as he went around the greenhouse, looking for certain plants. He returned with various leaves and added them to the mortar as she continued to grind them all into a paste.

Then, when he had all the ingredients he desired, he took over for her, his fingers easily taking the pestle from her hand. He stood just beside her, the warmth of his arm seeping into her skin.

'Just like this,' he said, showing her the contents of the mortar. He waved his hand and the paste thinned into a liquid with his magic. The sight was a delight; she hardly ever used her magic like that in the mixing process—she used more of her magic during the growing process—so it was a wonder to watch.

As if sensing she was impressed, Xander wiggled his eyebrows at him. Rolling her eyes, she shoved his shoulder, which only made him laugh quietly.

'Look,' he said, dipping a finger in, then showing her. It looked like a juice made from dark berries.

'Will it work?' she asked.

'Oh ye of little faith,' he said, shaking his head. She raised a brow, and he released a dramatic sigh. 'Yes, it will work.'

He poured the liquid into a teacup. Bisma followed him to Mei's side, where she gently raised Mei up and watched as Xander fed Mei the liquid. In her sleep, Mei drank it, grimacing slightly.

'Sorry,' he said, sheepishly. 'That can't have tasted good.'

After Mei swallowed, Bisma set her down. 'Now what?' she asked.

'Now we wait,' he replied.

Bisma released a long breath, exhausted. She realized then that more than an hour had passed. The rain had stopped, and the sky above the greenhouse was beginning to change colors to welcome the dawn.

'What's her story?' Xander asked. He was leaning against a table, arms crossed over his chest as he regarded her.

She arched her brow.

Color warmed his cheeks; he was shy, asking her like this. 'Unless you don't want to say, but . . . you all have stories, don't you?'

Every Unwanted Girl did, of course. Though no one ever bothered to ask.

Because Xander had, Bisma felt compelled to tell him. More than that, she wanted to. Their histories were part of who they were, and she wished for the girls to be known, truly, beyond simply being the monsters in the woods.

'She came to Enchanted Forest when she was five,' Bisma said, remembering. 'I was fourteen at the time. She explained that her parents were marrying her to a man in one of the neighboring villages—one of those small villages I can't even bother to remember the name of. Basically sold her off.'

'She was *five*?' Xander asked, eyes wide with horror.

Bisma nodded. 'She didn't even know what was happening; they told her she would get to wear a pretty dress and get gifts.' She clenched her jaw tight enough to make her head hurt. Her blood boiled at the story, but she continued. 'It wasn't until Mei's sister, who was about twelve at the time, came home for the wedding with *her* husband. She'd been sold the same way a few years back and warned Mei to run the night before the wedding. Her sister told her to go to the Forest, to risk death rather than to be wed, and so she did.'

'She must have been so afraid,' Xander said, his voice a whisper.

'She was. But the Enchanted Forest saved her.' She turned to look at Mei.

Worry turned Bisma's insides. The Forest had saved her then, but what about now?

'Don't worry,' Xander said, as if reading her thoughts. 'You'll save her now, too.'

Bisma hoped so.

'I suspect it will take a few hours, at least,' Xander said, coming round to Bisma's side. He set a gentle hand to her shoulder. 'Why don't you rest?'

Bisma shook her head, taking Mei's hand in hers. 'I won't leave her.' She turned to Xander. 'But if you must go to the Apothecary, by all means.'

'It's alright,' Xander said. 'I already told my mother I wouldn't be in today.'

She wrinkled her brows. 'You're allowed to do that?'

'I sometimes have cases of my own to tend to; she understands that. I was actually on my way to the greenhouse to get an early start when I heard you knocking on the door.'

He wasn't worried or stressed at all; what a marvel. Recounting Mei's story had made Bisma angry and frustrated, and to think of him as his own master, able to do as he pleased, and with his mother's support, no less—hideous envy seeped through her.

'I'll pay you for your services, do not fret,' she said tightly. She shook his hand off her shoulder.

His brows knit together. 'Bis, no, that's not—that's not what I was saying.' He took a step closer, and she saw the dark circles beneath his eyes; he was exhausted, too. 'You don't need to pay me.'

She set her jaw. 'Of course I do. I won't take your charity.'

'It's not—I didn't . . . mean it like that,' he said. 'I want to help you—' He broke off, looking away as he bit his lip. He ran a hand through his hair, letting out a frustrated sigh. The copper locks were wild and messy; she had the sudden urge to run her fingers through them, smoothing his hair down.

She mentally slapped herself. 'You don't have to stay,' she said, her back rigid. 'It'll be hours, as you said. I'll watch her.'

She turned back to Mei, who seemed to be trying to shift a little, as if uncomfortable. She moved forward to adjust Mei's pillow, but as she did, blood rushed to her head. Her vision darkened and she swayed.

Xander caught her, hands steady on her waist. She gasped, looking up into his darkened eyes. Her heartbeat was fast, a thunderous roar as exhilarating as a downpour.

'I'm worried about you,' he said, clenching his jaw.

A jolt of electricity splintered across her chest, as though she'd been struck by a lightning bolt. She blinked up at him, feeling dazed.

'Why don't you get some rest?' he asked, stepping closer. 'We have guest rooms in the house. Or you could go home, check on your sisters. I'll watch her.'

She felt his breath on her cheek, whispering against a tendril of hair. The sensation was heady, delicious. Her pulse raced, blood rushing in her ears. She wanted to draw closer, to wrap her arms around him, feel his warmth against her.

And that made her afraid.

She wrenched out of his grasp, glaring. 'Don't *touch* me,' she snapped, her voice laced with venom.

She was being mean, she knew she was, but she couldn't bear how he was looking at her, the tender care in his eyes. She was afraid of what it might inspire her to do.

Her words did the trick; his face became shuttered, wounded.

'I'll leave you alone, then,' he said.

Xander left her, shoulders drooping as he walked away.

Good, she told herself, even though the sight pierced through her.

But this was not the time to be soft-hearted, to be weak. She reminded herself of what had happened the last time she let a boy this close, remembered being young and foolish, and the way she had ultimately paid the price.

The shame that had remained. It lived inside her still, something she could not cut out, no matter how hard she tried.

She was right to be vicious to Xander. She was right to push him away.

Even so, she couldn't help the pain in her chest, how empty the greenhouse now felt without him here beside her.

But she had bigger things to worry about. She looked at her sister, the wet splay of her short black hair. Bisma held tight to Mei's hand, tears falling down her cheeks.

'Please be alright,' she begged.

7

Bisma didn't know when she dozed off, only that one moment she was looking at the soft rise and fall of Mei's chest, and the next, there was a gentle hand shaking her awake.

'Bis, wake up,' Xander said.

She startled, and a shawl fell from her shoulders. She shivered. *When did that get there?*

It took her a second to remember where she was and why. She looked up at Xander, who stood next to her.

'You'll want to see this,' he said. All the previous hurt on his face was gone, replaced with something akin to excitement. He had bounced back to normalcy with alarming speed, which was why she had to be even more on her guard around him. But for now she was more concerned about her sister. Bisma followed his gaze and looked at Mei. Gasping, she abruptly stood.

'Good grief,' Bisma gasped. Mei's skin was back to its original fawn tone, but the veins were such a dark purple they looked black. Even worse, they were bulging, as though there were slugs just beneath her skin.

It was a horrific sight, but Bisma did not look away. The image seared into her mind. This had happened on *her* watch. It was *her fault*.

'This is good,' Xander said, and she gave him an incredulous look. 'No, really! It means all the poison has been raised and is just waiting to be extracted now.'

He pulled out a large leaf from a platter, showing her. She touched her finger to the light green surface; it had a texture to it like tiny teeth and was nearly translucent. She didn't know what it was.

'Took some trial and error, but I made it,' Xander informed her. 'Now watch this.' He wrapped the leaf around Mei's arm, until the skin was covered. 'Wait for it . . .'

He was thrilled, practically vibrating with energy. She wanted to throttle him, but at the same time, his manner made hope bloom within her. She held her breath and watched.

Slowly, the leaf changed color from pale green to deep, dark green. When it seemed the leaf could grow no darker, Xander unwrapped it from Mei's arm, revealing the skin underneath. Unblemished and clear.

Bisma looked up at Xander with wide eyes.

His cheeks were pink, though now the excitement in his eyes had doubled. 'It sucked the poison out,' he explained, hair flopping as he nodded at her.

'That's . . . wow.'

She didn't know what to say, and she would usually rather die than let Xander know she was impressed by his magic, but this was too remarkable for her to scorn.

'That expensive schooling does pay off every now and again,' Xander joked.

He had gone away to a private school in Whitebridge for six years. Whitebridge was one of the biggest cities in Crownley and had one of the best schools in the entire kingdom of Fairendelle.

He was clearly much more learned than she was. Bisma had been taught basic things such as reading and math by her older sisters. Since none of her sisters were witches, she had taught herself garden-magic, with the Enchanted Forest supplementing her education, but Xander had had a proper education. Bisma wondered what that might be like. Being in a big city, with no responsibilities except to learn, read, practice. Growing better and better.

Bisma cut off the dream before it got out of hand. It could never be a reality; she would never abandon her sisters and the duties she had as their baji.

'Let's do the rest,' Bisma said, clearing her throat. She reached for a leaf and began wrapping Mei's upper arm. Xander got to work on her other arm, and they covered Mei's skin until every inch was beneath a curing leaf.

It took a great deal of time because they had to ensure the tiny teeth of the leaf were sinking into her skin, then they had to wait for the poison to be sucked out. It was tedious work. After a few leaves, Bisma was already tired, and she saw that Xander was, too, his usually chipper mood dimming.

'I can do it on my own,' Bisma said. 'You don't have to.'

He arched a brow, looking across the table to her. 'I'm positive you can,' he said. 'But not as good as me, surely.'

She narrowed her eyes, a fire flaring inside her. 'Is that so?'

'Go on, then,' he said. 'Prove me wrong.'

She scoffed. 'As if that is a difficult task.'

Bisma got back to wrapping Mei's skin, working faster than

before, and she saw Xander do the same. They were racing to see who could get more done.

They had to wrap some areas multiple times because the leaves could only hold so much poison, but eventually they did it. It took a great deal of time—a few hours, at least—and by the end, they were both exhausted, but Bisma had done more. She ended up on Xander's side, finishing Mei's leg while Xander worked his way down.

'Ha!' she said, when the last of Mei's skin cleared. 'I win.'

Instead of being vexed, as Bisma had expected, Xander surprised her by laughing. He looked almost . . . pleased. She gave him an alarmed glance.

'Since when are you so graceful in defeat?' she asked, eyes narrowed. 'You do realize I beat you, don't you?'

He smiled, shaking his head. 'Just happy to see you back to your ill-tempered self.'

She realized then that he'd done it on purpose. He had known that putting a competitive angle on their task would make the time pass faster, and indeed, it had. Tenderness for him poked her heart so powerfully, it was painful.

For a moment, Bisma considered doing something she would surely regret. But before she could act, a figure entered the greenhouse.

She and Xander both turned to see a slender woman in a long gown with intricate embroidery. It was a deep wine color that was striking against her creamy skin, and her copper hair was pulled back into a simple twist.

The famous and accomplished Eleanora Chapman.

'Mother,' Xander said, tone both vexed and affectionate.

'Oh, I'm sorry, darling. I didn't know you had company,' she said, smiling fondly at him. 'I was just checking in.' Her green eyes turned to Bisma, who suddenly felt raggedy and unkempt.

'Yes, just working on something,' Xander said.

'Why don't you and your friend join me for breakfast and tell me all about it?' Eleanora asked.

Xander turned to Bisma, and she felt like shrinking. A breakfast at the Chapman Estate was much too fancy for the likes of her; she doubted she would even know which fork to use. Rich people like Xander had multiple forks with their meals, which was just absurd.

Bisma shook her head.

Xander looked disappointed for a moment, but he turned back to his mother, saying, 'No, thank you, Mother, we're alright.'

'Of course, dear,' she replied. Her gaze turned curiously from her son to Mei on the table.

A protective edge came over Bisma; she stood in front of Mei, blocking Eleanora's view.

Eleanora smiled, then turned and left.

Releasing a breath, Bisma turned to Mei, and Xander came to stand beside her.

'It'll be a bit before she wakes, I think,' he said. He stretched, cracking his neck, then sighed. 'I'll be back.'

When he came back to the greenhouse, it was with a pot of strong tea, freshly baked bread, hard cheese, fried eggs, turkey bacon, and a decadent apple tart topped with vanilla custard. Xander set a blanket on the floor, then spread out the food. He sat, gesturing for Bisma to join him. She shook her head, heart beating fast. He was being too kind; it made her wary.

'You won't eat?' Xander asked, leaning back on his elbow as he took a bite of bread.

It would be too easy to say yes, to give in, but she needed to be strong, to be careful.

'No, I'm alright,' she replied, lifting her chin.

He shrugged. 'Suit yourself.' He pulled the apple tart toward him.

It really did look delicious. Bisma's convictions wavered. And besides, it wasn't as though she was going to give him her heart just because he'd brought her some food.

'Well, if you're just going to eat it all like a pig,' she said with a roll of her eyes.

He grinned as she sat down and ate with him. The tea was divine, just what she needed, and, oh, the cinnamon dusted atop the apple tart was truly heavenly.

They ate in companionable silence, until Mei roused.

Bisma jumped to her feet. 'Mei!' she called, rushing to her side. 'How do you feel?'

Mei groggily rubbed her eyes, pushing her short hair back from her face.

Holding onto Mei's thin arms, Bisma helped her sit up. 'Slowly,' Bisma said, as Mei swung her legs over the table. Xander came to Mei's other side; he and Bisma helped Mei stand. She felt as light as a feather.

'I'm . . .' Mei trailed off as she registered something. Her eyes opened wider. 'Is that custard? I'm *starving*.'

Bisma smiled. 'Come, I saved you some.'

Mei sat down on the picnic blanket, and Xander pushed the food closer to her.

'Ooh, fancy,' Mei said, holding up the heavy silver spoon.

She began to eat, and a weight lifted off Bisma's chest. *Mei was alright.* Bisma snuck a glance at Xander, who was smiling fondly, as relieved as she was. Something skittered across her chest, impossible to ignore.

Xander stood, coming to Bisma, and she stood as well, as if propelled by some force she had no control over, some sort of ancient magic she was not familiar with but which called to her all the same.

'Bis,' he said, giving her one of his usual smiles, though this time, she could see he was nervous. The pulse in his throat was racing.

She looked up into his eyes, which were the color of glistening evergreen trees after rain. They shone like jewels as he regarded her, the skin by his eyes crinkling softly. She inhaled the scent of cloves as he stepped closer. Her skin warmed.

'Perhaps, sometime, we could get a meal together under less stressful circumstances?' he asked, his voice low. She bit her lip, her heartbeat spiking as he reached for her hand, taking it in his. He ran his thumb across her knuckles.

She yearned to say yes—with every beat of her heart she did.

'Or maybe not,' Xander said, seeing her hesitate. 'Perhaps we could just go for a walk in the woods?'

And those words—that question—it was like a bucket of ice had been poured over her. Bisma snatched her hand away from his. Those words were too familiar. She would not open herself to such pain and ridicule again.

Alarm and confusion filled Xander's eyes.

'I don't give payment that way,' she snapped.

He was taken aback by her tone. 'That—that wasn't what I was suggesting,' he said, his brows knit together. He was upset. 'Bisma, you know that's not what I meant.'

'Do I?' She glared. 'You'll have your payment by the end of the week.'

'You are impossible—always finding some way to twist my words against me.' He let out a frustrated groan. 'I don't want your money.'

'Of course you don't!' she cried, not caring that he was right. Being cruel was the only way to keep him away, to keep herself safe. She couldn't trust him, no matter how much she yearned to. 'My hard-earned coins mean nothing to someone as frivolous and spoiled as you.'

He stepped back as if slapped, genuinely hurt, but Bisma didn't allow herself to focus on it. She couldn't, or she would do something idiotic like apologize. She could not let tenderness for him grow in her heart; she *would* not. Not after all she had been through. She knew better—she had to know better.

'Bis—' he started again.

But she had already turned away from him. 'Mei!' she called. 'We're leaving. Now.'

She headed for the exit, Mei falling into step beside her.

'Bisma,' Xander said, his voice a strangled whisper, but she did not turn back.

8

Bisma returned home with Mei. The storm from last night was gone; the sky was blue, filled with fluffy white clouds. The air had an autumnal chill to it, but the sun warmed their skin as they walked back to the Enchanted Forest.

Once they made it through the foggy border, Bisma felt she could finally breathe. She inhaled deeply, savoring the scent of damp earth. Then she walked through the mud and squishy moss of the wet woods as they journeyed to the treehouse.

There, Bisma pushed her cart back to the garden, and found Nori in the chicken coops, collecting eggs with straw in her messy hair. Luna was with the goats, milking them while Deeba sat beside her and watched.

'Baji!' Deeba squealed, the first to spot them. She waddled over, and the other girls followed.

'They're back!' Luna called up to the treehouse.

Azalea came down, her fingers stained reddish pink from peeling pomegranates.

'You're alright!' Nori said, crushing Mei with a hug and dropping an egg in the process. Deeba made it to Mei's legs, latching on as well, while Mei laughed.

'Nothing to worry about,' she said.

'Everything good?' Luna asked Bisma, coming to her. Azalea joined, the three eldest stepping aside.

Bisma nodded, forcing a smile. 'Like Mei said, nothing to worry about.'

'Are you sure?' Azalea asked, her brown eyes uncertain.

'Yes, Azalea, I am sure.' Bisma released a long breath. 'How were the girls?' This question was directed at Luna.

'Fine. We slept after you left, and when we woke up this morning, we had breakfast and have just been doing chores,' Luna replied.

Bisma nodded. 'Good,' she said. She suddenly felt exhausted, but there was no time to rest. She went to pick up Deeba, smothering her with kisses as the toddler laughed. She hugged Nori next, while Luna and Azalea hugged Mei.

'Mei, why don't you go rest?' Bisma asked, tucking a strand of silky black hair behind Mei's ear.

'Baji, what about my chores?'

'You get a break today,' Bisma said. She gave Mei a conspiratorial smile. 'We'll all cover for Mei. Nori, you'll help me cook, won't you?'

'Baji, noooo,' Mei said, trying not to laugh. 'Nori always adds too much salt!'

'No I don't!' Nori retaliated, offended. 'Baji, tell her! I always do it right!'

Unfortunately, Nori rarely did it right, but that's why Bisma needed to teach her.

'Yes . . . of course you do, sweetheart,' Bisma reassured Nori. 'But let's just be extra careful, okay?'

'Okie!' Nori said, jumping up. Her blonde hair was a mess, falling in front of her face, and Bisma surreptitiously tucked the strands behind Nori's ears, where they would remain for approximately three seconds before falling forward again.

Bisma helped Mei up the treehouse, Nori trailing behind her on the winding stairs with the basket of eggs. Luna finished up the chores with the animals, while Azalea gathered clothes to take down to the stream for washing. They would need to make good use of the sunshine before it rained again; already, Bisma could see the clouds circling.

Once again, they fell into the busy routine of ordinary life.

Slowly, Mei rebuilt her energy with daily fresh juice made of apples, beetroot, and carrots. The carrots were extra sweet this time of year. She rejoined the others with the chores after two days, helping Bisma make ghee from scratch.

The wooden chairs around the table were looking quite depressing, so one day they painted them, each choosing a different shade for their own chair. Bisma painted hers emerald green, while the others painted theirs yellow, pink, purple, and blue. It added some color to their house.

Then there were the wool sweaters and socks that needed to be checked and darned to prepare for the approaching winter. Already, the weather had turned; Bisma constantly wore a shawl wrapped around her shoulders and her tea consumption went up by about fifty percent.

The girls wore multiple layers—double the sweaters, double the socks—and fought over who could sit on the sofa in the patch of sunlight in the afternoon. The smell of citrus was constant in the house, as it was peak orange season now, and there was constantly one being peeled and split between them.

In the midst of all this, Bisma realized she had never replied to the mysterious letter she had received. When she was alone in her room or out in the Forest by herself, she read the page over often, folding and unfolding it until it became soft in her hands. Her heart warmed at the words: *perhaps we can be lonely together.*

Who *was* this mystery person?

Well, she would only find out if she asked.

Hello, and thank you for your kind words. They came at a time when I truly needed them, and for that I am grateful. You say you are a long-time admirer, yet you will not divulge who you are. Have we crossed paths? Do I know you? I confess I am curious.

I have thought over your proposition to be friends, and I would like to accept. I could use a friend, and it seems as though you could as well. I'm so overwhelmed by my circumstances; it feels as though I am an autumn leaf withering away on a branch, fluttering in the wind, holding on with all my might.

Falling—failing—feels inevitable. I have so many people counting on me, and I don't want to let them down. I'm afraid I already have, and I don't know how to fix it. But I suppose your previous advice still stands: to try, then try again.

It's nice writing to you, even though I do not know you. I am sorry to hear you are lonely. I hope this letter brings you a bit of joy, as your letter brought me.

Your friend,
Bisma

Bisma sent the letter the same way the first one had been sent: through the Enchanted Forest. It would know what to do, where to take it.

As she patiently awaited a reply, she had a more pressing mystery to concern herself with: what had happened to Mei?

Bisma couldn't figure it out. Mei retraced that day for Bisma, but it had been ordinary, spent in the Enchanted Forest, with all the girls. As far as Bisma recalled, nothing had been amiss.

Mei had not even been to town with Bisma that day; Bisma had gone alone. If the poison had come from the town, surely it would have been Bisma who was poisoned, not Mei, who had been in the safety of the Forest.

Perhaps something had occurred while Mei was cooking? Some sort of chemical reaction between ingredients? That was the last thing Mei had been doing before she fell. But Mei was a kitchen-witch; surely her magic would never have such a drastic reaction? She had gotten cheese from the village a few days prior; perhaps it had gone bad?

Bisma considered whether perhaps it had been sickness instead of poisoning, but either way, she had no conclusive evidence. It was maddening.

It rained again a few days later, and Bisma took the opportunity to make everyone pakoray, the fried vegetable fritters proving to be the perfect snack for the drizzly weather, especially when paired with cardamom and ginger spiced chai. The girls all had different cultures and backgrounds; they learned from each other.

After eating the last of the pakoray, Bisma went up to her room at the top of the treehouse, looking for her bag. She and Luna needed to go to town to deliver poisons and run errands.

The soft sound of rainfall pitter-pattered against the roof of her room, a quiet, constant melody. When she entered her room, she saw a small square of white on her bed.

Her heart rate spiked. It was a letter.

Forgetting her bag, she rushed to her bed, reaching for the dirt-streaked paper. She caught her breath as she unfolded the square, and a thrill shot through her.

> *Thank you for your reply, and for agreeing to my proposition. You cannot imagine how overjoyed I am to be writing to you. Even more so to be lucky enough that you've accepted my offer of friendship.*
>
> *You do not know me, not truly, but I would like you to, except for the small fact that I am a bit afraid of you, in the way one is afraid of people they admire, which makes me a bit shy. Hence why I am writing instead of approaching you directly.*
>
> *I heard in town that someone close to you has fallen sick. Is she alright now? I hope she is well, and that you are, too. It cannot be easy being in charge, but please take care of yourself as well.*
>
> *Your grateful friend*

Bisma sat on her bed, smiling to herself. She pressed a hand against her chest, feeling her heartbeat race against her palm. It was nice to have someone to talk to, beside her sisters, whom she could never be fully truthful with. She would not burden them with her worries and doubts.

Without a moment's delay, she stood to go to her desk, reaching for a piece of paper.

'Baji!' Luna's voice called from below. 'Are we going or what?'

Bisma suppressed a sigh. 'Yes, I'm coming!' she called back, folding the letter. She placed it in a box with the first letter, then locked it, slipping the key into the pocket of her burgundy dress. It seemed an unnecessary precaution, but she didn't want her sisters prying.

Years ago, she remembered one of her older sisters had a diary, and nosy eight-year-old Bisma had snuck into her room one day to read it. Her sister had been furious. Little girls don't mean to be terrible, but sometimes it can't be helped.

'BAJI!' Luna bellowed.

'I'M COMING!' Bisma called back.

With a final glance at the locked box, she went to tend to her duties as Baji.

9

After lacing up her boots, Bisma grabbed a black shawl and hurried down the spiraling steps of the tree trunk, all the way down to the very bottom, where Luna was waiting with Deeba.

The two-year-old wore a knitted white bonnet, her adorable chubby cheeks sticking out. It had stopped raining, but the air was still cold.

'Are you ready?' Bisma asked Deeba, scooping her up and kissing her.

Deeba laughed. 'Yes, yes!' she cooed.

Bisma set her down so she could pick up her basket of poisons, as well as another empty basket for their shopping.

'Ready?' she asked Luna, who wore a pale yellow dress. Her honey-brown hair was pulled back into two braids fastened with pink ribbons to match the embroidery on her dress.

Luna released a long sigh. 'I have *been* ready!'

They began walking, Deeba between them, and Bisma smirked. 'Someone is impatient to get to town,' she sang.

Luna held up a hand. 'I have no idea what you are talking about.'

Both girls exchanged a smile, then began chatting as Luna recited various poems from the poetry book she was reading, highlighting her favorite lines and dissecting what the metaphors meant. They passed by a brook, where toads were happily croaking.

A little while later, they passed rabbits munching peacefully on grass, until Deeba tried to reach out and grab them. They hastily hopped away, while Deeba laughed, looking back at Bisma and Luna. 'Them run!' Deeba said, clearly proud of herself.

'Yes, *they* run!' Luna said, smiling at the two-year-old.

The trio continued walking, and along the way Bisma plucked an apple from one of the apple trees, tossing it to Luna before plucking another for herself. It was red and ripe; when Bisma bit into it, sweet juice poured into her mouth along the crisp fruit.

The fruit in the Enchanted Forest was always perfect, a magical marvel. Often, fruits and vegetables could even be found growing outside their ordinary season. It would turn a huge profit if the Unwanted Girls wished to harvest and sell them in town, but the Forest fruits could only be enjoyed within the bounds of the Forest. Once the fruit or vegetables left the Forest, they rotted.

Something Bisma was sorely wishing wasn't true at the moment; she still had to pay Xander for curing Mei. It had been nearly a week and she'd avoided going to town as she figured out how to gather the necessary funds.

At least orders had come in, and she'd spent the better part of the week completing them, and now she could drop them off and collect payment.

When they made it to Old Town, Luna instantly brightened.

She smoothed her braids, checking the bows at the ends, then said, 'Let's go to the bakery, first.'

Bisma bit back a smile. 'Sure.'

The town was busier than usual as they walked toward the square, and Bisma carried Deeba to make sure she didn't get lost. Luna skipped ahead, and as they approached the bakery, Bisma inhaled the comforting scent of fresh bread.

They walked in; it wasn't very busy, and right away, Bisma spotted Haru behind the counter, wearing his usual apron. He was filling pastries with custard, but when he saw them, he immediately stopped, his face lighting up with a smile.

'There's the prettiest girl in town,' he said.

Before Luna could respond to the compliment, Bisma arched a brow. 'I do hope you're talking about Deeba,' she said.

'Baji!' Luna hissed, mortified.

There was no one around, so Bisma laughed as Haru's cheeks turned red.

'Yes, of course,' Haru sputtered, pinching Deeba's cheek. He cleared his throat. 'What can I get for you? The usual? I've just finished baking a fresh loaf of pumpkin bread, Lu.'

Lu? Bisma thought to herself.

Luna looked equally surprised by the affectionate nickname and doubly pleased.

'Oh, that sounds *divine!*' she squealed. She approached the counter, setting her elbows upon them to lean her face on her chin. Haru leaned forward across the counter as well, beaming at her.

There was a streak of sugar on his cheek, and Luna reached across to wipe it away, hand lingering.

Oh good god . . .

Bisma cleared her throat. She could not say she was enjoying witnessing her younger sister flirt with her crush. 'I'm going to go,' she said, approaching the counter. She deposited Deeba between Haru and Luna on the counter, and Deeba clapped her chubby hands in excitement when he picked her up.

Bisma gave Luna a sisterly warning glance, which only earned her a roll of Luna's eyes in response, but Bisma wasn't worried. Haru was genuine, and Luna wasn't stupid; she would be alright.

'Watch Deebs,' Bisma ordered. Luna hardly spared Bisma a glance; she was busy gazing at Haru. Deeba was currently snuggled against his chest, holding tight to his shirt with her little fists.

'Don't worry, we will,' Haru said, giving Bisma a winning smile. Even her cold, shriveled heart warmed at that.

'And make sure you go to the butcher's,' Bisma reminded Luna. 'You have the money I gave you, don't you?'

They got meat from the butcher in town because none of the girls wanted to slaughter their own animals; the younger ones would be traumatized if their best friends (the goats and chickens) were being butchered every week.

'Yes, yes, I have it,' Luna said, waving a hand absentmindedly. Clearly she was too preoccupied with batting her lashes at Haru to give Bisma any attention.

'I'm about to go on my break so I can help,' Haru offered, eyes kind.

'By all means,' Bisma said, taking her leave.

The poisons were in a basket on the crook of her arm, hidden beneath a plaid cloth. Even though Bisma herself was infamous, she hid the poisons for the sake of those buying them; they could not be seen doing business with her. Which was why, as the sun moved across the sky, she went to various previously agreed upon locations outside the square, finding gaps between rocks or hidden alcoves where money lay waiting for her. Each client had their own distinct drop spot.

After Bisma finished her deliveries and collected her money, she went to the final secret stop, which was for new customers to leave order requests; they either left the requests here or at the edge of the Enchanted Forest. This location on the outskirts of the town square could only be learned by word of mouth.

Thankfully, when she arrived, she saw a handful of new orders. She would need them.

Most of these would go to paying Xander, and she'd already given a chunk of money to Luna for the butcher, not to mention that Bisma still had errands to run: Azalea wanted new yarn to knit Deeba a sweater, Nori wanted paint, and Mei had sent an entire grocery list of ingredients.

While they grew most of their fruit, vegetables, and herbs in the Forest, some seasonings and ingredients could only be acquired from town. So, with a deep breath, Bisma headed back to the town square.

Now that it was late afternoon, many people were done with their work for the day and were getting their shopping done before heading home for the evening. More than once, Bisma had to push her way through a crowd, and there was quite a large line at the cheese stall, which she would have avoided entirely because of its strong smells had Mei not made a specific request.

Bisma wondered how long Old Town could last like this. It had been getting increasingly crowded over the past year and did not look to be slowing down any time soon. But she was glad for the busyness as it meant there was less focus on her. She could slither in and out without being noticed.

Or so she thought.

After Bisma had bought the paint for Nori and was exiting the art shop, she saw something hurtling toward her from the corner of her eye. She moved aside at the last moment, but rotten fruit splashed across her shoes and legs.

Heart hammering, she looked up to find an older man glaring

at her. She did not know him, but he shook his head with disdain, muttering, 'Filthy Unwanted Witch.'

An acidic feeling spread through her, equal parts fear and rage. She should have just moved on, but the rage took over. Instead, she hissed at him, baring her teeth.

Anger flared across his face, and he approached, spitting at her just as she felt an arm pull her back.

Bisma turned. It was Razan Al-Mansour, the bookshop owner. She was a kind, middle-aged woman with dense black curls and olive-colored skin.

'That's enough now!' Razan snapped at the old man. 'Be on your way.'

He huffed and puffed, but waved a hand, leaving them.

Bisma released a long breath, her heart still pounding. Shame ran through her for needing Razan's help; she needed to defend herself, not rely on others.

'Thank you,' she managed to say.

'Don't mention it,' Razan replied. She released a breath, then smiled. 'Is Luna enjoying the latest poetry book, then? It's all the rage in Whitebridge; apparently the author even came from Castletown to do a signing.'

'Oh, don't mention that to Luna, or she'll have us all traveling for the author's next visit,' Bisma said with a roll of her eyes, feeling calmed by the change in topic. 'Which is to say she is enjoying it quite a bit . . . perhaps *too* much.'

Razan arched a curious brow.

'She insists upon reading passages aloud to us,' Bisma explained. 'Azalea is just about at her wits' end.'

Razan laughed, dimples appearing in her cheeks. 'Oh yes, some passages are definitely not to be read aloud . . . at least, not to one's sister.'

They both shared a smile. Not all people in Old Town were

terrible. Throughout the years, Bisma and the other Unwanted Girls had made *some* friends.

Bisma went on to buy the yarn, depositing her purchase into her basket. That was the last of the errands, she realized with annoyance. Which meant the only thing left to do was pay Xander.

With a sigh, she turned toward the Chapman Apothecary. As if summoned by her thoughts, Xander stepped outside the door just then. He immediately spotted her across the square, despite how rushed it was, and a smile lit up his face.

He began walking toward her, his hair falling into place perfectly even as he took long strides in her direction. He wore a silver-gray waistcoat that matched the cloud-filled sky, and the color made his hair a deep mahogany-copper. His eyes shone like emeralds in his pale face as he came to stand before her.

'Well met, Bis,' he said, giving her that dazzling smile of his, as if she had never been vicious to him when they last spoke.

She was taken aback for a moment, confused. She had expected him to be standoffish at least, after he had done so much to help her and she had been so cruel in response, but it seemed no matter how hard she snapped, he would not be deterred.

On the contrary, he appeared to be . . . happy to see her.

Setting her jaw, Bisma threw a bag of coins at him. He caught it easily with one hand, his elegant fingers closing over the bag.

He looked as though he was going to say something, then thought better of it. 'Thank you,' he said, not even looking at the contents. He simply accepted it. Her eye twitched. But why wouldn't he? What care did he have about her hard-earned money?

'How are you doing?' he asked, that velvet smooth voice of his sending a shiver down her spine.

'I have orders to complete, so I'm much too busy to be wasting my time here with you,' she replied, lifting her nose up at him.

This was a lie, of course, but she was annoyed by his constant sunny disposition, and the only way to fight against it was to be dark as midnight rain.

'Is that so?' he asked, eyes sparking. 'Are you trying to rub in my face, how lucrative your business is?'

As two of the few garden-witches in Old Town, it was always a competition between them.

'If that's how you see it,' she said, tone haughty.

'Well, if you must know, I have my own business to conduct, as well,' he replied.

She scoffed. 'You mean your *mother's* business.'

The Chapman Apothecary was run by his mother, Eleanora, and before her had been run by his grandfather, who had passed away a few years ago.

At this remark, color entered Xander's cheeks, which gave her a jolt of satisfaction. She bit back a smile.

'I have my own private clients as well,' he said, giving her a pointed look.

Then it was her turn to feel heat rush to her face. Unfortunately, she would not be deterred.

'Right,' she said, drawing the word out, as if she did not believe him. 'Like who?'

'My clients prefer discretion, same as yours,' he said, mimicking her haughty tone.

She arched her brow. 'What do you need private clients for when you have your family business?'

'You said it yourself,' he replied, stepping closer. 'That's my mother's business, not mine.' He lifted and dropped a shoulder nonchalantly. 'Private clientele worked out for you—thought I'd try my hand at it as well. Give you a run for your money.'

'Ah, so it's about me, is it?'

He smiled, reaching a hand out to pluck a stray white flower from her hair; it must have come undone from the string of motia entwined in her braid. He twirled it between his fingers before looking back up at her.

'Darling Bisma, you are my greatest nemesis, my sweetest rival. Isn't everything about you?'

She ignored the way her heart skipped a beat at that. He was an incorrigible flirt. That didn't mean she had to lose her head.

Instead, she cocked her head, saying, 'While it makes sense for people to require discretion when it comes to purchasing poisons, why would they require such discretion to purchase your curing potions?'

'Maybe I'll explain it to you sometime,' he said, eyes glittering. 'Perhaps over dinner?'

That nearly made her laugh out loud. 'I'd rather drink my own poisons, thank you kindly.'

'If only to give me the chance to heal you?'

She mimicked barfing. He laughed, an open-mouthed, rich laugh that passed through her like the first delicious chill of autumn after a scorched summer.

'You'll change your mind someday, Bis,' he said, stepping closer.

She narrowed her eyes, taking a step forward as well.

'Don't hold your breath.' She paused, considering it for a moment before amending her previous statement. 'Actually, please do.' She smiled sweetly.

His only response was to grin, eyes lidded as he looked down at her. She felt a strange warmth unfurl in her chest.

'Did you find out what caused Mei to get sick?' Xander asked, changing the topic and only causing the warmth to unfurl further.

'It looked to be poisoning,' Bisma replied. 'But now I'm not sure; I haven't been able to track the source.'

'But by whom?' he asked, genuinely confused.

Forest, he really was thick in the head sometimes.

She gestured to the town square. 'Take your pick.'

For some reason, Bisma did not feel compelled to mention the old man who had just thrown rotten fruit and spit at her. She had an uncanny feeling Xander would react badly to that news, and she did not need his emotions on top of her own.

'Everyone hates us,' she simply said.

'Not everyone,' he said, his voice soft but firm. He stepped closer, close enough that she had to look up to meet his eyes, and as she did, her breath lodged in her throat.

She clenched her jaw, internally chastising herself. He really was insufferably handsome.

Without another word, she turned and took her leave, but not before a blush had already crept to her cheeks. She suspected he had noticed, for she heard his gentle laugh as she stalked away, but she refused to waste a moment thinking of it.

Bisma went back to the bakery, where Deeba was on the counter sucking on a pretzel stick and Luna was deep in discussion with Haru. In the background, Haru's mother and father looked to be quite frazzled as they dealt with the rush of customers.

'*Haru!*' his father called, but he did not notice.

With an exasperated sigh and glare at his son, Haru's father packaged another loaf of bread and handed it to a customer, then was immediately besieged by another.

Bisma came up beside Luna, who was just as oblivious to anything outside the little bubble she and Haru had created. Bisma aggressively cleared her throat.

'Oh, you're back!' Luna said, turning to her. Luna was grinning, face cheery, but when she spotted Bisma's expression, she furrowed her brows. 'What happened? Are you angry?'

'No. What do you mean?'

'Your face is pink.'

Bisma scowled. 'So is yours.' She gave a pointed look in Haru's direction, and he consequently looked away.

Luna made an outraged sound, giving Bisma an *oh-my-god-you-are-so-embarrassing* look quintessential for a fifteen-year-old.

'Let's go,' Bisma said, carrying her baskets under one elbow, so she could hold Deeba with the other.

'Bajiiii,' Deeba cooed, latching onto Bisma's side. Her little fingers played with the end of one of Bisma's gold baliyan as they made their exit.

Luna waved to Haru, then skipped out behind Bisma.

As they made their way through the square, Luna giggled, her baskets swaying. She was happy and carefree, and Bisma didn't have the heart to tell her to act unhappy. Instead, Bisma glared at anyone who so much as glanced at the girls.

Luckily, Bisma was scary enough for all three of them.

10

The cause of Mei's sickness remained a mystery, which frustrated Bisma to no end. She wrote about it to her new friend, an act she was growing increasingly fond of.

She loved her sisters more than anything in the world, but they could be a handful. Writing to her friend was something that was all her own, and she'd always had an inclination for secrets, something that had gotten her into plenty of trouble in the past. But this was different, she told herself. This was safe, comfortable.

More days passed in an uneventful blur. Bisma sent Luna and Azalea to town to do errands, for there was simply too much to be done at home. Bisma had not finished her new poison orders yet, so she spent most of her time in the garden (when she wasn't doing chores or being in charge, of course).

However, this morning she came to the garden early, before any of the girls were awake, hoping to finish off the last of the orders and go to town to deliver them, all before lunch.

She walked across the stepping stones in her garden, looking for certain ingredients. She spotted the old mehndi plant, which was withering away. She looked down at her hands, which had been bare for a few days now.

With a quick bit of magic, she renewed the mehndi plant, then plucked the leaves to make powder later, after which she would mix it into a paste with sugar, essential oil, and water.

After she finished with the last of the poisons, she went up to the treehouse to check on the girls who had awoken. She went to give Deeba a cuddle, feeding her some kaju barfi, which Bisma had made the day before by grinding and kneading cashew nuts into a dough.

She popped a piece into her own mouth, accompanying it with the milky tea Luna had just made, before heading out.

Once she'd finished dropping off the orders, she was glad she did not have errands to run, for the town was exceptionally busy, even busier than it had been a few days ago.

She was glad, too, that she'd come alone today. Anxiety prickled through her.

Everyone seemed to be there, waiting for something. The square was full of people of all ages and backgrounds—rich and poor alike—and Bisma realized that today was when Xander's uncle, that famous architect from Whitebridge, was arriving. There was a stage at the front of the square in front of the mayor's office, and it was decorated with banners and ribbons.

Drat. She should have come yesterday and avoided this entire affair, but she hadn't finished in time.

Frederick Chapman was probably the most famous architect in

all Fairendelle, for he had designed, at the king's special request, the renovations of the castle in the capital city of Castletown. Beyond that, he was known for his plans to improve the old cities of Crownley, the province which held Castletown, Whitebridge, and Old Town.

Old Town was one of the only remaining towns in the capital province that had not yet been redesigned, which was why Old Town remained, well, *old*. Despite attempts, the main reason Old Town could not expand was because of the Enchanted Forest.

It could not be tamed, so that land remained untouched, whereas with other villages, they'd had cut into the surrounding forests for their expansion plans.

Bisma felt smug about that, at least. No one could hurt the Enchanted Forest. No matter how many people had tried over the years, the Forest could not be felled.

Perhaps Frederick's plans were to expand west, but there Crownley lands bled into the province of Huntington, and inter-province politics usually stopped such expansions from taking place. Perhaps they had come to an agreement or found a loophole?

She wondered what, exactly, Frederick was planning, and it was this curiosity that made her linger on the edge of the square, watching. A man, who could only be Frederick himself, left the hotel front and was met by the mayor, Lady Charlotte.

He bowed toward her, then kissed her hand. Lady Charlotte was an older woman with her long hair in twists and dark skin. She wore a long gown, and beside her stood Xander's mother, Eleanora, who was also dressed in a long gown with gorgeous beading, her hair pulled up into a beautifully braided crown. She looked even more regal than when Bisma had seen her last, in Xander's greenhouse.

The wealthy did not mind wearing dresses so long that the hems tracked six inches deep with mud; such mess meant nothing to them. On the contrary, Bisma and her sisters always wore dresses that fell six inches above their ankles to avoid getting them dirty. Of course, they had to do all the washing themselves, and did not have new dresses to wear every day.

As Eleanora moved to stand with Frederick, Bisma mentally slapped herself for not making the connection sooner. They were brother and sister! Xander had mentioned Fredrick was his uncle, but she hadn't realized how close the relation was.

Now that he was standing beside his sister, the resemblance was obvious. Eleanora and Frederick both had the same copper hair as Xander and the same delicate bone structure and elegance.

Frederick was in his late thirties and was quite handsome, which led to the irritating realization that if Xander aged like his uncle, he would never stop being beautiful.

How annoying.

Bisma should have realized sooner that Frederick Chapman was *the* Uncle Fred Xander often spoke of, the same uncle he had stayed with in Whitebridge while he was completing his studies.

As if she'd summoned him, Xander appeared, standing beside his uncle, mother, and the mayor. His father must have been out on business, otherwise this picture-perfect family would have been complete.

Xander was wearing a fine topcoat above a waistcoat, both pieces of clothing a dark teal that Bisma imagined the deep ocean to be. The effect was quite regal, and she found herself staring.

Bisma did not even notice Lady Charlotte addressing the crowd to introduce Frederick, until everyone was clapping. She averted her gaze from Xander to his uncle, watching as Frederick stood up behind the podium.

'Good afternoon, dearest citizens of Old Town!' Frederick said, his voice just as charming as his nephew's. He gave the crowd a dazzling smile as they cheered. 'I am honored to be here, in this great town of my youth. As many of you know, my family has run the Chapman Apothecary since the very inception of Old Town; you may know my big sister, Eleanora.' He turned to toss a wink at her. 'Because of this, Old Town has a special place in my heart. No matter where I travel, I always come back to this little village,' he continued. 'Old Town has undeniable charm—where do you think I get it from?' The crowd chuckled along with him. 'I firmly believe this town, with its wonderful spirit, is an untapped gold mine.

'Now, you must be thinking, "Frederick, what are you going on about?" Well, let me tell you! As of now, because Old Town is well . . . *old*, most business passing through this area goes straight to Stoneville. However, if Old Town expanded and renewed, it could become as metropolitan—and successful—as Whitebridge, or dare I say, even Castletown! And that is exactly why I am here: I wish to see Old Town—and its people—prosper, and the king himself has commissioned me for this cause!'

Frederick finished his speech with a grand flourish. Immediately, the crowd erupted with applause and cheers. Beside Frederick, Xander clapped fervently, looking up to his uncle with stars in his eyes. He clearly idolized the man.

Bisma rolled her eyes. It was a grand speech, to be sure, but it lacked any actual specific plans. It didn't matter to her anyway; she did not care much for Old Town. The Enchanted Forest was her home, and it would always be safe and perfectly enough for her and her family.

As the crowd continued to cheer, Bisma turned to leave, though not without one final glance in Xander's direction. He was absorbed with his uncle, standing up there on the stage, and for once, he did not approach her.

Good, she told herself. She would not be bothered by him, which was excellent, though she couldn't help the strange twinge of disappointment she felt as a result.

Bisma made her way home. On the way, she saw a rose bush and plucked as many flowers as her basket could hold; she would put them in bowls of water around the house for the sweet smell.

As she continued her journey, she tossed some nuts and berries from her basket to the crows as she walked along, skipping over branches and waving to the rabbits.

When she arrived home, Bisma hugged and kissed all her sisters hello, then retired to her room to freshen up. The moment she entered her room, her gaze strayed to her bed, and a thrill shot through her.

A letter!

She had responded the other day to tell her new friend about her day, to describe what she had been busy with, and she was excited now to hear about his life. She had learned that the writer was a boy, a bit older than her, but there was still so much to learn about him.

Bisma was just about to unfold the paper when she heard a cry from downstairs.

'BAJI!' Azalea yelled.

Alarm cut through Bisma; she threw the letter down on her bed and hurried down the stairs.

When she arrived, she saw it wasn't anything serious. Bisma released a long breath.

'They're being so ANNOYING,' Azalea said, pointing at Nori and Deeba, who sat on the floor by her feet. It looked like Azalea was trying to do some embroidery on a dress.

'Stop bothering your sister,' Bisma scolded.

'We didn't even do anything!' Nori cried, outraged by the accusation, while Deeba giggled.

'Did so!' Azalea snapped. 'Now go away! Or I'll undo that hole I mended in your stuffed rabbit!'

Nori never slept without that rabbit, so this threat was enough to scare the wits from her.

'Baji!' Nori wailed, tears already filling her eyes at the prospect.

'Okay, okay, let's all stay calm,' Bisma said, coming toward them. 'Nori, I think you're hungry, let's have a little snack. Does Deeba want a little snack?' She reached for both their hands and helped them to their feet.

'I'm not hungry,' Nori said, crossing her arms and pouting.

'Hmm, are you sure?' Bisma asked. She crouched down so she was at eye level with the five-year-old, then pressed her ear to Nori's stomach. 'You are! Your tummy just told me so.'

A smile cracked through Nori's pout. 'No it didn't!'

'Oh yes it did.' Bisma felt around Nori's stomach, tickling her in the process. 'Look, I can feel it, too! Your tummy is empty.' She stretched her free hand to Deeba, tickling her as well. 'And so is yours!'

Both girls laughed, and Bisma pulled them close. 'Now, will you help me make chai? You can have some honey milk and nankhatai.'

'Make me some, too!' Luna called from the couch, where she was lying down, fighting with a spool of yarn.

'Fine, but watch Deebs,' Bisma said, depositing the two-year-old onto the floor in front of her.

'Yeah, yeah,' Luna said. She grabbed some painted wooden blocks and tossed them to Deeba, who quickly busied herself with playing.

'Azalea?' Bisma asked, pulling out a wooden stool for Nori to stand on by the stove. She set a pot with water on the stovetop, careful to mind Mei's work. Mei was in the kitchen as well, making a hot and sour soup for dinner.

'Yeah, duh,' Azalea replied. Only the older girls were allowed caffeine, and like most twelve-year-olds, Azalea took every opportunity to be one of the older ones.

After the water boiled, Bisma asked Nori to add in the loose tea, telling her to only put in a spoonful. Nori, of course, added a spoonful that could easily be counted as two, but Bisma had accounted for such an error; two spoonfuls was really the amount she needed.

As that brewed she added sugar and cardamom, then when it was ready, Bisma poured in the milk herself, adding milk to another small pot with honey, to warm for the younger girls.

When their drinks were ready, Bisma poured the chai and milk into teacups as Nori brought out the tin of nankhatai, giving each of her sisters a buttery shortbread cookie.

Bisma distributed the teacups, and when she gave Luna hers, Bisma's eyes caught on Luna's work. She seemed to be knitting a pair of colorful striped mittens and looked to be getting tangled in the yarn.

'Who are those for?' Bisma asked. They looked far too big for any of the girls.

Luna hid her nose in her teacup. 'No one,' she mumbled.

Bisma returned to the kitchen, exchanging an amused look with Mei who'd overheard.

They sat wrapped in their sweaters and shawls, feet clad in fuzzy socks, sipping their warm drinks, as candles glowed around them, their home filled with the smell of ginger and soy sauce. Luna hummed to herself, and Deeba happily babbled along.

'Baji, did I tell you?' Luna said. 'Last time Azalea and I were in town, Haru made this wonderful pumpkin dessert with the first pumpkins of the season. He knows I just *adore* pumpkin sweets, as I've mentioned it to him on more than one occasion.'

'Hmm.' Bisma had already heard this story about eight times in the past two days.

'But *he* also likes them,' Luna continued, 'so do you think he made them because *he* likes them or because he knows that *I* like them . . . ?' She trailed off, clearing her throat.

'Oh, thank god she stopped,' Azalea muttered.

Bisma wasn't really paying attention; her gaze was trained on the little ones, eyes jumping from Mei in the kitchen, to Nori at the table, and Deeba on the floor.

Bisma took another sip of her chai—then nearly choked on it as Luna shrieked.

'What is it?' Bisma asked, shooting to her feet. She turned to the living area, where Luna had dropped her knitting and was clutching her left arm with her right. Her hand was red as if burning.

'Lulu?' Deeba asked from the floor, alarmed.

Luna cried out, falling to her knees. Her face was contorted with pain.

'What happened?' Bisma cried, falling to her side. It didn't make sense. And then she saw the skin of Luna's hand and wrist, the veins turning dark blue.

Just as they had with Mei.

Luna had been poisoned.

All the girls had gathered round, but upon seeing her dark blue veins, Mei started back, face petrified. Her dark eyes were wide with fear.

There was no time to waste.

'Forrie!' Bisma cried out. She tugged on her shoes, and Azalea helped Luna into hers. A vine snaked into the treehouse, wrapping around both Bisma and Luna, taking them down to the ground.

'Azalea, you're in charge!' Bisma called, supporting Luna.

Then they ran.

11

Bisma headed straight for Xander's greenhouse. The entire way over, she'd hoped and prayed he would be in there. As she came bursting through the door, Luna hanging off her, she was glad to see he was.

He was in his shirtsleeves, the teal topcoat and waistcoat from earlier discarded. His shirt was undone at the throat, and his dark copper hair was unkempt; he seemed to be in the middle of something, but when he heard the door open, he looked up.

Shock cracked his features, followed quickly with consternation. He choked, taking in the wild look on her face and Luna. 'Bisma, what happened?'

He strode forward, immediately taking Luna's weight to bring her forward. Luna was whimpering with pain; Bisma had half dragged her here from the Enchanted Forest.

Even though the sun had set on their walk over, bringing a biting chill to the evening air, Luna was burning hot, her hair drenched with sweat. Her arm had gotten worse in the time it took to get here, the dark blue in her veins now extending up to her forearm.

'Clear that table,' Xander told Bisma.

She did as she was told and he swiftly lifted Luna and laid her down. He left, then quickly returned with a small roll of leaves; Bisma recognized the white willow, modified with something else she didn't know.

'Chew on this,' he instructed Luna. 'It'll help with the pain.'

Luna grabbed the leaves and started chewing them, and they must have provided some relief, for her face relaxed a little.

'It's—burning,' Luna choked out. 'It feels like there's hot coals on my skin.'

Heart twisting painfully, Bisma looked up to Xander. 'Can you do something?'

Xander ran a hand through his hair; he radiated tension. 'I—I don't know,' he said. 'It's different from last time.'

'But it has to be something similar,' Bisma said. 'Look at the veins.'

'Yes, but Mei was cold. Luna is hot—' He broke off, examining Luna's arm, which was red around the dark veins. 'I don't . . . I don't understand. It's traveling, as well, whereas Mei seemed to be infected straight away. Whoever is doing this has adjusted their poison . . .' He trailed off.

Bisma's throat closed. It didn't matter who had done this or why—right now, they needed to heal Luna. 'Xander, please,' she said, her voice broken.

He turned to look at her. Their eyes met and held.

He shook his head as if coming out of a daze, and his frazzled look cleared. He nodded firmly.

Luna was still whimpering, but what he gave her for the pain was helping a bit at least for she was no longer crying. She held onto Bisma with her unpoisoned arm so tightly that Bisma felt her bones shuddering beneath the pressure.

Luna buried her face against Bisma's neck, her chest shaking with quaking breaths.

Bisma stroked her sister's hair, glad she was not looking at her own injury. Luna's arm was blistering now, the skin peeling.

Xander returned, a mortar and pestle in his hand. He stirred it vigorously, and she saw the stretchy liquid of honey. Setting it down beside Luna, he cut a leaf from an aloe vera plant nearby, slicing it in half and scraping out the gel to add to the mortar.

The potion bubbled as he infused it with magic, but Xander's gaze was hardly on it. He looked around, searching for something.

'What?' Bisma asked, impatient. 'What is it?

'Peppermint,' he replied, agitated. He rummaged through different pots. 'I know it's around here somewhere.'

'Are you a garden-witch or not?!'

'It'll take too long—'

There was a pot nearby with a small plant. Bisma plucked the plant out and threw it on the floor, then stuck her hand into the soil. A moment later, another plant sprouted.

'Here!' she cried.

He blinked, staring at her with awe. Then he looked at the peppermint before looking back at her. 'Brilliant,' he said, jaw slack. 'You're brilliant.'

He picked the leaves, then used magic to make them bigger. After that, he dipped them into the mixture, then came to wrap the leaf around Luna's arm. It was a similar yet different process to what he had done for Mei.

Bisma held Luna as he worked, whispering consolations in her ear. The front of Bisma's dress was soaked with Luna's sweat, but she did not let go.

When Xander was done, he stepped back, rubbing a hand over his face. 'I don't know if it'll work.' He sounded afraid. 'I've never seen anything like this before, so I've never tried this before, either.'

They waited, and slowly, it seemed Luna was in less pain. She was no longer sweating as profusely, and her body ceased shaking. Bisma released a long breath. Xander rested both hands against the table, leaning forward and bowing his head.

'It's working,' Bisma said.

Xander nodded, taking a deep breath before looking up at her.

But it seemed she spoke too soon.

Luna cried out again. Before Bisma's eyes, Luna's veins turned dark blue once more, this time reaching above her elbow.

'Xander!' Bisma said, fear choking her.

'Baji!' Luna gasped. The skin of her arm was blistered red, the veins growing darker.

Xander's face went pale. 'Bisma, it's going to keep spreading,' he said, eyes wide. 'It'll spread to her heart. Look at the pattern. I—I don't know what to do.'

But she did not see what he saw; all Bisma felt was Luna's pain. 'What happens if it gets to her heart?' she asked, though she already knew.

Xander shook his head, and Bisma set her jaw.

'*No*. That's not an option.'

Luna was sobbing by then, and Bisma could not bear it, but she would not let Luna fall silent forever.

'The easiest solution would be to amputate,' Xander said.

'No!' Bisma cried. She wouldn't have Luna permanently altered. '*No*. Think of something else.'

Xander ran a hand through his hair, agitated. 'We could . . .' He trailed off, thinking. 'Leeches? No, they won't be quick enough.'

'Would bloodletting work?' Bisma asked.

Xander looked up at her. 'It might,' he said, and she could see him running through the process in his mind. 'The problem is the poison seems to have overtaken much of her blood supply; to let it all might cause too much blood loss.'

'What if we isolate the blood in her arm, then couple it with a fortifying potion?' Bisma suggested, mind racing.

'It might work . . .'

'We have to try,' Bisma said. They had no choice.

Even as they spoke, the dark veins had crept higher and were by her bicep now. The longer they took to discuss this, the further it would spread. There was no time.

Bisma held Luna's face in her hands.

'Luna, I'm sorry, but this is going to hurt,' Bisma said, her words clouded with tears. 'Sweet, I'm so sorry.'

'Please,' Luna begged, voice barely audible. 'Just make it stop.'

Bisma met Xander's eyes. 'I'll do the extraction; you make the potion.'

'We have to time it properly—' Xander began, but Bisma ignored him. She looked around to find a tourniquet, and Xander sprang into action.

He gave Luna something to help her sleep as Bisma tied the tourniquet around her arm.

'Make that potion quick,' Bisma ordered, picking up a scalpel. Xander was already at work, and without sparing him another glance, she put the blade against Luna's darkened veins and cut.

The first incision was like a dam breaking loose: blood spurted up in a gush, shooting over Bisma's hands, arms, and the front of her dress. Taken by surprise, Bisma squealed, stepping back.

'Bis!' Xander cried, coming to her side. His face was wild with concern as he reached for her, but she held up a bloodied hand.

'I'm fine,' she said. Her heart was pounding, but the extracted blood wasn't harmful. It was warm on her skin, seeping through the fabric of her dress, but it wasn't any hotter than blood normally was. If it was poisonous, it would have burned upon contact, since it seemed to be burning Luna from the inside.

'Here,' Xander said, handing her a bucket to collect the poisoned blood. Her dress was already ruined, her hands covered, but she held the bucket against Luna's arm, drawing more incisions to release the blood, which was thick and an unnatural purple so dark it was almost black.

Luna whimpered, her face contorted with pain despite the potion Xander had fed her to put her to sleep. Bisma's eyes burned with tears, her hands shaking as she held the scalpel over Luna's skin. There was already a row of cuts along Luna's arm, but Bisma hesitated to add more.

You have to, she told herself. She was already a monster, what was one more monstrous thing? Lip trembling, Bisma cut across her sister's arm, watching as more blood flowed out. An acidic smell filled the air.

'The potion, Xander,' Bisma called, her voice thick. He was busy mixing it.

'Almost done!' he called back.

But blood was pouring from Luna's arm freakishly fast, and Luna's light brown skin had lost all its warmth. A gray pallor came over her, her lips becoming dry and cracked. Bisma's stomach turned, dread seizing her.

'Xander!'

'Here!'

He dashed over with his mortar, the blue liquid inside splashing.

Grabbing a beaker from another table, Xander filled it. Then he fed it to Luna, who swallowed it.

'Is it working?' Bisma asked, unsure. There was no way to tell if any of what they were doing was effective; Luna's skin was still hot, the veins still dark. She had lost a lot of blood—too much.

'I think it is,' Xander said, feeding her more of the potion. 'Look.' He pointed to Luna's arm. 'It's stopped spreading at least. Now it's just a matter of extracting all the poison.'

But how much bloodletting would Luna survive? The fortifying potion had brought some warmth back to her skin, but it lasted only moments before she went pale again. Bisma's entire body shook with uncertainty, with fear.

What if it didn't work? Had she risked Luna's life? Should they have amputated her arm? How had this even happened to begin with? Questions swarmed through her mind. She felt she was in the worst nightmare, but there was no waking from it.

'Bis, don't worry,' Xander said, though even he did not seem sure. 'I'm sure if we just keep at it . . .'

Xander fed her more of the potion as Bisma watched Luna's blood pour out. She couldn't look at anything but the blood dripping down into the bucket, splashing, a hideous sight.

Luna's blood, her sister's blood. Each drop felt like a prick against Bisma's heart. Bile rose in her throat as the bucket filled up.

Then, finally—*finally*—the blood spilling from Luna's arm changed from purple to ordinary scarlet, no longer thick, with none of the acidic smell.

'I think that's enough,' Xander said, pressing a clean cloth against Luna's arm. Bisma was frozen in place, unmoving. 'Bis?'

She stared at the bucket, the contents now having fallen still.

The gruesome sight was Bisma's only solace. The poison was out of Luna. Even as Bisma abhorred what she had done, even as she blamed herself for it, at the very least, Luna would be safe.

Her vision swam, and she wanted to collapse, but the work was not over yet.

'We need to close the wound,' Xander said.

Time seemed to skip. Without her realizing, Xander was at her side, his hands gentle on her shoulders as he sat her down on the table by Luna's legs. In a daze, Bisma watched as he fed Luna more of the fortifying potion, then was transfixed by his long, clean fingers stitching up the cuts. Her gaze then went to her own hands, which were coated with black blood.

'You did excellent, Bis,' Xander told her, but he sounded very far away. 'Bisma . . . *Bisma.*'

She startled, turning to look at him. The room came back in brutal focus.

'She's going to be okay,' Xander said. His fingers were gently touching Luna's neck.

'She lost so much blood,' Bisma whispered.

'I know, but look,' he said, reaching for her hand, which was limp. She allowed him to bring her fingers against Luna's throat, pressing against her pulse.

For a moment, Bisma felt nothing, and her chest cleaved in two—until the pads of her fingers picked up a pulse. It was faint—so soft!—but it was there. She released a long breath, relief pouring over her.

'Why don't you get her more of the sleeping syrup while I finish up here?' he asked, busy cleaning Luna's arm. There were six ugly wounds along her arm, where Bisma had cut her. 'It's just there by the juniper berries. I'll apply more of the numbing jelly so she doesn't feel any pain in her sleep.'

She went to retrieve the vial, then emptied a dose into Luna's mouth. While Luna was still asleep, this second dose would help ease her into another cycle of sleep.

With nothing else to do, Xander and Bisma both stood back, exhausted and stunned.

Luna had almost died. The realization struck her like a physical blow. Suddenly the smell and sight of blood was too much. Nausea overcame her, and before she could stop herself, she doubled over.

She had just enough time to aim into a nearby dustbin before vomiting. The sound was awful. Her throat burned, but she couldn't stop until the contents of her stomach were emptied. Even then she stood dry heaving, gasping for breath.

It was only afterwards that she realized Xander was holding her hair back, gentle hand in her hair. She straightened, embarrassed, and he released her hair. It fell forward, and she wanted to hide, to bury herself in the soil.

Xander brought a clean cloth forward, raising it in his hand as if to wipe her face, but she turned her face, ashamed of the spectacle she'd made of herself.

'Bis,' he said, his voice soft, but still she would not look at him. She was on the very edge; even so, she did not wish to break down in front of him. Her body trembled.

As if realizing, he dropped his hand, stepping back. 'I'll just get some clean towels,' he said, but she hardly heard him. She didn't watch him walk away, only listened for the door closing shut behind him.

Once it sounded, she was alone. Pain spread through her and tears shot to her eyes. A sob rose in her throat, and she clamped a hand over her mouth, keeping it shut, not allowing it to release.

There was no one around to hear, but still, she would not allow herself to be vocal. The sob threatened to break, but she forced it back with both hands, as if she could stop this agony from overcoming her.

This was all her fault. Her entire body shuddered with the suppressed cries. She quickly wiped the tears away as they bubbled up in her eyes, catching them before they fell.

When the tears finally stopped, she uncovered her mouth, gasping for breath with only one thought going through her head:

What have you done?

12

As if sensing she needed time alone, Xander was gone for some time.

Luna slept while Bisma stared off into the distance, unmoving.

Xander returned about an hour later, and this time, she actually saw him. He had changed and freshened up. With him, he brought a tray of food balanced atop a pile of clean cloth.

Around him, things came into focus again: the greenhouse, the aftermath of the bloody procedure, and she realized the bedraggled state she was in. Her clothes were covered with blood and reeked.

Xander set the tray of food down on the table, then approached her with something else in his hands.

'Here,' Xander said, holding a folded piece of clothing out to her. His voice was kind.

'Oh.' She blinked, taking it. The fabric was thick and soft, obviously expensive.

'It's an old dress of my mother's,' he explained. 'Don't worry; she won't miss it.'

She looked down at her hands, which were still covered with her sister's dried blood.

'I'll show you where you can wash up,' he said.

She followed him outside the greenhouse, where a washing area was set up.

He lit the candles to reveal large basins filled with clean water, a small bucket for pouring, bars of soap, and a sponge. Xander pointed out the towels on a shelf, and she set the dress down beside them.

'I'll just be inside,' Xander said. 'If you need anything.'

'I—Thank you.' She met his eyes, hoping he understood just how much she meant it. 'Really, Xander.'

He swallowed. 'Of course.'

He left her, and Bisma tied her hair up into a knot, preparing herself. Then she stripped off her clothes, which she would be discarding now. It felt like peeling off a layer of skin, and she poured cold water over herself, then scrubbed with the sponge. She watched the water turn pink with the dried blood; she scrubbed and scrubbed until it was all gone.

Bisma took long, measuring breaths, her heart slowing. It was done now; there was no use in being upset about it. She ordered herself to be alright.

Grabbing the soap bar, she lathered suds across her skin, inhaling the scent. The soap smelled strongly of cloves, and when she washed it from her body, she found she smelled just like Xander.

Pressing her nose to her skin, she breathed it in. She closed her eyes, letting the scent calm her.

Once she was clean, she patted herself dry, then stepped into the dress. It was of a fine material, and the moment it touched her skin, she felt safe from the chilly evening.

The dress had a dark plaid print with full sleeves, though the neckline was wide enough that the sleeves were barely hanging onto her shoulders. The dress was long on her, for Eleanora was taller, but that was not the biggest issue.

The dress laced in the back.

Eleanora had maidservants to help her dress, of course, but Bisma had no such thing. She tried to reach across and lace it up herself but to no avail. The dress slipped off.

With a sigh, Bisma considered putting on her own dress, but she looked at the sorry state of it and her mouth soured.

Well, there was only one thing for it.

After drying her feet and putting on her shoes, Bisma slipped the dress back on. Holding the front of the dress in place, she walked back to the greenhouse.

Luna was still asleep, and Xander was leaning against the opposite table, watching her with careful eyes. When he heard Bisma come in, his gaze immediately went to her. His jaw went slack.

Suddenly, she felt exposed. Her wet hair was still up in a knot, tendrils falling down, but for the most part her entire neck was bare. His eyelids fluttered.

'It laces in the back,' Bisma said, hesitating. 'Can you—'

He looked her up and down, his gaze lingering. He clenched his jaw, then nodded. 'Come here,' he said, his voice a command.

A shiver ran through her.

She went to him, holding the dress tightly in place to keep it from falling. Beneath her palm, she felt her heart race. Suddenly, she felt shy, not wanting to turn, for her entire back was bare.

Xander slid his hand over her waist. With the barest pressure from his finger, he turned her. She couldn't help but gasp as he pulled the laces, pulling her closer to him. His legs bracketed her; she stood between his knees.

He began at the bottom, at the base of her spine, the pads of his fingers dancing across her bare skin. She imagined what it might feel like if he slipped his hands under the dress; it would be so easy—he could pretend it was an accident.

But he did not, which almost made it worse. The temptation hung there, like a sword swinging above her head, back and forth, waiting to fall. She wondered if he felt it, but she couldn't see his face, which she was almost glad for. Her skin grew hot.

He continued lacing her up, tugging the strings tight, and Bisma briefly forgot how to breathe. His long fingers worked deftly but slowly, as if he was savoring it. Desire pierced through her, sharp and bright.

She felt his scattered breath against the bare skin of her shoulders as he finished, tying the laces in place into a tight bow. The dress was secured, but Bisma still held onto her heart as it pounded thunderously.

A single finger went down the laces, as if he was checking them, and she felt an electric current tingle through her skin with the movement. Then his hand settled on her waist, holding onto her like an anchor.

He was quiet, deathly so.

'Is it done?' she asked, her voice a whisper.

She received no response, but she heard his hoarse breath. A moment later, she turned. His hand moved with her body, shifting over her stomach, leaving a trail of heat in its wake as he held onto her. Blood roaring in her ears, she faced him.

Because he was leaning against the table, they were finally eye level, though his eyes were closed. She stood between his knees, their faces separated by a distance so paltry she could almost taste him, if only she put out her tongue.

It was disconcerting to see his face this close; she had the urge to run her fingers through his hair, down to the planes of his cheekbones, drifting lower until she reached his mouth.

'What is it?' she asked.

He still had not opened his eyes. He leaned closer, inhaling deeply.

'You smell like . . .'

He opened his eyes, and the breath lodged in her throat. She could hardly see the green in his eyes; the pupils were blown wide, a bottomless black. He stood abruptly and she tilted her head back to look up at him.

His hand tightened at her waist, pulling her closer. His gaze went to her lips.

She wondered if he would kiss her. She had not been kissed in some time. Her terrible experience at sixteen had deterred her from love, but not from dalliances. She had kissed plenty of boys in the two years since that summer—always strangers, travelers who didn't know who she was, and most importantly, always just the once.

She never got her heart involved.

To kiss Xander now was surely a bad idea; she knew that. But the way he was looking at her . . . she couldn't help but draw nearer, her entire body pulsing in anticipation.

'Bisma,' he whispered, his voice strangled.

His free hand came up to tuck a stray lock of hair behind her ear, and he cupped her face, his fingers soft against her neck. His skin was so warm it felt intoxicating.

He was trembling, as if exerting a great deal of power in holding himself back.

She bit her lower lip, hard enough to feel pain. 'Yes?'

He opened his mouth—to say something or to kiss her, she would never know. For at that exact moment, Luna roused.

Bisma startled back, out of Xander's reach. Her heart hammered. Feeling hot all over, she rushed to her sister's side.

Luna groaned, blinking blearily.

'She's awake,' Bisma said, turning back to Xander.

He shook his head as if waking from a trance, or a dream, then slapped both his cheeks with his hands a few times. She thought she heard him mutter a curse to himself before he came over to Luna's other side.

Together, Bisma and Xander helped Luna sit up.

'What happened?' Luna asked, turning to Bisma.

Relief poured through her at hearing Luna's voice, at seeing her open brown eyes.

'You're okay,' Bisma said, pulling Luna into her arms. 'You're okay.'

'But what happened?' Luna asked. She groaned. 'I feel terrible.'

She pulled back, her gaze going to her arm, which was covered in stitches. Her eyes widened.

'You were sick—poisoned, like Mei was, I think,' Bisma explained. 'But you're alright.'

'I remember . . .' Luna trailed off, her face twisting.

'What?'

'I was dying,' she said quietly.

Pain pricked Bisma's heart. Luna looked so afraid.

'I wouldn't have let anything happen to you,' Bisma said, trying to keep her voice strong.

'Baji, I was *dying*.' Luna's eyes welled with tears, and she blinked them away rapidly, though they only came back. 'I felt it,' she continued. 'And there was nothing I could do. Everything hurt so much!'

'Lu,' Bisma said, wrapping her sister in a hug.

What Luna had gone through was a traumatic experience. Guilt needled Bisma; how could she have let this happen? Bisma wouldn't have let anything happen to her sister, but what if it had, anyway? What if Luna *had* died? She'd clearly come close.

'I'll give you a moment alone,' Xander said, quietly stepping back.

Luna cried, and Bisma held her tight. When it seemed Luna's tears had subsided, she let go, and pulled back to face Bisma.

'Do you have *any* idea how this could have happened?' Bisma asked. 'Something you ate? Touched?'

Luna shook her head. 'I don't know. I was at home all day. I didn't leave the Forest.'

Bisma didn't understand. Something was getting into their home, poisoning them right under their noses—under *her* watch—but what?

And by whom?

'Can we go home?' Luna asked, sniffling. She brushed her messy hair aside.

'Of course.' Bisma helped her stand, but as Luna swayed, she had her sit down again. 'Why don't you drink some water first?'

Bisma saw the tray of food Xander had brought earlier; there was a pitcher of water and glasses on it. She poured Luna a glass, then handed it to her.

Xander watched from a corner of the greenhouse, agitated, running a hand through his hair; she could see he did not approach because he did not wish to intrude.

'Just a second,' Bisma told Luna. She went toward Xander, and he immediately went to meet her.

'Anything I can do?' he asked. He was bouncing on his feet, restless. 'I can ask my mother for help, as well. She wouldn't mind.'

'It's alright,' Bisma replied. Eleanora would clearly do anything for her beloved son, but Bisma didn't want her help. She didn't quite know if she trusted Eleanora, and besides, even asking for Xander's help was already too much. 'I'll draw up strengthening potions and give her something for the pain.'

She shuffled on her feet, feeling awkward and unsure. She wished to go back to the mindless bliss of a few minutes ago, Xander's hand on her waist.

'If there's anything I can do, please let me know,' Xander said, his eyes kind.

She nodded. 'I'll send over payment soon; it'll just take me a while to arrange it.'

Anger flared on Xander's face. 'You can't be serious,' he said, making a sound of disbelief.

Bisma was taken aback; it was the first time he'd been truly upset with her. 'I—I'm sorry.'

Xander exhaled, his face immediately melting. 'No, I'm sorry for snapping,' he said, his voice gentle. 'I . . . I'm just—sorry.'

Bisma's composure shook. 'If there's anyone who's sorry, it's me,' she whispered. 'I don't know how I could have let this happen.'

'No, Bis, it's not your fault.' Xander brushed his thumb across her cheek, and she was unsettled to find it wet; she didn't even know a tear had slipped out. She didn't have the strength to push him away.

Instead, she shook her head. For once, she didn't have anything to say.

'Goodbye,' she whispered.

She went back to Luna and they left the Chapman Estate to return to the Enchanted Forest. They walked in silence through the cold night. Bisma could not find any words, not even as Luna silently cried. She didn't fully understand why Luna was crying; she was alright.

'Lu, you're okay,' Bisma said, trying to reassure her. She put her arm around Luna's shoulders.

'I just feel so afraid.' Luna wiped her cheeks. 'It was so dark.'

'Nothing is going to happen to you,' Bisma said. 'I promise.'

Luna nodded, though there was a distant look in her eyes. She needed time, Bisma decided. Then she would be alright.

Luna stopped crying when they reached the Forest, which was dark, though all the Unwanted Girls could easily maneuver it blind. However, at a turn, Luna tripped, stumbling.

Just as she was about to fall, Bisma reaching for her from behind, a branch crept out and caught her. Luna steadied herself, and the branch retreated.

As they walked on, Bisma looked back to where Luna's foot had caught: there was a small puddle of murky water. That was . . . strange. The Enchanted Forest never had random elements out of place in such a manner. The creeks and streams usually all flowed seamlessly.

But perhaps Bisma was imagining it. In truth, Luna was weak, exhausted. That was why she had tripped.

'Thanks, Forrie,' Luna whispered. A breeze lifted to kiss her cheeks, and Bisma felt the same breeze against her own face.

But Bisma didn't deserve to be consoled.

They arrived home, and from the bottom of the treehouse she could hear noise and commotion. Azalea was clearly bossing everyone around, and the girls were begrudgingly listening. They would have eaten dinner some time ago and must have been getting ready for bed.

Luna paused to catch her breath, and a branch reached down, twining around her body to carry her up. Bisma followed on the stairs, and she heard the noise inside fall dead silent as she came up the last step.

'Luna!' Nori cried, rushing to give Luna a hug.

'You're alright!' Mei called.

The other girls crowded around, Deeba waddling over with Azalea behind her.

'You look *awful*,' Azalea blurted. 'What happened?'

Luna's lower lip trembled, and tears sprang in her eyes.

'She's okay,' Bisma said. 'We got the poison out.'

But Azalea was right; Luna's skin was practically gray. She had lost a lot of blood.

Without another word, Luna went up the stairs to her room, disappearing from sight. Which left the girls to stare at Bisma instead. She saw the accusation in their eyes, the confusion and the fear.

'She's fine,' Bisma said, her voice weak. 'Everything is *fine*.'

The words were hardly consoling, to them or to her. In truth, nothing was fine. Two of her sisters had been poisoned, one barely escaping with her life. But Bisma did not say anything else, for she did not know what there was to say.

Deeba was the only one too young to understand; she sat on the floor, gleefully knocking over a tower of blocks. Bisma went to her, and Deeba greeted her baji with the usual affection, which Bisma sorely needed. She hugged little Deeba tight.

'Everyone get ready for bed,' Bisma said, standing with Deeba still in her arms.

Nobody moved.

Bisma cleared her throat. 'Come on, then,' she said. 'It's getting late. Nori, Mei, get changed.'

They went up the stairs. Azalea paused, looking back at Bisma as if she wanted to say something, but in the end, she didn't.

Bisma changed Deeba, then took her to Mei's room, laying her down in the cot with her favorite handmade doll. Mei was already in bed, though she was sitting up, eyes wide.

'Go to sleep, OK?' Bisma said, going to tuck her in. When Bisma grew near, Mei threw her arms around Bisma, hugging her tight. Bisma held her close.

Mei was trembling. When she pulled back, Mei looked afraid.

'Baji, why couldn't you help Luna the same way you helped me?' she asked quietly. 'She doesn't look fine.'

She was not accusing, she was merely curious and confused, but it was hard not to feel the words as a reproach.

'We tried, sweet,' Bisma said, tears pricking her eyes. She blinked them away. There wasn't anything else to say. She kissed Mei goodnight, then blew out the candles.

Bisma went to Nori's room, where she was in bed with her stuffed rabbit, the one she never slept without. Nori was holding it tight.

'All ready to sleep?' Bisma asked.

'Is Lulu going to be alright?' Nori asked.

'Yes, of course,' Bisma said, though she did not know for certain.

'Are *we* going to be OK?' Nori asked, nibbling on her bottom lip. Her blue eyes were clouded with worry.

'Yes,' Bisma said, brushing aside Nori's blonde hair. 'Always.'

But as she left Nori's room, she wasn't so sure about that either.

Bisma went across the hall to Azalea's room, where Azalea was sitting cross-legged on her bed, fiddling with her hair.

'Go to sleep, OK?' Bisma said.

Azalea looked at her, dark eyes slitted. 'I don't think Luna's fine,' she said. 'What even happened? How did she get poisoned? Who did this?'

Bisma's heart all but stopped at the accusation in her sister's tone.

'I–I don't know,' she said, her voice halting. 'I'm sorry.' What else could she say? 'I'm doing the best I can, Azalea.'

'Well, it's not good enough!' Azalea snapped, then stopped,

surprised by her own words. She quickly got into bed, pulling the covers over her and turning her back.

'Azalea—' Bisma started.

'Goodnight,' she replied curtly.

Tears bubbled in Bisma's eyes, falling down her cheeks, but there was no one to see. She went up to Luna's room to check how she was faring, but Luna was already asleep, which was good. Sleep would help.

After checking on the girls, Bisma went down to the garden. She made a strengthening potion, then grew something for the pain, and took both up to Luna's bedside table, leaving a note with instructions beside them.

Then there was nothing left to do. Bisma should have gone to sleep herself, but she knew sleep would not come despite how drained she was.

She went back outside, walking through the dark woods, letting her feet take her. As she walked, she listened to the sounds of the birds and crickets and frogs; she wasn't alone, but she felt so terribly lonely.

Thoughts swam around in her mind. Would Luna truly be OK? The poison was out of her, but Bisma was afraid Luna had been permanently affected by the experience.

Bisma ended up by Mirror Lake, the water a glistening black as it reflected the moon above. Bisma took off her shoes and clothes—thankfully the dress was much easier to undo than it had been to lace up—and waded into the lake, letting the calm waters fold over her. Though the night was cold, the magic of the Forest meant the water was always warm.

Bisma lay down, floating beneath the moonlight, staring up at the stars. Usually, such an exercise helped to soothe her, but tonight it hardly made a difference.

Sometime later, she dragged herself out of the lake. She did not wish to put Eleanora's old dress back on; she remembered Xander's firm hands lacing her up, and a shiver ran down her spine. She felt a dozen emotions sparking together inside her, and any moment now, she would burst into flames.

Luckily, the Forest had anticipated her needs and brought out clothes and a towel for her. She dried herself, then slipped on the thick, soft nightgown, relishing the cozy, comfortable fabric.

Bisma returned home, where everyone was sound asleep. She tiptoed up to her room, lighting a candle and pulled out a piece of paper.

Tears slid down her cheek as she wrote, one plopping onto the page. She brushed it aside, smearing the tear stain with ink. She continued writing her letter, as if perhaps by writing, she might remove these feelings from within her and seal them away on the paper.

> The most horrible thing has happened. My sister nearly died. I'm so afraid. What if this happens again? What if I can't save her, or any of them? I am not fit to be their baji, or to even be in this family.
>
> What am I doing here? What am I doing at all?
>
> How do I rid myself of all the bad parts? I suppose that's a trick question, for if I removed all the bad, surely there would be nothing left.
>
> I wish there was a way to quietly slip away from time, to no longer be known, to no longer exist or have ever existed at all. To simply be replaced by someone better, someone good.
>
> Bisma

13

A few days passed and Bisma continued to puzzle over Luna and Mei's poisonings. The two cases had been so different and yet the same person must have been behind both. In the meantime, Luna recovered. Her strength returned, and though her brown skin regained its warm color, there was a strange sort of emptiness in Luna's dark brown eyes that scared Bisma. Luna was on edge, afraid.

The girls helped in any way they could, and the Forest, of course, helped as well, but Bisma remained troubled. Mei had bounced back completely after being healed, whereas Luna seemed to be struggling with something. She was quiet, startlingly so.

Anytime she asked her what was bothering her, Luna would give Bisma a brave smile and say it was nothing, but Bisma knew better. She supposed coming back from the brink of death wasn't something one could easily recover from, and, as such, Bisma greatly admired Luna's willpower.

Sometimes Bisma was filled with such a force of love for her sisters that she couldn't believe how lucky she was to even know them, let alone be their sister. It felt like a gift to exist at the same time, at the same place as them, and an even greater gift to not only be allowed in their lives but to be counted as one of their closest relations.

For a week, Azalea kept her complaining to a minimum; Mei cooked the most delicious, comforting food; Nori did not cause a mess; and Deeba obliged everyone with extra kisses and cuddles.

Because it was getting colder and carrots were especially sweet this time of year, Bisma made them all a huge pot of gajar ka halwa, a sweet dish soaked in ghee that they all enjoyed as a special treat every late autumn, and she did not harass them about their chores. They all needed a bit of a break, anyway, so even lessons were suspended, much to Nori's relief. Things were calm—perhaps a bit *too* calm.

Bisma felt it, the lack of the usual chaos, but she thought that was what Luna needed: a bit of peace.

Until one evening, when they were all gathered round drinking tea and eating the last of a spiced vanilla cake. Nori finished her slice and, when Mei wasn't looking, swiped half of Mei's slice, too. By the time Mei turned, Nori had already shoved it in her mouth.

Ordinarily, this would be when Mei would complain, Bisma would then scold Nori, and they would all get involved with mediating a suitable punishment. But because they were all doing their best not to cause a ruckus, Mei quietly pinched Nori under the table, to which Nori then quietly kicked Mei under the table in retaliation.

So ensued a silent battle that they were all trying very hard to pretend wasn't happening.

'Enough!' Luna cried, pushing her chair back and standing up. 'I hate how well-behaved everyone is being! Act normal, for god's sake! Nori, that was so *mean*.'

'I only took a bite!' Nori exclaimed.

'YOU ATE HALF OF IT!' Mei cried.

'You're such a liar!' Azalea said.

'Azalea!' Bisma scolded.

'I mean, Azalea's right,' Luna agreed.

The spiced vanilla cake was very personal to them.

'Thank you, Luna. By the way, you need to wash your hair, you look terrible,' Azalea said. 'I've been meaning to say that for *days*.'

Bisma gave Azalea an incredulous look as Luna's mouth fell open in shock. But then Luna started laughing, sitting back down.

'I know,' Luna said, touching her greasy hair. Then she touched her cheeks. 'I need a face mask, as well.'

'I wasn't going to say it, but yes,' Azalea said, taking a sip of her tea.

'Well then, let's do it,' Luna said. 'Where's the haldi? Baji, do we have yogurt?'

'Ooh, face masks!' Nori said, clapping. 'Me want!'

So they mixed honey and turmeric into yogurt, then lathered the mixture over their faces, trying their best not to move their facial muscles as the masks dried, which of course, only made them giggle.

Later, as Bisma taught Nori basic math, Azalea let Luna use the special soap she had gotten from town to wash her hair, informing Luna that the soap cost her most of her allowance, so Luna now owed her. As recompense, Luna offered to read to her from her poetry book, to which Azalea vehemently shook her head.

'Forget I said anything!' Azalea pleaded, then reconsidered. 'Actually, I'll take you NEVER reading from that dreadful book again as payment.'

Luna gasped, affronted. 'This book is EXCELLENT,' Luna said, clutching it to her chest. 'You just lack DEPTH.'

'Riiiiight.'

And things were once again back to the usual chaos.

The next day, Bisma made plans to go to town, and asked Luna if she would like to accompany her, hoping the excursion would further lift Luna's spirits. At first Luna seemed willing, but when Bisma mentioned they might stop by the bakery, Luna quickly changed her mind, letting out a quick and harsh, 'No!'

Bisma was confused. 'What do you mean? I was thinking of getting pumpkin cookies for everyone.'

'No,' Luna said again, this time her voice quiet. 'I don't want to go.'

Before Bisma could press further, Luna retreated to her room, her shoulders stiff.

'Baji, take me,' Mei said, getting up from where she was churning the butter. They all loved going to town.

'Okay, sure,' Bisma replied, running a fond hand over Mei's silky hair.

'And can I get a new cake pan?' Mei asked, excited. 'I've been saving my allowance!'

'Yes, of course, love,' Bisma said.

Saying goodbye to the others, they left the treehouse and began walking toward Old Town. It was a bright, sunny day, and she savored the warmth on her cheeks. Scorching sunlight and cold wind were one of her absolute favorite weather combinations, and she relished it now.

Mei skipped along beside her, humming to herself. When they reached a grapevine, Mei stopped to pick a few, popping them in her mouth.

'Yuck,' Mei said, immediately spitting them out.

Bisma furrowed her brows. 'What is it? Sour?'

'No. They taste *weird*.' She picked one, handing it to Bisma. 'You try.'

Hmm. The fruit in the Enchanted Forest was always perfect and ripe. Bisma approached the vine, touching some of the green grapes. They had an odd texture, and she saw that most of the grapes had already fallen, rotting on the earth.

'That's strange,' Bisma said.

Further along, they passed an apple tree. Bisma picked one, biting into it, and it was just as sweet as always, so whatever was happening with the grapevine must have been an anomaly.

In town, Bisma completed her tasks, dropping off poisons and picking up payment, Mei accompanying her. She saw Frederick Chapman busy at work; she couldn't tell exactly what it was he was doing, just that he seemed preoccupied, an entire team surrounding him.

Bisma paid him no mind. She went to the bakery, where Haru gave Mei a fresh cookie, then packed a dozen for the girls back home.

He looked as if he wanted to ask Bisma something—surely about Luna—but was too shy to bring himself to voice his question. Bisma put him out of his misery, offering the information up herself.

'Luna was going to join us but she's been a little unwell,' she told him.

Immediately, his face contorted with alarm. 'Is she alright? What happened?' he asked, and he might have asked a dozen more variations of the same questions had Bisma not replied within the next second.

She explained how Luna had been poisoned and the only way to save her had been to bleed the poison out.

Haru looked crestfallen. 'How is she doing? Can I see her?'

'You know that no outsiders are allowed in the Enchanted Forest,' Bisma said. 'Don't worry—I'm sure she'll visit you herself, when she's ready.'

'If I write to her, will you give her the letter? And if she responds, could you bring it back next time? And then if I write to her again, will you take it?'

Bisma had no aspirations to be a messenger owl, and she doubted Luna would appreciate her sister being involved in such a personal, intimate matter.

'I have a better idea,' she said, inching closer as she lowered her voice. Haru came nearer to hear. 'Leave a letter at the edge of the Enchanted Forest; the Forest will deliver it to her either through the soil or via a woodland creature. As for her response, that is up to her.'

'Thank you,' Haru said. 'I will do that. And in the meanwhile can you tell her . . .' He trailed off as he tried to decide what the best thing to have Bisma tell Luna would be. 'Tell her that I am thinking of her.'

'I will,' Bisma said, her heart turning fondly for this sweet-faced boy.

'Oh! And one more thing.' He disappeared, then returned a moment later with a small box. 'It's a pumpkin cake, part of a larger catering order, but I doubt they'll notice.'

'Is that so?' Bisma asked, smiling.

'Well . . . better take it quick before I get told off,' he said sheepishly.

She snuck the box into her basket, covering it with cloth. 'I'm sure Luna will appreciate it,' Bisma said.

'And if there's anything I can do or anything that she needs, please tell me.'

'I will.'

Bisma put a hand on Mei's back, making to leave when she noticed how busy the bakery was. As people waited in line for their orders, they chatted and gossiped.

'Actually . . .' Bisma turned back to Haru. He grew alert, and she motioned for him to come close so he could hear her. 'If you hear anyone talking about us, tell me. I still don't know who poisoned Luna, or Mei, for that matter.'

'You've got it,' Haru said, saluting her. 'I'll keep an ear to the ground.'

'Thank you,' she said.

As they left the bakery, she tried to think of her more extreme cases, husbands or fathers who had been killed by her poisons, but in all of those instances, it was mere speculation, or the wives and daughters would have been held to trial.

Bisma always made poisons that could not be easily traced or recognized. Other than Xander, no one had ever been able to recognize her hand. As much as he vexed her, as cruel as she could be to him, she knew he would never rat her out.

Unless . . .

Unless he had not done so intentionally? An idea turned over in Bisma's mind, but it was not concrete. But it pointed in the direction of Eleanora Chapman.

But if whoever was doing this was doing it to exact revenge, why wouldn't they come after her directly? Why go after her sisters?

To hurt her?

But to what end?

She couldn't figure it out.

14

Bisma remained lost in thought as she and Mei walked to the blacksmith's. She did not notice someone approaching until she felt a gentle tap on her shoulder. She turned to see Xander. He wore a navy-blue waistcoat, and with the sun shining, he painted a radiant picture, though the expression on his face was quite frazzled.

Bisma turned to Mei. 'Why don't you go in, honey? I'll be just a second.'

Xander waved at Mei, smiling at her. She looked at him with curiosity, then at Bisma, then back at Xander again. Something must have clicked in her mind, for she gave him back a slow, sweet smile before giggling at Bisma.

'Inside,' Bisma said, not amused in the slightest. 'And don't bother Diego, alright?'

Diego was the blacksmith who had taken over the shop after Luna's father was unable to continue. He was not an outright friend, but not an outright enemy either, and that was much more preferable to Bisma.

Mei went on ahead, while Bisma turned back to Xander. He ran a hand through his copper hair, and it flopped to one side. She took a closer look at him and despite his usual smile and glittering eyes, he looked exhausted.

'Sorry, I've just got a moment, then I need to head back, I'm helping Uncle Fred with his plans,' he said, words rushing out of him. He reached into his pocket and held something out.

It was a narrow bottle full of iridescent liquid that shimmered pale blue and purple.

'What's this?' she asked, inspecting it.

'It's a sleeping potion,' he explained. 'Well, a sort of "freezing" potion, really, but it'll seem like whoever drank it is asleep. At least, that's what it's supposed to do. If anyone else gets poisoned, give them this; it'll put them in a frozen sleep state so the poison can't spread.'

She looked up at him, shocked.

'I've been working on it since you left and I've finally cracked it,' he continued, speaking fast. 'I've been trying to suss out a cure, of course, but it's been giving me trouble, since the poison mutated. I tried to work on the blood we extracted from Luna, but since the blood was cut out, the poison seemed to die as well. So that's always an option!' He stopped, eyes wide. 'That was a bad joke, forgive me, of course I am not suggesting . . . I mean I didn't . . . ahhh.'

He broke off, rubbing a hand over his face while still holding the potion in his other hand.

Bisma stared at him with wide eyes. It was a brilliant idea, rather than attempt bloodletting again. It had been a close call with Luna, and she did not wish to take that risk again.

'I haven't rested, so forgive the profusion of words,' he said. 'I've been working on this, and Uncle Fred's been working me nonstop, as well.'

Bisma was overwhelmed by the urge to throw her arms around him then. *She* should have been working on a cure and coming up with such precautions, but she'd been so busy making sure everyone was alright.

'How did you have time for this?' she asked, incredulous.

'I make time for what's important,' he said, giving her an easy shrug, but there was an intensely genuine quality in his green eyes.

Their gazes met and held. A current ran down her spine, like lightning striking a tree.

Xander looked away first, suddenly nervous. Then he added, as a joke, 'Unfortunately my beauty routine has suffered, so do not look at me too closely.'

He was trying to make her smile, and it worked: the corner of her mouth lifted.

'Hmm, I can tell you've missed a step or three,' she said, pointing to under his eyes, attempting levity herself.

'Ah!' He covered his face with his hands. 'I said, don't look at me!'

She smiled, nearly laughing. He peeked out at her between his fingers and saw, which caused him to laugh.

'Truly,' she said. 'Thank you.' She wanted to simply be grateful, but old habits died hard. Suspicion rose in her. Her smile vanished. 'Xander, why are you helping us?'

He blinked. 'Isn't it obvious?'

Time seemed to slow down as he stepped closer, his expression softening. His eyes were warm, and she felt his gaze deep in her core. Her heart skipped a beat, which agitated her to no end.

'No,' she said, feeling stupid, which made her angry.

He smiled, shaking his head. His soft expression was replaced by something closer to his usual mischief as he considered her question.

'Well?' she prompted, getting annoyed.

Which was why he was pretending to think for so long.

'It's an interesting case,' he finally said. 'From an academic perspective.'

She frowned—her sisters were not a case study! As she geared up to say as much, she looked at the potion in his hands and softened slightly. Besides, him helping her because of personal curiosity was better than him helping her for other reasons.

Part of her was disappointed, having expected a more... personal answer. But perhaps he had finally grown tired of trying to entrap her. He'd certainly had the perfect opportunity to kiss her senseless the other day and had not taken it, she remembered (with some disappointment).

What other reason could there be?

'Where did you learn all this?' she asked, curiosity of her own taking over. 'Most of my magic is just intuition, nothing this disciplined.'

'I apprenticed under a garden-witch in Whitebridge,' he told her. 'Just for a few years, but I learned a great deal. While witches here are one in a hundred, in Whitebridge, it's easily double or triple that number. It's a great place for learning, a true metropolitan hub, for witches come there from all over Fairendelle to apprentice and learn.'

'You have your mother to learn from, don't you?' she asked.

'Yes, of course, and my mother is very skilled, indeed,' Xander said. 'She studied in Whitebridge as well before coming back to work with my grandfather. She never continued her studies, but I'd like to.'

Bisma's brows knit together. 'Well, why don't you? You obviously have the funds and the free time; you could do whatever you wanted.' Such freedom seemed impossible to her. 'What's keeping you here?'

'Ah, an excellent question.' He smiled.

He took another step toward her, that same intensity returning to his glinting green eyes. Something about the way he was looking at her made her feel very uneven. Her pulse scattered.

'Well, someone has to be your competition,' he finally said, teasing.

'Please.' She exhaled shortly. 'You're not competition—you're a nuisance.'

He laughed. 'Thank you for the reminder of my inadequacy. In truth, I was away for so many years—I missed my parents, and, old as it is, Old Town is home. For now, I think I'll stay.'

That sounded absurd to her. She would have jumped at the first opportunity to go to Whitebridge and study, to be as skilled and knowledgeable as the witches there. She would miss her sisters, yes, but once Luna turned eighteen, Bisma would have no chance but to leave the Forest, anyway. Of course, she did not say any of this to him, but it was as if he read her mind, for he gave her a conspiratorial smile.

'Perhaps one day we'll go to Whitebridge together,' he said.

She rolled her eyes—that was never going to happen.

'Didn't you say you were in a rush?' she asked.

He jolted, remembering, and the frenzied energy returned to him. 'Ah, yes,' he said, holding out the potion for her to take. 'Here.'

She hesitated.

'Come now!' he said. 'Take it just in case.'

'I don't—'

He tsked. 'Must you argue about everything?'

'I don't argue!'

He gave her a pointed look. 'Then prove me wrong and take the damn potion, Bis.'

'Fine.' She took it, slipping it into her basket. Begrudgingly, she added, 'Thank you.'

His face lit up. 'If I knew all it would take for you to be civil was to bring you gifts, I would have tried much sooner.'

'The civility is a one-time thing,' she informed him. 'Don't test your luck.'

'Ah, but when it comes to you, I am always testing my luck.'

She covered her mouth so he wouldn't see her smile, feeling more normal than she had in days. Giving him a wave goodbye, she entered the blacksmith's, but she must have not done a good job hiding her smile, for when Mei saw Bisma, she began giggling again.

Bisma tried to give her a stern glance. 'Come now, let's hurry and get home.'

They paid for the cake pan, then skipped on home. At the treehouse, Bisma kissed everyone hello. Luna was watching Deeba as she folded laundry. Azalea and Nori were cooking; their home smelled like brown butter and sage, which would be spread over potatoes. Nori layered tomatoes onto a sheet of pastry for a galette.

As Mei went straight to the kitchen to put her new cake pan to use, Bisma went up to her room to set down her things and saw there was a letter on her bed. Catching her breath, she rushed to unfold it, but then hesitated as she recalled how she had spilled her guts after the ordeal with Luna. Embarrassment spread through her, but as she read, she realized there was nothing to be ashamed of.

Dearest Bisma,

I wish you would not speak of yourself in such a manner as you did in your last letter. It is not your fault, not in the slightest! You must not blame yourself, I beg you. If not for your own sake, then for mine: please be kind to yourself.

I cannot bear to think of you so unhappy. How is your sister doing now? She is strong and brave, just as you are. I know it.

I saw you in town today. I wished I had the courage to tell you just how beautiful you looked. The sunlight was touching your cheeks in a manner that made me most envious, and leaves were blowing in the breeze around your head, making a golden crown just for you.

You looked fit to be worshipped.

Your reverent friend

Bisma's cheeks heated up, reading that last bit. She touched her face and the skin was, in fact, warm; she pressed her cold fingers against her cheeks, hoping she wasn't red.

Not for the first time, she wondered exactly who the writer was. She did not usually like being seen by the residents of Old Town; she kept their glances at bay with her dark clothes and permanent scowls.

But something about the way this stranger saw her, really saw her, made goosebumps rise on her arms as potent desire simmered deep within her.

She thought this feeling was a disease she was cured of, but now she realized the craving to be loved and wanted was something that had not left her.

It had gotten her into trouble before, and she was afraid it would get her into trouble again.

The last time she had yearned for a connection this deeply, she had been sixteen. Though Bisma did her best to keep the memories of that time locked away, today the box slipped open and the memories unfurled.

She thought of another boy. He was a year older than her and had been in Old Town for the summer, accompanying his father, who had come to sell his landscape paintings.

Bisma saw him in town one day as she was running errands; the sight of him immediately made her stop in her tracks. He was beautiful, with curling brown hair the color of bark and deep blue eyes a gorgeous shade of twilight.

And it wasn't just her who saw him; he saw her. When she left the fabric store, a gust of wind loosened the ribbon from her hair and it flew off. As she turned to catch it, he already had.

'I'm Gregory,' he said, stepping close to hand the ribbon back to her. He smelled like parchment and paint.

'Bisma.'

She found excuses to go to town nearly every day, and the next time Gregory saw her, he asked her to go on a walk together. They meandered through the woods, then sat and ate the picnic he had packed for her, and talked and talked.

She loved listening to him speak of Springfield, the village in Huntington where he was from, and all the other towns he'd visited with his father, who sold paintings.

She fell in love. She did well to make sure he never found out she was an Unwanted Girl, nor about her reputation as a garden-witch, and with him, she felt like a different person. Like she could be normal, just another girl. She was so careful.

Or so she thought.

One evening, after their walk, he brushed the hair from her face and pressed his lips to hers. It was her first kiss, and it awakened something in her, a deep hunger. She snuck away daily to see him, and they would explore each other's bodies.

Then, a few weeks later, on a blanket in a hidden corner of the woods, they went all the way. It was painful, but she had never been so connected to someone, and finally she felt that there was someone all for herself, someone who could be hers and she could be his.

She had never felt happier.

Until the next day, when he didn't meet her at their spot.

A day passed, then two, then three.

Finally, she paid another visit to Old Town, hoping to spot him, worried that something terrible had happened to him or his father. It was then that she found him, surrounded by other village boys, laughing. He looked fine. But then why hadn't he come to see her?

She snuck closer, hoping to catch his eye and that was when she overheard the others congratulating him for bedding the most unwanted of the Unwanted Girls. At first, she was confused; she didn't understand who they were talking about, until, with dread, she realized they were talking about her.

Her older sisters had been right. Gregory did not love her; he had used her.

She was just a plaything to him, and now that he'd had his fun, he saw no need to entertain her anymore.

Tears burning her eyes, Bisma stepped back, but as she did, a branch broke. The boys heard; they all turned to look at her. The moment they recognized their eavesdropper, they began to laugh, clutching at each other with glee. Gregory turned to her tear-stained face and for a second she thought he might show some remorse, and if he did, she would forgive him, of course she would.

But there was not an ounce of guilt on his beautiful face; he only laughed.

She had never been so humiliated. She ran all the way home, not stopping until she reached the Rushing River, letting the roaring waters drown out the sound of her crying.

Worse than the humiliation was the heartbreak, and worse than that was the hatred she felt for herself. She had been so *stupid*. To think he had meant all those pretty things he'd said, to think he could actually want her—that anyone could.

Well, she had learned her lesson.

Too embarrassed, she didn't mention it to her sisters; instead, she buried it. Soon thereafter, the summer ended, and Gregory left. She did not even get a chance for revenge; she was too busy being heartbroken and ashamed.

After he left, she thought that was it, but the village boys still snickered whenever they saw her.

So Bisma did what she did best. She poisoned them.

She noticed that they all liked to chew on a particular plant while they stood around and talked in their corner of town. It didn't take long for her to deduce the plant to be betel leaves. And so, the night before the harvest festival dance, with a simple bit of magic, she modified the leaves.

The boys didn't notice. Not until it was too late.

The festival dance was notoriously the most romantic day of the year, with many couples spending the night together. None of the boys received such an auspicious fate.

Bisma watched as the effects of the plant kicked in just in time and one by one of the village boys soiled their pants on the dance floor. All the village girls avoided them as though they had the plague. While ordinarily the Unwanted Girls did not attend the festival dance, Bisma snuck out just to see her handiwork. She stood in the dark edges of the woods, her smile like a wolf's.

The boys did not snicker after that.

She thought Gregory had understood her, but of course he hadn't, not really, not truly. She was just projecting what she wanted onto him, her own light reflecting off him in a convincing facade. She had deluded herself into believing that he was all that she desired, settling for the crumbs of his attentions and affections.

It made her furious to think back on now, to see how little she had accepted from him, how highly she had regarded him. He had not deserved any of it.

She was always there for him, whenever his father scolded or yelled, she was the one he came complaining to, and she'd felt so important, so special, that it was she he unburdened his heart to. But, no, she was not special; he was just using her.

He did not care about her, not at all—not like this mysterious letter writer seemed to. It filled her with a strange sort of hope, that foolish romantic part of her heart that she thought had withered away, coming alive once more.

All these years she'd convinced herself she was content with stolen kisses, secret rendezvous, purely physical things, nothing more, but deep down, she craved affection. She yearned for love, even though she'd been smited by it.

Bisma wrote back, then went down to join the girls. As she went down the stairs, she saw Luna's light on. Bisma entered, holding the cake Haru had given her. Luna had a blanket wrapped around her shoulders and was reading.

'Special delivery,' Bisma sang, smiling as she deposited the pumpkin cake onto Luna's bed and sat down. Luna looked up from her book. 'Haru sent this and said to tell you that he's thinking of you.'

Emotion crossed Luna's face, so quickly that Bisma couldn't decipher it.

'I don't want it,' Luna said, turning back to her book. 'Give it to the others.'

'What?' Bisma asked, confused. 'You've never turned down a cake before, and from Haru, no less.'

'I'm just not hungry.'

'Luna, what's going on?' Bisma took a closer look at her sister, and Luna buried her nose deeper into her book. 'You're not going to ask me *exactly* what Haru said and how he said it?'

Luna shook her head.

Bisma didn't understand. Luna had been cured; she was alright, now. The scars on her arms had all but healed and Bisma had offered her a salve that would make the deep lines disappear, though Luna had refused.

She frowned. 'Lu, tell me what's wrong,' Bisma ordered.

'Nothing,' Luna mumbled. She absentmindedly ran a hand over the scars on her arm, which concerned Bisma. 'I just want to read.'

She would not look up, even as Bisma lingered. Sighing, Bisma stood. She placed the cake on Luna's bedside. 'Alright.' She didn't understand why Luna was acting so strangely. 'Why don't you come read downstairs?'

'In a little while,' Luna replied quietly. She still did not look up.

Bisma nibbled on her lower lip. With a sigh, she went down to the main area, where Mei was now playing with Deeba, having put her vanilla cake in to bake.

'Baji, why is Mei telling me Haru gave her a pumpkin cookie and yet I see no cookies for the rest of us?' Azalea asked, arching a brow. She and Nori were done cooking. While Nori played with her stuffed dolls, Azalea was making candles at the table.

'Goodness,' Bisma said, bringing the box forward and setting it on the kitchen table in front of Azalea. 'If you would only *wait* a moment.' She opened the box, and the room filled with the scent of cinnamon, ginger, and nutmeg.

Nori cheered, rushing to the table to take the first one. Mei left Deeba in the living room, coming to get a cookie herself, and Bisma took one, as well. It was delicious, and the girls were all exceedingly happy.

Bisma was bone tired, having been up most the night working on poisons, but all that hard work was worth it when it meant she could afford a treat such as this.

Deeba whimpered from the other room. 'Baji.'

'Aw, no,' Bisma cooed with a laugh. 'Did we forget to give Deebs a cookie?' She picked one up and went to her.

The cookie fell as she stopped in her tracks.

Both Deeba's pudgy little hands were covered in dark blue veins.

'Deeba!' Bisma cried, going to pick her up. Deeba's skin was hot like Luna's had been, the dark veins tracking up her arms.

'Mei!' Bisma called from the living room. 'Go up to my room! There's a vial on my bedside table. Get it. Quickly!'

'What's—' Mei poked her head in, then saw Deeba. She froze, petrified.

'Mei, *now*!' Bisma called, rocking Deeba back and forth. Azalea and Nori came in to see what was happening, then stopped in their tracks with similar horror.

'What's happening?' Nori asked.

Azalea held Nori to her side, anger contorting her face. 'Who's doing this?' she cried.

But Bisma was not focusing on their questions, not as Deeba held onto her tightly, fussing. She did not cry out, but fat tears rolled out of her eyes.

Bisma's heart splintered. 'Shh, it's OK, baby, it's OK,' she cooed, holding Deeba's head against her.

Bisma heard Mei run down the stairs, then Mei was beside her, holding out the potion Xander had given her.

'What's happening?' Luna asked, coming down the stairs. She froze when she saw Deeba's hands. 'Baji, do something!' she cried.

Bisma tuned them out, focusing solely on Deeba, who was whimpering in her arms.

'I know it hurts, I know,' Bisma said, holding Deeba tight as she wriggled. This hurt her more than her other sisters getting poisoned—Deeba was just a baby.

'Azalea, come hold Deeba's head steady,' Bisma ordered. Azalea came and did as she was told. Bisma held Deeba steady, then said, 'Mei, feed her the potion now.'

Mei brought the bottle to Deeba's lips, but the smell must have been strange, for Deeba tried to twist her face away.

'Shh, it's OK,' Bisma said, as Azalea held Deeba's head back. 'Mei, now.'

Mei poured the liquid into Deeba's mouth. Bisma hoped Xander being a know-it-all would pay off as Deeba swallowed.

After Deeba drank the potion, Bisma set Deeba down on the couch, holding a hand over her heart. It beat steadily as Deeba closed her eyes, but slowly her body froze completely. Her skin turned gray, as though she had turned to stone; it was a horrifying sight.

Nori screamed, then burst into tears.

'No, don't worry!' Bisma said. 'Come, look, she's alright.'

Nori haltingly came forward, and Bisma brought Nori's hands to Deeba's little chest, where she could feel her heart continuing to beat. Luna, Azalea, and Mei came to do the same, needing reassurance as well. The poison had also been frozen in its tracks.

'She's alright,' Bisma whispered, exhaling. She sat back, heart hammering.

The question was: now what?

15

'I need you to not be insufferable about what I'm about to say,' Bisma told Xander, pacing in his greenhouse early the next morning. She'd rushed in without thinking and only realized at the end of her sentence that he was asleep, his copper hair sticking out in every direction.

He rubbed his eyes, disoriented.

'Bis?' His voice was groggy with sleep. 'Am I dreaming?'

Her face heated, not at all helped by the fact that he was shirtless under his paltry bedsheet. She spotted his shirt draped over a chair and threw it at him. 'Put some clothes on.'

He sat up, frowning. 'Usually in the dream, you're telling me to do the opposite.'

She flushed at the thought. Pushing the rest of his blanket off, he stood, and she could unfortunately see why a dream version of her might make such commands. He was slender and well sculpted, all lean muscles from his broad shoulders down to his narrow waist, and she couldn't help but stare.

It had been a long time since she'd been up close and personal with a shirtless man, and she sure had missed it, if the way her body hummed in response was any guess.

'Like what you see?' he asked, grinning as he caught her ogling.

She scowled. 'Remember when I prefaced this with how I need you to *not* be insufferable?'

'Sorry,' he said, grinning more stupidly. 'Didn't hear much beyond "I need you".'

She didn't have a clever response to that, since he chose that moment to slowly put his shirt on, lazily tucking it into his trousers, and she watched his muscles move beneath the thin fabric, the image searing into her mind.

Remembering herself, Bisma glared. She turned to leave but Xander caught her hand, pulling her back with a firm tug. She whirled, almost colliding into his chest. He did not let go of her hand; she inhaled the sweet scent of cloves.

'Sorry, Bis,' he said, looking at her with a lopsided smile. 'You're too easy to rile—my little porcupine.'

'Porcupine!' She made an outraged face at that, wrenching free from his grasp.

He laughed out loud. 'Alright, alright, I'll behave.'

Xander ran his hands through his hair, tidying it a bit, and she felt disappointed she had not been afforded the honors. He cleared his throat, straightening up, then crossed his arms over his chest. 'Alright,' he said, green eyes focused. 'I'm listening.'

Giving him a final withering look, she released a breath. 'The freezing potion worked.'

Now he was alarmed. 'Another poisoning?' he asked, concerned, and she nodded. 'Who?'

'Deeba,' Bisma replied. 'The two-year-old.'

He swore.

Bisma looked away, blinking rapidly to force back the tears welling in her eyes. She had spent all night trying to figure out what to do and had come up with nothing substantial. There was no choice but to find a cure, and no matter how she had tried, she couldn't do it alone.

Which was why, as dawn broke, she had decided to come to Xander. He had helped her twice already and had expressed an academic interest in the case. He was vexing, irritating, *annoying*, but she had no one else to turn to.

'What's her story?' Xander asked, his voice gentle.

She turned back to him. 'Why do you ask?' No one ever did. He had asked about Mei's story, as well. He hadn't asked about Luna's story but hers was more known in Old Town.

'It's important,' he said. 'Your sisters are part of who you are; I want to learn more about them. About you.'

Her heart skipped a beat. She cleared her throat, ignoring how his words warmed even the coldest parts of her.

'Deeba came to us at nine months old, about a year ago,' she told him. 'She was in a little basket with a note, which explained that she was an orphan and that her wards were neglecting her. The neighbors were the ones who took her away one night and left her in the Enchanted Forest; they couldn't care for her themselves but hoped that the Forest would look after her.'

'Goodness,' Xander said, alarmed. 'They just . . . took her? And risked the baby being rejected by the Forest?'

'The note detailed just how neglected Deeba was there,' Bisma explained. 'Apparently for the first month, they heard her cries all day and night until eventually the crying stopped. The neighbors thought perhaps this meant that things were well, but when they went to visit, they saw that the baby was practically starved.'

Rage flared through Bisma, still fresh.

'The lack of crying was not a sign of contentment; it was an eerie sort of silence. She hardly stirred or made a sound because she had become conditioned to realize that crying out for help yielded no results. So she simply . . . stopped. That was when the neighbors realized they needed to intervene, that the chance of life in the Enchanted Forest was better than a life in the village, which would surely end if things continued the way they were.'

'A baby not crying at all?' Xander asked, horrified.

'She still hardly cries,' Bisma said. 'At first, we all thought it awfully disconcerting, but of course we got used to it. Even now, she'll whimper or fuss a bit, but she never cries out fully, the way most babies do. Even last night—' Bisma broke off, mouth trembling.

She took a deep breath, releasing it slowly. 'She was the first baby to come to the Forest when I was older,' Bisma said. 'I mean, Nori was left as a baby as well, but I was thirteen at the time and had sisters older than me who held more responsibility, so it wasn't the same. But with Deeba I was second eldest, with only Baji—*Eva*—above me. And of course Eva was busy with everything else, so much of looking after Deeba in those early months fell to me.'

Why was she telling him all this? Just because he had asked one question didn't mean he wished to hear her ramble on.

'Anyway,' she said, clearing her throat. Xander had been listening intently, which made her feel . . . strange. Shy. She wasn't used to speaking in such a manner with anyone outside her family, or now with her new letter-writing friend, but writing was different from speaking aloud, watching the other person watch you, seeing their face shift with emotions.

'She'll be alright,' Xander said, his voice sure. 'The freeze potion will protect her. Just imagine she's taking a long nap.'

'Yes, but now what?' Bisma asked. 'That's why I've come, really. Can I see what you've been working on? You said you've been puzzling over a cure.'

'Oh, yes!' Xander said, brightening at the chance to help. 'Can I see Deeba? I want to make sure the freeze potion is really working, and perhaps we can extract some of the poison from her and study it?'

'I'll bring her here,' Bisma said.

'I can go with you,' Xander said. 'Save you the trip, meet the rest of your sisters.'

Bisma gave him a stern look. 'No.'

Though outsiders were not allowed in the Enchanted Forest, she knew she could probably bypass the Forest's border fog with her magic to allow Xander in, and the Forest would allow it if she asked nicely, but that wasn't the issue.

They needed to proceed professionally. She couldn't have emotions meddling in, and if he went to her home, met her family, things would surely get messy.

'If we're to work together, we'll work here. Away from the Forest and away from my sisters.' She looked around his greenhouse; it was clearly equipped with everything they might need.

'But I've met your sisters before,' Xander said, confused. 'Mei and Luna, of course, and the others, when they're in town with you.'

'You haven't been formally introduced, and it's going to stay that way,' Bisma said. She didn't want them to get attached to him. They would work together to find a cure, then go on as they had before. 'This is strictly a business arrangement, as in we are working together as colleagues and nothing more.'

'Right,' he said, blinking.

He swallowed. She could tell he was disappointed, and she felt guilty, but this was the only way to stay safe: to keep him at a distance.

'And what exactly would I have to do to earn the honor of meeting your family?' he asked, bouncing back from his melancholy mood with determination. His eyes sparkled.

Bisma could not help it; her heart warmed. No matter how difficult she was, Xander was always willing to rise to the occasion.

With Gregory, Bisma had always had to be on her very best behavior in case she upset him. He had been so mercurial, and Bisma had always needed to be so easy-going, and even then it was never guaranteed that he wouldn't grow cross with her over the littlest thing.

But why on earth was she comparing Xander to Gregory? It wasn't as if she was in love with Xander as she had been (foolishly) with Gregory.

Bisma pretended to think about his question. 'Hmm. Stop being so insufferable and I'll consider it.'

He clicked his tongue. 'Damn, that's half my personality, Bis.'

'Half? I'm impressed, Alexander; I wasn't aware you had a personality beyond that.'

He held a hand over his heart as if injured, though he laughed as well. 'You don't even need poisons,' he said. 'Not with a tongue like yours.' His gaze dropped to her mouth. 'Positively deadly.'

Her lips tingled. 'Don't test it,' she warned.

'Not even a taste?' he asked, stepping closer.

She arched a brow, lifting her chin. 'You wouldn't survive. You said so yourself—positively deadly.'

She ran her tongue over her teeth. He watched the movement, his eyes dark. A little thrill buzzed through her.

'Ah, but with your tongue on mine at the very least I would die happy,' he said, voice low.

Imagining such a prospect, her heart leapt.

'I can't have you dead yet,' she replied, trying to get back to the topic at hand. Hadn't she just said something about professionalism? And yet there they were, going back and forth. It was so easy—too easy—to lose herself with Xander. She cleared her throat. 'Not before you've made a cure for Deeba.'

But the words lacked her usual bossy nonchalance. Her face felt flushed, and it must have shown, for Xander smirked.

She hissed at him, which only made him smile.

'Come then, let's get to work, my darling strictly business colleague.' Xander motioned for her to follow him to one of the tables, where there were variously sized plant pots, as well as a variety of tools and bottles of ingredients: dried herbs, aloe vera gel, essential oils, infused waters.

Bisma had spent most of the night panicking about Deeba's safety, but the freeze potion had held. Deeba would be safe while they worked on a cure.

At least, that was what she told herself whenever she felt her composure unraveling. She needed to focus on things beyond being worried: the cure, preventing more poisonings, not to mention discovering who was poisoning them.

'What is all this?' Bisma asked, lifting a bottle and smelling its contents. She wrinkled her nose—*wormwood.*

'I've been testing different concoctions,' he said, quickly paging through a journal. She didn't focus on or read the exact words, but it was clear he was being very methodical.

'Oh.' She was a little impressed, really. Her process was so far from this.

'You don't keep notes?' he asked, intrigued.

'No, I do,' she replied, then thought about it. 'Well . . . not really.'

This seemed to both deeply alarm and fascinate him. 'How do you keep track of your mixtures?'

'I don't really mix as much,' she said. 'I usually rely on my magic when I'm growing the plant, then just supplement it a bit?'

'And that works?' he asked, interest lighting his green eyes.

'It's kind of like cooking,' she explained. 'If you've got the main ingredient, like meat, or bread, or cheese, or potato, you don't need to do much to make it into a meal?'

Her words sounded like nonsense to her, but he hung on to every word.

'How fascinating!' he breathed, genuinely interested.

She gave him a curious glance. 'Why?'

'As far as I know, most witches don't operate in that way,' he told her. 'Even in Whitebridge, I met a few garden-witches who worked on potions, but most focus on mixing magic rather than growing magic. Going off your analogy, mixing is more like—you can grow wheat, but you still need to alter it a great deal before you can have bread. Whereas with growing, you've already got the flour and basically just need to add water and bake, and there you have your bread.'

'Oh.' She hadn't realized there were different subsets of skills in garden-witchery. It really was fascinating. 'You learned all this in Whitebridge?'

He nodded. 'And from my mother and grandfather. Their focus was on mixing as well—same as mine. From what I've gathered, focusing on growing is rather rare because it's more difficult.'

'I've never thought of it that much,' Bisma admitted. 'I've just grown what I've needed or wanted.'

'Yes, but how do you communicate that with your magic, with

the soil? To receive the product you desire?' He was practically buzzing with excitement, and she could tell he had a dozen questions to ask.

'I don't know,' she said, feeling shy. 'It doesn't always work. Sometimes it takes me a few tries and modifications, but it's just something I *feel*, I suppose. How do your lungs know how much to breathe in and breathe out? Or how does your heart know how long to wait between beats? It just does.'

'You're a marvel, Bis,' Xander said.

She rolled her eyes; he was being superfluous.

'No, really, I mean it,' he insisted. 'The reason growing magic is so rare is precisely what you just said: it's hard to explain, which makes it even harder to teach. Mixing magic can be learned quite easily; it relies very little on intuition. It's why most of what I learned was focused on mixing rather than growing.'

'I hardly know any mixtures, though,' Bisma said.

'Well, that's no problem at all!' Xander said with a smile. 'It's easy to learn.'

Bisma did wish to learn more, she always had, but she'd never had any education or books to study from. Xander had a wealth of knowledge in his family, not to mention his education in Whitebridge, but she had obviously never asked him or Eleanora to teach her.

Perhaps she should have.

'I'll teach you all I can about growing magic if you teach me about mixing magic,' Bisma said, feeling brave.

Xander's face lit up. 'Would you really?'

She nodded. 'Absolutely.'

He was even more excited now; he was practically bouncing like a puppy. 'Brilliant. That would be brilliant.'

His enthusiasm was infectious, but Bisma guarded herself from it. She would not allow Xander to sneak into her affections; she could not. She was afraid that if he ever did, it would be impossible to be rid of him.

Bisma did not wish to go back to the way things were after discovering Gregory's true colors, the acute heartbreak she had felt. The nauseating realization that it had all been a lie: every moment they had spent together, every word, every touch. The disappointment had been a heaviness on her chest, infiltrating all her bones, which had been followed with the shame.

She would not open herself up to such a wound again, not when the previous one had been so hard to heal. Even now she felt the scar, the bruised, bumpy skin of it, cutting through the center of her, a jagged welt still tender to the touch.

She would have given Gregory her whole heart, and it would have meant nothing to him; on the contrary, he would probably have complained about what a large, bloody mess it was.

She'd stopped trusting herself after that incident. How could she have not seen it? Was she so easily deluded? So easily fooled? Bisma had always prided herself on her mind, but Gregory had proved that it was not always to be trusted.

But that wasn't going to happen with Xander.

He was only interested in the cure from an academic standpoint. As for the rest, he was an incorrigible flirt, but as long as he didn't start to mean anything more to her, she would be fine.

She would stay vigilant; they could work together as colleagues. She had always yearned to know more about her magic, as well, and perhaps this was the only opportunity she would ever have.

It was these thoughts that occupied her mind as she returned home to pick up Deeba, as well as some things from her garden to take to Xander's. She placed the frozen, sleeping Deeba in a basket, wrapping her in a blanket.

'Is she going to be alright?' Mei asked, worried. They were all staring at Bisma as she prepared her things in the garden.

Bisma turned to give them all a reassuring glance. 'Yes, she will be. I'm working with a very skilled and clever witch to find a cure.'

Xander was not here to witness it, so she could freely admit that he really was very clever.

'There's absolutely nothing to worry about, really. In the meantime, just think of Deebs as taking a very long nap,' Bisma said. 'Nothing at all to fret over.'

'At least this means I get a break from changing diapers,' Azalea joked half-heartedly.

Bisma and Luna exchanged a glance before they both laughed out loud.

'Azalea, you're such a little demon sometimes,' Luna said, shaking her head, but she said it with fondness. Azalea blew her a kiss in response.

'Oh, we were all thinking it,' Azalea said, shrugging.

Seeing the older girls laughing, Nori and Mei joined in, their shoulders relaxing.

'Now back to your chores,' Bisma said. 'I'm going to be busy working on this cure, so I need you all to be good and to listen to Luna.'

Azalea groaned.

'You heard Baji!' Luna said, grinning wickedly.

The girls dispersed before they could be told what to do, and Bisma pulled Luna aside.

'I'm sorry we didn't have the freeze potion for you, Luna,' she said. If they had, Luna wouldn't have had to go through the awful bloodletting process. 'Can you ever forgive me?'

'Baji, it's not your fault,' Luna said, squeezing her hand. 'I'm just glad you have it now for Deebs, so she won't have to go through what I did.' Her hand absentmindedly went to the scars on her arm again, a darkness entering her eyes for a moment. Then Luna shook her head, and Bisma wondered if she imagined it.

'You'll find the cure,' Luna said. 'I know you will.'

But as Bisma carried Deeba back to Xander's greenhouse, she couldn't help but doubt herself, her thoughts racing. She still needed to find out who had done this, and why, but finding the cure was more pressing. She just hoped she'd be able to do everything and that her sisters' faith in her was not misguided.

Letting herself down was something she could survive.

Letting her sisters down was something she could not.

16

'Alright,' Xander said, rubbing his hands together. 'Let's get to work.'

She was back at the greenhouse and had laid Deeba down on a small cot Xander had procured from Forest knew where. The advantages of being rich, she supposed.

'I'm glad to see the freeze potion is holding,' Xander said, after examining Deeba. 'Now to make the cure . . . It would be easiest to run trials if we had the poison to test on.'

'Right,' Bisma agreed. 'Can we extract it from Deeba?'

'Precisely what I was thinking,' Xander said. 'If we take some of her blood, we should be able to separate the poison from it.'

'But the poison won't stay alive outside of the body,' Bisma said. 'Didn't you say the blood we extracted from Luna wasn't viable to examine?'

'Yes, that is a problem . . .' Xander ran a hand through his hair, thinking.

'What if we manipulate the freeze potion and apply it to the poison to keep it from dying. Would that work?'

'Possibly,' Xander said. 'But I don't know if manipulating the poison in that way would affect how it would interact with a cure. Also, how would we do that in the first place?'

They both puzzled over it, until Bisma was struck by another idea.

'Wait,' she said. 'What if we simply put the poison on something else living, but make sure it can't kill the host?'

'That would work,' Xander said. 'With your speciality in growing, particularly. You could make a plant that could survive that sort of thing, and we could inject it with the isolated poison.'

'Alright,' Bisma said. 'I'll work on that; you work on extracting and separating the poison.'

They both attended their tasks, working in comfortable silence. Bisma was used to working alone, so she anticipated working with Xander to be a nuisance, but she was glad to see that he was just as serious as she was when it came to their magic.

He gave her space, working at a different table, as she tried to create what they needed.

It took some time, but Bisma created a smaller version of an evergreen tree, though of course it was manipulated with magic to become something more. Evergreen trees survived the harshest of winters without dying; this magical plant would survive this poison.

'I'm just about finished as well,' Xander said, spreading a fine white powder over a small dish of Deeba's blood.

Bisma went to watch, standing on her tiptoes to look over his shoulder so she wouldn't be in the way. The blood was a strange color, a kind of dark purple, red and blue mixed together.

A moment after the blood absorbed the powder, the dish made

a hissing sound. Bisma watched as the liquid separated itself, until there was red blood to one side and dark blue liquid on the other.

Xander released a breath. 'Finally.'

'Now to test it,' she said.

Xander put the poison into a syringe and brought it to the other table, where her magical evergreen tree was waiting. It was about a foot tall and perfectly lush, though the green leaves were threaded through with iridescent silver.

As Xander injected the base of the tree with the poison, Bisma held her breath.

The poison spread through the branches, giving the leaves a darker tint. She waited to see if the tree would wither and die, but it continued to hold on.

It had worked!

'Brilliant,' Xander said, turning to her. 'You're absolutely brilliant, Bis.'

The validation sparked embers deep within her. She lifted her chin, trying not to smile. 'Was there any doubt?'

He laughed out loud. 'None whatsoever, but credit must, of course, also be given to me.' His eyes crinkled. 'We make a good team.'

The sparks inside her fizzed into a fuzzy feeling at that. She cleared her throat. 'So this is our test subject,' she said.

'Now for the cure . . .'

They started their work. It was difficult to figure out how to treat something when they could not diagnose what was causing the symptoms. If Bisma knew exactly what the poison was, she could simply grow something to counteract it. Cures were the opposite of poisons; they canceled one another out.

But it was near impossible to make a cure from nothing, which was why they focused on a mixing approach rather than growing.

A WITCH'S GUIDE TO LOVE AND POISON 163

Bisma's lessons began, as Xander enthusiastically told her the theory behind the magic, explaining that much of the knowledge witches based their potions or magic on was already pre-established by other witches, kind of like tried-and-true recipes in cookbooks.

'I'll lend you one of my beginner-level books,' Xander said. 'It has all the common mixtures and their effects. As you learn more, you can use those common mixtures as your base, then add onto it.'

She listened intently, absorbing every word, thrilled to be learning.

'So for the cure to this poison, I've been using myrrh, which is a common base for cures,' he said, moving to another table, where there was a pile of the sap-like yellow resin.

He threw some into a bowl, then used his magic to turn the little rocks into a thick syrup, stirring it with a spatula. 'And then yarrow leaves are also often used for cures; I've found drying the leaves in direct sunlight helps bring out their properties.' He had a case of dried leaves, which he measured out into a spoon, which he added.

'Can you mix that?' he asked.

She did as she was told, watching as the dried leaves blended into the myrrh syrup.

Xander looked at the color and consistency, then added in a touch more of the dried leaves. 'Perfect.'

She stopped stirring.

'Now, I've found that adding fresh flower petals of yarrow brings out different benefits of the plant, which might be beneficial for this. Since the poison is strong, we want our cure to be stronger.' He brought over a pot with little white flowers. 'I haven't tried it yet, so let's see, but this won't be nearly enough—'

He stuck his hand into the soil, and the plant grew. Quite slowly actually, compared to Bisma's magic. Wanting to help, Bisma put her hand in the soil as well, and the plant immediately sprouted, the flowers tripling.

Xander's eyes widened. 'I felt some of your magic there,' he said in awe. 'It was like a roaring fire compared to my candle flame.' He blinked. 'Incredible.'

She bit back a smile, her cheeks warm.

'Now we want to make a paste of these leaves,' Xander said. 'Why don't you try?'

He slid over a mortar and pestle, then plucked the white petals and added them in.

She began to crush it, and his eyes widened.

'Goodness, not like that,' he said, coming closer. 'Use your wrist. Clockwise and—no, no.'

With an impatient sound, he came behind her, his head above her shoulder.

One of his hands covered hers above the mortar, holding it in place, as he placed his other hand around hers on the pestle. His palm enveloped her knuckles, his long fingers slotting just above hers.

'Like this,' he said, his voice soft. His breath moved a tendril of hair against her cheek, and it tickled her jaw. She blinked twice, trying to focus.

His hand moved hers to gently crush the petals in a twisting motion, dragging it across the petals.

She felt the warmth of his chest against her back; she leaned against him, feeling the press of his body. An ache spread through her, deliciously painful.

'That's it,' he said, the words fluttering against her neck.

She bit her lower lip, heart leaping. She continued with the motion he had shown her, both of them moving together. The difference in technique was obvious: the petals crushed more easily this way, dissolving into a smooth sap.

'Perfect,' he whispered, his cheek against hers.

She jolted as if struck with lightning.

'I've got it now,' she said, her face flaming. She brushed him off her, and he stepped back. She immediately felt cold, but she focused on her task, refusing to look at him, despite how her heart thundered.

They continued working. It took some time—there were more than a dozen steps, all with different ingredients. Xander had been testing different combinations and measurements and ingredients, bringing him closer and closer to the cure, but it was not quite there yet.

She was glad to be doing this with him, otherwise she'd have no idea where to begin, and the process was much too tedious for her to undertake on her own, nor was she nearly as organized as one apparently needed to be to concoct such a delicate potion.

As she worked, Bisma considered who might have gone through all this trouble to craft such an intricate poison. The more difficult the cure was to make, the more difficult the poison was. Whoever had done this had put a lot of thought and effort into it.

It was clear the aim wasn't to get rid of the Unwanted Girls, as some hateful villagers had wished over the years. That would have been much easier and simpler.

In contrast, this was slow and painful . . . a punishment, almost. And it seemed to be directed at her. Why else would it occur so soon after she had become Baji?

But who hated her that much?

Luna's father, her first victim? No, he wasn't nearly conniving nor intelligent enough. If he wanted to hurt her, he would have done it years ago, and he would have been savage but quick about it.

Mei's family, then? But they ran from town shortly after failing to uphold their end of Mei's marriage agreement; Bisma had never even exacted revenge upon them.

Deeba's wards, perhaps? Bisma had gotten retribution in that instance. She had poisoned them with something that made them constantly feel like they were starving, no matter how much they ate, which was a fitting punishment for neglecting Deeba.

Bisma had made them suffer for a few weeks but she didn't think they ever knew it was her—they had assumed it was some sickness.

Most of her poisons were used on people who could not be sure they were, in fact, being poisoned. Much of Bisma's reputation came from exaggerated legends.

Unable to pinpoint *who* might be behind the poisonings, Bisma considered *how* they were occurring, but she could find no conclusive answers in that line of thought, either. It was impossible to keep track of what the girls touched or ate because they were constantly moving, and there were so many of them.

They spent most of their time in the Enchanted Forest, but the Forest was safe. Only Unwanted Girls were allowed in; the fog around the perimeter ensured that.

As for the Forest itself, there were, of course, some berries, mushrooms, and plants that were harmful if eaten, but the girls knew those like the backs of their hands. So if not from the Forest, the poison had come from town, but there was no reason for that, either. Neither Deeba, Luna, or Mei had got sick after a trip to town, where they could have ingested or touched something.

So then *how*? How was the poison getting in?

To make such a poison also required a skilled witch, and the most skilled witch in town was—without a question—Eleanora Chapman. There were a handful of other garden-witches, as well, but none clever enough to sell potions as a business as the Chapmans and Bisma did, so there was no way any of them could concoct such an intricate poison.

Bisma thought about how the poison had changed from Mei to

Luna, how Eleanora could easily have adjusted the poison when she saw Xander heal Mei. But why would she do so?

And then came a horrifying thought: was Xander complicit? He was the only witch with power to rival Eleanora's. The pair could be working together to create such a poison.

But then why would he help her create a cure? Deep down, she did not believe he would do such a thing. He was insufferable, not deadly.

Eleanora could create a poison on her own . . . but why? Bisma thought through her previous customers and anyone affected by her poisons, trying to see if there were any links between them and Eleanora.

But she didn't know her customers that well; they told her their blights and she gave them solutions. Bisma did not ask them personal details.

Rubbing her temples, Bisma groaned. This was so *frustrating*.

At least running through her tangled thoughts kept her busy.

Soon enough, the cure was ready.

'Only one thing for it, now,' Xander said, taking a deep breath. Bisma held her breath, as well, hope creeping up on her as he injected the cure into their testing tree.

At first, nothing happened. Then the tree began to lose its branches. The trunk splintered.

Xander swore, rubbing a hand over his face.

'Lovely,' Bisma said, her eyes slitting. Her back hurt. They'd been at it all day, and it hadn't even worked.

Xander frowned. He was practically wilting at the edges, his earlier excitement long gone. More than that, he looked exhausted.

An idea planted itself in Bisma's mind.

'Why don't you take a nap?' She blurted out the question before realizing how out of character it was.

Xander gave her a funny look. 'Since when are you so attentive to me?' he asked, though he did not seem suspicious. Rather, he looked quite pleased.

Bisma made a face that portrayed just how ridiculous she considered him.

'You look horrible,' she said, trying to bring back the usual bite back to her tone. 'And I'd prefer if my partner didn't drop from exhaustion in the middle of a trial.'

Though she had insulted him, he only grew more pleased. 'I'm your partner now, am I?'

She rolled her eyes, not bothering to give him a response.

'No, no, I can't take a nap,' he said, sighing. 'I might have some tea and take a break, however. And I've got to drop something off.'

That would work for her plan. 'To whom?'

'I have my own private clients,' he said, sounding quite pleased with himself by the fact. 'I like to experiment with new techniques, and since Mother doesn't want me to take such risks under the official Chapman Apothecary name, I do so with my own personal clients.'

'What's the case?'

'The patient has shaking hands, and the Apothecary doesn't have anything strong enough for it. We have potions to help with the pain, and some to help with mild shaking, but none for his condition. I think I've puzzled it out, though.'

He went to a cabinet, rummaging around bottles until he found a short, fat one.

'I used a base of dried chamomile leaves and celery seed, then mixed in vanilla and nettle,' he said, removing the cap and showing her the salve.

She smelled it. 'Hmm, seems good to me,' she said. 'I wonder if it'll work.'

'Only one way to find out,' he replied, putting the cap back on. 'I was meant to head over hours ago, but . . .'

He would be gone, which meant she could investigate Eleanora. She recalled what he'd once said about guest rooms in the house.

'You should go now.' Bisma yawned, a bit theatrically. 'While you do, perhaps I'll take a nap.' She rubbed her eyes for good measure.

'Of course,' Xander said. 'Make yourself at home.'

He gestured to the bed in the greenhouse, which was really just a mattress on the floor. It had no frame, just an abundance of blankets and pillows. At the moment it was a mess, which made her think of Xander lying there, sleeping.

Her face warmed at the thought. Her gaze jumped away from the bed. He seemed to follow a similar train of thought, for his face turned pink, as well.

'We have guest rooms in the house, as well,' he added quickly.

'Oh.' She pretended to think about it. 'Is anyone home?'

'No, Mother's at the Apothecary, and Father's away on business.'

Perfect.

17

Xander took Bisma into the Chapman Estate, which was a sprawling mansion unparalleled in grandeur and beauty. She felt just as intimidated as when he'd previously tried to usher her in. Whereas other cottages were old and worn in with splintering stones and soft edges, the Chapman Estate looked newly constructed. Everything was immaculately clean and polished, sparkling with crisp lines made of the finest materials.

As they walked up the winding staircase, Bisma ran her hand along the dark wooden banister; it felt like silk under her fingers. She wondered what it would be like to grow up in a place like this.

She adored the Enchanted Forest and their treehouse, but this place was undeniably gorgeous. There were servants quietly bustling around, taking care of anything that needed attention.

Xander was clearly the apple of his parents' eyes. There were paintings of him everywhere, capturing different ages, some solo portraits and others with his parents and grandparents. Alongside them were framed certificates from his school days, as well as awards.

It was sweet—so sweet she felt a sharp pang of envy along with it, as though her teeth were rotting from sugar.

There were other portraits as well: an older couple that she assumed were Xander's grandparents; the same couple many decades earlier, with two children standing before them (this pair she deduced to be Eleanora and Frederick); then portraits of Eleanora alone, as well.

To make the perfect home with the perfect family even more complete, there were also numerous portraits of his parents, who were clearly besotted with one another.

Bisma had never seen a healthy relationship, and wondered what it was like. She knew the older girls had had such paramours, but she had never witnessed any of the couples together. It was an unspoken rule to keep such romances away from the Enchanted Forest and their home.

'This way,' Xander said, leading her down the hall. He opened a door to reveal a spacious guest room, double the size of her room at the treehouse. It was tastefully decorated and fastidiously clean.

'Thank you,' she said.

He smiled. 'If you need anything, just ask any of the servants,' he said. 'I've told them you're my guest. I'll see you when I get back.'

He closed the door behind him, leaving her alone. For a moment, Bisma was sorely tempted to lie down on the plush bed and sleep; she had an inkling it would be some of the best sleep in her life.

But she had more pressing matters to attend to.

Exiting the guest room, Bisma walked around, familiarizing herself with the building. Under the guise of needing a glass of water, she ambled over to the kitchen, where cooks were busy preparing the evening meal.

Goodness, the *stove* was the size of their entire kitchen at the treehouse! And everything was so neat and clean, perfectly orderly and matched. Bisma tried not to gawk.

After finishing her water, she continued her survey, spotting the laundry, which led out to a courtyard where clothes were hung out to dry. It seemed to be a weak spot in the estate's security; if she ever needed to sneak in later, this would be where to do it.

'Can I help you with anything, miss?' a cleaning lady asked her when Bisma headed toward the main area.

Bisma smiled. 'No, thank you. I just needed to quench my thirst before I take a nice long nap.' As Bisma went up the stairs to the second floor, a few servants gave her strange glances. Making a show of yawning, Bisma closed the guest room door loudly. Then she waited a good few moments before sneaking out again.

Upstairs, she walked down the hall, quickly and quietly checking each room only to reveal more guest rooms, a library, a study, a gallery.

Until finally she found it: Eleanora's office.

It was in the wing opposite that of the guest room, next to what she assumed was Xander's parents' bedroom. There were a few more bedrooms in this wing, and Bisma guessed one would be Xander's, and another his uncle's.

Checking to ensure none of the servants had come up, Bisma snuck into the office.

The room was as neat as the rest of the house but a bit more personal and lived in than the guest rooms. The walls were decorated with certificates and awards in Eleanora's name, and Bisma was distracted by Eleanora's many accomplishments.

If Bisma was not investigating Eleanora's possible hand in the poisoning of Bisma's sisters, she might have even been impressed. Bisma had never had another garden-witch to look up to, to aspire toward, but Eleanora could easily fill that gap.

She understood why Xander was so close with his mother; she'd seen them together a handful of times in town, not to mention that time in the greenhouse when Mei was poisoned, and it was clear he held his mother in the highest esteem.

Guilt needled Bisma for a moment; surely Xander wouldn't be happy to find Bisma snooping around his mother's office. Bisma quickly shoved the thought aside. She would do whatever it took to find out who was hurting her sisters; she would *always* do whatever was necessary when it came to the ones she loved.

After a quick scan, Bisma approached the mahogany desk, the main feature of the office. Behind it was a portrait of the Chapman family: Xander's grandparents, his parents, and, in the center, Xander himself. He looked to be about ten years of age, before he went away for school, and he still had that same boyish grin. On either side of the portrait were floor-to-ceiling shelves of books pertaining to garden-magic, potions, and horticulture.

Desire swept through her. What it would be like to sit in the sunlight and read all those books! That vast wealth of knowledge within her reach. Unfortunately, right now she needed to focus.

Under the portrait were wide drawers. She pulled the top one open, then the bottom, parsing the files, skimming through the papers. There were lots of recipes and notes, as well as accounting files for the Apothecary strewn with numbers and balances.

Shutting the drawers, Bisma turned back to the desk, where something caught her eye. On top of the desk, beside candles and a framed picture of Eleanora and her husband, was a beautifully carved wooden box. It looked special, and when Bisma went to open it, she found it locked.

Special, indeed.

Bisma searched the desk drawers for a key, but found none. *Hmm.* There were little potted plants atop the drawers under the portrait.

Putting the wooden box beside a pot, Bisma slipped her hand into the soil of one of them. With magic, a little twig sprouted. Concentrating, Bisma grew the thin, twisted twig until it reached into the keyhole. The lock resisted, but she morphed the twig until it fit perfectly.

The box clicked open.

Anticipation laced through her. She opened the box, finding it filled with keepsakes. There was a twisted lock of copper hair that must have been Xander's from when he was a baby. Bisma touched a finger to it; the hair was feather soft.

There was also an old pocket watch, which had perhaps belonged to Eleanora's father. Beside that, there were dried roses stuck to a piece of paper with a date on them, dating back twenty-two years; she wondered if they were the first flowers Xander's father had given to Eleanora.

The box held other trinkets but none piqued Bisma's interest until she spotted a small painted portrait of two girls.

One was obviously a young Eleanora, but what made Bisma pause was that the other girl looked a little familiar. She had brown skin and long, wavy hair. Bisma could not quite place who she was, but the image remained in her mind even as she closed the keepsake box, using the twig and magic to lock it once more.

She searched through the desk drawers, finding even more notes and old letters. Her eyes skimmed the words. She did not know exactly what she was looking for, and part of her hoped she would find nothing, while another part of her knew deep down that there was something to be found.

And indeed there was.

A letter made her halt her search. It was from a friend, clearly a very close one. The writer seemed to be angry with Eleanora for not helping her, saying she would find help elsewhere; none of which meant anything to Bisma—until she saw who had signed it.

Leilani.

Memories turned over in Bisma's mind. A few months ago, a woman had come to Bisma for a slow-release poison. The woman's husband was abusive in every sense of the word, and she wished to kill him slowly so as not to raise any alarms.

Bisma had not known the woman's name, only that she signed her letters *L*. Now she recognized that handwriting. She recognized, also, that the woman was the same girl in the portrait with Eleanora.

Bisma had only met *L*—Leilani—once, but she was clearly wealthy, so it was no surprise she was Eleanora's friend.

As with all her other customers, Bisma completed the order, giving Leilani what she needed. Bisma did not hear from her again, but she didn't exactly follow up with her clients.

Now she wondered what had transpired. Had something happened to Leilani? She was evidently a close friend of Eleanora's. If something had happened to Leilani, did Eleanora blame Bisma? She could have easily worked out it was Bisma who had given Leilani the poison.

But Bisma didn't have time to think about it further just then. She heard something—someone—heading in her direction. Slipping the letter back into the desk, Bisma ensured everything was back in order before quickly sneaking out of Eleanora's office. Luckily, the hallway was empty, but she saw a shadow rounding the corner.

Bisma ducked into the first room she saw. It was larger and more lived in than the guest room Xander had shown her to and there was more furniture. There were bookshelves and a desk, and the side tables had various knickknacks. She realized with a jolt that this must be Xander's room.

She wondered if he had a box of keepsakes, as well, and what might be inside.

Before her curiosity allowed her to search for such a thing, she heard someone approaching. She froze, trying to figure out what to do. Should she hide? Jump out the window? Pretend like she was meant to be there? The options paralyzed her.

Just as she was deciding, the door opened. She prepared to explain herself until she saw who it was.

Xander.

'Oh!' he said, surprised to see her. His cheeks and nose were flushed, as if he'd just come in from outside. 'What are you doing here?'

'Um . . .' She looked around, biting her lower lip.

He took off his coat, giving her a sly look. 'Intrigued, were we?'

She rolled her eyes. 'Not in the least.'

He smiled as if he didn't believe her and almost looked . . . pleased. Well, it was as good a cover as any, and it wasn't exactly a lie. She *was* intrigued by him. That wasn't a crime. Bisma held her chin up, unrepentant, then assessed her surroundings.

His room was quite bare compared to the greenhouse, which felt more like him. This room did not even smell like him; she could only faintly catch the scent of cloves.

'If you're going to snoop, at least light a candle,' Xander said. He walked past her to the desk, reaching into a drawer for a pack of matches.

Outside the windows, the sun was setting, casting the room in dark shadows. She hadn't even noticed.

Xander pulled out a match to light the candle when someone called for him.

'Xander, dear!'

It was Eleanora. Bisma's heart leapt.

'Oh, good, Mother's here,' Xander said, long strides heading directly for the door. 'We can all have tea and I can introduce you properly!'

'No!' Bisma cried, grabbing his arm and pulling him back. He gave her an alarmed glance, his green eyes wide, but before he could object, she shoved him into the closet, following behind him and shutting the door.

'Xander, are you home?' Eleanora's voice came closer.

Bisma covered Xander's mouth with her hand before he could consider replying.

'I'm meeting Lady Charlotte for dinner,' Eleanora continued, 'but the cook's prepared a roast and potatoes for you, so do—' This last part she said as she knocked and opened the door. Seeing the empty room, she said, 'Oh, I must be hearing things.'

She closed the door and left, and a few moments later, Bisma and Xander listened as the house's front door opened and closed.

Bisma released a breath.

It was then she realized just how close she and Xander were standing; their chests were practically touching. Her hand was still over his mouth; she felt his lips brush against her palm as he shifted.

Heat bolted through her.

She snatched her hand back, trying to step away from him, but there was hardly any room, and the clothes merely pushed her right back.

'Well, that was dramatic,' Xander said, giving her a funny look. But then he seemed to notice how close they were, how her head tipped back so she could meet his eyes, and his voice turned husky. 'Not that I'm complaining.'

Her heart skipped a beat.

'You're ridiculous,' she breathed, trying to regain her senses. 'Why do you have so many clothes?'

'On? Or in my closet?'

He gave her a wolfish grin, to which she responded with an unamused glare.

'In your closet, you idiot.'

It looked like he had seven of the same white shirts and an array of colorful waistcoats. She spotted her favorite, the emerald-green one, and almost reached out to touch it, before she recalled she was not a lovesick fool.

'Nothing wrong with a man who cares about his appearance,' Xander replied easily. 'As much as I'm enjoying this, can we get out of here now? My arm is cramping.'

She didn't dignify that with a response. Instead, Bisma threw open the closet door and hurried out, Xander close behind her.

'Let's get back to work,' she said, trying to catch her breath.

18

They returned to the greenhouse and worked in silence. Bisma needed to ask about Leilani, but how to do so without arousing Xander's suspicions? He was unnaturally nosy and would only ask a hundred questions.

'I've been thinking about who might be ordering the poisons to happen,' Bisma said, keeping her tone casual. 'A few months ago, I gave a client a slow-release poison for her husband. What if he found out and is trying to get revenge on me?'

Xander dropped what he was working on, his wide eyes focused solely on her.

She swallowed. So much for being inconspicuous.

Shaking his head, he rubbed a hand over his face. He stalked over to her table, stopping in front of her.

'Good *god*, Bisma.' He was angry, one of his eyes twitching. 'This is why I say you should stay away from this poison business. You shouldn't be getting involved with people like this! Making enemies!'

How dare he scold her!

'Someone asked me for help!' she said hotly, scowling. 'I wouldn't refuse them, and anyway, it's my business.'

'You can do business in other things!' he exclaimed, refusing to back down.

'I am a garden-witch! I make poisons!'

'You don't have to! You could make perfectly reasonable and harmless potions.'

She scoffed. 'You know full well that is not an option, not as long as your family's apothecary stands—as long as you continue to create in bulk and sell at lower prices. Why would anyone buy from me? But poisons are different.'

'If you worked at the Apothecary, like I suggested, you wouldn't have to worry about that.'

Her eye was twitching by then, as well. The gall of him! She glared at him and he shrank back a little.

'Or you could work with me,' he continued, his voice gentler. 'We could be partners.'

She scoffed louder this time; she had a mind to stomp on his foot for even suggesting it!

'You can't just go around poisoning people, Bis!' He was back to lecturing, waving his hands about dramatically. Indignation flared through her. His face was splotchy, his hair a mess. 'See how it's hurting you to see *your* loved ones poisoned, how do you think others feel?'

'How *dare* you? He abused her; he deserved it!' she snapped, her heart beating furiously fast. 'Are you saying Deeba or Luna or Mei deserve to be poisoned? They've done nothing wrong! I'm not entirely heartless—I don't just poison people for no reason, or sell to anyone with coin. Each client always explains their predicament to me and I refuse cases that I feel like are based purely on malice—but why am I explaining myself to you? You've clearly already made up your mind.'

Who was he to her that she needed his approval? His good opinion? He didn't matter. She was wasting her breath, she knew she was, but, even so, it hurt that he thought so little of her.

She could bear everyone else thinking she was a monster, but not him.

It was just because they were working together, she told herself. They needed to be civil with one another.

But deep down she knew it was more than that.

'I didn't know all that,' Xander said, sheepish now.

'As much as you like to think so, Alexander, you don't know everything.' She turned her back to him, focusing back on her work. She heard him walking over to his table, and she stewed silently, itching for a fight.

If only he would yell at her, she could argue with him, but he said nothing. Even his last words had been calm. It gave her nowhere to direct this energy.

She took deep breaths, sinking her hands into the soil, making different herbs and plants for them to use in their research. Though she felt him watching her, she ignored him.

After a little while, when the worst of her emotions were gone, he finally spoke.

'I'm sorry, Bis,' he said, his voice gentle. 'I judged you harshly. I shouldn't have.'

'Yes, you shouldn't have,' she said, not looking up.

'I really am sorry,' he said, coming to stand in beside her. She refused to look at him. 'Bis,' he said.

'What?' she snapped, finally turning to him.

'I know you're doing the best you can to take care of your sisters,' he said. 'I see now that you use your magic for good, to help people.'

His sincerity doused her anger like water over a flame. She hated how his validation made her feel, but she couldn't ignore it.

'I do just want to help,' she said quietly.

'I know that,' he said, giving her a small smile. She felt warm. 'I just wonder—and don't bite my head off for this—but why not go to the authorities, have them deal with it?'

She sighed. 'It isn't so simple, nor so easy.'

'Why ever not?'

'People like you are taken seriously by the authorities,' she said. He was rich, powerful, important. 'But people like me . . . the people I help . . . we aren't.' These were women, the poor; those who were abused, overlooked, discarded, undervalued. 'Sometimes you have to take things into your own hands.'

'Oh.' He considered this. 'I've never thought of it that way.'

Of course he hadn't. Why would he? But that wasn't his fault, either; she knew that. It was getting harder and harder to be cruel to him, especially when he seemed so adamant on not being frightened away by her.

'I'm sorry,' he said again. 'And thank you for explaining that to me, though it was not your duty to do so. You know I've—' He broke off, suddenly shy.

That piqued her interest.

'What?'

He laughed nervously before fixing his green eyes on her. 'I've always been interested in you,' he said. 'From that very first time, when you did what you did to Luna's father. Even when I didn't agree with your poison work, from an academic standpoint, I was always fascinated—in awe, really. You motivated me; I wanted to be as good as you, even when I was away at school. I thought of you often.'

His cheeks were pink, and he looked away, clearly embarrassed by what he'd said, but his words cooled her like a salve against a burn.

She had always wanted to be as good as *him*, even when he had been away. She had thought of him, as well. She still did. More than she would ever care to admit.

But she didn't say any of that. She couldn't say anything, not until her heart stopped pounding so hard.

She cleared her throat. 'The reason I brought up the woman poisoning her husband,' she said, trying to get back to the topic at hand, 'was because I didn't hear from her again for a second dose, which I was expecting since I gave her enough for a month, but told her it would take three before her husband died.'

'Does that happen often?' Xander asked. 'What if she changed her mind?'

'I don't think so,' Bisma said. 'She was determined to end her suffering. But what if the husband found out about the poison and is trying to get revenge on me? She said he traveled for business sometimes, so he could have hired a witch to make the poison for him.'

Or Eleanora, she thought to herself.

'It's possible,' Xander said, considering it. 'Though it's also possible that the woman ran away, isn't it?'

'I suppose.' Bisma hadn't thought of that. She certainly wanted to believe it. For some odd reason, Bisma didn't want Eleanora to be guilty, and she suspected the reason was standing right in front of her.

'Even so, do you know the man's name?' Xander asked. 'With a bit more information, I could try and find out.'

'No, but I do know the wife's,' Bisma said. 'Leilani.'

Xander froze. His face flashed with pain so severe that Bisma felt sorry for bringing it up.

'What is it?' she asked, unable to keep the worry from her voice.

'I knew someone called Leilani—she was like an aunt to me,' he said, voice thick. 'She was like a sister to my mother; they grew up together and were the best of friends.'

'Do you think it's the same woman?' Bisma's heart pounded. 'Wait, what do you mean *was*?'

'I never knew her husband . . .' He trailed off, horrified. 'But, Bisma, she died in her sleep two months ago. That's why you never heard from her.'

Bisma's suspicions were confirmed.

This gave Eleanora a clear motive. Leilani's husband must have found out about the poison and used it—or something else—on Leilani. Eleanora must have known it was Bisma that sold Leilani the poison and was the cause of all this.

Oh *no*.

Bisma's mind whirred, but she did not want Xander to notice or he would ask questions, grow suspicious.

'It's getting late,' she said, reaching for her shawl. 'I think we ought to call it a night.'

'Won't you stay for dinner?' Xander asked, adapting to her change in topic. 'I know the promise of my company won't tempt you, but surely a roast and potatoes will?'

'No—No, I'll eat with my sisters,' she said, distracted. She headed for the door and Xander followed, grabbing a dark coat.

'I'll walk you,' he said, slipping the coat on.

'There's no need,' she said, already walking away. Lifting his collar against the chill, he easily fell into step beside her. *Damn him and his long legs.*

'It's no trouble,' he said. 'Besides, it isn't safe.'

She gave him a funny look. 'I walk home alone all the time.'

He frowned. 'Yes, well, seeing as three of your sisters have been poisoned, I'd rather not take any chances,' he said, agitated.

This tickled her. 'And what might you do if someone shot out of the bushes now, ready to poison me?'

He gave her an unamused glance. 'That isn't something to jest about,' he said, which made her laugh.

'*Alexander*, scolding *me* on what and what not to jest about!' she said, donning a scandalized tone.

He glared, huffing and puffing as she laughed.

'Forgive me if I don't find the prospect of you being wounded entertaining,' he said hotly. 'And to answer your question, just let someone try and hurt you in my presence. You'll quickly see what I might do.'

She had another sarcastic response ready at the tip of her tongue but stopped when she saw his face. He was scowling.

Oh. She felt a little sorry for teasing him, for he seemed genuinely upset now.

They walked on, Xander silently stewing until Bisma bumped his shoulder with hers. He was so shocked that he practically went flying, nearly tripping over a branch.

He gave her an incredulous look. 'What was that for!'

'Quit pouting,' she said. 'You'll get wrinkles.'

His hands instinctively went to his face.

She smiled.

A moment later, he smiled, too, the tension leaving him. He bumped her shoulder with his, and she nearly went flying as well. His rich laughter filled the air.

Then they walked in companionable silence; it was nice. He stayed by her side as they walked all the way to the Enchanted Forest, the moon shining bright above them, the stars glinting as they watched, as if giggling to a private joke.

They stopped at the edge of the Forest. There was the usual

foggy border along the Forest's perimeter, and though it looked daunting, Bisma wasn't afraid. Xander didn't seem to be, either.

'Goodbye,' she said.

'I'll see you tomorrow?' he asked, sounding hopeful.

She nodded. 'Goodbye, then.'

She passed through the thick fog until she was fully in the Enchanted Forest. She walked on, thinking over the day's events, letting her feet carry her along the usual path home.

Until she realized she was lost. Where there should have been a slowly running creek, there was not.

But—no, she couldn't be lost.

Bisma looked around. Everything else was the same: the trees, the position of the moon in the sky, the little rabbit hutch, the big red maple tree. She stepped closer to where the creek ought to have been, touching the land.

It seemed like the creek had simply run dry. The soil was cracked, parched.

Strange.

The Forest must have had a reason for it, Bisma told herself, as she continued home. The Forest always knew what it was doing; she had nothing to worry about. Even so, unease needled the back of her mind.

Back home, Bisma ate dinner with the girls, a soothing chicken and corn soup with crackers. Nori made quick work of her dinner, then went directly to dessert, eating the pumpkin cake Haru had sent for Luna.

'Nori, isn't that Luna's?' Bisma asked.

'Baji, she said I could have it!' Nori said, crumbs falling from her mouth.

'I don't want it,' Luna said.

Bisma looked at Luna, but Luna avoided her gaze.

Why was Luna acting weird? That night, after they had played games and gotten ready for bed, Bisma stopped by Luna's room on the way to her own.

'Why don't you come to town with me tomorrow?' Bisma asked gently. 'You can get a batch of gingersnaps for us to eat with tea.'

Luna was sitting on her bed, brushing her dark honey hair, not looking at Bisma. 'Take Azalea,' she said.

'Lu, what's going on?' Bisma frowned. 'You never miss an opportunity to go to town or to go to the bakery.'

Luna set the hairbrush down and promptly burst into tears.

Shock poured over Bisma; she hesitated, then rushed to Luna's side.

'What is it?' she asked, wrapping Luna into a hug. Luna clutched Bisma tight, her tears falling onto Bisma's shoulder. Confusion coursed through Bisma.

'I'm just so scared,' Luna managed to say through shuddering breaths.

'Scared?' Bisma repeated. The volatile emotions of fifteen-year-olds were quite something to grapple with. 'Of what?'

'I almost died,' Luna replied.

'But you're alright,' Bisma said, not entirely understanding. 'You're safe. Nothing is going to happen to you, I promise.'

'I know,' Luna said, pulling back to wipe her face with the edge of her sweater sleeve. Her eyes were red. 'I trust you, Baji, I do. But no matter how hard I try to be brave, I still feel scared. It feels like something is *wrong* inside me, as if *I* am wrong. And what if he sees? What if he *sees* that there is something wrong with me?'

Her eyes welled with tears again. She did not need to specify who *he* was.

'First of all, there is nothing wrong with you,' Bisma said, holding Luna's face in her hands. 'You're perfect! You always have been.'

She wiped Luna's cheeks. 'Secondly, you needn't worry about Haru. He likes you, Luna.'

Luna shook her head, bottom lip trembling. 'You don't understand.'

Bisma didn't, not really. She opened her mouth to say something else, but Luna pulled her blanket up, getting into bed.

'Goodnight, Baji,' she said, her voice quiet.

Unsure what to do, Bisma stood. With a sigh, she stroked Luna's hair. 'Goodnight, Lu.'

As she left, guilt knifed through Bisma—but it morphed quickly into rage as she went to her own room.

She would find out who was behind the poisonings, and she would make them pay. She swore it.

Even if it was Eleanora Chapman.

19

Bisma and Xander continued to work together on the cure. She spent every free moment she had with him, and along with her poison business, running errands, trying to find evidence of Eleanora's involvement (the only lead she had) and the general work of being Baji, she felt she was constantly running from one place to the next.

After a few days of relentless work, Bisma was at her absolute wit's end. They had tested out numerous different mixtures. In the beginning, Xander had suggested consulting Eleanora on the matter, which Bisma had vehemently refused. She knew Xander trusted his mother wholeheartedly, but Bisma did not.

Besides, Xander had no shortage of theories himself, and while some didn't work right away, others seemed promising before failing. He made more of the freezing potion in case any of the other girls were poisoned.

It was no wonder that Bisma and her sisters were in low spirits. Nori began crying at every little thing, particularly because Deeba wasn't there to play with her; Mei was just sad, letting out great big sighs; Azalea was angry, more sassy than usual; and Luna still refused to go to town, which made both her and Haru forlorn.

The Enchanted Forest seemed to be influenced by their drab energy, as well, for one day when Bisma went down to Mirror Lake, which was usually as clear as a glass—hence the name—it was murky.

It was unnerving, and only gave her a heightened sense of urgency. While working with Xander was a necessity, it was also exhausting.

Some days they worked startlingly well together, so well, in fact, it felt they operated as one entity. Often, they worked in silence, but that did not undermine their communication skills; they could almost read each other's minds now, knowing what the other required before they even had to say it.

Then, other days—like today—Xander was his usual, insufferable self.

He was standing beside her as they worked, and she felt him staring at her, smiling to himself.

'What?' she finally snapped, turning to him.

He leaned against the table so they were facing each other.

When he didn't reply, she said, 'Well?'

'Come to dinner with me.'

She balked. 'Excuse me?'

He smiled. 'You heard me.'

'I don't like to be commanded,' she said, though this was not the complete truth. But he did not need to know about the types of situations she liked to be commanded in.

'Darling Bisma, won't you accompany me to dinner?' he asked sweetly. He plucked a red rose from one of the bushes in the greenhouse and offered it to her.

Bisma pretended to consider it. She gave him a sweet smile, then said, 'No.'

He frowned, sighing. He must have been bored and more than that, tired. She had to confess, she was exhausted as well. But that did not mean she intended to take leave of her senses and go out with him.

'Why don't you direct your efforts elsewhere?' she asked, just to bother him. 'You're sure to be met with more favorable responses.'

He looked peeved. 'I don't know what you mean.'

Bisma rolled her eyes. He was being willfully obtuse.

'Step outside, I'm sure you'll have an offer from a number of girls within the minute,' she said. The idea of it added an edge to her tone.

Suddenly, Xander didn't look irritated, but amused. 'Is that so?' he asked, cocking his head. 'Are you quite sure?'

She scowled, thinking of the village girls she routinely heard talking about him.

'Yes, I'm quite sure. I've heard Christina and Racquel going on at length about your ridiculous hair on numerous occasions, not to mention Famke and Umamah's obsession with your height.'

'Keeping track of all my admirers, are we?' He smirked.

She rolled her eyes.

'Of course not,' she said, her cheeks warming. 'They're all so loud and obnoxious, one cannot help but overhear.'

'Ah, of course.' He echoed, tone amused. He thought about what she had said for a moment, which vexed her. 'I really would take your suggestion if only one name was added to that list.'

This immediately intrigued her. 'Who?' she demanded.

'I'm not sure you know her,' he replied, and Bisma furrowed her brows. 'She's whip-smart, probably the cleverest person I know, definitely the cleverest in town—second only to me, of course. And beautiful—fierce as the rising sun, lovely as falling snow.'

Bisma scoffed. He was being dramatic, as always. 'I doubt she even exists,' she said.

'Yes, sometimes I do imagine I dreamed her.' He laughed, a fond expression on his face.

Irritation laced through her. *Who was this perfect girl?*

Xander straightened from where he was leaning against the table, taking a step forward to dip his head by hers.

'Here, I'll give you another hint,' he said, whispering into her ear. Little electric jolts skipped over her skin. 'She's terribly ill-mannered, but I'm growing rather fond of her bad temper.' He pulled back, looking into her eyes.

With a start, Bisma realized who he was speaking of. Heat flushed through her.

Heart beating unreasonably fast, she looked up at him. Even though he was surely teasing her, she saw his green eyes were genuine, kind. She couldn't tell if his earnestness was better or worse than his jests.

'You are so full of shit,' she scoffed. 'I am *definitely* cleverer than you.'

He looked surprised for a moment—then he laughed out loud, dispelling the tension.

She laughed, too.

'Now focus.' Bisma grabbed his arm. She turned him to face the table, hoping he didn't notice the color that had undoubtedly risen in her cheeks. 'Come, I'll teach you how to grow.'

'Oh yes!' he said, delighted. 'I've been waiting for this.'

She brought a fresh pot of soil in front of him.

He made an excited sound, like a child about to receive a toy.

'What shall we grow?' he asked, practically bouncing.

She thought she would be irritated by his enthusiasm, but she found she rather liked it. It was nice having someone who was as excited by magic as she.

'In the beginning, I didn't know what to do with my magic,' Bisma explained. 'I just knew I had it, and when I put my hands in the soil, I could focus and grow something that I needed, based on what I was feeling. So just try to feel and see what comes out.'

His mouth gaped open as he gave her an incredulous look. 'Those are your instructions?' he asked. 'To *feel* and see what happens?'

'Yes.'

Bisma could see how this would be disconcerting to someone like Xander, with his precise notes and outlines and instructions and plans. But she had never had any of that, and this was *her* specialty.

'But—' he started. 'I need more than that—I need details!'

'That's all I have,' she said. 'Now do as I say!'

'Have you ever considered being a teacher?' he asked dryly. 'It might be an ideal profession for you.'

'I've been following your mixing instructions fastidiously,' she told him, 'despite how tedious it's been, and now you must follow *my* instructions.'

'Alright, alright,' he said. Taking a deep breath, he put his hands into the soil.

'Focus,' she said. 'Close your eyes and *feel*.'

He did as instructed, a wrinkle appearing between his brows as he concentrated. Some time later, he peeked open an eye, looking for results, then sighed.

'It's not working.'

He frowned like a petulant child, which made her bite back a smile. She wondered if anything had ever been difficult for him; it tickled her that this one thing she had never had trouble with was what would give him a tough time. The superiority she felt added a little pep in her step, actually.

'Here,' she said, taking one of his hands out of the soil. He let her, pouting like the dramatic person he was. She cleaned his hand with a cloth, then set it against his heart. Then she put her other hand into the soil.

'Do you feel that?' she asked, holding his hand above his heart.

He swallowed, looking down at her.

'I sure feel something,' he said. His eyes were dark.

Shoving aside her murderous impulses, she gave him a disapproving look. 'Focus, Alexander.'

'Yes, right, but how exactly to do that with a pretty girl's hand on my heart?'

She scowled. 'Be serious.'

'Bis, I am deathly serious.'

He was telling the truth, she could feel it in the soil, and in the pound of his heart. He was allowing himself to feel, opening himself up to the magic. She drew closer, pulled in by the magic, and felt the heat of his body beside hers. She inhaled the sweet scent of cloves.

'The magic will wait for instruction inside you,' she said. 'Don't think about it too much; just imagine what you want to happen and make it happen. You have to be a little bossy with the magic.'

He smiled at that. 'I'm not at all surprised that you excel at the magic in which a key quality is being bossy.'

'Now do it,' she said.

He released a long breath, and she waited, watching. Then, slowly, something began to grow.

A flower sprouted from the soil: it was pretty, pink with red streaks. They both pulled their hands out of the soil, and she let go of his hand.

'I did it!' Xander exclaimed, clearly proud of himself.

They both looked at the flower. Xander held it up between them. It had a sweet scent.

She breathed it in.

All of a sudden, she felt . . . parched. But not for a drink, for *him*.

She looked up at him, into those gorgeous eyes, a perfect glinting green the color of grass after summer rain. Though there was hardly any green left now; his pupils were blown wide. His eyelids fluttered as she looked up at him, and he set the flower down, his hands empty for hardly a second before they came to seize her waist.

With a swift tug, he pulled her close. Her heart started pounding in response, a haze coming over her. Everything around him blurred, fading away until all she could see was him: the fall of his copper hair, the cut of cheekbones, the full shape of his mouth.

He was similarly focused on her, his attention razor-sharp. His fingers dug into her skin, the pressure deliciously painful. She brought her hands up to his neck, slipping her fingers into his beautiful hair.

'So soft,' she whispered, running her hands through the locks. She twisted his hair around her fingers, pulling.

He made a strangled sound.

'Bisma,' he choked out, his nose brushing her cheek.

Heat flushed through her.

She *needed* him.

'Xander,' she sighed back, nipping his ear.

He held her tighter, gasping. His teeth grazed the sensitive skin of her throat. As her heart hammered, she didn't understand why he wasn't already kissing her. The bed was right there. What on earth was he waiting for?

She pulled back. His eyes were almost entirely black. He was focused solely on her, drinking in the expression on her face. She didn't even care to hide just how much she needed him, but it seemed to confuse him.

He blinked.

Then his gaze jumped to the pink flower on the table beside them. He released her, which almost drove her mad. As she was about to pull him back to her, he snatched the flower and plucked it from the soil.

He ripped it apart in his hands, then ran halfway across the room before she realized what had happened.

Bisma felt as if she'd been doused in ice water. The fog that had come over her cleared, leaving her lightheaded.

'What was that? Xander, what did you grow?' she asked, catching her breath. Her head was spinning. She grabbed a nearby glass of water, drinking it with shaking hands.

'Nothing!' Xander replied, his voice high. He was standing behind a table, gripping it so tightly his knuckles had turned white.

Dots connected in her mind, drawing a most infuriating conclusion.

'Alexander Chapman, did you grow a *lust* plant?'

How quickly his face turned red was answer enough.

'XANDER.'

'You're the one who said to just feel it!' he complained.

She groaned into her hands before glaring at him. 'Oh, I'm going to kill you.'

'God, Bis, don't look at me.'

He had very purposefully not stepped out from behind the table.

She forced herself to turn around, still reeling from the fog of lust that had overcome her. Her entire body pulsed.

She felt nauseous, her stomach in painful knots.

The sooner she found the cure, the sooner she would be free of Xander's company—free of all these *emotions*.

20

Back at the treehouse, Bisma busied herself, but, even so, she kept thinking of Xander's dark eyes, his hands at her waist. Just the memory of it made her stomach twist, made her jittery.

At the very least, at home she could hardly hear her own thoughts, the girls were being so loud. Bisma was at the table, opening up the hem of one of Mei's dresses to make it longer, while Mei and Luna were in the kitchen, chatting.

From the living room, Bisma heard Azalea's third consecutive frustrated groan in the past thirty seconds.

'NORI,' Azalea snapped, 'why don't you know how to spell?'

'I do!' Nori cried, outraged by the (accurate) accusation.

It was Azalea's turn to teach the five-year-old, a task that drove one to the very edge of sanity.

Luna and Mei snickered from the kitchen, and Bisma gave them a scolding glance.

'OK, so how do you spell *land*?' Azalea asked.

'Uh . . . um . . .' Nori stuttered. 'J-J?'

'No! *L!*' Azalea cried. 'Baji! I literally cannot do this anymore! My head hurts, and I'm tired, and she's not learning *anything*, and I want to take a nap.'

Bisma sighed, her fingers working along the dress's hem. 'Azalea, quit complaining. We could easily switch tasks but you need to have some patience. You're always huffing and puffing; try calming down a little. And, Nori, do try to pay attention, sweet.'

Azalea was quiet then; she must have been in one of her moods. Releasing a breath, Bisma looked over her shoulder.

Azalea was frowning at her hand and Bisma's heart missed a beat when she saw it was shot through with blue. She leapt to her feet, immediately going to her, while Nori's eyes welled with tears.

'I'm sorry,' Nori said. 'I'll try harder, I promise!'

'Great!' Azalea grimaced with pain, leaning back against the sofa. Bisma turned to ask Luna or Mei to grab a dose of the freezing potion when Mei arrived by her side, holding the potion in hand.

'You're going to be just fine,' Bisma said, sitting down next to Azalea.

'Tell me it doesn't taste awful,' Azalea said. She was shaking with pain, face pale, but still had time to be sassy.

'No promises,' Bisma said. She emptied the liquid into Azalea's mouth, and Azalea swallowed.

'At least I get to take a nap now,' Azalea said. Then, her eyes closed, and her skin went gray. She was frozen. Bisma released a breath, turning to look at her sisters—those who remained.

She pulled Nori into her lap, wiping the little girl's cheeks.

'At least we won't have to listen to her complaining,' Luna said, attempting levity, but they were all dispirited. The treehouse felt so much quieter without Azalea's noise, without Deeba's.

'I'm going to the greenhouse.' Bisma lifted Nori to her feet and stood. With the Forest's help, she put Azalea onto her pushcart, then brought her sister over to the Chapman Estate.

When Xander heard her approaching with the pushcart, he left what he was doing and rushed to her side, taking it from her.

'I'm sorry,' he said.

She nodded, unable to speak. Frustration and anger coursed through her. Who was doing this? Why? If someone had a problem with her, she wished they would be upfront and say so, attack *her* if need be, but leave her sisters out of it. She *hated* this.

'What was her story?' Xander asked.

She blinked, looking at him. 'Azalea was left as a one-year-old,' Bisma explained, as together they transferred Azalea to a cot beside Deeba. 'There was no note to explain her story, so nobody knew it. Azalea never wanted to learn it either because that way, she got to choose and craft her own past.'

'She was never curious?' Xander asked.

Azalea was settled, and Bisma took a moment to look at her frozen face.

'For a while, she tried to convince us she was the child of the king,' Bisma said, smiling at the memory. 'She told this elaborate tale of how she must have been kidnapped and left in the Enchanted Forest for safekeeping, but one day she would return to the castle and be the princess she was always destined to be.'

'Don't worry,' Azalea would tell them. 'When I'm back at my castle, I won't forget about all of you. You can even come stay with me! Only so long as you're nice to me, of course. Mei, get me another biscuit, will you?'

This was when Azalea was around ten; as she got older, she

stopped believing in the stories, but sometimes in jest she would still remind her sisters that she was a lost princess.

On Azalea's birthday, they called her Princess Azalea all day, and she spent the day wearing a crown of twigs and flowers.

Azalea's birthday was coming up soon—would she be awake for it?

'Let's get to work,' Bisma said, clenching her jaw.

For the next few days, Bisma worked twice as hard, spending most of her time with Xander in his greenhouse. Luna was left in charge of Nori and Mei and the housework, while Bisma tried to keep up with selling her poisons and working on the cure.

She still thought that if she found out who had made the poison, it would help with formulating a cure. As much as she tried to fight it, her thoughts went back to Eleanora.

Xander extracted the poison from Azalea's blood and compared it with the extraction from Deeba, finding both samples to be identical. This was a good sign, for it meant that the poison was no longer mutating or changing, and once they made a cure, it would work on both of them.

If only they could make it!

Xander focused on mixing the perfect potion (they did not attempt another growing lesson after the previous disastrous outcome) while Bisma tried to use magic to break down the poison in order to find out how it was made, which might in turn give them a clue about *who* had made it.

She had not forgotten that Xander's mother might be involved in all of this, but she would not make an accusation without solid proof.

Unfortunately, this was impossibly difficult to accomplish. She didn't know the exact science behind it, and neither did Xander, so she eventually stopped trying and went back to focusing on creating a cure. Once the girls were alright, she could discover who had done this and plot her revenge.

Bisma was so preoccupied that she hardly slept or ate, and her health quickly deteriorated, a fact she did not even notice until one day she entered the greenhouse and Xander gave her a look so filled with worry that even she grew apprehensive.

'This won't do, Bisma,' he said, shaking his head. 'You need to take care of yourself.'

'It's fine,' she said, but her voice was weak. She tried to clear her throat. 'I'm fine.'

'You're clearly not.' He frowned. 'I've seen you in that same outfit for a week now.'

Ugh. He was right. Not that she admitted it to him then, but the next day she showered and came in wearing a fresh dress.

'Happy?' Bisma asked, gesturing pointedly to the clean outfit.

He smiled, about to nod, when he saw her hair. The smile faded.

'You haven't brushed your hair,' he said.

She was appalled. 'You know it isn't exactly nice manners to point that out.' She touched her knotted hair self-consciously. 'Brushing it is an entire effort, and I've been too tired.'

'Allow me,' he said, rummaging around a desk for a hairbrush. Of course he kept a spare hairbrush in his workspace!

'What? No.'

'Come on, it'll help you think.' He held up the hairbrush, then strode toward her. 'You need blood circulation.'

'Blood circulation?'

'Yes, blood circulation. We learned about it in school and everything.'

'Of course you went to a school where they taught you the importance of brushing your hair.'

'The only class I ever got full marks in, too.'

He was in front of her now, and put his hands on her shoulders, steering her to sit down on a stool. She really was too tired, so she let him, sighing.

With gentle hands, he undid the knot of her hair, then sectioned it off, his long and elegant fingers working deftly through the tangled mess. Then he began brushing, tugging lightly, and it was, to put it simply, heavenly.

Bisma closed her eyes as he worked, both of them silent. She listened to the sound of his breathing and of her hair being tamed. It was lovely, so lovely.

She had brushed her sisters' hair for years, but hadn't had hers brushed in a long, long time. It was so kind—so sweet to be taken care of—that she felt tears well up in her eyes, which was just absurd.

Why are you crying? She hastily blinked the tears away, glad he was behind her and would not see.

As Xander finished, she felt another wall around her heart come crumbling down. Bisma was afraid of how few of her defenses remained.

Spending so much time with Xander—she had gotten into the habit of him, and it was one she did not want to let go of. Even so, she was afraid: not only of the damage he could do to her if she let him in, but the damage he might find within her if he got too close. How repulsed he might be by the truth of her.

'There,' he said, gathering her smooth hair in his hands, then setting it down. She ran a hand over her hair; it was soft.

'Thank you,' she said, turning to face him.

'Of course,' he said.

There was an expression on his face she could not quite decipher, but his eyes were very green, bright and dazzling.

Bisma felt her face grow warm, and he inched closer. For a moment, she thought he might kiss her, and she resolved not to stop him. Not this time.

She closed her eyes, waiting.

But the kiss did not come. Instead, she felt cool air on her cheeks. She opened her eyes to find Xander smiling fondly.

'Your face was red,' he said, his voice low. 'Thought you might need help cooling down.'

She was flustered, but she did feel fresh, much better than she had in the past few days. She felt ready to think, and indeed she did.

'Xander,' she said, standing. 'Do you think your mother might know?'

'My mother?' he repeated. He ran a hand through his hair. 'Wasn't particularly thinking of her at the moment, but do go on.'

'I was just thinking . . . Well, she might have a recipe for a mixture that you haven't thought of so far,' she said, trying to keep her tone normal.

'Unlikely, but I can ask her,' Xander said. 'I did offer to ask her for help before, if you recall. I spend most of my time here with you and talk about you often enough.'

Alarm bells rang inside her. 'You haven't told her what's happened, have you?' Bisma asked, her tone sharp. 'What we're working on?'

'No, don't worry,' he said. 'I do tell her everything, but not what isn't my business to tell.'

Relief flowed through her. 'Good. I don't want her—anyone—knowing.'

He looked as if he was about to say something, then stopped. After a moment, he said, 'What do you suggest then?'

'I was thinking . . . what if we took a look at her notes for the Apothecary potions? Perhaps we might find something?'

Bisma was hoping she to find something relating to the poison, something that would connect Eleanora to it. She had snuck into Eleanora's office at the mansion again in search of such material, but had found nothing, and wondered if Eleanora kept more sensitive files at the Apothecary.

Xander thought about it. 'I know how most of the Apothecary potions are made,' he said, 'so I'm not sure there will be anything new. I grew up learning how to make those potions, and they are all entirely tried and true. My mother—like my grandfather before her—is meticulous about what she sells at the Apothecary.'

'Yes, but isn't she ever developing anything new?' Bisma asked.

Xander considered this. 'I suppose so,' he said. 'If you like, we might as well try. Those types of notes and products will be in her office at the Apothecary.'

Excellent.

They went over that evening, after Eleanora had left. The manager gave Bisma a harsh look, recognizing her as the Unwanted Witch, but because she was with Xander, he did not stop her as they strode directly into Eleanora's office.

It was smaller than her office at the estate but overflowing with papers and far less tidy. There were also loads of vials of potions made of that special Castletown glass customary of the Chapman Apothecary. The space reminded her of Xander's greenhouse in a sense.

'Time to get reading,' Xander said, taking a deep breath.

They started paging through piles of paper, looking at instructions for different potions, as well as handwritten notes for products that Eleanora was testing out.

Bisma searched for notes that might tell her how the poison was made, but found none, for of course it would not be that easy. As she continued her search, she understood where Xander got his affinity for diligent record-keeping from, but she didn't find much else that was useful.

Until Bisma spotted the words *Enchanted Forest* written on a piece of paper.

Making sure Xander wasn't watching, Bisma pushed the papers on top to the side, until she could see the file.

She froze. It had information on each of the Unwanted Girls, and at the very top was Bisma's name.

'Did you find something?' Xander asked, looking her way.

'No,' Bisma said quickly, discreetly covering the paper. She cleared her throat. 'I thought I did, but it's nothing.'

Xander sighed, paging through more papers. 'I don't think there's anything here that I didn't already know.'

'Yes,' she agreed. 'Let's go.'

'Oh, wait!' Xander paused, pulling a sheet out from the pile. His eyes scanned it quickly, and Bisma came to read it over his shoulder. It looked to be a cure recipe.

'This is new,' he said. Bisma didn't know enough about the mixing recipes to see anything particularly of interest in it, until Xander pointed to a line. 'I've never thought of using star anise this way.'

She looked at him and could see his mind was whirring, possibilities clicking in and out of place.

'I have an idea,' he said, stashing the sheet back. With a grin, he grabbed her hand, pulling her along, and they made a quick exit from the Apothecary. Xander was in such a hurry he did not notice the man entering just as they were leaving, and he collided straight into him.

'Xander, my boy!'

'Uncle Fred!' Xander exclaimed, stopping in his tracks.

Frederick smiled at him. He really was even more handsome up close, which only bothered Bisma.

'Where are you running off to?' Frederick asked, grabbing his nephew's shoulders. His gaze turned to Bisma. 'And who's your lovely friend?'

'This is Bisma,' Xander said, pulling her forward to introduce her. He was still holding her hand, and she knew she should have let go, but she did not want to. 'Bisma, this is my uncle.'

'Pleased to meet you,' Frederick said, bowing a little.

'Charmed,' Bisma replied, attempting a pleasant smile.

Frederick grinned, turning to his nephew. 'Well done, Xander,' he said.

Xander's cheeks turned pink.

Bisma arched a brow. 'I wouldn't congratulate him just yet.'

Frederick laughed out loud. 'I like this one, Xander—be sure not to muck it up, now.'

'And that's enough embarrassment for today.' Xander pulled Bisma away, and she bit back a laugh. He was still flustered when they arrived back at the greenhouse, but he quickly went into his focused research mode, asking her to grow certain ingredients as he prepared a new trial.

He ground ginger into a paste, and she added fresh nutmeg shavings in, which he then mixed together. Bisma grew bok choy, and Xander plucked the long leaves off, spread the paste over the inside, then rolled it. As he held the roll in place, Bisma pierced each roll with a toothpick to keep it from unraveling.

Then he grabbed star anise and added it to boiling water, brewing it as he did something with his magic, making the water level stay the same, rather than decrease with steam. When the water had changed color, he added the bok choy rolls in. They cooked them until the rolls had wilted entirely and the water had thickened.

Xander strained the liquid out; it was amber, threaded with gold flecks.

'It's ready,' he said, holding up the bottle of liquid.

Bisma grew another test tree, injecting it with the poison as Xander brought over the potion. He poured it over the soil, then they waited and watched.

Slowly, the tree began to drink the potion up, and they saw it travel through the trunk and into the branches, dispersing to the darkened leaves. They were getting close; Bisma could feel it. She and Xander complemented each other in skills, and now, as they watched, she wondered if they had finally done it.

Then, just like magic, the leaves changed, morphing from their poisoned state back to their original health.

'Oh my god,' Bisma said, covering her mouth with her hand.

'It's working,' Xander said in awe.

They looked at each other with wide eyes.

They waited to see if it would hold—and it did.

'Bis, it worked!' Xander whooped, and before she knew what was happening, he scooped her into his arms, spinning her around. She laughed out loud, holding onto him, until he set her down on her feet again.

'It worked,' she said, elation making her heart soar. They both looked to their test tree to make sure they had not deceived themselves, but, yes, it really was perfectly healthy once more.

'Should we try it on Deeba?' Bisma asked. Hope made her feel as if she was floating.

'I think—' he began, but he was interrupted by the greenhouse doors opening.

Luna and Mei entered, Luna holding Nori.

Nori, who had been poisoned.

21

Bisma's stomach lurched. 'Nori!'

'Baji,' the five-year-old cried, face wet with tears. The veins of her hands were dark blue, the poison spreading up past her wrist.

Bisma and Xander turned to one another at the same time, the same thought crossing their minds.

'We have to try,' she said.

Xander didn't hesitate. He grabbed the potion they had just concocted, and Bisma gathered Nori into her arms. Nori clung tightly to Bisma, both arms wrapped around her neck.

Hot tears fell onto Bisma's shoulder, and her heart twisted painfully. 'Shh, you're going to be fine,' Bisma said, voice soothing as she sat down, Nori in her lap. 'Nori, look at me.' But Nori wouldn't let go of Bisma's head. Over Nori's shoulder, Bisma exchanged a glance with Luna and Mei.

'Nori, come on,' Luna coaxed. 'You have to take some medicine, okay?'

'I don't want to!' Nori cried, clutching Bisma tighter. Bisma stroked her back.

'Nori, please,' Mei said. 'Otherwise you won't feel better.'

'Don't you trust your baji?' Bisma asked. Nori nodded slightly. 'Now, come, be a good girl.' With a sniffle, Nori pulled back, and Bisma brushed aside Nori's messy hair. 'That's it.'

Bisma turned Nori so she was facing forward, still sitting in her lap. She nodded at Xander, who was ready with a small vial of the cure.

'It's going to be okay,' Bisma said, addressing this to Mei and Luna as well. 'We made a cure; she'll be fine now.'

'Hello, brave girl, can you open your mouth, pretty please?' Xander asked Nori, crouching down in front of her.

Nori looked at the vial, then shook her head, whimpering.

'It's medicine, sweet,' Bisma said, giving the five-year-old a squeeze. 'Just a sip and you'll feel better, OK? Pinkie promise.'

Tears rolled down Nori's face as she shook her head again.

'Nori, please?' Bisma asked, her voice breaking. The poison was spreading up Nori's arms. 'Just a little bit, I promise.'

Finally, Nori opened her mouth. Without delay, Xander emptied the liquid into her mouth, and she swallowed it, quickly dissolving into tears once more.

'No taste good,' she cried, turning to bury her face against her sister.

'I'm sorry,' Bisma said, stroking Nori's hair as she blubbered against Bisma's chest. 'But you did so well!'

They waited, holding their breath.

Mei hugged Luna, while Xander stayed crouched in front of Bisma.

She looked at him. Without thinking, she reached for his hand only to find he was already reaching for her. They clutched each other, holding on.

A few long moments passed before Nori stopped crying.

Bisma watched Nori's arm. 'Xander, look,' she said, gasping. The poison was receding. Bisma stood Nori up so they could all see.

'It's working,' he whispered.

But the relief lasted only a second.

Nori threw up, vomiting out the cure, and the poison immediately began spreading once more. Nori wailed, breaking Bisma's heart.

Xander swore, rushing to grab the freeze potion as Bisma gathered her little sister into her arms. She held onto Nori tight, the crash from hope to despair too much for her to bear. Xander fed it to Nori, who froze and fell asleep just like the rest, then he scooped her up and set her beside Deeba and Azalea.

Bisma could almost convince herself that Nori was just asleep—except she couldn't because Nori was quiet. There were none of her usual loud snores to be heard.

Suddenly, Bisma rose to her feet, rage taking over. She let out a screech, kicking a table. The contents went crashing, but she did not notice. Blood roared in her ears, and she wanted to scream, to drown it all out.

'Hey.' Xander was suddenly in front of her. She couldn't see straight; she couldn't see anything.

He cupped her face in his hands, saying her name once, twice, rubbing his thumbs over her cheekbones, and finally, she saw him. She looked up into his green eyes.

'Get some fresh air,' he said quietly.

Over his shoulder, she saw Mei and Luna, both startled. Tears sprang to her eyes. Bisma was horrified with herself for succumbing to her despair in front of them.

She ran outside, gulping in cool air. She fell to her knees, sticking her hands into the soil, letting her magic flow through her. A thorny bush sprouted, and she felt her breathing grow more even, some of the more potent emotions leaving her.

With a sigh, Bisma walked and went to town, hoping to clear her head. She still felt Nori's little body in her arms, the way Nori had clung to her. The front of Bisma's dress was still wet with her tears.

It broke her heart.

In town, she spotted Haru leaving the butcher's shop, presumably on his way home. When he saw Bisma, he came over.

'Everything alright?' he asked, looking concerned.

'Yes, it's nothing.' She attempted a smile.

'How's Luna doing?' he asked. He always asked.

'She's doing a bit better,' Bisma said, her heart breaking for him now, as well. Why was everything so horrible and sad?

'Tell her I'm thinking of her,' Haru said, then paused. That warmed her, this thread of hope persisting among all the awfulness. 'No, tell her I miss her. She hasn't replied to any of my letters.'

'I'll tell her,' she reassured him.

He went on his way, and Bisma went back to the greenhouse.

When she returned, she saw Xander excitedly showing Luna and Mei around different plants, the three of them sucking on toffees. The sight was a balm to her heart.

Xander was good at that, distracting them away from their sorrow. He was a bright light, the glimmer of a rainbow shining through the rain.

Bisma walked over to Luna and Mei, pulling both of them into a hug. 'I'm sorry,' she whispered. They both held her tight, and when they separated, both Mei and Luna gave Bisma a reassuring smile.

She turned to Xander, who held up a toffee. 'A sweet for my sweet?' he asked, giving her an inane smile.

Bisma gave him an incredulous look as Luna and Mei giggled behind her.

'Thank you,' she said through gritted teeth, approaching him to take it and discreetly kick his shin in the process. He yelped, which finally made her smile.

'I should have known it would be torturing me, and not sweets, that would bring you joy,' Xander grumbled, rubbing his leg.

Bisma smiled sweetly, popping the toffee into her mouth. 'It can be a combination of both.'

He shook his head, amused.

'Let's go home,' Bisma said, turning to the girls.

'Wait,' Xander said, touching her wrist. 'Before you go—what was Nori's story?'

'You want to know?' Mei asked, intrigued.

Xander nodded.

'Why?' Luna asked. She arched a suspicious brow. 'Morbid fascination?'

'No, just curious to know your stories,' he said with a shrug.

'He's asked after everyone's,' Bisma explained to the girls. Nori was the only one left. She obliged Xander, just as she had with the others. 'Nori was the youngest of eight children; she came to the Forest when she was three. She was lost and just wound up there one night, and the Forest accepted her after trying its best to scare her home.'

'Didn't her family wonder where she'd gone?' Xander asked.

'We met them in town once,' Bisma said. 'Nori said, "Oh, I used to live with them," and pointed them out. They saw her, too, but weren't interested. One of the older kids came over and said Nori was better off wherever she was, for their mother had recently run away, and most of the kids were scattering the first chance they got.'

Xander blinked. 'That's . . . something.'

'That it is,' Bisma said. She sighed. 'Well, I'd better get these girls home.'

'I'll go with you,' Xander said. He walked them to the Forest, then she, Luna, and Mei went the rest of the way home.

When they entered the treehouse, it was quiet . . . empty. Bisma hated it.

She went to her room, feeling restless. She drifted to her table, pulling out a piece of paper to write to her friend.

> I'm sorry I haven't written much lately, I've been so terribly busy. The hours in the day fly by and I don't know where they go. It feels like trying to capture light in my hands, but I cannot get a grasp no matter how I try.
>
> I don't know if I can do this, be what my sisters need. I feel as though I am failing constantly, and every time I pick myself up and think, yes, perhaps now I can stand, I last but a moment before I lose my footing and fall again.

After writing, Bisma went down for dinner, which the three of them ate in a strained silence, unsure of what to say. Everything felt strange. There was an uncanny energy in the air, coming from the Forest itself.

It would not leave even after they finished eating. Since Mei had done most of the cooking, she went up to her room while Bisma and Luna cleaned up.

'I saw Haru,' Bisma said. 'He said he misses you.'

Luna stopped washing the dishes, catching her breath.

'Lu, just talk to him,' Bisma said gently.

'I can't.' Luna's voice broke.

'Why?'

'I told you,' Luna whispered. 'I'm afraid.'

'You can't live your life in fear, darling,' Bisma said.

Luna just shook her head, sighing. She finished washing the dishes in silence, then left, leaving Bisma alone.

Bisma released a long breath, listening to it fill the empty house. She checked on the girls, then got ready to head back to Xander's greenhouse. It had been two weeks since they'd put Deeba to sleep, and they were so close now.

They just needed to keep at it.

At the greenhouse, Xander was already at work. He was as dedicated as she was—even more so. She didn't understand it.

'Why are you working so hard?' she asked, coming to stand beside him as he ground ginger into a paste. 'They're my sisters, but why would it matter to you?'

He looked at her as if she was daft. She didn't understand what she was missing that seemed so obvious to him.

'Because it's important,' he finally said.

'Why?'

'Why?' he repeated. He looked ready to tell her something. Her heartbeat quickened. 'Look at my notes.'

'What?' She didn't understand what that would prove. 'I asked *why*, not *if*.'

He ran a hand through his hair, seemingly agitated. 'Because—' But then he broke off, shaking his head. 'Don't worry about it, Bis. We have more important things to focus on. I added chives to the last attempt, but we're out of test trees. Can you grow me another?'

'Yes, just a moment,' she said, going over to where her sisters were sleeping. She wanted to check on them first, hoping it might give her heart some ease.

They were lying side-by-side: Azalea, Nori, Deeba. She hated to see them so frozen and still, quiet. They almost looked—

She touched each of their hearts to reassure herself, but the faint pulses weren't much consolation.

She was stroking Deeba's hair when she noticed Deeba's expression was . . . different. It was hardly perceptible, but Bisma could tell. There was a slight crease between Deeba's brows.

'Xander,' she called.

He walked over just as she lifted Deeba's sleeves, and her suspicion was confirmed. The poison had spread further.

'No,' she whispered. Panic seized her with its icy claws. She turned to Xander, her eyes wide.

He swore to himself.

'Bis, it's going to be okay,' he said, his voice sure. 'Don't worry. It's only moved a little bit.'

'What if it moves more?!' she cried.

'It won't, not that fast. Give me—give me a second.'

He rolled up both Deeba's sleeves, then ran back to grab one of his notebooks. He seemed to be tracking the spread of the poison since they had fed Deeba the freeze potion, calculating the speed. She saw him doing complicated math in his head, until he released a breath.

'We have two more weeks before it spreads to her heart,' he said. 'That's just a few days after the harvest festival.'

'Two weeks?' Her anxiety spiked. 'Can't we give her more of the freeze potion?'

'No,' he said. 'Giving her too much will stop her heart; each dose is a precise amount to keep the body still so the poison won't spread, as well as just alive enough so the heart can beat. Of course, it won't last forever, and will start to wear off. I should have thought of that, but I thought . . .'

They had two more weeks to find a cure.

Two more weeks, or Deeba would die.

22

Two weeks seemed like a lot of time, but days passed in the blink of an eye. Bisma had to keep up with her orders, for people were counting on her, and she continued working with Xander, but nothing they did seemed to be working.

Even the Enchanted Forest was upset. The fog around the perimeter had thinned, fruit was rotting, the lake was murky, creeks had run dry, and the animals were quiet.

Bisma tried to be cheery for Luna and Mei's sakes, but she was unbearably frightened. Paranoia was setting in as well; she felt at any moment, her remaining sisters would fall.

What was the end game? To eliminate them all? Why not get it over with?

But more likely, the goal was to make Bisma suffer. If Eleanora was getting revenge for losing her best friend, who was like a sister to her, it would make sense to make Bisma feel that same pain again and again and again.

Whenever Bisma felt herself spiraling, she thought of the last letter she had received, and found strength from the words.

> *I confess I have also been feeling that way as of late, as though I cannot get my footing. I am dealing with a problem that is proving difficult to solve, and I have never dealt with anything like it before. But for both our cases, I think we need to focus on the good, the little steps we are taking. We must hold onto hope, for it is hope that will carry us through.*
>
> *Don't give up, Bisma. I believe in you. I don't think there is any reality in which you will fail.*
>
> *Your friend*

Bisma hoped she would not fail, and, even as she worried, she refused to expose that worry to her sisters. Which was why she allowed Mei to do her hair every day.

'Who am I trying to impress?' Bisma asked, as Mei finished off a complicated braid.

'Mmm, no one,' Mei sing-songed, giggling. 'There.'

Bisma ran her hand over the braid, which was perfectly neat. She wrapped a string of motia around the braid, inhaling the scent of jasmine.

'I like Xander, by the way,' Mei said, tucking her silky hair behind her ear.

Bisma gave her a funny look. 'That's nice . . . And why exactly are you informing me of this?'

'No reason,' Mei said, smiling.

'I like him, as well,' Luna added from her position on the sofa, where she was reading a book.

Bisma furrowed her brows. 'It doesn't matter if you like him; we're only colleagues.'

'*Colleagues*, right . . . right . . .'

Bisma narrowed her eyes at Luna. 'Mei, love, why don't you go check on the chickens?' After Mei had gone, Bisma said to Luna, 'Speaking of boys you like, I don't think you should be ignoring Haru so vehemently.'

Luna looked up from her book to give Bisma a glare. 'Just drop it.'

'I'm not going to drop it,' Bisma said, getting up. She went to the sofa, plopping down on Luna's legs.

'Ow!' Luna cried, trying to kick Bisma off. 'Baji, get off!'

'No.' Bisma settled in on Luna's legs, reaching over to close Luna's book. 'Haru is such a sweet boy. Why are you living in fear? Put yourself out there!'

Bisma knew he wouldn't hurt Luna; every time she saw Haru, he asked after Luna. He was clearly sad to not hear from her, and if he did not genuinely care about her, he would have gotten over her by now.

Luna's mouth fell open. 'Oh, that's *rich* coming from you!'

Bisma flinched. 'What is that supposed to mean?'

'Xander is so great—he's so *kind*—but you don't trust him!'

Bisma bristled. 'That's different.'

Luna gave her a superior glance. 'Oh really? How?'

'It just is.'

Luna was wrong—Bisma *did* trust Xander, of course she did. Why else would she have gone to him for a cure and keep going to him? The problem was she did not trust *herself*. She had been wrong about Gregory, and she could be wrong about Xander, too.

But Luna saying that Xander was great did make Bisma feel a bit better. She trusted her sister's judgment, and knew Luna only wanted what was best for Bisma, just like Bisma only wanted what was best for her.

Bisma groaned, sinking back into the pillows.

'How about a deal?' Luna said, sitting up. 'If you let Xander in, I will let Haru in.'

Bisma narrowed her eyes. 'Since when were you so conniving?' Luna smiled. 'Fine. Deal. As long as you uphold it.'

'I will!' Luna said, though she looked daunted and fiddled with the ends of her braid.

'Good. Because I'm going to town, so you're coming with me.'

'Ah, wait! I need to get ready first!' Luna cried. She was immediately nervous.

Bisma smiled, getting off the sofa. 'Mei!' she called down the stairs. 'We need you to do Lulu's hair!'

'Yay!' Mei called back. She ran up the stairs, joining them, grinning with excitement. They went up to Luna's room, and as Mei did Luna's hair, twisting it up, Bisma pulled out Luna's favorite dress with matching stockings and shoes.

'Baji, pinch me,' Luna instructed, sitting down in front of her mirror.

Giving her sister a strange look, Bisma reached over and pinched Luna's arm.

'Ow!' Luna shrieked. 'I meant my cheeks! I need a rosy flush.'

'Oh.'

'Should I slap her?' Mei offered.

Luna gave her an arch look in the mirror's reflection. 'You focus on the hair, will you?'

Mei giggled, then Bisma pinched Luna's cheeks until they were suitably flushed as Mei finished her hair. As Luna got changed, Bisma got dressed as well, chatting with Mei and Luna from the top of the stairs.

It was nice, even with just the three of them; their home wasn't entirely empty.

When they were ready, Bisma and Luna left Mei in the Forest and went to town. Luna took measured breaths, but as they grew closer and closer to the bakery, Luna's steps slowed, until she stopped entirely.

'Oh no,' Luna whispered. 'My tummy hurts. Perhaps I should go back.'

'You're alright, Lu.' Bisma held her hand and squeezed.

Luna squeezed back, her brown eyes wide. 'I'm just so scared . . . If I don't want him, then it's my choice and I can live with that hurt. But if I reach for him and get rejected . . .'

Bisma released a breath. 'I know . . . trust me, I *know*. But you—*we*—need to be brave.'

Luna shuddered and then took a steadying breath. 'Yes. And we can be. We're Unwanted Girls! The villagers fear us!'

Bisma laughed, and Luna joined her.

'Go on,' Bisma said, nudging her forward.

Bisma stayed outside and watched as Luna entered the bakery. At first, Haru didn't notice; he was sitting forlornly with his chin in his palm, sighing as he stirred a bowl with his other hand. But then he did a double take, registering who was there before him, and he lit up. He was so happy to see her.

'Luna!' Bisma heard him cry. Without hesitation, he dropped what he was doing and went round the counter to greet her. Haru scooped her into his arms, hugging her. 'I missed you.'

He pulled back. There was a streak of flour on his face.

Luna lifted her hand, brushing it aside, and he held her hand to his cheek.

'I'm sorry I've been avoiding you,' she said.

'Come, sit, let's talk,' Haru said, holding her hand.

Bisma left them, then. She knew they would be alright.

Luna had upheld her end of the deal, now it was time for Bisma to uphold hers. The prospect was only slightly nauseating.

Bisma went to the greenhouse, where Xander was happy to see her. She noticed it now. He was always bright and energetic, but when she arrived, he grew even more so. She felt like a hissing stray cat, while he was more like one of those adorable puppies rich people carried around in their baskets.

As they got to work and the day carried on, Bisma allowed herself to notice Xander more—how kind and considerate he was toward her. When they were working together, he always gave her a bit of space, not being invasive, and he was always glancing up at her in case she needed something, anything.

Once she started noticing, she couldn't stop.

Had he always been like this? Had she truly never realized?

Bisma wanted to let him in, but it felt as though her heart was so tightly secured she could not reach it. It tried to break free from its restraints, but it was as if she had locked her heart away so long ago, that she no longer knew where the key was.

A part of her, too, was afraid that once her heart was set free, she would regret the mess it would make.

And yet—she still wanted to. She *wanted*.

She couldn't stop wanting; she didn't know how. It clung to her all day, like a film over her skin, heavy like a stone sitting in the pit of her stomach, demanding to be acknowledged, to have something done about it.

In the afternoon Xander brought in a tray of food from the main house for them: bread and a lentil stew, along with a pot of tea. They ate, discussing various theories for the cure, as well as talking about random, mundane things.

It was often like this, them talking about things she later could not remember precisely. All she could recall was how easy it was talking to him and listening to him talk. Comfortable and always interesting. She was never bored, not with him.

Today was no different. After they ate, Xander poured her a cup of tea, making it how she liked, and she supposed he had done so numerous times over the past two weeks—surely, she had poured him tea sometime in all these hours they spent working together—but today was the first time she really paid attention.

He knew just how much milk she took, just how much sugar. He had watched and noted and thought it worth *remembering*, storing this information until it could be useful to him, then applying it to make her this perfect cup of tea, which warmed her hands and soothed her parched throat and made her feel all types of cozy.

Luna was right. He was so *kind*.

It suddenly made her want to cry.

Her hands shook as she set down the teacup, and she quickly blinked away the tears filling her eyes. And he noticed—of course he noticed. He always did.

And that only made her eyes well up again.

'What is it?' he asked, worried. He was sitting across from her and scooted closer. 'Bis, what did I do?'

'I'm just not used to . . .' The words felt impossible to say, but she had to try. She had told Luna she would, and she wouldn't break a promise to one of her sisters, no matter how embarrassing it was. 'I'm not used to being taken care of like this.'

'What do you mean?' he asked, his voice gentle. He waited patiently for her to speak, giving her due time to collect her thoughts, to formulate them into something coherent.

She swallowed.

'A few years ago, I was involved with someone,' she said. There was that familiar pang, the shame. 'He didn't . . . care about me—he wasn't very nice, but I liked him so very much . . . I was young and foolish. And it's been years, but it still feels so jarring to be treated with kindness from someone who isn't family.'

'You deserve all the kindness in the world,' Xander said, as if this was a foregone conclusion. 'I'm sorry he made you doubt that—you didn't deserve to be treated the way you were. I hope you know that.'

'I know,' Bisma said, and a tear rolled down her cheek. She swiped it away angrily. 'That's what—that's what makes me so upset. I know I didn't deserve it, but I was a fool, and I accepted it anyway.'

She stood up for the village girls who needed poisons to fight their bullies, she fought against Luna's father and her sisters' abusers, but the first pretty boy who had given her any attention at all, she had fallen at his feet, she did whatever he said, and she was *thankful* for it, which was what disgusted her the most.

She truly thought he had liked her! But all he had liked was what she was giving him: all her affection, her energy, her time. Everything he wanted, exactly when he wanted it, how he wanted it.

She hated to remember that point in her life; it filled her with absolute horror.

'That's why when you're kind to me it's . . . unnerving,' she said, pushing forward. 'It feels like a gift I'm not meant to receive, which makes me feel as though you're trying to trick me, that you're only doing it for a certain reason, because you want something from me.'

She shook her head. 'Gregory was nice in the beginning,' she said, covering her face with her hands, 'but then once he got what he wanted from me, he changed, and I was a fool for clinging onto the memories of how he was instead of facing the reality in front of me.'

'You weren't a fool,' Xander said. 'Hey.' He pulled her hands away from her face, and she looked into his eyes. 'You were in love,' he continued. 'And this Gregory character is the real fool, for not cherishing the treasure that is your affection.'

Xander swallowed, edging closer.

'Bis,' he said, taking her hand in his. His skin was warm, soft. 'I really like you, and I think you like me, too. I understand that you're scared and hesitant—but I just want you to know that I am not like him. I would never treat you like that.'

At this he broke off, forcing himself to take measured breaths as he clenched his jaw. He was angry on her behalf, angry just at the thought of how she had been treated.

'As I was saying,' he continued after a moment. 'I genuinely like you, and I like spending time with you; it's why I agreed to help you find the cure in the first place, silly.'

'I thought it was because you said it was interesting from an academic viewpoint!' she said, positively shocked by this news.

'Yes, I mean, of course it is,' he said, flashing her a smile, 'but *you're* more interesting. From a Xander viewpoint.'

Her face got warm at that.

'See,' he said, running his knuckles against her cheek. 'Your face gets just slightly pink, hardly noticeable.'

'Then how do you notice?'

'I'm always paying attention when it comes to you, Bisma.'

She narrowed her eyes. She believed everything he was saying, she did, but old habits die hard. She couldn't help being prickly and untrusting, she just couldn't.

'I'm not being kind to trick you,' he said. 'Or to seduce you! I simply enjoy being nice to you.'

'Why? Particularly when I am not nice to you.'

'I don't know.' He shrugged. 'And I know you don't mean it, not really.'

'*How* do you know?'

'I just do . . . I know you.'

'How?'

He laughed. 'I pay attention.'

'Why do you pay attention?' She was being petulant, but she couldn't help it.

'Because you're . . . *you*. You're interesting and fascinating, and I like learning about you.'

'Hmm . . .'

He smiled, bumping her shoulder with his. 'I'm not like him,' he said in a more serious tone. 'Can you try to see that? If I was simply trying to find someone to seduce, I'm sure it would be much more efficient to approach any of the admirers you mentioned the other day.' He considered it. 'Actually, it would be much easier, really. You're incredibly difficult, did you know that?'

'Well, what if you're just trying to "tame" me, like all the village boys wish to do with Unwanted Girls?' she asked, scowling.

He laughed at that. 'Why would I want to *tame* you? I'm sorry, but that sounds thoroughly impossible. Besides, from what I recall, I've already given you full leave to bite me whenever you want.'

His eyes warmed with heat.

She chewed on her bottom lip. 'Hmm.'

He was right.

He was an incorrigible flirt, but he wasn't aggressive. Gregory had tried to kiss Bisma the second time they went out together, but in all this time, Xander had not made any attempts—even when she had wanted him to. And whenever Xander touched her, it was always gentle, not presumptuous.

So she could no longer be afraid; she had promised Luna, after all.

She sighed. 'FINE.'

'"Fine" what?' He knit his brows.

'Take me out for dinner.'

He was startled. 'Bisma, that wasn't what I was trying to—'

'Xander, why are you arguing with me?'

He geared up with a response, then paused. He blinked. 'You're absolutely right, why *am* I arguing with you?' He shot to his feet. 'Be ready at seven!'

Before she knew what he was doing, he quickly kissed her cheek. A tingle went down her spine; she touched a cold hand to her warm cheek, as if to capture the kiss.

'Wait!' she cried, realizing that he was leaving. 'Where are you going?'

'I have a beauty routine I must get to!' he called back, not bothering to turn. 'I have a date and must look my absolute best!'

She laughed, feeling giddy. But she was frightened, too.

She didn't want to ruin this, whatever it was.

23

Bisma returned home to get dressed and arrived shortly after Luna.

'How was it?' Bisma asked Luna, who was in the kitchen with Mei. They were making hot chocolate, and their home was thick with the sweet smell.

Luna giggled at Bisma, which adequately answered Bisma's question.

Bisma squealed.

'How was it for you?' Luna asked.

Bisma smiled.

Now it was Luna's turn to squeal.

Mei giggled, looking between the pair of them, the three sisters positively giddy.

'I need a complete and total debrief,' Luna said, pouring hot chocolate into three mismatched mugs. Mei topped them with whipped cream, while Bisma reached for the jar of marshmallows.

'You first,' Bisma said.

The three of them grabbed their mugs and sat down on the sofa, Mei between Luna and Bisma, all their legs pulled up and over one another. With a pang, Bisma wished all her sisters were present, but she was thankful these two were at least.

As if having the same thought, Mei said, 'Azalea will be so jealous to be missing the gossip.' Her tone was teasing yet sad.

'Nori would be jealous to be missing the chocolate,' Luna added.

'And Deebs would just want cuddles,' Bisma said, reaching for both her sisters' hands.

They all sighed.

Luna cleared her throat. 'Baji, you were right,' Luna said. 'I wasn't giving Haru enough credit—he is wonderful. Just . . . wonderful.'

'Aw, Lulu,' Bisma said. 'Details, please. I need all of them.'

And so Luna recounted every word she and Haru had shared, along with every expression, and about five interpretations for various key moments throughout the encounter. By the time she was finished, their mugs were long empty.

'Now tell me all about Xander!' Luna ordered.

'We talked and . . . we're going out for dinner tonight,' she said, hiding her face as Luna and Mei squealed.

'When?' Luna asked.

'At seven.'

'WHAT?' Mei cried. 'That's in an hour! We need to get you ready!'

They rushed Bisma up to her room, where Luna pulled out dresses and ribbons as Mei did Bisma's hair. As Bisma got ready, she felt a little guilty; should she be going at all? When her sisters were sick?

But taking a break would help her think better, and an hour or two wouldn't be the end of the world. The freeze potion was holding up, even if the poison was slowly spreading. Bisma watched it every day, tracking its movement.

When she was ready, Mei and Luna walked her down the stairs of the treehouse—giggling profusely—from where she kissed them goodbye before walking to the end of the Forest on her own. She passed through the thinning fog to find Xander waiting for her.

He looked unbearably handsome, dressed smartly in a charcoal gray suit that complemented every line of his body. When he saw her approaching, he broke into a dazzling smile, which he tried to bite back but couldn't—he was giddy, and the sight made her giddy as well.

'Well met, Bis,' Xander said, handing her a bouquet of lilacs that matched the light purple embroidery on her plum-purple dress.

'Hi,' she said, pressing the flowers to her nose.

He looked over her shoulders. 'Your sisters aren't with you? I was hoping to meet them properly.'

'Oh . . . um, no,' she replied.

'I'm still not allowed to meet them?'

'You have met some of them,' she said. 'You get to meet them every day!'

He gave her a dark look. 'Them being poisoned and asleep in my greenhouse does not count, Bisma.'

She knew it didn't, but she was still hesitant to introduce him to her sisters.

'I'll wear you down someday,' he said, bouncing back with a smile. 'Now, shall we go?'

He offered her his arm, which she took, the fabric of his jacket soft under her hand. Warmth radiated from him, and she found herself drawing closer. With her other hand, she held the lilacs, the sweet smell drifting to her nose every now and then.

They walked to town, and she tried to mask her anxiety and excitement by looking at anything other than him: the trees, which were nearly bare of leaves now; the buildings, which were mostly closed for the night; the well, the waters of which were strangely murky.

'Right this way,' Xander said, as they arrived at their destination. He held the door open for her.

She should have figured he would bring her here. It was the only tavern in town and was frequented by most villagers, which was why when they entered, it was entirely packed.

The sight of so many villagers made her immediately don her harshest scowl and nastiest glare. Her heart beat fast, and she tensed, on guard.

When Xander entered behind her, Bisma felt everyone turn to look, a gasp going through the crowd. More than a few people looked at the bouquet of flowers in her hands, then turned to whisper to one another. She bit the inside of her cheek.

She was so used to being alone with Xander in the greenhouse that she didn't realize how this would feel, for everyone to see *her* with the town's precious golden boy. Embarrassed for some reason, she felt like she did not belong, that she had somehow tricked Xander into bringing her here.

Then a worse thought came: did they all think it was like how it was with Gregory? That she was being . . . conquered?

She swore she heard someone snickering.

Bisma turned back to look at Xander, who seemed to be enjoying the attention. He put a hand on her back, a self-satisfied smile on his face.

She bristled at the sight. Without another word, she pushed past him and stormed out.

'Bis, what's wrong?' he cried, following her. He sounded confused, but really, he could not be so thick.

She threw the flowers on the ground.

'Where are you going?' He jogged up to catch her, grabbing her arm. 'Bisma.'

'Why did you bring me here?' Her voice broke.

'Um, it's the only decent place to eat,' he said. 'I thought you'd be more comfortable there than at a formal dinner with my parents.'

'No, that's not why.' She shook her head. 'You wanted them to see me with you.'

He blinked. 'Well . . . yeah.'

She let out a scoff. He wasn't even ashamed!

'I knew this was a bad idea,' she said, her voice hardening. 'I'm going home. Don't follow me.'

'Bis, wait!'

She whirled on him. 'Why?'

'Of course I wanted people to see you with me—look at you.'

'Now you're being cruel.' Unbearably, her eyes welled with tears. 'I know what I am. I'm the monster in the wood, the Unwanted Witch. I *know* what I am.'

'No, I don't think you do.' He stepped closer. 'Look at you! You're stunning. Fit to be worshipped.'

Those words stopped her in her tracks. They sounded familiar, but she couldn't recall why. Her cheeks warmed.

'I wanted everyone to see you were with me so they could witness my good fortune,' he said, face gentle. 'I wanted them all to be jealous—you're the prettiest girl in town.'

She rolled her eyes. 'You are so full of shit.'

His mouth fell open as if he couldn't believe she thought he was lying.

'Bisma, I am being deathly serious,' he said, his eyes vividly green. 'You're . . . breathtaking. As in you literally take my breath away every single time I look at you, worse when you look at me. It's better than magic, that gaze of yours.'

She didn't believe him, how could she? Xander couldn't mean all those words, not about her anyway. She crossed her arms, scowling.

He let out a frustrated sound. 'I don't understand why you're upset,' he said.

'Of course you don't!' she snapped.

He flinched. 'I'm not *him*. Please don't punish me for what he did,' he said, sounding angry.

This time she was the one who flinched.

Then something changed in his expression. His face softened as if he realized something. 'Don't punish yourself, either, Bis,' he said.

She shook her head, hearing but not truly understanding what he was saying. She wouldn't look at him.

'It is not your fault you loved an idiot who did not deserve even a fraction of your affection,' he said.

But it *was* her fault. It was completely, entirely her own fault.

'Let me let you down,' Xander implored.

'What?' She brought her gaze back to him.

He sucked in a breath. 'Disappointment is inevitable,' he said. 'I can't promise that I'll never upset you. But allow me to make amends, allow me to improve, allow me to be better. Let me let you down, if only so I can pick you up again. Please, Bis. Just give me a chance.'

His voice was a whisper on those last words, as though he was praying.

She bit her bottom lip, thinking about it, even though she didn't want to think; she just wanted to say yes and yes and yes to everything he ever said, ever asked of her.

But she didn't trust herself enough for that yet. So she thought. And thought. And thought again.

'Alright,' she finally said, releasing a long breath.

A smile broke out across his face. He held a hand to his heart. 'Phew.' Catching his breath, he fanned himself.

She rolled her eyes; the dramatics never ceased with this one.

Tilting her head back, she looked up at the stars. It was a bit cloudy, but she could still see a few between the clouds, shining bright.

Xander tipped his head back to look as well, and she took the opportunity to look at him unobserved: the long column of his pale throat, the sharp line of his jaw, the tilt of his mouth. His bright eyes.

Fondness crept into her heart, spreading across her chest. She was overwhelmed by the urge to hold his face in her hands, to look at him, to just look.

'I'm sorry,' she said.

His brows knit. 'For what?'

'For storming out like that.' Her gaze went to the lilacs on the ground. 'And for throwing away your flowers.'

'Don't worry, silly. I'm a garden-witch, remember?' he said, stepping toward her. 'I'll grow you new flowers—I'll grow you flowers forever.'

'And thank you,' she whispered. He brought his gaze to hers, and a current ran through her. 'For what you said.' She swallowed. 'For thinking I'm pretty.'

'Pretty is an understatement,' he said, taking a step closer.

Her breath hitched.

He ran his knuckles down her cheek, and she leaned into his touch. 'That's like calling the stars pretty.'

His hand opened, his thumb rubbing against her jaw as he cupped her face in his hand. He stepped closer, his voice lowering, and she felt the heat of his skin filling the space around her, banishing the cold night. She wanted to tuck herself into him, to wrap herself in him so tight she could never be extricated.

'"Ethereal" is a bit more accurate,' he whispered.

His gaze went to her mouth, and he released a slow sigh. Her body pulsed in anticipation as they grew nearer, cheeks almost touching. They were breathing the same air now, lips mere inches apart.

All it would take was one step . . . just one—

'Baji!'

Bisma whirled to see Luna. Her stomach lurched.

'What is it?' Bisma ran to her sister.

'It's happened again,' Luna said, catching her breath. 'Why does this keep happening? Why won't it stop!'

Bisma grabbed Luna by the shoulders. 'Luna, what's happened again?'

'Mei,' she sobbed. 'She's been poisoned again.'

24

*L*una had given Mei the freeze potion, so she was alright, but it meant that there was no time to mentally unpack the brief evening she'd had with Xander.

They went to his greenhouse, straight to work, and Bisma hoped Luna would stay safe. With Mei poisoned, Luna was the only one left other than Bisma.

But then, a day after Mei was poisoned, while Bisma was away, Luna drank the freeze potion, leaving behind a note.

I'm sorry, Baji, but it feels inevitable that I will be poisoned again next, and I can't live with the fear. I thought I would get ahead of it and take a nice long nap. The house is terribly boring, anyway. I know you'll find the cure. I'll see you soon.

Kisses,
Luna

A WITCH'S GUIDE TO LOVE AND POISON 237

So Bisma was the only one left in the Enchanted Forest, which made her feel utterly alone and afraid. The treehouse was cold and empty, and the next morning, she did not want to get out of bed.

But she needed to keep working; there was less than a week left, now. The harvest festival was in a few days, and the poison would reach Deeba's heart two days after that. She kept at it all day, which at least kept her away from her silent home, kept her away from her thoughts. She worked herself to exhaustion, hoping that the moment she returned home, she would be able to sleep.

And yet she could not get any rest.

> I cannot sleep, not without my sisters here. Our home always seemed to be cramped—in a cozy way but tight nonetheless. We never had any concept of personal space; we were always sitting with our elbows and knees touching round the table, or on top of each other on the sofas, or huddled beneath the same blankets. I rarely got through a meal without one of my sisters snagging a bite from my plate or even directly from my hand. I used to think it would be nice if we all weren't so close all the time, but I realize now that things were just right.
>
> I miss everyone desperately. I feel so utterly alone, more alone than I have ever felt before. That was not real loneliness, I can see that now, not when I compare it to this. This is a living thing, and I fear it will eat me whole. It makes me afraid, and I have never felt afraid in the Enchanted Forest before, which only makes it worse.
>
> My home no longer feels like home.

She wrote to her friend, hoping that might ease her heart, but it did not help much. The Forest seemed as upset and lonely as her; everything felt strange and wrong, not the way it was meant to be. There was an absence of noise; the trees were still, and even the birds and forest critters were quiet.

She spent all night twisting and turning in bed, until exhaustion took over and she slept for two hours before dawn arrived and she woke again. Even then, it seemed all the color was gone from her world.

All day the fatigue scratched at her, wearing her down. She was so tired she could hardly see straight. She wanted to cry—no, what she really wanted was to sleep.

But even that night she couldn't.

Finally, she gave up, lighting a candle, and that was when she noticed she had received a letter.

It is not strange that your home no longer feels so without your family. What is a home without its inhabitants? But do not think of yourself as entirely alone, I implore you.

You are not as alone as you think.

Your friend

He was right; she was not entirely alone. Which was why she got out of bed and descended the stairs of the treehouse, letting her feet carry her along the familiar path until she had left the Enchanted Forest, going to the one place that might feel like home.

'Bis, is everything okay?' Xander asked, worried. It was late, later than they had ever worked. The candles in the greenhouse were blown out, there was just the one in Xander's hand now as he held it up between them.

He looked as though he'd been asleep; his hair was messy, his shirt hastily pulled on, open at the neck.

She didn't know what to say, so she said nothing. As if understanding, Xander stepped aside from the doorway, letting her enter. Like a ghost haunting her family, she floated to where her five sisters lay.

They were all sleeping peacefully behind a wall of sheets, closed off. She checked each of their heartbeats, feeling them beat in tandem with her own. Xander trailed after her, saying nothing, just patiently holding up the candle so she would have light.

When she was done, she left that section of the greenhouse, pulling the curtain behind her.

'Bisma, is everything okay?' Xander asked, a hand on her arm.

She turned to face him, looking into his eyes. Moonlight streamed into the greenhouse, shafts of white light illuminating his face.

'I didn't know where else to go,' she whispered. 'The Enchanted Forest doesn't feel like home anymore.'

He set the candle down, then pulled her into his arms. She didn't hesitate; she hugged him back, bringing her hands up against his shoulder blades. His skin was deliciously warm. She inhaled the sweet and spicy scent of cloves.

Placing her cheek against his chest, she listened to his heartbeat, the sound like the steady fall of rain, just as comforting and sure.

Xander pulled back. He cupped her face in his hands, tilting her head so he could look into her eyes. He scanned her face. 'Feeling a little better now?'

'Yes,' she breathed. She had immediately felt better once she saw him, like he was the cure to chase the poison from her veins. 'I'm just so tired.'

'Come,' he said, leading her to sit down. Her shawl slipped from her shoulders, but he reached out and caught it, adjusting it, his fingers warm on her skin. He sat beside her, their knees bumping against each other.

'I never asked,' he said, 'but what's your story? I know all the others' now.'

Bisma hadn't spoken about it in a number of years, but she found she wanted to tell Xander about it now. She wanted him to know everything about her, every single tiny little thing. She wouldn't mind being dissected by him.

'I came to the Enchanted Forest when I was three,' she said, 'but I didn't learn my story until years later, when I began looking into it. Before then, what I understood was this: I never knew my father. All I knew of him was that he was the source of all our problems, my mother's and mine. He had left us destitute, for we never had food, or money, or clothes, or warmth, or anything, really. My mother left one day when I was three and didn't return, so then I didn't have her, either.

'I don't remember much from that time, just that I waited for her for days, weeks maybe. I remember the hunger and a fear I'd never felt before—I was so afraid. The hunger eventually got so bad that I went in search of food and saw a crop of carrots in someone's backyard garden. Well, I stuck my hands in the soil to steal one, and when I did, I felt this strange pull.'

A smile played on Xander's face. 'Magic.'

'Precisely. I followed it and ended up in the Enchanted Forest. It wasn't scary, like it was for the other girls. The Forest didn't frighten me at all. I was just following the magic, and it led me there. I passed through the fog, and, once I did, I felt safe, at home.'

The memory warmed her, then brought a harsh pain to her chest as she thought of the stark difference between then and now. Tears pricked her eyes, and she blinked against them.

'The Enchanted Forest doesn't feel like home anymore, not when it's so empty,' she said.

'Did you ever find out what happened to your parents?' Xander asked.

'My mother was hanged,' she said. 'My father had apparently drunk himself into an early grave, leaving my mother and me penniless. She turned to crime for cash: theft, prostitution, and a long list of other crimes. Apparently, it was well known she was bad news, but she was never directly caught—well, until she was. It was only a matter of time, really.'

'What was the final crime?'

'She killed someone,' Bisma said. 'Apparently she had stolen a lady's purse and when she was caught, she tried to fight her way out with a knife and ended up killing the lady, who was rich and important enough for the authorities to have my mother hanged for it.'

'God,' Xander breathed.

'It's why . . . well, it's why I can't be good, no matter how I try. I'm just like my parents; I have their blood in my veins after all. My mother didn't mean to kill the lady; all accounts said it was never her intention. But what could she do? It's why I don't mind making poisons, being the monster. Someone has to do it.

'Even my sisters—they all have their demons to battle, and I don't have any of my own, so I want to fight theirs for them. It feels like I owe them somehow, for coming to the Enchanted Forest so easily. Not everyone survives the Forest, you know; it chooses who to keep.'

She stopped. 'I don't know why I'm going on and on,' she said, sighing. She didn't want him to say anything, though she could tell there was a lot he wished to say. 'I'm tired. I should go.'

She stood, but he squeezed her hand as she was about to leave.

'Don't go,' he said. 'Your home is here, too.'

He gestured to where her sisters lay asleep on their cots, but she felt the deeper meaning in his words as he pulled her closer to him.

'Please stay,' he whispered, looking up at her.

She yearned to, desperately, and she couldn't think of a reason why not. She reached for his face, and he closed his eyes, leaning into the touch.

'Alright,' she whispered. Her gaze went to his rumpled bed, where he had been sleeping not long ago.

'I'll go into the main house,' he said, swallowing. His eyes were dark. 'You sleep here.'

This time, it was Bisma who grabbed his hand as he made to leave.

'No,' she said, voice quiet. 'Stay.'

His eyelids fluttered.

They went to his bed, slipping in on opposite sides but facing one another.

She stared at him, feeling unsure.

'Close your eyes,' he whispered, touching her cheek.

She did.

Finally, Bisma slept.

The next morning, she woke with her limbs entwined with Xander's.

She lay on his chest with his arm around her, gently rooting her in place. He did not lock her there; if she wished, she could slide out, but she didn't want to. She watched him breathe, so comfortable that a sense of peace enveloped over her.

In these quiet moments at dawn, she could almost believe this was all a dream.

She looked at his throat, his jaw, the cut of his cheekbones, the fall of his hair. His copper locks were messy, and she wanted to reach out and smooth them. That blasted hair of his—she always wanted to run her hands through it.

But she didn't want to move her hand from where it was resting against his chest, in the empty space of his open shirt. Her fingers were directly on his bare skin, which was warm, and she could feel his heart beating just beneath her palm, so steady and sure.

She loved the feel of it. If she closed her palm into a fist, could she capture his heartbeat forever? It sounded like the melody of magic, the energy that pulsed through the earth when she grew plants.

Bisma watched him for some time, tenderness overcoming her with such a force that she ached. But it was a lovely ache, the kind that came after a day of hard work that had yielded immeasurable success.

She looked at him with such fondness, such peace, that she fell asleep once more.

25

A few hours later, when she woke again, she and Xander were facing one another, the way two sunflowers face each other on a cloudy day. Sunlight slanted in over them, illuminating the rumpled sheets and blankets in rectangles of light. When Bisma opened her eyes, she found he was already awake, looking at her with an expression so soft that it made her feel shy.

They were in bed together after all, even if all they had done was sleep.

She buried her nose in her pillow. 'Don't stare.'

'How can I not?' he asked, tucking a tendril of dark hair behind her ear, exposing her cheek. She looked back at him; his green eyes were bright.

They looked at each other for a while, cocooned in an emotion she could not name, but whether mere moments passed or hours, she could not tell.

'Thank you,' Xander said, breaking the silence.

'For what? I should be thanking you for letting me stay.'

'Thank you for asking me,' he said. 'Nobody ever asks anything of me.'

'That bothers you?'

He nodded slightly, as if shy himself.

She gave him her fullest attention. 'Tell me why.'

He smiled at that. 'Always bossy,' he said. 'Well, it's just that my life is . . . perfect, so perfect I feel utterly useless at times. I want to do something with my life, to help people—the way you do. I've seen you with your sisters; it's extraordinary. They need you. No one ever needs me . . . or depends on me, or trusts me.' He swallowed. 'So you needing me is nice because then at least I can be useful to you.'

'You like being needed?'

'Yes,' he breathed. 'Especially if it's you. I'll feel like I've done something with my life even if it's solely you that I can be useful to.'

'Oh.' She had never thought that could be a possibility. And she couldn't help but think of Gregory who had wanted her to never be needy and to just be content with whatever he was giving—in fact, requiring her to put up with *him* being needy. And now here was Xander, who rather than feeling burdened by, it was outright pleased.

It was hard for her to ask for help, but he made it so easy. He was always there for her.

Perhaps needing people wasn't such a bad thing; perhaps it could even be . . . good.

She missed being needed by her sisters now that they were all asleep. She had never seen them as a burden—yes, it was difficult being Baji, but she loved them, and she loved showing that love through acts of service and care. So why not allow others the opportunity to do the same for her?

She'd always thought she didn't need it, but everyone needed someone.

And she needed Xander; she could admit that now. Not only needed but wanted.

She was overwhelmed with the urge to kiss him but held back for it was quite a frightening feeling. It wasn't just physical desire, lust that could flare and eventually burn out—it was a feeling deep in her core, a flame that if stoked would keep her warm and never die out.

So instead she smiled at him. 'What I *need* now is some breakfast.'

He smiled back. 'Of course, darling Bisma. What will you have?'

'Hmm.' She pretended to think. 'A dozen eggs, a loaf of bread, exorbitant amounts of raspberry jam, and a pot of your very best tea. Please.' She added the last word as an afterthought.

'Only because you asked so sweetly.' He tapped her nose, then got up, stretching. She was about to get up as well but stopped to languidly watch the muscles in his back and shoulders shift.

He was so . . .

There were no adequate words.

He disappeared to the main house to get breakfast, and she freshened up, checking on her sisters. She whispered a secret to each of them, smiling to herself as she shared the impossible news, even though they were not conscious to hear it.

Just saying the words aloud made her heart pound.

Xander returned in a fresh outfit with his hair tidied and a large tray of breakfast. They ate together, and he was so lovely and kind and caring and sweet, she wondered how she had ever thought of him as anything else.

After eating, they got straight to work, just as they had all those days before, and steadily kept up at it until halfway through the day, when Xander realized they needed more empty bottles for their sample potions.

Bisma accompanied him to town, needing a break. Like the night they went for dinner together, she was aware of people watching, but this time, instead of worrying that Xander was flaunting her, she was more concerned about how out of place she felt.

Bisma was so used to spending time alone with him in the greenhouse, away from watchful eyes, that she felt exposed to be walking across the square with him. She wanted to hide in his shadow, but Xander matched his steps to hers, never leaving her side.

She was no longer worried people would laugh, but that they would judge her, or, worse, feel sorry for Xander. She could see it on their faces; they were wondering what he was doing with her. The Unwanted Witch with the town's golden boy. They didn't fit together. He was as bright as sunshine, and she was dark as midnight rain.

'You go in,' Bisma said, when they arrived at the pottery store that sold the glass bottles they needed.

'I'll just be a sec,' Xander said.

After he left, she sighed. She did not know what to do. She didn't know what was right or best in this moment that would determine her future. If she pushed Xander away—to protect herself—would she regret it? Or if she allowed him in, opening herself up to heartbreak, would she regret *that*?

Bisma was so lost in thought that she did not see Xander exiting the shop, just as an angry woman was approaching Bisma.

In slow motion, she saw the woman upend a vial of liquid into the air; she smelled the sharp scent of acid.

All Bisma could do was brace for the attack.

But it never came.

'Xander!' she cried, horrified.

Her heart dropped as she took in his injury. He had blocked the attack. His skin hissed from the acid, and he groaned with pain. The woman ran off, but Bisma didn't have time to chase after her. She held Xander up. He was shaking.

'Come on,' she said, half carrying him. She didn't think—if she was thinking clearly, she might have led him to the greenhouse, which was closer—but her brain wasn't working. Her feet moved on their own accord, leading her to the Enchanted Forest.

She could fix this; she knew she could.

'Just hold on,' she said.

Xander was gripping her tightly, and she didn't stop to assess the damage—it would only slow her down, and she needed to get him to the Forest as fast as she could so she could heal him.

When they got to the border of the Enchanted Forest, a foreboding wind whistled. The Forest was not happy at the prospect of a stranger entering.

'Please!' Bisma cried. 'I need to heal him!'

The wind calmed, the Forest acquiescing to her request. Holding Xander up, she walked into the Forest. The fog was thin, hardly there, and provided no resistance.

'Help me,' Bisma said.

The Forest was slow to react—she wondered if it was discontentment or something else—but then finally a branch reached out from a tree, carrying half Xander's weight as she brought him to her treehouse. There, the branches carried him all the way up to her room as she caught her breath. Xander groaned, and her heart squeezed.

This was all her fault. Tears blurred her eyes as she ran to her garden. Without thinking, she stuck her hands into the soil, letting her magic take over. The Forest was lacking its usual power, so her magic did not flow so freely. The connection felt weak, but she couldn't think about that now. She pushed her magic, and a surge of energy poured from her hands.

Something like an aloe vera plant sprouted from the ground. It was what she needed; she knew it. She plucked the thick leaves and ran up the stairs, grabbing a knife from the kitchen then heading straight for her room.

Xander was lying on her bed, the skin of his cheek, neck, and chest an angry red. His waistcoat and shirt had burned through in the attacked area, and the skin beneath was blistered.

'Bis,' he said, lifting his hand to reach for her.

'I'm here.' She squeezed his hand. 'I'm going to take this off,' she explained, using her knife to cut off his waistcoat, then doing the same with his shirt, discarding both.

'Not quite how I imagined you undressing me playing out,' he said, gasping with pain yet still attempting levity.

She wasn't amused in the slightest.

'Shut up,' she said, her voice stern.

He nodded. 'Right away.'

Once he was disposed of his shirt, Bisma cut open the plant she had grown. Inside the leaves was a slippery, clear jelly threaded through with marigold-orange lines. She sliced out the jelly, warming it in her hands with magic until it became a thin gel.

Xander closed his eyes, nodding. His hair was matted with sweat, his throat working hard as he swallowed. He was trembling.

'This will heal you,' Bisma said, applying it to his cheek first. Her voice broke on the words, but it seemed to be working; his skin immediately cooled, the blisters withering away.

'Mmm,' Xander said. 'That feels better.'

Bisma continued spreading the gel, working her way carefully across his skin, making sure to get every affected inch. As she moved down to his neck, he stopped shaking, and by the time she reached his chest, he was breathing deeply, asleep.

Only when Bisma had finished applying the salve did she stop to catch her breath. Her hands were quaking, and she closed them into fists. She couldn't tear her eyes away from Xander.

He was fast asleep now, shirtless in her bed. Standing, Bisma pulled a blanket over him, tucking it under his body. He didn't even stir.

That was normal; she knew that. He needed rest to properly heal, but, even so, she couldn't help the hot tears that filled her eyes and fell down her cheeks, as she looked at his still form.

The attack had been meant for *her*. Why had he stepped in front of her? Why had he risked himself? She was so angry with him!

But deep down she knew she was really angry with herself. Every time she felt she had moved forward with him, something threw her off course, again.

She had been so concerned about what people would think of Xander having her by his side that she hadn't even paused to consider the danger he was opening himself up to by associating with *her*.

26

Xander slept for the rest of the day. She knew the potion was doing its work, but, even so, she couldn't bring herself to leave his side. Which was why she was there when he woke later that evening. He stirred, blinking slowly.

'Oh thank goodness,' she breathed.

'G'morning,' he said sluggishly.

'It's evening,' she told him.

'Ah, no wonder it's so dark.' He tried sitting up, then groaned.

'Do you remember what happened?' she asked, lifting the pillow for him to lean against. As he got comfortable, he thought about it—then his eyes widened.

'Oh god, yes,' he said. His gaze trained on her. 'Bis, are you alright? You didn't get hurt, did you?' He scanned her face, her hands, searching for signs of injury, and a lump formed in her throat.

'I'm fine, nothing happened to me,' she managed to say.

He released a breath. 'Good.' He seemed perfectly alright, then, while she was still left feeling frayed, even more uneven than when he had been asleep. Wasn't he angry with her? It was her fault, after all.

But he seemed preoccupied, taking in his surroundings. He realized he was in her room, slowly perusing every inch to his satisfaction before turning back to Bisma with a small smile.

'Of course it takes me being terribly injured for you to finally bring me to your home,' he said.

Bisma surprised them both by promptly bursting into tears. She hardly saw the shock on his face before she covered her own with her hands.

'Bis, I'm sorry!' he said. 'I was only joking.' His hands came over hers, gently prying them away from her face. 'Look, I'm fine! I promise. I'm alright.'

He *was* alright, but, even so, she sniffled, taking her hands out of his to wipe at her cheeks.

'I'll be back,' she squeaked, and before he could protest, she ran down the stairs. She went to the kitchen, stopping at the basin to run cold water over her hands.

With a deep breath, she looked about to find him something to eat. He must be hungry, and his body would need fortification.

There wasn't much food, but there were shaami kebabs, the tender patties made of beef and yellow split peas with onions and spices. She fried him a few, then made a pot of chai with extra cardamom. Busying herself with cooking relaxed her a little, until she began to think of all that had transpired between her and Xander these past few days.

Her heart hurt to think of him, in ways that were both good and bad.

She wished Luna was here so she might ask her advice; maybe all those poetry books she read would give her some insight. Or even Azalea, who would roll her eyes and make a snarky remark, or the little ones, who would giggle—any of them, really, she would talk to any of them. She missed them all with a pain that felt heavy.

Worse than that, she felt guilty. Xander had been hurt because of her. What if he wanted nothing to do with her after today? She didn't want to lose him, but didn't that make her selfish?

He was so good and kind and optimistic and bright, and she was so dark and twisted and messed up—how could someone like him ever love someone like her? The town's golden boy with the most unwanted of Unwanted Girls.

It was almost comical.

When she returned upstairs with the tray of food, Xander was looking around her room again from his position on her bed. Bisma found she didn't mind at all. She wanted him to see.

Setting the tray across his lap, she inspected the skin of his face, neck, and throat, glad to see that the gel she had applied was being absorbed into his skin, gradually returning it to its previously smooth and unscathed state.

'You didn't have to bring me food,' he said, his voice quiet as he regarded her.

She didn't say anything, but perched on the bed beside his legs.

She wanted to take care of him, and it was the least she could do after all he had done for her. Nibbling on her lower lip, she poured him a cup of tea, adding a spoon and a half of sugar, then offered it to him. She knew how he liked his tea, as well.

'Mmm, thank you,' he said, taking a sip.

She was quiet and he noticed. It was like he could read her energy and see there was something upsetting her.

'What is it?' he asked.

'Nothing.'

He gave her a look. 'Bisma.'

She looked at him closely. 'Well . . . you aren't . . . angry?' she asked. 'It's my fault you got hurt.'

'Oh, that.' He waved a hand, taking a sip of tea. 'Is that why you're brooding? You should have said sooner. I would have told you how preposterous the notion is. And anyway, you're the one who brought me into your home, healed me, and are now feeding me, so really I am in your debt.'

'Oh.' Apparently, she no longer had a grasp on language and could say nothing clever beyond *oh*. He was just so sweet, it made her want to cry. She needed to stop feeling the urge to cry every time he was nice to her; it really was not a sustainable way to live with the way he carried on!

'Then that's settled?' he asked.

She nodded.

'Good. Now eat with me, I'm sure you haven't eaten all day, and this is too much food for me.'

So she ate with him, until she saw that he looked tired again. She took the tray back downstairs, then rummaged around the kitchen for a pain relief potion she had on hand for any of the girls who might need it. She found it at the back of a cabinet and brought it up.

'For the pain,' she said, handing it to him. 'You ought to rest some more.'

'Thank you,' he said, tipping the liquid into his mouth.

She helped him get comfortable, and soon after realized why this particular potion was hidden so far back: it made one temporarily lose their senses.

Which was why Xander looked up at her with a foolish expression on his face, blinking slowly.

He reached for her hand, pulling her closer.

'Darling Bisma,' he said, hand in her hair. 'I wish you didn't hate me, not when I adore you so.'

'Shh,' she said, heart hammering. 'You don't know what you're saying.'

'You're right,' he said, his voice sleepy. His eyes were closing. 'I don't simply adore you, I—'

But he fell asleep before the end of the sentence, and Bisma could not tell if she was relieved or disappointed.

27

There were two days left to find the cure.

Bisma and Xander worked ceaselessly; there was no time to stop and ponder the very complicated emotions she felt for him. He did not bring it up either, and she considered that perhaps he had forgotten about what had transpired.

But then, Xander surprised her, like he always did.

'Will you go to the festival dance with me this evening?' he asked.

She blinked. They were in the greenhouse, and he was at a table behind her, mixing a potion. Pulling her hands from the pot she was growing white willow in, she turned.

'What?' she asked, convinced she had misheard him.

He walked around to her table, coming to stand next to her. He took her hand gently in his.

'Darling Bisma, will you go to the festival dance with me?' he repeated, smiling that charming smile of his. His green eyes sparkled. 'I know there isn't much time left for the cure, but a break will help us get refreshed. Anyway, sugar helps stimulate the mind. We learned all about it in school, no, really.'

'You wish to go *with* . . . me?'

He looked at her as if she was positively obtuse. 'Yes,' he said, furrowing his brows. 'That's why I'm asking you.'

'Oh.'

'Besides,' he added, stepping closer. He tucked a tendril of hair behind her ear, his finger running over the curl. 'I want to pick up where we left off the other night.'

His gaze went to her mouth, and she recalled nearly kissing him. Her cheeks felt warm. For a moment, she thought he might kiss her right then, and she stepped closer.

But he only kissed her cheek, sending a tingle down her spine.

'OK,' she squeaked. 'I'll go to the dance with you.'

There was a skip in his step as they continued working for another hour before she went back home to get ready. As she walked through town, which was busy with preparations for the festival, she caught snippets of a conversation.

'The water has been awful, hasn't it?'

'It has, it has.'

'Do you think it has to do with what the architect has been up to?'

'Frederick Chapman? No, I doubt it. He's the king's architect; whatever he's doing, I'm sure it'll only benefit Old Town. My bet would be those Unwanted Girls.'

'You're absolutely right. The water supply passes through that forest of theirs, does it not?'

Bisma didn't hear what else they said, but it presumably involved speaking ill of the Unwanted Girls. It was just like the villagers to blame them for anything that went wrong in town.

She wondered if the villagers even knew that all her sisters were asleep, that she was the only Unwanted Girl left. She had hardly spent any time in the Enchanted Forest these past few days.

The problems with the water had nothing to do with her or her home; it was more likely Frederick's fault, something to do with his expansion plans, but of course no one would ever blame *him*.

Even though it irritated her, Bisma put the thought from her mind as she approached the Enchanted Forest to focus on a more pressing matter: The fog along the border was thin, practically gone. When had *that* happened?

And that was not the only cause for concern. Inside the Forest things felt . . . wrong. She couldn't put her finger on it, but there was a strange energy in the air.

Bisma put a hand to a tree, stroking the bark. The wind whistled weakly, almost forlorn. The Forest must have missed the girls just like she did. Bisma's heart twinged. For the first time, Bisma considered that the Enchanted Forest needed the girls just as much as they needed it.

'Hold on a little longer, Forrie,' she said. 'We'll all be home soon. Promise.'

Whoever was poisoning Bisma's sisters was not only attacking her family but her home. Everything that mattered to her, everything that was important. It was the perfect revenge.

Her thoughts strayed to Eleanora again—could she do such a thing to make Bisma suffer? To get her vengeance?

The answer was obvious: yes, she very well could. There was no one else Bisma could think of who could exact such a punishment against her.

But then the next question was: *Would* she? Would Eleanora be this cruel? To use Bisma's sisters as collateral damage, to hurt the Enchanted Forest.

She didn't know Eleanora well enough to deduce that, but from the way Xander spoke of her, Bisma wasn't sure. But Bisma clearly couldn't think logically when it came to Xander . . .

Maybe going to the festival dance was a bad idea. She should be working on the cure.

But she did want to go. She couldn't bring herself to cancel on Xander. There was a time when being cruel to him came easily, but now? She was afraid the opposite was true.

Bisma returned to the treehouse, which was quiet and empty. There was a darkness cast over it, whereas usually it glowed warm and golden. A cold wind blew, and a chill ran down her spine.

Shivering, Bisma went up to her room. There was a letter waiting for her. She realized she hadn't replied to the last one—she hadn't been writing as often with everything going on, and felt badly for it.

The letter was short.

I hope you will save me a dance.
Yours

Her heart started beating fast. Practically everyone went to the dance, so it wasn't crazy for him to assume she would be there. They would finally meet in person—the prospect unnerved her. She wondered who her strange friend would be.

Bisma got ready, missing her sisters even more. Mei was not here to do her hair, nor Azalea to critique her dressing. Nori would have wanted to twirl with her, Deeba cooing as she watched, and surely Luna would have been reciting love poetry dramatically in the background, giving Bisma inane tips.

Even if Bisma was not going to the dance, they would have been excited. The Unwanted Girls usually did not go, but the next day, when the leftover food was left out for people to take and most of the town was asleep, recovering, the Unwanted Girls would go to town and eat caramel apples and dance to imaginary music under the hanging lights, treating it like their own private party.

She would only go to the dance for an hour or two, Bisma resolved. That was enough time to refresh her mind. Then she would get back to work. She missed her sisters desperately, each and every one of them, and that ache stayed with her as she walked back to town.

Some of the pain was soothed by the general splendor of the party. The entire town square had been cleared for it and decorated with crisscrossed strings of hanging lights.

Children carved pumpkins, while teenagers played games, a band playing lively music in the background for the adults to dance to. The evening was cool, but the square so packed that the air was warm. Everyone was enjoying themselves, having a merry time.

Her correspondent would be here, among the crowd. She wondered if he would approach her and when, but the thought left her mind as she spotted Xander.

He saw her a moment before she saw him and strode toward her.

'Well met, Bis,' he said with a smile, handing her a bouquet of red roses so dark they looked maroon.

'Xander,' she said, pressing the flowers to her nose to hide her smile. She adored them, but it would be tedious to carry them around, so she quickly made gajre out of them, wearing them as bracelets.

She held out her wrists to show him, and he smiled.

He took her hands, kissing her knuckles.

'Beautiful,' he said, but he was looking at her.

She smiled to herself. 'Not so bad yourself,' she replied, which was an understatement.

He was always gorgeous, but tonight especially so. Even though they had spent so much time together these past few weeks, every time she saw him again, she was struck by his beauty.

He wore the emerald-green waistcoat, the one she loved best—it made him look like a prince from a fairy tale, the type of story that only had happy endings, no sorrow, no grief. She was wearing her birthday dress in a similar but darker shade of green. Her hair was half up, strings of motia hanging with the rest of her hair.

As they walked through the crowd, he trailed behind her. She felt his feather-light touch at the end of her hair. When she turned, catching him, he smiled shyly and her heartbeat quickened.

He offered her his arm and she took it, trying not to fret over being seen with him in public. Even so, she glanced around. Some people were giving them looks, whispering to each other, and whenever she noticed, she felt more and more distressed, yet she could not keep looking. She was used to attracting negative attention, but she didn't want Xander to be the recipient of such derision.

'I bet you can't beat me at the potato toss,' Xander said, interrupting her thoughts.

It was a game with different baskets worth varying amounts of points, and to win one had to achieve the most points.

'And what will I win when you inevitably lose?'

'Win and maybe you'll see,' he said, his tone playful.

Her pulse sped up.

She won the first round, then he won the next, and in the last round, she won again.

'Ha!' She whooped, jumping up. He smiled, unbothered, and she found she had not noticed or cared about anyone watching; Xander had successfully distracted her. Her heart glowed.

'And now time for your prize,' Xander said, steering her to a stall that sold apple slices covered in caramel.

'Ooh, yummy.' He paid for a portion and they ate. The caramel apples were so sweet her teeth hurt but she didn't mind the ache, not one bit.

Bisma's gaze went to a nearby booth, which was selling cider donuts. She was about to demand they get some when she recognized who was standing there: Eleanora and Frederick.

Xander's gaze followed hers, and he smiled. 'Oh, let me introduce you!'

She shook her head quickly. 'Let's not disturb them. Besides, I've met them before.'

She had been avoiding crossing paths with Eleanora ever since and successfully managed it, despite Xander's many attempts to the contrary.

'A brief moment in the greenhouse doesn't count,' he said, grabbing her hand. 'Even if you won't formally introduce me to your family, I want you to meet mine.'

She tried to resist, but he pulled her along, and her chest tightened with fear.

When they reached Eleanora and Frederick, the pair of siblings were sipping a bubbly drink from goblets, deep in conversation.

'As I was telling Charlotte this afternoon, Phase One is nearly complete,' Frederick was saying. 'After that, the expansion—' He stopped when he saw Xander approaching with Bisma. A smile broke across his face.

'Uncle Fred, Mother,' Xander said, stopping in front of them. He was still holding Bisma's hand. 'This is Bisma.'

Eleanora and her brother were as beautiful as the portraits she had seen at the Chapman Estate. Bisma smiled at them, but it might have been more of a grimace as she braced herself for Eleanora's reaction.

'So this is the infamous Bisma!' Eleanora said, her green eyes sparking with interest. Bisma flinched, until Eleanora continued, 'Xander speaks of you so often I feel I know you. I'm pleased to meet you properly.'

Before Bisma knew what was happening, Eleanora stepped forward, gathering Bisma into her arms in a perfumed hug. Xander wasn't even ashamed. His cheeks did turn a little pink, but he grinned at Bisma.

'Oh.' Bisma blinked, not knowing what to say. 'He speaks of you often, as well,' she continued as Eleanora smiled.

'Clever girl,' Frederick said with a grin. 'Always compliment the mother.'

'Uncle Fred,' Xander said in a warning tone.

'Just teasing, Xandy-boy,' Frederick said with a wink. He took Bisma's hand to kiss the back of it, his touch lingering as he squeezed her palm with his gloved hand. 'Delighted to meet this wonder again.'

Bisma bit back a laugh. *Xandy-boy?* she mouthed at Xander.

He rolled his eyes, but the act was affectionate. It was evident that Xander's mother and uncle adored him, and that adoration was now being extended to Bisma, as well, which felt . . . lovely.

'Alright, we'll let you kids go now,' Eleanora said, squeezing her brother's arm.

'Have some fun on our behalf, as well,' Frederick said. 'Though not *too* much fun, mind you!'

Eleanora nudged her brother scoldingly.

Xander and Bisma waved goodbye, walking away, but Bisma looked over her shoulder to find Eleanora watching her.

Eleanora waved, smiling.

Was she that good of an actress? Did she not hate Bisma for the hand she thought Bisma had played in Leilani's death?

Bisma couldn't think of it further for something else required her attention; a handful of village boys were approaching. She recognized some of them. The unfamiliar faces seemed to be from the richer set; she could tell as much from their outfits.

'Xander!' one said, laughing as the group drew nearer. His eyes settled on Bisma, recognizing her; even if she did not know the boy personally, all the villagers of Old Town knew who she was.

She scowled.

'What's this?' the boy said, turning to one of his friends. They all snickered, clearly amused by the fact that Xander was here with her.

Embarrassment burned through her, though she had nothing to be ashamed of. Bisma turned to Xander and saw his face was red and splotchy. Her heart crashed. He was embarrassed as well.

'Strange choice of prize, Xander,' one of the boys said.

'Get lost,' Xander snapped, his voice lethal.

And she realized he wasn't embarrassed. No. He was *furious*.

While he was usually verbose, now he could hardly grit out the two words. That seemed to frighten the boys enough that they stopped laughing, but they didn't make any move to leave.

Suddenly, Bisma did not feel embarrassed anymore.

'Didn't you hear him?' Bisma said, glaring. 'Or do you need some encouragement?'

She reached into her bag, pulling out a closed fist as if to blow poison on them. They screamed, sprinting away, faces white with fear.

For a moment, Xander looked surprised, until she showed him her empty palm.

She inched closer to him, then revealed the contents of her purse.

'Just an energy potion,' she said.

Xander was surprised, but then he began laughing—they both did.

'Well played,' he said.

'I thought so,' she replied. Her reputation had come in handy.

She felt silly now for being afraid of stupid boys from the village. It was hard to be afraid of anything, really, when she was with Xander.

Not even her own heart.

'Come on,' he said, flashing her a smile. 'Let's dance.'

28

'I don't know how,' Bisma said automatically, but that wasn't true.

She did know how to dance. A few years ago, back when she snuck out to the festival dance to see if her poison on the village boys had worked, she stayed and watched, yearning to join in the revelry. She had watched enough to learn.

She would hum the music to herself and dance in the Enchanted Forest, eventually teaching her sisters, and they would all dance together. She missed her sisters with an ache, and perhaps that was what made her hesitate, now.

'Please,' Xander said, holding out his hand.

She lifted her hand to take his, but then she looked around at all the people who would watch and judge.

Xander stepped forward. 'Focus on me,' he said. 'Just on me.'

So she did. With a smile, he swept her off her feet—literally—twirling her in the air, which got a surprised, delighted laugh out of her. People turned to see, but by then she really didn't care.

They joined the group of people dancing. The music was upbeat and loud. The steps to the dance were quick, but she remembered them. They all danced in a line, moving their feet and hips, clapping along with the music, then spinning with their partners.

Then the music shifted, and she didn't know the dance, but with Xander beside her she had nothing to worry about.

'Just follow me,' he said.

She was a quick learner and had soon learned all the steps, moving with Xander flawlessly.

'That's my girl,' Xander said, twirling her, and she grinned.

They danced and danced until they took a break to get some drinks. As Xander went to get them, she sat on the side, waiting, until she spotted Haru, who was sulking in a corner.

She walked over to him.

'Don't be sad,' she said, squeezing his arm. 'Luna will be alright soon.' She had told him about Luna taking the freeze potion the last time she was in town.

'I hope so,' Haru replied, sighing.

Xander returned with two goblets, handing her one, and she waved goodbye to Haru. They walked to the side as she took a sip of her drink.

It was cold and fizzy, tasting of spiced maple and sugared oranges. She had never had anything like it, but it tasted wonderful. The bubbles popped in her mouth, making her giggle, and Xander laughed, too, as if they were both in on a secret, which perhaps they were.

Standing beneath the lights, she gazed up at him as music played all around them. Everyone else was dancing to the slow song, but they were both simply standing and looking at one another. Xander finished his drink, watching her over the glass, and she looked at the long line of his throat as he swallowed, his tongue as he licked his lips.

She set her glass down unfinished.

'Do you want to dance?' Xander asked, putting his glass down. His voice was raspy.

'I'm all danced out,' she replied.

'I don't really want to dance,' he admitted, eyes sparkling. 'I just wanted an excuse to hold you.'

She laughed, feeling fizzy even though she was no longer drinking. 'Well, if you're looking for an excuse . . .'

She stepped into his waiting arms, and they started dancing, swaying slowly with the music. Her arms wrapped around his neck, while his hands were warm and steady on her lower back.

She yearned to slip her hands into his hair; it would be so easy. Bisma scanned his face, taking in every little detail as if seeing him for the first time.

A slow smile spread across his face. 'You're staring.'

'Just checking to see if your beauty routine worked,' she replied.

'Did it?'

'Yes,' she breathed.

'Oh, thank god.'

She threw her head back and laughed, and as she did, she saw the lights hanging above them. Everything was golden against the night, a juxtaposition of light and dark, and he was the brightest light of all.

Bisma began playing with the ends of his hair, unable to help herself. They were so close now, their bodies pressed together. She felt the heat of his skin. She could almost feel the pound of his heart.

They were aligned, moving together to the music. It was an effort to keep her mouth away from his as their feet moved slowly, swaying. She could almost taste the cloves on his skin.

She wanted to kiss him and could see he wanted it too. His gaze dropped to her lips, his eyes growing darker by the moment. He clenched his jaw as she inched closer, her nose grazing his.

He took a shuddering breath, and they stopped dancing. She stood on her tiptoes, lifting her head to meet his, anticipation thrumming within her.

Just as her lips brushed his, he let out a strangled gasp and stepped back.

Oh, Forest. Had she misread the situation that badly?

Her heart hammered. Clearing her throat, Bisma looked around, the noise of the gathering coming back to her. Suddenly, everything felt too bright—bright enough to burn.

'Maybe we should get back to the greenhouse,' she said, her voice high.

He opened his mouth, about to say something—but then he pressed his lips into a line, clenching his jaw, and nodded.

Taking a deep breath, Bisma exited the town square, Xander trailing behind her. She thought she felt the phantom touch of his hand at the end of her hair, along her dress, but she didn't turn.

Walking away from all the noise, they made their way to Xander's neighborhood, cutting through the back to reach his greenhouse at the back of the Chapman Estate. The minute they entered, Xander discarded his coat, throwing it onto a chair. He ran a hand through his hair, making it messy.

He was agitated, but she couldn't understand why.

'Maybe I should go,' she said, though she didn't want to.

His eyes widened. He crossed the room in two strides and caught her hand.

'No, don't,' he said, his voice low. He drew her near. 'Back there . . . I wanted—I *want* to. But I didn't want you to think that's why I asked you to the dance. I know it's largely regarded as the most "romantic" night of the year, to put it delicately, but that wasn't my intention—I just wanted to dance with you, spend time with you. See you laugh. And I know you don't want to be flaunted in front of the whole village—'

He was speaking quickly, his cheeks pink, and she realized he was nervous. *Oh!* She was so used to confident Xander, with his endless flirtations and clever remarks; this version of him was impossibly endearing.

Her chest glowed with warmth.

'It's alright,' she said, smiling. She saw his pulse racing in his exposed throat. She wanted to press her lips just there. 'I know that wasn't your intent, but if you're quite done with all your good intentions . . .'

She put her hands on his shoulders, moving them up to his neck. He was trembling, and she rose to her tiptoes again, pressing a kiss to his throat feeling his pulse beat against her lips. He gasped.

'Actually,' she said, opening her mouth to run her teeth over his skin. His eyelids fluttered, his head tipping back. 'If you have any *bad* intentions, I really wouldn't be opposed . . .'

His gaze snapped to hers. 'I don't want to pressure you,' he said softly.

She gave him an incensed look. 'Why are you arguing with me?'

He blinked, her words sinking in. 'You're absolutely right,' he said, as if in a daze. His eyes were dark.

'Aren't I always?'

He did not waste another second. He seized her face with both his hands and crushed his lips to hers.

Finally, her body sang.

He lifted her up off the floor, and she yelped in surprise but kissed him back. Her legs wrapped around his waist as he continued to kiss her, surely bruising her mouth, but she did not care.

'Bis, there's something I want to tell you, to show you,' he said, breaking away, but she hardly heard him. The moment his mouth was gone from hers, she wanted it back again. She pulled him closer, kissing him again, and he forgot whatever he was trying to say.

He walked her to the bed, then promptly deposited her there, and she laughed against his open mouth, positively giddy. She had been numb for so long she had forgotten what this felt like, but now it was all coming back, coming alive, every beat, every pulse, every inch.

His body slid over hers, a wondrous weight. She undid the buttons of his waistcoat, and he shrugged it off. He tasted like spiced maple sugar, and she felt fizzy all over again.

'I've wanted to do this for so long,' he breathed, kissing her jaw, her throat. 'I almost did so many times.'

'You should have,' she said, her fingers tightening in his hair.

'Suppose I'll have to make up for it now,' he said, making her gasp with the way he kissed her just above her beating heart.

'Is that a vow?'

He brought his face up to look into her eyes. 'All my vows are yours.'

Her heart soared. She pushed him off her, turning with him so she was on top. He sat up, and she straddled his lap, running her hands through his hair as his long, elegant fingers moved across her skin, pressing deep enough to hurt, yet still gentle.

She knew he would not hurt her. He was handling her with care still, even as she felt how desperate he was, how much he wanted her.

His hands slid up her thighs, slipping beneath her dress, and she ripped his shirt off.

'Hope you didn't like that one,' she said, throwing it aside.

'I rather did,' he replied with a laugh. 'Though not nearly as much as I like you.'

She laughed, and then he grazed his teeth against her neck, which promptly made her stop laughing. She closed her eyes, body aflame as her hands roamed over his chest. There was so much to touch and explore.

His skin was hot, burning hers, and his heart was beating wildly fast.

Too fast.

'Your heart is beating rather quickly,' she managed to say.

'I wonder why,' he replied, words slurring. His hands were on her waist, fingers digging in as he pulled her even closer. He sucked on her jaw, and she couldn't think straight.

'Xander, wait,' she gasped. Despite how heavenly this all was, something felt wrong.

She opened her eyes the same time he did, and he let out a startled cry. She shifted off his lap, and that was when she saw.

The veins of his forearm were dark blue.

Her face must have been horrified, for he looked down. His eyes widened with alarm.

'Shit,' he said.

Her hands were red, hot from his skin; she hadn't even noticed. 'No. No, no, *no*.' She scrambled off the bed.

Xander fell back on the bed, groaning, and Bisma rushed to find the freeze potion, but she was shaking.

He cried out with pain and the sound speared through her.

'Xander, hold on!' she called, her voice high.

Where was that blasted potion?

She moved aside ingredients and herbs, rummaging through bottles, until she found it.

She rushed over to him and hauled him up, holding his head in her hands. His mouth was clamped shut, his jaw clenching against the pain. He was trembling.

'Drink,' she ordered. 'Please.'

He forced open his mouth and she emptied the potion into his mouth. Some of it dribbled down his chin, but he swallowed the rest of it. She hoped it was enough.

'Bis,' he whispered, before his eyes closed. He felt heavy, frozen, still, when only a moment before he had been so alive. She laid him down gently.

Taking in a shuddering breath, she stood.

Bisma was completely and utterly alone.

29

She had one day left to find the cure, and everything to lose if she didn't. The poison had spread past Deeba's little arms to her chest, the dark veins reaching for her heart like the claws of death.

Bisma was her baji; she would not let that happen.

Mind whirring, she walked to Xander's worktable, which was covered with ingredients and plants. They had gotten so close, but she didn't know the exact measurements of what they had been mixing—Xander usually handled that, making meticulous notes.

That was it: she just needed his notes.

Rummaging around the table, she searched for his notebook, moving from space to space until she finally spotted it. But as she picked it up, she noticed something beneath it.

A keepsake box, the same as the one on Eleanora's desk in her library.

She wondered if his would be locked, like Eleanora's was. This wasn't the time to investigate, but she couldn't help but to indulge her curiosity. The keepsake box hadn't always been there; she would have noticed it.

Something struck her then: what had Xander said, just minutes—what felt like hours now—before? That there was something he wanted to show her.

Setting the notebook aside, she tested the clasp of the box, and it opened with no difficulty. The box easily displayed its contents to her. She should not have let her curiosity take the best of her—not when there was so much to be done in so little time—but it felt like there was something she needed to know.

Then she spotted something familiar.

A spot of ink on the edge of a page. A tear-stained smudge, to be precise.

One she had put there.

Bisma pulled out the folded papers. They were covered with streaks of dirt.

With a start, Bisma realized Xander was her anonymous friend.

These were *her* letters, kept safe in a keepsake box.

Blinking fast, Bisma turned back to Xander's notebook, flipping it open. The evidence was there: his handwriting.

All this time! If she had only *looked* at his notes—looked even once!—she would have seen. Her heart hammered. She recalled Xander asking her to on numerous occasions, the expectant look on his face. But she had never been interested.

If only she had looked! He had been her constant companion, the person she wrote to when she felt there was nobody else she could unburden herself to. The friend who slowly but surely helped her lessen the fortifications around her heart.

All this time! And she had not appreciated it. She had not seen how wonderful he was!

It made sense now that her correspondent did not mind that she wrote less the more time she spent with Xander.

Xander. Of course it was Xander. Deep down, Bisma recognized that she'd always had an inkling it was him—had hoped for it even. At the festival he had been the only one to ask her to dance, after all.

Her heart ached at the memory. She yearned to go back to that moment, hours ago, when she was in his arms, her mouth sweet from sugared oranges, dancing beneath a thousand twinkling lights.

Bisma flicked through the keepsake box, finding every letter she had ever sent him until she found the very first one. The paper was worn as if it had been folded and unfolded many times. It was streaked with dirt and had little teeth marks on it.

So the Enchanted Forest had sent her letter to him.

A week ago, she might have wondered why, but now, lips still bruised from kissing him, she knew why. There was no more denying it.

She loved him. It was that simple.

Bisma had thought what she had with Gregory was love, that that was all love had the capacity to be, so of course she had scorned it all these years and kept away from it even as she longed for it.

But that wasn't real—*this*, what she felt for Xander, what he felt for her, was true love. Him brushing her hair, the soft touch of his gentle hands; him, constantly forgiving her, even as she was cruel to him. Him knowing when to push, when to be silent. Letting her down only to pick her up again.

She had found him overbearing, too much, but now she saw that for him to fill her life with such brilliance was not a burden, but a gift, the very best gift she could ever hope to receive.

He was a flirt and overly cheery and liked her too much, but those were all good things—the very best things!—for it finally gave her the courage to like him, to adore him, to love him, to release the floodgates of all the love that was bubbling within her, the love that had previously been reserved only for her sisters, for the Enchanted Forest.

She had never thought such affection would be given to a man again, that she would ever feel this type of love, but now that Xander was still and motionless—and that love taken from her—she knew she wanted it back, that she would do anything to bring it back, just as she would do anything for her sisters, for the Forest.

They were all as much part of her as her magic, as her heart, as her soul. Xander was part of her now, and he was frozen, his life in danger. Bisma could not believe she had not realized what she felt for him sooner—she should have recognized it, appreciated it, basked in it.

What if he did not wake, and their love was lost forever?

She'd thought herself so clever. She'd thought she was being so careful, so cautious, that she was protecting herself, but really, she had been a fool all over again not to recognize the very best thing she had. She had conflated it with the worst thing to happen to her.

Tears filled her eyes. She had been punishing herself for having such a big heart, for thinking Gregory was better than he was, but that was not a character flaw in *her*; she saw that now.

The true character flaw was to be too bitter to see a good man even when he was right in front of her.

She would rather be too kind, too open, too accepting and be proved the fool—as she had been with Gregory—than be too closed off, too mean, too angry and be proved the fool—as she had been with Xander.

To open your heart to love was not foolish; it was brave. And she wanted to be brave. Wasn't that what she had been telling Luna all this time? To trust in others, in good people? To try, then try again?

Bisma took a deep breath, wiping her cheeks. With trembling hands, she put the letters back in the keepsake box, closed it, then turned to Xander's notebook.

She had a long night ahead of her, and she would not fail.

She would not rob herself of the chance to do better.

Determined, Bisma read through Xander's notes, her heart twisting painfully at the familiar script. She focused on the trials; they had gotten very close these past few days.

Even the trial with Nori, which seemed forever ago now, had been close to being successful. They had adjusted that potion with a dozen different ingredients, but it had not yielded results.

But what if they had been focusing on the wrong thing?

What if it was simple?

Mind whirring, Bisma recalled how the potion had seemed to work on Nori until she threw it up.

What if all they needed to add to the potion was something to help keep it down long enough for it to expel the poison?

Bisma got to work, growing different plants. After that, she grew the potion, mixing it precisely as Xander's notes instructed, then added in the new ingredients—but the problem was how to test it? They could not test it on the magical evergreen trees, like they had been doing.

She needed to test it on someone.

Well, there was only one thing for it.

Taking a deep breath, Bisma drank the potion. It felt cool going down her throat, like an iced drink after a long, hot day, and for a moment, she felt energized—*good*. Until it soured in her stomach as if someone had reached in and squeezed.

Before she could help it, then she retched into a bin.

Wiping her mouth, Bisma stood. She drank water—then got back to work.

Bisma worked all night: growing plants, making potions, taking notes the way Xander would have. She tested each trial on her body, each time upending the contents of her stomach.

It was horrible, awful, but she kept glancing at the still bodies of her sisters, at the still body of her love, and turned back with renewed vigor until the early morning came, and she passed out in her seat for a few hours, completely spent.

When she woke, she ate some of the cheese and dried fruit Xander kept at the greenhouse, along with a fortifying potion, then began again.

After half a dozen more failed attempts, she was exhausted. Her throat burned, but she kept going until the afternoon, tears streaming down her cheeks.

She had only until the evening before Deeba would die. The thought of losing her sister forced her to carry on, even as her body resisted such abuse.

Bisma took heart in the fact that she was getting closer and closer; she could feel it. The intensity of the vomiting was decreasing, until—

The vomit did not come.

She held her breath, not believing it.

'Can it be?' she whispered aloud, holding a hand over her mouth. Along with the hope, fear beat through her. She waited, standing perfectly still.

Then she felt the irritation in her throat heal, as if she had drunk a glass of cool water after a long day of thirst. The exhaustion from earlier faded away. The terrible taste of vomit left her mouth and was replaced by a fresh minty taste.

She felt . . . good. Wonderful even. Intensified further by the fact that she had done it.

She had found the cure!

Or had she?

Bisma waited, making sure the effects would continue to hold.

Her mind raced. But she had not been poisoned. What if the cure reacted differently in a poisoned body?

She could poison herself and test it, but what if it didn't work and she died? There would be no one left to wake the others.

Her only choice was to test it on one of them.

But who?

She approached Xander, sitting beside him on the bed. If the cure failed, he would be fine, since the poison had spread the least in him. If it didn't work, she could give him another dose of the freeze potion and try again.

But she really hoped it would work.

'Please,' she whispered, holding Xander's head in her hand. She poured the cure into his mouth and waited.

For a moment, nothing happened, and she worried.

But then—he moved.

'Xander?' she whispered, curved over him, watching and waiting.

He let out a groan, eyes crinkling. 'Bis?' he said, voice rasped. And then his eyes opened, that brilliant emerald green, her favorite color, and her heart soared like a bird taking flight for the very first time.

'Xander!' she cried out. She leapt on him with a hug, arms going around his neck.

He wrapped his arm around her immediately, holding her.

She pulled away to make sure this was real—that he was really alright. She ran her hands through his hair, coming down to rest her fingers along his neck. His free hand came up to cup her cheek, and she pressed a kiss to his palm.

'You did it,' he said, mouth spreading into a slow smile. 'That's my girl.'

She surprised them both by pressing her lips to his.

He was so shocked he did not react for a second, but then he pulled her close, deepening the kiss. She smiled against his mouth then pulled back, breathless.

Absently, she felt relieved by the addition of mint into the cure's recipe.

'I'm sorry it's taken me so long to see how wonderful you are,' she said, eyes pricking with tears. She held his face in her hands. 'But I can see you now. And you are a treasure.'

'No, don't apologize,' he said, a soft expression on his face. 'Every moment with you is a gift.'

'Can you stand?' she asked with a smile. 'I want you to meet my sisters.'

30

With Xander's help, Bisma made more of the cure. She told him to rest—that she could do it herself—but he wanted to see how she had accomplished the feat that had eluded them all these weeks.

'Brilliant,' he said, shaking his head in awe as she showed him how she had grown gulkhaira, a single-blossom flower that was rose pink, shading into pink and white. She had used the root of the plant to treat stomach disorders before, and with some magic and manipulation it was just what their cure needed. 'Bis, you're absolutely brilliant,' he said, looking at her with wonder in his green eyes. She smiled to herself, cheeks warm.

When the cure was ready, they treated her sisters together: Deeba first, then Azalea, Nori, Mei, and, lastly, Luna. They were all groggy and grumpy, as if waking from a midday nap that had accidentally turned into a day-long slumber.

'My tummy hurts,' Nori said, pouting, while Azalea groaned.

'I feel awful,' Luna said.

'Owie,' Mei added, rubbing her eyes.

Deeba whimpered as Bisma scooped her into her arms, cuddling the toddler.

'Nori, get off,' Luna complained, as Nori stretched out on top of Luna.

'But you so warm,' Nori said, cuddling closer, smiling at having successfully vexed Luna.

'Go bother Azalea—she's warmer,' Luna said.

Azalea shot up. 'Do *not* bother Azalea,' she warned.

Bisma had never been happier to hear their noisy complaints; the greenhouse was brimming with them. With all the girls awake, the private space that was hers and Xander's now felt crowded, but in the very best way, all of them snuggled tight and cozy.

'I missed you so much,' Bisma said, going to kiss each of them.

Deeba jumped from her arms onto the cot to snuggle with Mei, while Bisma hugged Luna tight. Azalea waved Bisma off when Bisma approached.

'It's too early in the morning for this,' Azalea fussed, but Bisma didn't care, she plopped a kiss onto Azalea's cheek.

'Where are we?' Nori asked, looking around with wide blue eyes.

'I'm *starving*,' Luna added.

They were all sitting up now, taking in their surroundings.

Bisma felt Xander's hand at the small of her back, and she turned to look up at him.

'You girls get reacquainted. I'll get some food,' he said.

'Thank you,' she said, reaching up on her tiptoes to brush a soft kiss against his cheek.

His face lit up with such innocent cheer that she wanted to kiss him properly, but she was aware that all her sisters had stopped their complaining and curious glances to watch with shocked faces.

'EW.'

'What was THAT?'

'BAJI?!'

Xander laughed as he walked away, leaving Bisma to face the girls.

She smiled shyly. '*That* was none of your business,' she said, walking over to Xander's bed to grab a blanket. 'Mei, help me set this down.' She and Mei placed the blanket on the floor for them all to sit, and Azalea grabbed pillows. As the girls crowded on, getting cozy, she continued, 'Xander helped me find the cure that saved you all.'

The girls had a thousand questions, ranging from asking how the goats were (Nori) to how long they were asleep (Mei) to what exciting gossip they had missed (Azalea). Bisma answered all of them, everyone talking over one another as they came up with more and more questions. She had missed them so sorely: each of their voices, their expressions, their touch. Her heart panged.

Then Xander joined them with food—a hearty vegetable soup with warm bread and baked potatoes topped with golden butter and melting cheese—and the girls ate their fill, growing more and more energetic as their weakness wore off, their voices and laughter increasing in volume by the minute.

They all laughed and teased. Deeba looked on in wonder at all of them, speaking her own gibberish, her little chubby hands squeezing Bisma's.

Bisma held Deeba close. She had nearly lost all of this . . . that could never happen again. Now that they were all alright, she needed to find out who did this. She would get revenge.

Eleanora was the only promising lead she had come up. But how to bring it up? How to investigate?

And there was now a glaring hole in her theory—why would Eleanora poison Xander? Even if only to hurt Bisma, it was hard to consider that Eleanora would risk her precious son.

'What is it?' Xander asked, as if he could sense her thinking.

She turned to him, to his patient, kind face, the face that she loved so dearly. She couldn't do it—she couldn't tell him her suspicions, not without evidence. 'I—'

She broke off, noticing a figure lurking behind Xander. In the shadows outside the greenhouse, Frederick was watching her.

When her gaze met his, he spun on his heel and disappeared.

Why was he watching them?

'Bis,' Xander said, brows furrowed. 'What's wrong?'

She cleared her throat. 'Nothing.' She stood. 'I'll be back in a moment,' she said, smiling reassuringly at the girls and Xander.

'Anything I can do?' he asked.

She touched his cheek. 'No, thank you.'

Bisma slipped away from the greenhouse, leaving them chatting and laughing. She went to the mansion; she knew where the back door to the laundry was and it was easy to sneak in from there.

Inside, she ducked away from servants, not wishing to be seen. Lurking quietly, she made her way upstairs, going to the wing that housed all the family's rooms. She soon found it—Frederick's room.

Bisma slipped inside, closing the door behind her. A grandfather clock ticked in the corner, as she looked around, her heart beating fast. Frederick's desk was clean, but she pulled open the drawers, finding vials from the Apothecary; she recognized the special glass bottles imported from Castletown.

They were regular-looking potions, nothing suspicious or strange. In his papers she saw maps of town, blueprints, nothing of any use.

Bisma glanced out the window behind the desk. Down below, Frederick was talking to a group of men who looked to be workers—surely the workers on his expansion project.

Her thoughts raced. It couldn't be a coincidence that the poisonings began soon after Frederick came to town. Bisma had been too preoccupied suspecting Eleanora to consider someone just as powerful and resourceful. She had ruled him out because he was not a garden-witch, but what if . . . ?

Bisma looked out the window again, and this time, Frederick and the men were gone. Logically, she knew that she should have left his room before he returned, but she wanted answers. And she wanted them now.

Setting her jaw, Bisma pulled out the leather chair in front of Frederick's desk. She sat down, making herself comfortable. Then she waited.

A few minutes later, the door opened and in came Frederick.

He didn't look surprised to see her; he looked as if he had been expecting her.

Anger flared through her. What was going on?

'That is my seat, you know,' Frederick said, entering the room. He closed the door behind him.

'Why were you watching us?' she asked, her voice hard.

Seeing that Bisma had no intention of getting up from his chair, Frederick pulled out the chair across the desk from her, taking off his coat and setting it on the back of the chair before sitting down. He crossed his legs languidly, as if he had all the time in the world.

'I wondered when you might put two and two together and come see me,' he said, and it was unnerving how similar the cadence of his speech was to Xander's.

All of it was unnerving, really: the green of his eyes, the fall of his hair. This was her beloved's uncle, and though on the surface, they may have resembled each other, he was missing all the heart that made Xander, well, *Xander*.

'Put what together?' Bisma asked, grinding her teeth. She was horribly confused.

'It might be simpler if I showed you,' Frederick said. He stood with ease; he didn't seem alarmed to have Bisma in his room, questioning him. The man was just as confident, just as secure— even as he pulled something out from one of the desk drawers and set it upon the table.

It was one of the vials she saw earlier.

'Wouldn't open it, if I were you,' he said, sitting back down, and suddenly she understood. It was the poison.

She itched to inspect it, and he noticed as much. 'Alright, go on,' Frederick said, his voice amiable. 'I suppose it doesn't matter whether or not you get infected now that you've found a cure.'

'You're the one who's been poisoning us? Why?' she demanded. 'What have I ever done to you?'

'Xander always talks about how intelligent you are.' Frederick glanced at the grandfather clock, then smiled, leaning back in his chair. 'Why don't I give you a moment to figure it out, dear?'

Her mind was racing—Bisma's original theory was that this was all about Leilani. Xander had said Leilani was like an aunt to him, that she and Eleanora were best friends . . . What if Frederick had loved her?

He and Eleanora could be united in seeking revenge—the poison had clearly been made by Eleanora. The bottles were made of special Castletown glass, which only the Apothecary used. Even so, one thing still didn't make sense.

'Why poison Xander?'

Frederick nodded. 'Ah, yes, a small hitch in the plan,' he said. 'He wasn't meant to be poisoned. That was meant for you.'

She furrowed her brows. But then she recalled meeting Frederick at the festival, how he had kissed the back of her hand and squeezed her palm. He had been wearing gloves.

'The poison was meant for me,' she said, blinking. She understood how the poison worked then. 'The poison is transferable.'

'Yes,' he affirmed. 'Transferred through a touch or a kiss, maybe.'

Bisma felt as if she'd been kicked in the stomach. That was how her sisters were poisoned, even when they hadn't left the Enchanted Forest, when they hadn't even left the treehouse, because *she* was the one bringing it straight to them.

'You didn't account for the risk of me transferring it to Xander?' she asked. 'Even though we were at the festival together?'

'I am not so callous with my beloved nephew's life,' Frederick said, for the first time seeming offended by her words. 'I gave you a more potent dose that night, which should have affected you immediately, but I should have accounted for my nephew's charms on the most romantic night of the year. Again, a slight hitch in the plan, but it's no matter.'

'What plan?' she demanded. She was still so confused; she had so many questions.

'I'll answer all your questions, dear, so do take your time,' he said. She didn't understand that, either.

'Why are you answering my questions?'

He shrugged nonchalantly. 'Well, the jig is clearly up so I might as well feed your curiosity,' he replied.

Her thoughts were all jumbled. She didn't know where to begin. 'You said the poison is transferable,' she said.

'Yes. It was easy enough to have someone brush by you in town, transferring the poison to you,' Frederick explained. 'Then you would take the poison home and transfer it to one of your sisters. You lot are always so affectionate. And before you ask, "Well,

Frederick, why not just poison the girls directly when they came to town?" I'll tell you that, too. I needed the girls to be poisoned at home for it to really be effective.'

'You and Eleanora were in this together,' she said, a fact more than a question. 'Only she could design such an intricate poison.'

'Yes, all Elle's genius, though I wouldn't say we were "in this together". She merely designed the potion; she doesn't know what I used it for.'

'But . . . I thought this was about Leilani . . . that Eleanora was getting revenge on me, that you both were?' Her theory made no sense if Eleanora was not aware of what the potion was being used for.

'Leilani?' Frederick tsked, disappointed. 'I thought you would understand by now!' He stood up. 'No matter, let me give you a hint.'

He came around the table, opening the drawer she had looked through earlier. Pulling out a roll of papers, he laid them flat on the table, showing her what looked to be the finalized blueprints for the town's expansion project. It included tearing down the eastern neighborhoods—but where would they go?

As if sensing her question, Frederick lifted the page, showing her the answer.

'But that land belongs to the Enchanted Forest,' she said quietly. This was never about revenge.

'Yes! Now you're finally understanding!' Frederick said, pleased. 'Why do you think I said the girls needed to be poisoned at home?'

Finally, *finally*, Bisma understood.

The rotting fruit, the Forest's strange behavior—the thinning border fog. The Enchanted Forest was weak, and it was weak because the girls had been sick.

'You poisoned us to weaken the Forest so you could cut it down,' she said.

'Now you've got it!' He sat back down. 'Nothing personal, of course, you must see that, dear girl? I figured out that the Enchanted Forest gets its power from you girls—what is a home without its inhabitants, after all? So I picked you off one by one to gradually weaken the Forest so we could demolish it.'

It had never been about her sisters, never about her. It had always been about the Forest.

Bisma was shaking with anger, but Frederick was as cavalier as ever. He leaned forward, resting his elbows on the desk.

'Oh, I am not evil,' Frederick said. 'I never wished to kill your sisters, or this all would have been much simpler! I knew if I poisoned your sisters, you would eventually find a cure, which is why I intended to poison you last. And I knew that even if you didn't, then Xander would figure it out, or at the very least, Elle would, and by then Phase Two would be complete.'

Bisma's mind reeled. Rage burned through her, making it difficult to move. She looked around for a weapon but found none. It was no matter; she would claw his eyes out with her own hands. He would suffer. But something he had said made her pause her plans for violence.

'Phase Two?' she repeated. 'No.' She stood. 'Your plans have failed. The girls are awake, and the Forest still stands. We are healed, and the Forest will recover, as well. It was all for nothing.'

He gave her a look of pity then, one that chilled her down to her bones.

'Oh, sweet girl,' he said, frowning as if he felt very sorry for her indeed. 'I never wanted you girls to stay ill forever, just for as long as I needed. You all woke earlier than scheduled—but you're already too late.'

Her heart filled with dread as she thought of the men she had seen Frederick talking to outside the mansion, the workers. He had *made* her see him outside the greenhouse; he had *wanted* her to come ask him these questions. To stall her.

He had kept her here while the workers went to the Enchanted Forest to enact Phase Two—to tear down her home.

Bisma ran.

31

Bisma ran back to the greenhouse, where Xander and the girls were sitting and laughing at something ridiculous Nori was doing.

'Hey, where did you go?' Xander asked, standing. He reached for her.

She took his hand, then looked past him to the girls. 'We need to go now,' she said, out of breath. 'The Forest is in danger.'

The girls jumped to their feet, questions tumbling out of their mouths.

'What?'

'What's happening?'

'From who?'

Bisma held up her free hand to silence them. 'The Forest is weak—the border fog is gone—and they're going to cut it down. We need to go and stop them.'

Fear entered each of their expressions, followed by resolute anger. They would fight to protect their home.

'What we going to do?' Nori asked.

For a moment, Bisma blanked. She didn't know.

'I'll get Haru!' Luna said. 'He can help!'

'I can ask Diego!' Mei added.

'And Razan!' Azalea said.

Bisma hesitated, the old habit kicking in—she did not want to ask for help—but then she looked at the girls; she wouldn't jeopardize them because of her misplaced pride.

'Go,' she said, her voice thick. 'Get whoever you can and meet me by the Forest. I'll try to hold them off as best I can.'

The girls ran off, and Bisma turned to Xander, who was watching with a worried expression.

'What's happening? Who's cutting the Forest down?'

'Your uncle,' she said miserably.

'Uncle *Fredrick*?' he said in surprise.

'It's his expansion plans. The Unwanted Girls are tied to the Forest. He's been poisoning us so the Forest would be weakened, and now that it is, he's going to cut it down. Eleanora made him the poison, but she didn't know what he would use it for.'

It was a lot to throw at him, but she didn't have time to ease him in.

Xander stumbled back, shocked. Seeing the grief caused by his uncle's betrayal made her glad she had been wrong to suspect Eleanora—well, she was right to suspect Eleanora *made* the poison, but wrong about the rest of it.

'I—Wha—How did you find out?' he asked.

Her heart broke at the sadness on his face. 'He just told me,' she said. 'I'm sorry.'

'You're—Bisma, *I'm* sorry,' Xander said, stepping forward to hold her face in his warm hands. 'I had no idea—I swear I didn't. And my mother . . .' He was upset. 'How could she?'

'I don't blame her,' Bisma said.

Hadn't Bisma made poisons and given them to people, trusting they would use them for justice and good?

'I know she would never do this if she knew what Uncle Fred was using the poison for, I know it,' he said. 'She adores you. But Uncle Fred . . .' He paused, realizing something. 'That's why Uncle Fred was always asking me about the Unwanted Girls . . . Bisma, I'm sorry. I always answered his questions, I never realized he might be plotting something like this.'

His green eyes were wide with fear now.

'Please forgive me,' he said.

She reached up to take his hands in hers, squeezing them.

'I forgive you, Xander,' she said. 'And I trust you.'

It was the truth. She did trust him, and she trusted herself, as well. Xander would not betray her; he had proven himself over and over. She had no reason to doubt him.

Her words seemed to make him melt and he released a long breath, pressing his forehead against hers.

'Good,' he said, his voice a whisper. 'I was afraid . . .' He paused, swallowing. 'Well, I was afraid if I ever did anything wrong . . . that you wouldn't want me anymore.'

'I'm sorry if I've made you feel that way,' she said, pulling back to look into his eyes so he could see she meant it. 'That isn't fair to you—you don't have to be perfect all the time. We'll both make mistakes and let one another down. I'm sure to be prickly and unruly, and you're sure to be too trusting and too good, but as long as we're in this together, we can do anything.'

'We *are* in this together,' he said. 'Always. Forever.'

She wrapped her arms around his neck, hugging him, and his arms tightened around her, holding her close.

He smiled down at her. 'My little porcupine.'

She smacked his chest. 'Don't call me that!'

'Fine, fine.' His eyes glinted. 'How about my feral kitten? Pumpkin? Honeybunch?'

He was trying to make her laugh now, and it worked.

'We need to work on your terms of endearment,' she said.

'Anything you say, darling dearest,' he said.

She smiled. 'That's better, beloved.'

His entire face lit up. It was the first time she had called him a term of endearment and would most certainly not be the last.

Hand in hand, they ran back to the Enchanted Forest.

32

Bisma and Xander arrived at the Enchanted Forest to find more than a dozen workers already cutting down trees. The fog that usually protected the Forest's border was completely gone, making the home of the Unwanted Girls easy prey.

A weak whistle sounded in the air—it was the Forest crying out for help.

Rage cracked through Bisma with the force of a whip. She dropped her hand from Xander's and sprinted straight to the workers, picking up a branch along the way. 'Stop!' she cried, swinging. Beside her, Xander was fighting another worker, trying to unhand the worker from his ax.

Bisma hit one of the men, knocking him over, and he cried out. As Bisma reared to attack another worker, she felt an arm lock around her from behind, hauling her back.

She screamed, trying to wring free.

'Don't touch her!' Xander cried. He was there in an instant, striking the worker who held her with the hilt of an ax.

The worker released her, falling back, unconscious.

Xander's green eyes were wild. 'Are you alright?' he asked, caressing her cheek.

She nodded. Then something caught her eye behind him. 'Watch out!'

Xander turned in time to see a worker running at him.

He ducked, and Bisma fell to her knees, sticking her hands into the soil. Usually, her magic was stronger in the Enchanted Forest, even just outside its borders, but as she felt deep in the earth, she knew the Forest had no magic to lend her.

She called upon her own, drawing up vines which sprouted from the ground, hitting the worker Xander was fighting.

The worker was thrown back, and Xander turned to her, a bruise forming above his cheekbone.

The sight splintered through her. She pushed more of her magic into the earth, and vines emerged everywhere, reaching out to strike workers with vicious precision. Satisfaction coursed through her as she watched them scatter and fall.

But it wasn't enough. The workers got back up, redirecting their axes to her vines, while some trees were lined with dynamite.

'No!' she cried, as they lit the matches, the flames flickering in the darkening evening. Explosions sounded, one after another, and she shut her eyes, her heart tearing.

Mighty trees fell, and dew slid from the other trees' leaves, as though the Forest was weeping. Bisma felt each loss keenly. She focused on her magic, calling for it to help her, to help her home, and Xander was doing the same. But they were outnumbered—they couldn't do this.

Just then, Bisma heard a feral scream. She turned and saw the Unwanted Girls running toward the Forest, and they weren't alone. Behind them was Haru and his family, Razan and her husband, Diego and his teenage kids, as well as a few other villagers who she had sold poisons to, people she had helped.

They attacked the workers, striking them and taking away their axes. Nori bit at hands and kicked at shins. Mei was to the side with Deeba, keeping her safe, while Azalea and Luna threw dirt into the workers' eyes, temporarily blinding them. The villagers helped her sisters, watching their backs, fighting and pushing back the workers.

Bisma's heart flared with hope, and she realized she had been wrong.

It was not a weakness to ask for help; rather it was a strength to open yourself up to it, even if it was frightening.

She could not save her home by herself, but perhaps with her community she might be able to.

Spirit renewed, she had an idea. 'Xander!'

He was protecting her, fighting off anyone who came near. 'I'm here,' he said, his eyes bright. 'What do you need?'

'Your magic,' she said. 'If we grow poisonous hedges along the border of the Forest, the workers won't be able to pass through.'

'Brilliant idea.' He flashed her a smile, coming down to his knees to put his hands in the soil beside hers.

'Feel with me,' she said. 'Let your magic connect with mine, and I'll guide it.'

'I'm all yours, Bis.'

He closed his eyes, focusing. It took a moment, but then she felt his magic pulsing in the earth. She took hold of it, and it did not resist her. With double the strength, she grew thorny bushes all along the border, one sprouting after the other, each six feet tall.

A worker lifted his ax, trying to cut at it, but as he did, a leaf from the hedge brushed his hand. He screamed, falling back, revealing blistering skin.

The poisonous bushes coupled with the efforts of the Unwanted Girls and the villagers was enough to act as a ward to protect the Enchanted Forest. The battered, bruised, and poisoned workers looked at one another, then promptly dropped their axes, running off.

Bisma's home was safe.

'We did it!' Nori cried, jumping up.

'Woo!' Luna shouted, twirling and laughing with Haru.

'No one messes with us!' Azalea said. She clapped hands with Razan.

Everyone cheered, euphoric at the victory.

On the ground, Bisma and Xander both sat back, spent. Catching her breath, she leaned against his chest, and he wrapped an arm around her as they breathed together.

After a moment, they both stood, and everyone joined together into a circle.

'Is everyone OK?' Bisma asked, scanning their village friends and the girls. They were a bit dirty but seemed unharmed. 'Thank you all for your help . . . truly. It means the world to me and my sisters.' She looked at the girls, and they echoed back a chorus of thanks.

'Do you want us to stay?' Diego asked. 'In case they come back?'

'No, I think it's alright,' Bisma said. 'The poisonous hedges should keep them away.'

If the workers came back in greater numbers, the hedges could not do much, but for now it was enough. She would think about what else to do until then.

'If you need help, please just let us know,' Haru said. He was standing with Luna, holding her hand. Their fingers were entwined.

'Or if there's anything you need,' Haru's mother added.

'Thank you all,' Bisma said, feeling touched. 'Really.'

The villagers said goodbye, all except for Xander, who stayed by her side. She leaned against him, feeling anchored.

'Lu, take the girls home,' Bisma said, addressing Luna, who was staring at Haru as he walked away. Haru turned back to wave, and Luna beamed at him. '*Luna.*'

'Yes, I am paying attention!' Luna said, corralling all the girls together. 'Girlies, let's go!'

'Get some sleep, OK?' Bisma said, kissing Nori and Deeba. 'It's been a long day, and Forrie needs you all to be at your strongest so it can recover.'

'What about you, Baji?' Mei asked, coming to give Bisma a hug.

'I'll make some more bushes to keep the workers away.' Bisma tucked Mei's silky hair behind her ear. 'I'll be home soon, promise. Now give me a kiss, and off you go.' Mei kissed her cheek, and Azalea and Luna settled for blowing kisses before skipping into the Forest and taking the path home.

When they had gone, Bisma and Xander reinforced the poisonous bushes along the border of the Forest as best as they could, until they were both exhausted.

Then they sat down against a great walnut tree, resting. Moonlight shone above them, its milky white light illuminating their faces as soft wind rustled the remaining leaves on the trees. The night was cold, but as long as she was with him, she felt warm.

'I'll speak to my uncle,' Xander said. 'I'll stop him from doing this. And I'll have Mother speak to him, too—I don't know what's gotten into him to be so blinded by greed.' He ran a hand through his hair, clenching his jaw. 'I'm really sorry for all of this.'

'You have nothing to be sorry for.' She kissed his cheek. 'How do you feel about all this? I know you and your uncle are close . . .'

'I feel . . .' He released a long breath. 'Sad. Really sad, to be honest. It will be a loss, but I cannot keep my ties with him after all he's done.'

'I don't want to pit you against him,' Bisma said, feeling badly.

'It isn't your fault,' he said. 'It is his, entirely.' He stood, offering her his hand and helping her stand. 'I should go and speak with him now, though I dread to do it.'

She held onto his hand, squeezing. 'Speak with them tomorrow,' she said, voice soft. 'I don't think the workers will come back tonight, so hopefully we're safe for now. You deserve some rest.'

'You're right.' He ran his free hand over his face, rubbing his jaw. 'I can hardly think straight. I suppose I should go, then—let you get some rest as well.'

'Stay here,' she said, not letting go of his hand. 'Stay with me. I want you to.'

The Forest had accepted Xander now, and anyway, even if it hadn't, it was too weak to cause a fuss. Xander looked at her as though she was a wonder.

'I'd like that,' he said, cheeks pink. 'I'd like that very much.'

Hand in hand, Bisma led Xander home. Together, they walked up the steps of the quiet treehouse, which was finally full again. The candles were blown out. The girls were already asleep. She listened to the sound of their breathing, to Nori's snores, before leading Xander up to her room.

Once there, she lit a candle, setting it down on her desk. Then she released a long breath. She was tired, but more than that, she was worried.

'What's going to happen?' she whispered, turning to Xander.

'Hey,' he said, pulling her into his arms. He held her as if she was something precious.

Melting against him, she inhaled the sweet spice of cloves,

comforted by the familiar scent. Her hair was twisted up in a knot, held together by a twig, leaving her neck bare. His nose grazed her skin, sending a shiver down her spine. She relished the feeling.

'Everything is going to be alright,' he whispered against her ear. 'I promise.'

'Is it?' She pulled away, looking at him.

He took her hand in his. 'Build your home here,' he said, holding her hand over his chest. 'In my heart. Where you will always be safe, warm, and loved. That is my vow to you. I am forever yours.'

Her heart overflowed. Even though there was still danger out there, here with him she felt safe, like everything would be alright. The world was so much better because he was in it. She wanted to keep him close always and forever.

'Can I tell you a secret?' she asked, her voice soft. She slipped her hands up from his chest up around his neck, holding his face.

His hands came around her waist, anchoring her. 'Always.'

'I love you,' she said, looking deep into his beautiful eyes. His breath hitched. 'Truly, deeply, madly. I thought I knew what love was until I met you and you expanded the very definition of the word, as if you were the one to invent it, this tailor-made emotion just for me.'

'Bis, I love you, too,' he said, pulling her closer. 'I've been waiting for the right time to say it, but I'm glad you've said it now because I could hardly wait another moment without telling you. You're the very best thing I've ever known—you're pure magic.'

Warmth spread through her, filling her with starlight. She felt so lucky to know him, luckier still to be known by him.

She lifted her face and he pressed his lips against hers, kissing her deep enough that she felt it in her bones. She opened her mouth against his, tasting him.

Her hands roamed over his chest, feeling his heart beating against her palms as his hands moved up her body, trailing up her arms with a feather-light touch until they reached her collar, then her neck.

His hand came around her throat, fingers gently pressing into her skin, and her heart rate spiked against the delicious pressure. As they continued kissing, his hands slipped further up, into her hair, which was still twisted up.

'Take your hair down,' he said, his voice gravelly.

She shivered, doing as she was told, and something glinted in his eyes.

'So you *do* like to be commanded,' he said.

'Shut up.' She pushed him back onto the bed.

'So bossy.' He grinned, pulling her onto him, then rolling her over so he could trail kisses down her skin. She gasped in delight, holding tight onto his hair as he went further down, kissing her just where she wanted.

A starry eternity later, when they were both thoroughly exhausted, they fell asleep, bodies entwined.

She hoped he was right—that everything would be perfectly fine—but even as she fell asleep to the steady pound of his heart, her own heart dreaded what was to come.

33

Bisma woke to howling winds.

The Enchanted Forest was crying out. She didn't understand; the poisonous border should have kept the workers away, and even if it hadn't, they couldn't have caused that much damage in such a short time.

'Xander,' she said, untangling herself from him. 'Something's wrong.'

She sat up, throwing the blanket off. When she stood, Xander was right behind her, groggily blinking.

'What is it?' he asked.

She went to the window, but she couldn't see anything beyond the flying leaves and the shaking branches of the trees.

She quickly threw on a sweater and her boots, then ran down the stairs, Xander following. They left the treehouse, heading for the border. As she ran, she had a terrible feeling.

The Forest was in pain; she could feel it in the air. It was worse than when the workers had cut down the trees. Those had been scratches, while this felt like a deep wound.

What was happening?

Then she saw the smoke. She stopped in her tracks, horror cutting through her.

They had set the Enchanted Forest on fire.

'Xander, the Forest,' she said, her voice breaking.

He was beside her, seeing what she was seeing.

She started running again, heading for the smoke.

As they approached the border, she felt the heat and saw the flames. Everything was covered with thick black smoke.

'Forrie!' she called, coughing. The fire was spreading fast. A branch reached out and lifted her and Xander from the ground, depositing her up high on one of the trees so they could see exactly what was happening and breathe more easily.

The poisonous border had been reduced to ash, and all the trees beyond that were aflame. The sound of crackling wood was loud in her ears, over the pounding of her frightened heart.

'There!' Xander said, pointing.

She followed his gaze and saw Frederick and his workers. They had enough kindling and oil to set the entire Forest on fire.

'They're going to burn it all to the ground,' Bisma whispered, appalled. Tears pricked her eyes.

'Uncle!' Xander cried.

Frederick looked around.

'Uncle!' Xander called again, and this time Frederick spotted them. 'Stop this!'

'Leave while you can!' Frederick replied matter-of-factly. 'The Forest will be flat come morning!'

'This is our home!' Bisma cried. 'We won't leave!'

'Uncle, please!' Xander tried again, his voice cracking. 'There are children! Don't do this!'

'They can leave if they please!' Frederick replied.

'Never!' Bisma snapped.

Frederick addressed only his nephew then. 'Xander, you *must* go,' Frederick implored.

'I won't!' Xander said.

Frederick clenched his jaw, and for a moment Bisma saw remorse on his face. She thought he might call it off, do something—but he only shook his head. 'You're a fool, Xandy-boy,' he said. 'A besotted fool.'

And then he walked away.

Xander made a sound of pain, and she reached for his hand, holding him steady.

'We need to get down,' Bisma said. She touched a hand to the trunk, and a branch carried them to the ground. The heat was getting closer, the smoke thicker. Xander's face was wet with tears.

'Xander, go,' she said. 'Go—I'll get the girls.'

He shook his head. 'I'm not leaving you.'

He squeezed her hand, and they ran back to the treehouse. Some of the smoke had begun to reach here; she could smell it in the air.

'Luna! Azalea! Wake up!' Bisma called, rushing up to Nori's room and shaking her.

'Mei, Deebs!' Xander called, going to Mei's room, where she and Deeba slept.

'Bajiiiii,' Azalea groaned, but she must have sensed something was wrong because she instantly went quiet.

'What's going on?' Luna asked, her voice high.

They were all gathered on the winding staircase, looking at each other.

'We need to go, now!' Bisma cried. 'The Forest is on fire!'

The treehouse erupted in chaos as the girls grabbed their shoes and sweaters, putting them on. Xander held Deeba in one arm as he helped Mei into her sweater. Bisma fastened the laces of Nori's shoes while she buttoned up her sweater.

'But our things!' Nori said, turning for her favorite stuffed rabbit.

'There's no time, honey,' Bisma said. 'The fire is spreading fast; we need to go. *Now*.'

They all ran down the steps, Xander first, then the girls, then Bisma last, ensuring that no one had been left behind.

As she went down the stairs, she looked back at her home, at all their things: the teacups hanging in the kitchen, the ceramic pitcher full of flowers, the knitted blanket on the sofa. Luna's poetry book, Azalea's needle and thread, Mei's favorite mixing bowl, Nori's dolls, Deeba's little bonnet.

Tears welled in her eyes.

'Baji, come on!' Luna called from below.

Bisma ran down the last of the stairs, looking over her shoulder again, afraid it would be for the last time. She wanted to climb up all the way to the very top of her room to see the view just once more: the trees, the lake, the river.

Suddenly, an idea popped into her mind: the Rushing River. If she could use her magic to direct the river through the Forest, it could stop the fire. The Enchanted Forest was far too weak to accomplish such a feat on its own. The howling winds had stopped.

The Forest was dying.

'Xander, get the girls to safety,' Bisma said quickly.

He still held Deeba in one arm. With his free hand, he grabbed Bisma, stopping her, the question evident on his face.

'I'm going to the river. I have an idea.'

'I'm not leaving you,' Xander said, shaking his head.

'I need to make sure the girls are safe,' she said. 'Please.'

His face broke. Around them, the smoke was thickening. Deeba buried her face into Xander's neck, whimpering. Azalea held onto Nori, both coughing, while Mei clung to Luna.

'Please, Xander,' she said, eyes pleading. 'Make sure they're safe.'

He swore then pulled her close, crushing his lips to hers. He kissed her hard.

Her heart broke. She wanted to cling to him, but their paths were going in opposite directions tonight.

'I'll be back,' he said, pressing his forehead against hers. 'I promise.'

She nodded, pushing him away. She ran to the Rushing River, not looking back. She knew Xander would take care of the girls and make sure they got out safe.

The river was deeper into the Forest, away from the fires, and as Bisma ran, the temperature cooled, the air clearing from the smoke.

When she arrived at the river, its waters roared. She knelt on the banks, pressing her hands into the soil. Magic sparked up her arms; she could feel the river and its power.

'Come on,' she whispered, forcing her magic into the land. 'Please.'

Bisma pushed herself to continue. Slowly, she felt the waters beginning to change direction; a trickle separated from the river to head toward the fires, then a small stream.

But it wasn't enough, not nearly enough. At this rate the Forest would be burned down by the time the waters reached it.

So instead of pushing herself, Bisma pushed her magic. All of it, every ounce she could muster, every bit that was inside her. She poured it into the earth, willing it to take.

The breath was knocked from her as the magic connected with the soil. She felt the change. Whereas before her magic had felt like molding something in her hands, now it felt like she was bleeding.

The small stream expanded as half the river redirected and began rushing toward the fires.

It was working!

She continued to push, letting the Forest take her magic; she would give it all.

But she felt herself dwindling, her energy depleting. She looked at the Rushing River—it still wasn't enough. She could see red in the distance; the fires were still blazing.

She needed more. Closing her eyes, she pushed once more.

Then—a hand in her hair.

'Xander,' she gasped, looking up to see him.

'The girls are safe,' he said, rolling up his sleeves. 'I've got you, Bis.'

'Xander, no,' she said, her breath hitching as the magic continued to pour out of her.

It was leaving her, and she didn't know if it would come back. She did not want to condemn him to that.

He fell to his knees beside her, putting his hands into the soil. She saw the moment he felt what was happening, as the magic was pulled from him. The stream doubled, roaring past them more quickly.

'Xander, don't,' she said, shaking her head. 'You can still save yourself. Go!'

He gave her an incredulous look, his eyes wild. 'I'm not leaving you!'

'This is my home,' she said, tears streaming down her cheeks, 'but you don't have to do this—you can still go!'

'Don't you understand?' he cried. '*You* are my home.'

A surge of magic entered the soil. She felt it immediately; he was giving all he had to it, and it might just be enough.

The river rushed forth.

She heard the hiss of the flames being put out as her vision blurred.

The last thing she saw were the fires dying out before the world disappeared into darkness.

34

Before Bisma woke, she knew: her magic was gone.

Or it was somewhere she could not access, as if she had been bled dry, every bit of it given to the Enchanted Forest with none left for her to keep. She could feel a faint echo of it, the way she felt the magic of the Forest, but it was far away.

She was completely drained, tired down to her bones. In that half-consciousness her heart broke, and so she fell back asleep, not wanting to wake just yet.

Hours later, her body tried to wake again. She wanted to refuse it—she was still so tired—but then she felt somebody warm beside her, she inhaled the scent of cloves, and she decided she'd actually really rather be awake.

Bisma opened her eyes. She was in her bed in the treehouse.

Sunlight poured in from the window, and the air had a chill to it as it did on late-autumn mornings. It was almost winter now, and the weather was making sure they knew it.

She took in a deep breath, the crisp air refreshing in her throat. Bisma turned, and lying beside her was Xander. His hair was a mess, and his arms were around her, their legs entwined as though they were one person, not two.

She moved her hand from his neck down to his heart and felt it thump against her hand. She remembered that final moment, the magic pouring out of her, the two of them fighting a forest fire, together.

He had saved her home. He had saved her—in more ways than she could count.

'Xander,' she whispered. She rubbed her thumb over his heart, trying to wake him.

He took in a deep breath, groaning. 'Mmm?' he asked. He still didn't open his eyes.

'Are you awake?'

He grazed his nose against hers. 'I sure hope so,' he whispered back.

Before she could properly wake him up, there was a sound at the door to her room. Bisma turned to see Mei standing there with a blanket in her hands. Her face was shocked, her dark eyes wide.

'Mei—' Bisma began, but it was too late.

Mei turned to the stairs and bellowed, 'SHE'S AWAKE!'

Footsteps pounded up the stairs as five girls all ran into Bisma's room, crowding around her bed. When Xander finally opened his eyes, it was to the sight of half a dozen girls staring at him.

'Oh.' He blinked. 'Hello.'

'You're FINALLY awake,' Luna said, on her knees to be eye level with him and Bisma.

'Here, hold Deeba,' Azalea said, propping the toddler atop Bisma and Xander.

Deeba giggled.

'Baji, I've been asking this for DAYS and no one is answering me,' Nori started, pulling at Bisma's sleeve.

'Oh, here we go again,' Luna muttered, rolling her eyes.

'Why is there a BOY in your bed?' Nori demanded. Her eyebrows were furrowed with indignation. The treehouse was a clear boy-free area.

'Umm . . .' Bisma trailed off.

'Oh, this should be good,' Azalea whispered to Luna, both giggling.

Bisma gave them an unamused glance.

'Nori, I already told you,' Mei said, sighing. She was sitting on the bed by Bisma's feet. 'It's because Baji was scared and needed someone to sleep with.'

'So why not sleep with one of us?' Nori asked, confused. 'I give the best cuddles!'

Azalea snorted. 'Because you snore.'

'I DON'T SNORE.' Nori was outraged. She turned to Bisma. 'BAJI, DO I SNORE?'

Absolutely; her snoring shook the walls. 'No, of course you don't . . .'

'Hush now!' Luna scolded. 'Stop bothering Baji! And I told you all to be on your best behavior in front of Xander. He's our guest!'

'Here she goes again,' Azalea said, rolling her eyes. 'Baji, I'm glad you're awake because Luna has been on an absolute power trip these past few days.'

'*Days?*' Bisma disentangled herself from Xander enough to sit up, and Deeba took the opportunity to crawl onto her lap. Xander tried to rest his head on Bisma's lap as well, but Deeba promptly kicked him in the face.

'Um. *Ow.*'

They ignored him.

'It's been three days since the fire,' Mei said. 'When we saw the fires stop we came home and found you here, asleep.'

'Soooo romantic!' Luna cooed.

'Ew, stop, I'm going to gag,' Azalea interjected.

'The Forest must have carried us home,' Bisma said, ignoring them.

'You both looked terrible,' Azalea informed them. 'But now you look a little better, though you could probably use some more sleep. And food.'

'You know, more sleep *would* be nice,' Xander said, nestling deeper into the bed. His face was half covered by the blanket, and he closed his eyes.

'Fine, you can take a short nap but only because we haven't made breakfast yet,' Luna said, picking Deeba up. Mei stood as well, and they all made to leave. 'But be down in thirty minutes. Or else.'

As quickly as they came, the girls all shuffled out, and once they were gone, Bisma felt Xander pull at her foot. She yelped, sliding down beside him, and he made quick work of wrapping her into his arms. He closed his eyes, ready to sleep again.

'How are you sleeping?' she asked, lightly smacking him.

'We have twenty-nine minutes.' He sighed.

But she was already wide awake. She could have gone down to her sisters and let him sleep peacefully, but when did she ever let him have any peace?

'I can think of something better to do,' she whispered, licking his throat. His eyes shot open.

'Oh, definitely a better idea,' he said, shifting so he was propped on his elbows above of her.

She laughed. 'Not sleepy anymore, hmm?'

'Not in the least,' he said, kissing her long and sweet.

Giddiness bubbled inside her, and she smiled against his mouth. Remembering something, she giggled, then pulled back.

'By the way,' she said, holding his face in her hands. 'I figured out you were the one writing me those letters.'

'Finally caught on, did you?' he said with a smirk. 'Imagine my surprise when that first letter showed up in my room, stained with dirt. I knew it was from you immediately, though I figured you hadn't ever meant for the letter to be sent.'

'Why did you write back?'

'I wanted to be close to you, even if it meant I was just a stranger sending you letters.' He kissed her palm. 'I wanted to be your friend.'

'I really needed a friend,' she said, her voice soft. She looked deep into his eyes. 'Not just a friend—you. I needed you, Xander.'

'And now you have me,' he said, his eyes dark as he kissed her neck. 'You'll always have me,' he swore.

She pulled him closer, bringing her lips to his once more.

They made very good use of their twenty minutes until finally it was time to get out of bed, for they were both starving.

They freshened up and Bisma changed. Downstairs, she heard the girls laughing and chatting and bickering, and her heart soared to have her home back. The Forest seemed to be in great spirits as well; outside the birds sang, and the wind joined in with the melody. Sunlight created patches on the floor, and she pressed her toes against the warm wood.

Holding Xander's hand, Bisma went down the winding stairs and joined her sisters in the kitchen, which was in absolute chaos as the girls all prepared breakfast. Deeba had her hand in a jar of jam, while Nori arranged the flowers. Mei was instructing Azalea how to cut the potatoes, while Luna set the table.

The treehouse was back to normal, and there was no sign of any damage done from the fires. They must have put it out before it reached here, and Bisma wanted to cry with relief. Everything was as it should be—better, actually, because Xander was here, too. She wanted to wrap herself in him once more but refrained from making Azalea gag again.

They sat round the table, squeezing in. Azalea passed round the eggs while Luna poured tea, and Mei opened a new jar of orange marmalade for the toast as Nori popped cubes of sugar into everyone's teacups.

'You can have my chair,' Mei told Xander, batting her lashes at him.

'Aw, thank you, lovely,' he said, giving her a dazzling smile.

'We'll have to get another chair,' Mei said, holding Deeba in her lap in Deeba's chair.

'What happened to the strict No-Boys-Allowed-in-the-Treehouse rule?' Azalea asked, arching a brow.

'I think we can make an exception.' Bisma gave her a look. 'Seeing as Xander *did* help save our home.'

He had sacrificed his magic for it—for *her*.

'Come on, girls, let me be allowed,' Xander said, pouting at them. 'This breakfast looks delicious, by the way.'

'If he's allowed to visit, does that mean I can have Haru over?' Luna asked excitedly.

'Hmm.' Bisma pretended to think, then took a bite of her buttered toast. 'No.'

'What!' Luna cried. She actually stomped her foot. 'That's so not fair!'

'I'm Baji, so I'm in charge,' Bisma said, taking a sip of tea. *Mmm*, delicious.

'And we don't want this place overrun by boys,' Mei said, making a face.

'Yuck!' Nori said.

'Besides, even if Xander is allowed to visit, he won't be here all the time,' Bisma said. 'This is still our home, just for the Unwanted Girls, and nothing will change that. Ever.'

She gave Xander an apologetic look, but he held his hands up. 'Just happy to be here whenever you want me. Who made the marmalade? It's excellent!'

'Oh, I did!' Mei said, pleased by the compliment.

Xander asked her—and each of Bisma's sisters—loads of questions, easily winning them all over with his charm.

It warmed Bisma's heart to see him with them, and they painted a cozy picture huddled around the table, laughing and bickering light-heartedly. Everything was perfect. Just perfect.

So perfect, in fact, that Bisma's thoughts did not cross to all that happened. Not until a rabbit hopped up the stairs and into the kitchen, a letter between its teeth.

'What's this?' she asked, taking the letter. Nori picked the rabbit up to feed it strawberries, while Bisma unfolded the letter.

'That's my mother's handwriting,' Xander said.

Bisma moved the page so he could read it along with her.

Dear Bisma,

I am sorry for not writing sooner, but there was a great deal I wished to be sorted before I reached out to you. I can understand completely why you and Xander should keep your distance. I saw one of your sisters in town yesterday and asked after you both, but your sister refused to say anything other than you were both resting after your ordeal, which I cannot blame her for. You must both hate me, but let me assure you I had no idea what Frederick was doing.

I created the poison at Fred's request because he had explained to me that the police in Whitebridge planned to use it to track down smugglers. Xander did not tell me what happened to your sisters or I would have realized sooner. I apologize for the hand I have played in the suffering of your family, but please know it was not my intention at all. I am glad to hear your sisters have all recovered and that you are safe.

Truly, I would never hurt you; I hold you in great esteem. For one, my son adores you, and I adore him. For another, I am indebted to you. Some months ago, my dearest friend, who was like a sister to me truly, asked me for help with something and I refused her. I later found out she went to you for help and that you did not refuse her. She has passed now, and I wish I had helped her when she asked, but it comforts me to know she was not entirely alone during that time—you were there for her when I should have been, and for that I will be eternally grateful.

I could never have imagined Frederick would resort to such violent lengths to achieve his goals, but please rest assured that he will not harm you again. He is not to step foot into Old Town for as long as he lives and the expansion project commissioned by the Crown will not endanger the Enchanted Forest. I have spoken with Lady Charlotte on the matter and ensured that the Enchanted Forest will be protected by law. Apparently, the water supply to the town passes through the Forest, so to harm the Forest is now considered a direct attack on the town itself, which the mayor takes very seriously, I can tell you.

I am not sure if you care for the details, but they will expand Old Town to the west. Frederick will deal with the nasty business of provincial lines and speak with the king himself if need be, but the Enchanted Forest will not be touched. Your home is safe.

You may wonder how I have accomplished this and what guarantee there is that Frederick will behave. As you know, I am his elder sister. When my father died, he split his inheritance between us, but his will had the caveat that should either one of us harm the other, their right to the inheritance would be void. Well, Frederick nearly got Xander killed in that little fire of his, so if he does not behave, he will lose his fortune, and I assure you that is enough to motivate him to stay in line.

You may also wonder why I do not simply take Frederick's fortune or have him arrested. The truth is, having him arrested would be difficult, seeing as he is the king's favored architect. As for his fortune, it will be of more use to you this way: he will pay you and your sisters a monthly allowance. Additionally, Xander mentioned to me once that you hoped to study in Whitebridge someday; Frederick will pay for your schooling as well—in fact, for anything you should require. Do extort him for all his fortune is worth, dear.

I hope you will find it in your heart to forgive me.
All my very best,
Eleanora Chapman

P.S. Perhaps you and Xander might join me for dinner tonight?

'Goodness,' Bisma said, folding the paper and setting it on her lap.

'Goodness, indeed.' Xander sighed.

She turned to look at him. 'How do you feel?' she asked.

'How do *I* feel?' he repeated, blinking. 'How do *you* feel?'

Bisma thought about it for a moment. The truth was, she felt . . . calm. She had her home, her sisters, and Xander. With all that, she found she didn't really need revenge if Fredrick was being punished. And with the monthly allowance she could look after her sisters properly.

'Eleanora clearly meant no harm,' she said. Eleanora did not harbor a grudge toward Bisma for what had occurred with Leilani, as Bisma had assumed. 'And Frederick will be free, yes, but the Forest is safe and he can spend his whole life repaying me and my sisters for what he's done, which does not seem like such a bad deal.'

'What happened to my bloodthirsty Bisma?' Xander asked, confused. 'I thought for sure you would concoct elaborate poisons to make them both suffer.'

She laughed, leaning back into her chair, then sighed. 'I'm thinking of taking early retirement. The monthly allowance will do far more for the girls than my revenge.'

'How sensible of you,' Xander said, positively shocked.

'How do you feel?' Bisma asked again.

'I believe my mother meant no harm,' he said. 'Of course there are no excuses for Uncle Fred, and from this day forth I will cut myself off from him, which is a loss.' He looked at Bisma, smiling. 'Though not so much a loss at all when I have you.' He glanced at her sisters. 'And all of you.'

'Are we supposed to be following what's happening?' Azalea whispered to Luna.

'I don't think so,' Luna whispered back.

'I'll explain later,' Bisma said to them, and they went back to their breakfast.

'This could be good, actually,' Xander said. 'You'll finally get to study in Whitebridge—perhaps we'll get the chance to go together, after all.'

'I can't go now,' she said, her voice low. 'Luna isn't eighteen for another three years.'

'I don't mean now,' he said, taking a sip of tea. 'I'm sure the offer stands for whenever you wish to accept it.'

'What about you?' she asked. Would he be leaving so soon, just when she had finally gotten him?

He let out a small laugh. 'I am in no hurry to leave Old Town so long as you are here,' he said. 'We can have our adventure in three years the same way we might have it tomorrow.'

She blinked at him stupidly. 'You're thinking of having a future with me?'

'Of course,' he replied, giving her a funny look. 'You *are* my future, Bis. What on earth would I do without you?'

'Oh.' Her heart glowed. 'Well, in that case, I suppose we'll have dinner with your mother tonight.'

'Splendid! I hope she has the cook make a good roast.'

'Baji, are you and Xander done talking?' Nori asked, her voice loud with irritation. 'Can you pay attention to us now?'

'Yeah,' Mei agreed. 'We have a hundred thousand things to tell you!'

'Me first!' Azalea said.

'Me!' Deeba shouted with glee. 'Me, me, me!'

They all laughed.

'Yes, I'm listening, love,' Bisma said.

They sat round the table for an hour longer, drinking tea and telling stories and bickering over biscuits. Outside, the wind whistled, rustling the leaves, and the sun shone bright. Surrounded by warmth, Bisma felt so utterly whole—so utterly happy.

She had lost her magic, but she had gained everything else: her home, her family, her future, her love.

For now, that was enough.

EPILOGUE

*I*t was Luna's birthday, which meant it was time for goodbye.

But before the goodbye came years of love and happiness and, yes, magic, too. About a month after the fires, Bisma felt that familiar pull inside her, and when she went to her garden and stuck her hands into the soil, a little plant sprouted.

It had taken about a month for the Enchanted Forest to recover the trees it had lost, but once it did, it gave Bisma back her magic. She ran to find Xander and found that he had his magic back as well, along with a small mark on his wrist, black ink in the shape of a vine. Bisma had the same mark beside the tattoo that marked her as an Unwanted Girl.

Her magic felt different, she realized; it felt as if she carried a piece of the Enchanted Forest with her wherever she went. She was stronger, more energized. Xander felt the same, and he could freely visit the Forest whenever he wished.

They were permanently tied to the Enchanted Forest.

Theoretically it meant Bisma could be Baji forever—she never had to leave—but that wasn't what she wanted. Frederick still needed to pay for what he had done, and she wanted to study in Whitebridge. She wanted to see the world, to learn, to grow. All with Xander by her side: teasing, exploring, kissing, talking, laughing, kissing again.

But that would come later. She particularly enjoyed being Baji when, four months later, they were blessed with a new sister. She was a darling six-month-old with curly hair and dark skin.

'Great!' Azalea exclaimed upon seeing her. 'More diapers!'

But even she could not mask her excitement.

The baby arrived with a note detailing her past: her mother had died in childbirth and her father was terminally ill, expecting to pass any day. He could not take care of Halle and hoped the Unwanted Girls could. Despite their reputation, he had seen the way the sisters always cared for each other and loved one another. That was all he wanted for his little girl: for her to have a home.

While many in the village would always ostracize the Unwanted Girls, and the girls would never truly *belong* there, it was alright, for they belonged in the Enchanted Forest, and they belonged with each other. And they had some friends, which was proved by the people who had showed up for them when it mattered, and that was enough.

Moreover, Bisma had Xander. They could not see each other all the time, for she had her business and he had his—so it was a good thing they were already practiced in sending each other letters.

They went on early-morning walks and afternoon picnics and had evening chai and late-night swims in the lake. They had family dinners with his parents—who were truly lovely—and family dinners with her sisters—who were constantly fighting for his attention.

And the years passed so quickly she did not realize.

Suddenly it was Luna's eighteenth birthday, and it was time for Bisma to leave.

It was one last perfect day, and like all things, it had to end. Bisma hugged her sisters goodbye, looking up at the treehouse one final time. She would miss those weathered wood floors; the view from her room; the winding staircase; the scent of dried lavender; the dining table with its painted chairs; the mismatched teacups; the flowers; the stray socks—she would miss all of it. But she had to go.

Luna walked Bisma to the edge of the Enchanted Forest, both with tears in their eyes.

'You can do this. I know you can,' Bisma told Luna, giving her sister a smile. 'You're going to be great, Lu.'

'I'm going to miss you,' Luna said, cheeks shining in the moonlight with tears.

'I'm going to miss you, too,' Bisma said, pulling her into her arms. 'Desperately.' They held onto one another tight. 'But we'll see each other again.'

'What?' Luna asked, eyes wide. 'How?'

Bisma wasn't quite sure how, but those were the words spoken to her by her baji, and she was saying them to Luna now.

'Trust me,' she said, kissing Luna's cheek.

'I do,' Luna said.

'Goodbye,' Bisma whispered into Luna's hair.

Then she stepped into the fog bordering the Enchanted Forest. Bisma looked down at her wrist, at the mark that branded her as an Unwanted Girl. It was gone, now, but the black vine remained.

Bisma would forever be tethered to the Enchanted Forest, which meant she did not *have* to leave, but she wished to. She understood why the Forest had its rules, why it forced the baji to leave when the next girl came of age. It wasn't a punishment—it was freedom.

The fog cleared, and on the other side, Xander was waiting for her. He flashed her a dazzling smile, his green eyes brilliant and bright.

'Ready?' he asked, holding out his hand.

'Ready,' she said, and together they walked toward a new adventure.

ACKNOWLEDGMENTS

Alhamdulillah for another book published! That's book six, which is so exciting; everything that I've accomplished or done is by the blessings of Allah (SWT). If you've been reading my work since book one, thank you for keeping up with me, and if this is your first book of mine, I hope you'll be interested in my other works as well!

I am so grateful to publish this book, and I wouldn't have made it this far without all the wonderful people in my life who support me. Thank you to my incredible agent, Emily Keyes, for your endless effort; I appreciate everything that you do. Thank you to my amazing editor, Nazima Abdillahi, who has been such a joy to work with and whose faith in me has been such a blessing. Thank you to Jenna Mackintosh, copy-editor Jennie Roman and proofreader Zainab Ahmad.

Thank you to the entire team at Hachette Children's Group for being such a fantastic home for my book! Thank you to Jennifer Alliston for the cover and interior design. Thank you to Melissa Castrillón for the cover illustration. Thank you to Bec Gillies in Marketing for your work in promoting my book. Thanks to Joelyn Rolston-Esdelle, Karis Pearson, Katherine Fox, Annabel El-Kerim and their respective teams, too.

Thank you to my family: Mama, Baba, Sameer, Zaineb, and Ibraheem. Thank you to Papa, Mimi, Khala, and all the kids. Thank you to my best-friend-cousins, Hamnah, Umaymah, Noor, and Mahum. Thank you to my best friends: Arusa, Isra, Sara, and Justine. It's easy to write about sisterhood when I've got friends like you; I love you all so very much!

Thank you to my early readers for your enthusiasm and support so early on, especially Umamah, whose commentary always makes me giggle. Thank you to the authors who blurbed this book: [insert here].

Thank you to anyone who's spread the word about my books, recommended them to people they know, requested them at their library, left reviews, and/or bought copies. The reason I get to write books is because of you! I appreciate it so sincerely.

Please pray for me. Until next time x